Arm and a Leg

Also by David Ralph Martin

I'm Coming to Get You

David Ralph Martin
Arm and a Leg

HEINEMANN : LONDON

First published in the United Kingdom in 1998
by William Heinemann

1 3 5 7 9 10 8 6 4 2

Copyright © David Ralph Martin 1998

The right of David Ralph Martin to be identified as the author of this work has been asserted by him in accordance with the Copyright, Designs and Patents Act, 1988

This book is sold subject to the condition that it shall not, by way of trade or otherwise, be lent, resold, hired out, or otherwise circulated without the publisher's prior consent in any form of binding or cover other than that in which it is published and without a similar condition including this condition being imposed on the subsequent purchaser

William Heinemann
Random House UK Ltd
20 Vauxhall Bridge Road, London, SW1V 2SA

Random House Australia (Pty) Limited
20 Alfred Street, Milsons Point, Sydney, New South Wales 2061, Australia

Random House New Zealand Limited
18 Poland Road, Glenfield
Auckland 10, New Zealand

Random House South Africa (Pty) Limited
Endulini, 5a Jubilee Road, Parktown, 2193, South Africa
Random House UK Limited Reg. No. 954009

A CIP catalogue record for this book is available from the British Library

Papers used by Random House UK Limited are natural, recyclable products made from wood grown in sustainable forests. The manufacturing processes conform to the environmental regulations of the country of origin

Typeset by SX Composing DTP, Rayleigh, Essex
Printed and bound in the United Kingdom by
Mackays of Chatham plc, Chatham, Kent

ISBN 0 434 00439 1

1

A soft tap at the bedroom door and Joe came in murmuring his apologies to the Macmillan nurse. He handed Baz a black plastic binliner, stood back and waited. Baz turned his back on the nurse and took two padded Jiffy bags out of the binliner. One contained the short-barrel Smith & Wesson .38, the other the Browning 9mm automatic. Baz paid Joe for keeping them with three fifties from a thick roll and Joe left saying he was sorry for the disturbance.

Baz packed the Jiffy bags inside his leather jacket and said if God was to stand before him now, he'd shoot the Rass. The Macmillan nurse, who was as black as he was, looked at him askance. 'Forty years a life,' said Baz, 'and my Sis, she the only one ever nice – why shouldn' I? He bad, man, He worse than me.'

The nurse told Baz he should hold his sister Evelyn's hand, let her feel his life and try to be a good last companion.

Baz sat alone with his sister for an hour. It was a spacious first-floor room on a tree-lined street off the Finchley Road, north London. Evelyn, who was forty-seven and seamed up with cancer, had been carried there from her basement by Baz and her cousin Joe. Even with the camp bed and rubber mattress they used as a stretcher she had felt very light. Baz had fixed up a pair of split-cane roller-blinds to remind her of home. Thin winter sun shone through, striping the room with light but no heat. Her hand lay on top of his, skin translucent, blue veins showing. The previous night she had suffered a stroke which left her unconscious and Doctor

Rao said the cancer had reached her brain. The flesh on her oval face, once so calm and full, had melted like ice and the skin had tightened into concave curves around the sharpness of the bones. She was still beautiful, to Baz, but she was hardly there. He sat very still and upright, and although he did his best to love and mourn her he felt himself slowly filling with black volcanic rage.

Needing to move, he stood up, kissed his sister on her damp forehead, murmured 'Love you, Sis' and left. Once out in the street his pent-up rage erupted like a fireball. When it had passed, and nothing had changed, he felt both weak and free. He walked along the winter streets, fighting the ache in his bad leg, and let the cold air clear his head.

That afternoon he collected five kilos of cocaine for delivery to Bristol. At eleven o'clock that night, sitting with Evelyn, holding her hand, he felt her slip away. There was no rage now, just loss and cold disbelief in the way people said things were. Things had never been the way people said they were. During the long night's wake he kept for Evelyn, Baz figured he had always known how things were. Pitiless. What happen, happen. All there was to it.

Because he was chief mourner, he said he should postpone the delivery a week or so, and the North London brothers agreed. The delay gave him time to make his moves. First off was a call to Chingola, his contact in Bristol. Chingola was a musician kid, white but from Africa, one of them Z-places, Zambia, Zamibia, seriously into smack.

Baz said, 'How you doin', man?'

Chingola said he'd call him back off the street.

The phonebox outside Belsize Park Tube was ringing when Baz walked in.

'Where the fuck is it, man?' said Chingola. 'I got people's tongues hanging out down here, you said five fucking keys, man—'

'Family business,' said Baz. 'I got bad family business.'

'Oh right,' said Chingola. 'When then?'
'What our situation?'
'Viz-a-vee what?'
'Your cop fren',' said Baz.
'Oh, right.' There was a silence. Baz could hear Chingola's breath wheezing in and out. Then Chingola said, 'I think he's nobbing her.'
'Who that?'
'The widow.'
'What you talkin' about, man?'
'You know, I told you, that other cop, got killed. What's his name, Webber, Inspector Webber.' Chingola was toking down long and hard on a joint now, and when his voice came on again he was half laughing, half choking. 'Well, our guy, Detective Chief Inspector Barnard—'
'That fucker, put me in the fuckin' hellhole—'
'Yeah-yeah-yeah,' said Chingola. 'Well, he's not only investigating her case, he's sniffin' her snatch, man.'
'How you know?'
'I'm in this Watershed joint waiting for our weekly meet and he's only buying her fucking lunch, isn't he? Nodding and smiling and patting the back of her hand and going tut-tut-fucking-tut and all the time his eyeballs have got fucking hard-ons.'
'Heh-heh-heh.'
'So if he's not got it yet, he's gagging for it. He's fucking grey-haired, man—'
'We all got weakness, y'know?'
'Don't tell me.'
Baz said, 'You don' tell 'im me an' 'im, we know one another?'
'Fuck you think I am, Baz?'
'What else he say?'
'Wants to know the ins and outs of the cat's arse, man. How much coke, where to, packed in what, where we going to stash it on the night—'
'An' you tell 'im?'
'I don't fucking know, do I?' said Chingola. 'Not yet.'
'That right,' said Baz. 'You don', not yet.'

'I reckon he's got his own little private fucking mojo working—'

'Who ain't? Tek care now—'

'Baz.' Chingola sounding urgent.

'Yah?'

'Bring some fucking smack, man. Because it's fucking thin on the ground down here, and I'm pretty fucking strung out—'

'Heh-heh-heh. Talk to you soon.' Baz put the phone down.

Outside a thin-legged, blue-lipped white girl was glaring at him, smoking furiously. He held the door open for her. She walked past him saying nothing, not even looking at him.

Back home in the eighty-degree heat of his basement flat Baz took a glass of pale gold rum and picked away at the deal. The way Baz saw it, him and Chingola and DCI Barnard were supposed to be pulling on the same end of the rope, supposed to be setting up a sting on the local dealers to get them off the streets and into jail. That way DCI Barnard got the credit and Baz and the North London brothers got Bristol . . .

Was life like that?

Was it *shit*.

Everybody always had their own deal going. Chingola did. DCI Barnard did. Either one could put Baz inside for ten, fifteen years. On the other hand, as Evelyn used to say, 'All you got to do is watch which way the fish swim.'

In between talking to the undertakers and the minister and the ladies from the choir Baz was talking to the Turks. Jesus, it was hard work. Every time you asked for Shabbahatin they said Sabbahatin. You say OK, Sabbahatin, they say Who? He ain't here, he gone back, nobody seen him in months. Then some big, dark blue BMW 7-series would follow him round all day, not hiding, just showing him, three guys in the back, one guy in the front. Shit man, like crawling through one macca thorn-bush into another. But Baz kept on because he knew Sabbahatin and he knew it was Christmas and he knew they'd have a shipment coming through Bristol or Southampton or somewhere. He also knew the Turks never liked to stick their heads up out the trench driver-wise when they could watch and pay somebody else to do it for them. So he was seriously pissed off when finally Sabbahatin did come on and say, 'Sorry, Baz, you're the wrong colour.'

'Heh-heh-heh.' Baz taking his time.

'We need a white guy.'

'Whiter than you, you mean?' Knowing Sabbahatin had that dirty newspaper-yellow look.

Now Sabbahatin took his time. These Turk guys could pass it out but they couldn't pick it up. 'Yes, Baz. Whiter than me.'

'OK. Why?'

Sabbahatin ignored that and said, 'Somebody who can drive, looks clean, not like some chip-fed shavehead Millwall shit.'

Baz said he'd see what he could do, and by the time the funeral had come and gone, everything was set, all fruit ripe, and apart from Evelyn, Baz was feeling pretty good.

It was a mother of a deal. Deliver and collect. And the collection was awesome. Was a pension, no more, no less, and Chingola and the cop Barnard were disposable.

Yah.

Baz swirled the rum round the stubby little shot-glass and looked at what he knew about Chingola. First off, the kid was a smackhead, so he got no loyalty to nobody but the needle. Second, he was a musician, and all dem come feckless as shit. And third, he was white and in the cop's pocket, so the only way to work him was keep him in the dark until the last minute.

And then he'd be disposable.

The cop, Barnard, was a different matter. Ever since the guy had got him sectioned to that psychiatric fucking hellhole name of Hillside, Baz had been figuring ways to mash and juke the fucker the way the fucker had done him. Yah, Barnard, you got it comin'. Thinking about it, about it happening soon, made the juices run in Baz's mouth.

Heh-heh-heh.

Baz raised a last thimble of pale gold rum to his dead sister. It was a mother of a deal, justice and profit all the way. Yah. *All you got to do is watch which way the fish swim.*

Only thing he needed was a cyar and a white-kid driver. Also disposable.

On a fine, bright late-December Friday morning Baz Baxter stepped up into a hired blue Land-Rover driven by a fair-haired English ex-public schoolboy and set off for Bristol to deliver, collect, maim, burn and kill.

2

Inspector Frank Webber's widow, Rae, woke up in her parents' house to see her mother holding out a cup of coffee and the portaphone from the kitchen.

'It's Mr Barnard wants a word, love.' Her mother gave her the phone and pulled the curtains. The light was low and blinding. 'Hello?' Rae pushed a hand through her short cream-pale hair and looked at her eyes in the dressing-table mirror. Morning-slitty as usual. 'Hello?'

'Sorry to wake you, Rae,' DCI Barnard had his caring voice on. 'I just thought I ought to, you know, check up how you were. How you're bearing up—'

'Fine. I'm fine.' Rae looking at her mother.

'Also,' the DCI's voice becoming official, 'I thought you ought to know there's going to be quite a few of us there. At the crematorium.'

'Yes, you mentioned that.'

'Did I?' A pause then, 'He was a good man, Rae.'

According to the official autopsy report and what DCI Barnard had told her, Frank had had his windpipe and jugular slit wide open in one of the gynaecological examination rooms in the basement of the Bristol Maternity Hospital, while trying to save a young nurse from a chisel-wielding psychopath called Nigel who had subsequently hanged himself in his cell. Even at the time, Rae found herself thinking, How convenient.

Rae's mother said, 'What was that all about?'

'He said there's going to be quite a few of them, at the crematorium.'

'And afterwards, I suppose.'

'I suppose.'

'I hope they don't all eat like him.'

The previous afternoon Detective Chief Inspector Barnard, a solid fifty-year-old man in a boxy dark blue Italian suit, had seen off all but one of a plate of ginger biscuits explaining pension and compensation schemes to her parents, all the while chomping away and staring hungrily at the front of Rae's black satin shirt. 'This day and age,' he concluded, his gaze still fixed on her breasts, 'violence sadly affects all our lives.'

'Mmm,' said Rae's father.

'Awful,' murmured her mother.

Rae, who had put up with DCI Barnard twice already, once in his office at the Bridewell and once for lunch at the Watershed on the Docks, where he'd suddenly left her to speak to a scruffy guy he told her was a musician, said nothing.

They were in her parents' extended lounge in Henleaze, a comfortable suburb of Bristol close to the Downs. It was a low, wide room, buff with white woodwork and dark oak furniture lined up against the walls. The armchair Rae was sitting in faced the picture window and the frost-gripped garden.

Behind her, the ceramic logs in the fireplace swam with veils of blue and yellow flame and the Ebac dehumidifier sucked her father's pipe smoke into its slats. As always, the room smelled of beeswax and pipe tobacco, and after eight days the mild peace of her parents' existence was driving Rae mad.

'Rest assured,' said the DCI, pushing himself upright with thick hands on bulging thighs, 'we shall do all we can about everything.' He nodded to her father and mother and looked straight down the front of Rae's shirt into her bra.

Her breasts, he thought, were mean but perky.

The question was, if he got his hands on five kilos of coke, would she get her nice little titties out and rub their nipples through his lips? On balance DCI Barnard thought she would. For money if not for love. She'd got that look in her eye . . .

So all he had to do was see Chingola, sort out the drop, see where the stash was, set up the raid and bingo – coke and titty time.

After breakfast Rae's father got his red Rover 216 out into the Close and told Rae to watch out for black ice on Bridge Valley Road. It was always in shadow and the trees dripped. Her mother said, Look out for the other fools. They didn't want her to go. Not on her own, back to the house. But she needed her clothes, and underclothes. They had said they'd get them. She had shouted at them. Last night after DCI Barnard had left. Her pudgy-faced, hurt, bewildered parents, drawing together as she yelled at them through a blur of librium and Waitrose Zinfandel, her voice bursting out, piercing the blur.

I don't want you going through my things, Mother! For God's sake don't you understand? Driving me mad. Fussing! Leave me alone!

Her voice a yowl, rising to a scream. Then tears, hot and gulping, and sobs sinking down through the octaves into silence.

Her father took his pipe out of his mouth, laid it in its tortoiseshell and silver rest, put an arm round his wife and reached out a veined hand towards his daughter.

Now, still in a haze, disorientated, thoughts jumping like fish, she was walking out of the house. Her thighs felt as if she were wading through waist-high water. Eight-fifteen. Funeral eleven-thirty. She hit the bright cold air. First time out on her own in nine interminable days. Be careful Rae. Don't be late will you love. And the daylight shouting at her:

Rae Webber! Widow!

Her father scraping the frost off the rear window, mother spraying the front. She sat in the red Rover with the fan blasting. Their faces leaning in through both windows. Christ, would they never go away?

'Use the wipers, Rae, before it freezes again.'

'Yes, Dad. I know.' Switching them on.
'It's all right love, we know you've got to do it.'
'What's that, Mum?'
'Get your confidence up,' said her father.
'Say goodbye,' said her mother.

She drove out into the white street, past the big gabled-and-timbered houses and their bristling white hedges. Mid-December in north suburban Bristol. Some of the front rooms had had their trees up and their twinkly lights on for a fortnight. Only number 47, her parents' friends Gil and Eva Parsons, had its curtains drawn out of respect. Her mother had said, Well, all that was going out now.

She stopped at the junction, glanced in the mirror. Her father was out in the road, her mother at the gate. Both waving. She put the radio on, turned left and drove south.

On the day Frank was killed, Rae had found out she was eight weeks pregnant. Now she was nine, and her father had already been down to Ashton to start decorating the spare room.

The Circular Road round the edge of the Downs, next to the purple-brown cleft of the Avon Gorge, had been gritted but Ladies Mile was still white so she went down that. It slashed straight through two hundred acres of mown and frozen parkland, a mile long with a blind, dropping ninety-degree bend at the end. She was doing sixty, hallucinating on the sapphire sky, the sage-pale grass, the azure tree-shadows flailing across the windscreen—

And the bend came swinging at her.

Two joggers standing by the bushes with the breath pluming out of their mouths were turning to watch the crash. The Rover slid, skated, gripped. A twin-tone car horn blared. A charcoal-grey Volvo 850 estate heading for her, heaving round her, scrabbling uphill as she plunged down. Children's faces agape in the back, red-striped dresses and blazers. Going to Redmaids' School. Where she'd gone. She pulled up, slewing six feet over the white line into the traffic coming up Bridge Valley

Road. They all solemnly toured round her. A fat pink-shirted man in a Granada slowly shook his head in disbelief. She smiled weakly back at him.

You stupid cow, said Frank's voice at her shoulder.

She got stuck behind a yellow gritting lorry going down Bridge Valley Road. Amber lights spitting flashes at her, rock-salt and gravel rattling on the undertray.

She had an image of her father carefully examining the stone-chips in the bonnet's scarlet gloss, wincing as if they were his own wounds. She turned the radio up to drown the bony rattle.

Inching along the Portway through the morning rush she saw the Clifton Suspension Bridge dropping diamond splinters of thawed yellow ice into the Avon mud 250 feet below. It was dead low water and flocks of gulls were palpating the whaleback mudflats with their webbed feet, waiting for worms.

Up on to the flyover, the traffic flowing out of the city now, thinning, speeding. Past the big white sign arrowing The South West, the lazy, thudding wingbeats of Fleetwood Mac's 'Albatross' pulsing out of all four speakers. Through her chest and into her heart. She wanted them to go on playing it for ever, healing her. She wondered what would happen if she just went on driving.

Instead, she U-turned back into dull old Ashton and looking neither right nor left pulled up outside the grey pebbledashed semi. Most of the neighbours out working or taking their kids to school. Good. She couldn't face their jealous sympathy, and Frank had screwed the pair on either side anyway.

One sniff was all it took. Maybe it was the uniform, or the boredom. Or maybe everybody was like that.

There was a pile of dog mess outside the squeaky front gate. It didn't take long did it? For things to decay. Death or no death, nobody had bothered to shovel it away for her.

The front door lock was frozen. She dug in her bag for her lighter, and played the yellow flame over the brass, watching it sweat. Frank had showed her how to do that. Her father had said all it needed was a squirt of WD40 every autumn, but they'd never got around to it. Frank said Life was too short.

Inside, there was already a smell of damp and dead flowers. Her father, that careful man, had switched the central heating off without telling her. She could hear him saying to her mother, No sense in wasting heat, Wyn.

'Bloody people!' Her voice, harsh, fell into the dead rooms. She wrenched open the boiler door. Stuck on it with a Snoopy fridge magnet was a frayed piece of lined paper from a reporter's notebook. TO RESET, said her father's slanted engineer's capitals, SWITCH ELEC ON AND HOLD DOWN BLACK BTN 10 SECS. WAIT FIVE SECS THEN PRESS RED. H. N. HAMMOND.

The boiler whoffled into life and belched a blast of damp gassy air at her. Metal began to tick. She went round all the radiators turning their thermostats back to 23°C – her father kept theirs at 18°C, 'for the furniture' – and went upstairs. A 'WET PAINT' notice had been stuck on the spare room door.

There was a spider in the bath. A big one. Rae looked at it, wondering whether its legs would fold up enough to go down the plughole. As she moved her hand to the mixer tap, she saw its eye-stalks swivel. It started to scamper up the apple-green fibreglass. Rae smashed it to pieces – three-four-five times – with the bristles of the toilet brush. When she washed the legs out under the mixer tap, she felt sad. The spider had done nothing, had he? Maybe it was a she. Maybe it was pregnant. Could you be pregnant if you laid eggs?

She went into the bedroom, felt hot and fluey and sat down on the edge of the bed. Her mother had already stripped it. Frank's clothes were packed in his suitcases in the middle. Rae heaved them to one side so she could lie down, and saw they had been covering an archipelago of come-stains.

Your mother wouldn't like that, said Frank's voice. She lay down on the slippery patterned green satin and for ten long still seconds felt bereft and inconsolable. Not for Frank, for herself. She stared at the ceiling, crossed her hands on her breast. So this was what it was like to be dead. Cold, and boring. She sat up and felt her back. Nine bloody days and even the bloody bed was damp—

'Ohhhhhh God damn you all!'

The shout rang satisfyingly loud off the triple mirrors of the dressing table and the double mirrors of the swung-open wardrobe. Dust motes swam and swirled in the sunlight. She went to the window. There was a thin film of pale grey dust on the brilliant white paint. *You've missed something here, Mother.* She dabbed a finger to her tongue. Salt. Salt air from the river, condensing in the cold house.

She leaned the tips of her fingers on the sill and looked out at the view. There was no mist on the river today, otherwise it was the same as the Saturday morning before last. Red rock, trees, Georgian terraces, their limestone warm and gold against a hard blue sky. On that Saturday morning Frank had come at her as she stood now, lifted her nightdress and tried to shove his prick up her from behind. She hadn't known she was pregnant then, and to tell the truth, she was fed up with being shafted all the time to no good end. She had told him to save it for the match.

Now, not far below the grey cloud layer that librium put between her and the world, she could feel herself wanting to fuck her brains out. Instead, she turned to the dressing-table mirror and posed herself this way and that, first one hip forward, then the other.

So how's widowhood treating you, Mrs Webber?

No sign of a bulge. Not even that nice one other slim women had, rising from under the belly button and then falling away to the mons. Showing they had a womb, were women. While she was flat as a board. She jiggled her head in defiance. Her heavy pale hair still swung immaculately along her jawline, accentuating the length of her neck. Her narrow grey eyes were a bit bruised and slitty-looking, but they always were in the morning. How much make-up were you allowed for a funeral? There'd be the black veil of course; sheer, she'd chosen, like Jackie Kennedy's. She poked her tongue out at herself. A bright healthy pink. And her gums. She pointed her tongue, ran it round her lips and teeth. He used to like her doing that. Her mother always ended up with lipstick on her teeth. But hers were smaller, small and even, like her father's. Used to be. Why didn't death show? Why didn't being pregnant show? How could everything change and nothing leave a mark?

Quarter to nine: get on with it, woman.

She stripped off quickly. Her breasts were no bigger, her nipples no browner, her tan was still a pale dusty gold. Good. Black bra, suspender belt, stockings, steel-grey and black french knickers and slip. Long, black silk chinese jacket – but what skirt? She wanted to wear the chinese trousers that went with the jacket but couldn't face what they'd do to her mother. Or Mrs Webber. She'd be brick-faced, nearly as tall as her dead son, hard as nails in thunderous black, purple and mauve.

Now then, pencil-skirt or long? Long, with knife-edge one-inch pleats. Boots or shoes? Boots; and the black straw gaucho hat. Flat top, narrow brim. With the veil down she looked like Zorro's vicious younger sister. All she needed was the whip.

Is that all right, Frank?

Yeah. Great.

She packed the top-clothes in their tissue and Image of Bath carrier bags and laid them beside Frank's suitcases on the bed. Her mother said she had to ask Frank's mother if his brothers wanted any of Frank's clothes before they went on to Cancer Research.

Don't be stupid, Mother.

It's only right, Rae love. And you know what she's like.

Not wanting to, but needing to know what her mother had done, she opened both suitcases.

There was his silver-framed portrait on top. Clean-jawed, eyes cold and hard even in soft focus. Just promoted to Inspector. Staring at her bold as brass from under his shiny peaked cap.

Hi there.

His picture and his smell. What was her mother thinking of?

We know you've got to do it, love. Say goodbye.

Her knees went. She sank on to the bed between the suitcases and the Image of Bath carriers and curled up with her hand over her mouth to kill the sobs. She tried to think kindly of him, his hard young body, his ever-eager prick, but the reality refused to melt away. The truth was he was a cold, ambitious grammar-school grabber, and she was the spoilt tennis club kid he had set out to humiliate with his mirthless copper's grin and his aforesaid mighty prick. Which was just about the only thing he was generous with. In the end her convulsive sobs, her body heaving up and down on the damp green satin, were for herself. What would she do? Where would she live? What would happen to her? And the baby. Would she love it or feel doomed by it? She hoped it wouldn't look too much like Frank but expected it would. A boy, another male, his fucking image come back to haunt her for fucking ever. Weep, you poor cow, because your life's over, same as his.

The marriage probably wouldn't have lasted more than another couple of years. He had got his confidence up, sucked out of her at first, then fed on his own successes with work and women, until he was moving down the track, way ahead of her, speeding away without so much as a backward glance.

This is Rae, my ex.

She was supposed to be Stage One of the Frank Webber Apollo rocket launch. There to be used up, burnt out, and then cast off to fall slowly back to earth, end over end. Except it hadn't happened like that. It was Frank who fell, toppling sideways through her imagination like a bullock in a slaughterhouse. Definitely not part of the plan—

Hearing herself asking, *So why feel grief, you stupid woman?*

Slowly, as if she was coming out of an anaesthetic, she watched the answer taking shape in her mind.

It wasn't Frank she grieved, or herself. No, not the

Frank-that-was, but the Frank-that-would-never-be. The Frank-that-could-never-have-been. The Frank she felt her need manufacturing inside her, just as the rest of her body was manufacturing their baby.

Frank the father. The calm, modest, kind, smiling father, standing proudly beside her, arm round her waist, gazing down on his wife and child with his heart full, loving and protecting them for ever.

Frank the husband, Frank the daddy, Frank the perfect father. That was what she'd lost. That was what had been stolen from her, what she was grieving for, a father for her unborn child—

Leave it out, Rae, said Frank's voice. *You've never felt any fucking grief.*

She lay there, her mind shocked blank. It was true: she felt nothing. Not grief, not rage, not pain. Not even guilt. If she searched the silent empty sterile room in which she found herself – the recovery room, was it? – the only hint of feeling that she could detect was relief. Relief that she had outlived the bastard.

Thanks a bunch, Rae.

She shoved Frank mentally to one side and began thinking about the future. Being a widow was OK, there was something powerful and dark and female about it. Being pregnant, unfortunately, wasn't OK. Not at all—

Maybe she'd meet somebody at the funeral?

She smiled, told herself that was wicked.

Then, because she knew retribution was never far away, she realised the only person she'd be likely to meet at the funeral was DCI Barnard. He'd be there like the bloody Berlin Wall, all the way round her, blocking out every other form of life – practically blotting out the light.

What was it with him? She'd only met him a couple of times, at coppers' do's. He'd seemed perfectly all right then. Of course, he'd had his wife with him, a big sandy-haired South Walian, teacher or something, but even so—

Maybe it was something pervy, and he was some sort of death-freak and the idea of fucking a dead man's wife was a big turn-on. She felt his eyes crawling over her skin like bluebottles, shuddered and sat up.

'Yeurch—'

Looking at three different angles of her face in the dressing-table mirrors. Then realising it wasn't just DCI Barnard, although he was the worst. They were all the same, the way they looked at her. Eyes flicking over her, never meeting hers, sympathetic but sort of hiding, smirking – one of those nightmares where everybody knows you've got horrible facial cancer but you – even the Chief Constable, even the police surgeon who'd done the post-mortem, what was his name, Calder—

All quiet, noncommittal, slightly ashamed, none of them looking her in the eye – even when she'd gone in to identify him, his face already sunken, skin already tightening, that toenail pallor – and all of them murmuring what a hero he was, all using the identical bloody words practically, and not one of them daring to look at her—

Why?

The answer leaping at her out of the mirror like the late-night-smack-in-the-face revelation of adultery: I don't know how to tell you this but—

Frank hadn't died the way they said he'd died.

So how had he died?

What were they hiding?

And why bother to hide it in such a lazy, sloppy way?

The realisation grew that the only answer to that was contempt – the contempt of the group for the individual, the strong for the weak, the male for the female—

The phone rang, sharp as a drill in the still room.

'Hello?'

'Is that you Rae?' said her mother. 'Are you all right, love? You won't be too long, will you? You know the state your father gets—'

'I'm fine, Mum. Don't worry, I'm nearly done here. I shan't be much longer.' Her voice sounded strong and clear inside her head, as if she'd had cottonwool taken out of her ears.

Before she left, she set Frank's picture on the dressing

table so that she was looking at an infinite series of smiling contemptuous coppers.

Right, you bastards, if you're all so fucking superior – let's see how you like it.

She closed the front door and walked down the path. For the first time in yonks she felt calm, shining, triumphant, purposeful and alive.

3

The CC was standing waiting in the courtyard of the Bridewell, headquarters of Bristol Central CID. He was capped, gloved, and had his Chief Constable's baton under his arm.

Detective Chief Inspector Barnard, awkward in his unfamiliar uniform, hurried down the Well steps to meet him.

Under his peaked cap the CC's bony face shone in the slanting sun as if it had been sprayed with a mixture of blood, milk and latex. Although there were only a few years between them, the CC's austere black and silver figure made DCI Barnard feel as if he'd been caught skipping school assembly. He remembered to salute.

'Sorry sir.'

'Morning Barney.'

'Morning sir.'

'Nippy enough for you?'

The DCI excused himself by waving a couple of Xeroxed sheets. 'Bloody photocopiers—'

The CC took in DCI Barnard's uniform from toecaps to cap badge, caught a whiff of aftershave, and turned on his heel towards the gleaming black 1978 Daimler DS 420 limousine they shared with the Lord Mayor and Council. Its exhausts dribbled condensation and fumed massive amounts of lead-laden steam into the raw morning air. He jack-knifed his angular frame into the rear compartment, mouth compressed to a thin line. Aftershave for God's sake, aftershave at a colleague's funeral. Pollution and corruption were everywhere.

At prayer, alone with his Presbyterian God in the

narrow red sandstone nave of his choice, Chief Constable Royston Perry convinced himself once a week that he truly loved his fellow men. Outside, in the blare and mess of the real world, he could barely tolerate his own officers.

Given his steely view of justice and discipline it was hardly surprising, and he accepted the inconsistency as part of his daily life. Daily life was, after all, meant to be difficult, and his fellow citizens, the half million or so souls who swarmed and transgressed through his patch, deserved neither sympathy nor charity, let alone unconditional Christian love. Once a week and in the abstract was enough. Monday to Friday he served the God of justice, and did his best to see that was what people got.

Now, at the peak of his career and close to its end, the CC considered that, unlike the heads of certain other constabularies, he had kept his men more or less up to the mark and, in consequence, given his fellow citizens a service far better than they deserved. He had, many years ago, found it easier to retreat into a silver and black monasticism: the uniform suited his spare frame and thirty-seven years later he could still, just about, get into his first PC's serge tunic and trousers. He was proud of that; both he and his wife – a woman who remained the worn and patient whetstone to his keen-edged sense of righteousness – considered that in all those years there had been no other significant changes, mental or physical.

They had had two children, a boy and a girl; both had been to university, both had got married, and both now lived abroad, one in Canada, one in Australia. His wife sometimes wondered about that. The CC did not. He considered it the best thing Jane and Richard could possibly have done. Even so, in two years, when he retired, they were both looking forward to seeing their three grandchildren for the first time. The Chief Constable also keenly anticipated crossing the entire breadth of the North American continent on the Canadian Pacific Railway, and having a critical look at Ayer's Rock, scene of the so-called dingo murder.

Leaning back, inhaling wood and leather and being wafted past the grey limestone spires and brown glass office blocks that filled the city's heart, he found himself looking forward to his visit to the crematorium. The grounds were well-landscaped and meticulously kept, the Chapel was light and airy, and the acoustics, thanks to a mixture of curved blond wood and burnished concrete, excellent. It would make a pleasant oasis in the day for half an hour. If only the rest of this bloody Webber business weren't such a pigging mess.

Riding with the CC made Detective Chief Inspector Barnard nervous. It was meant to, and it did. Every time he shifted his stocky short-armed body on the creased grey hide, the leather made grunty farting noises. Despite the cold air from the blowers he could feel his meaty face beginning to sweat and his swept-back iron-grey hair itching under his shrunken cap band.

DCI Barnard felt uncomfortable, unreal even, in anything but a boxy Italian suit. This bloody uniform made him suck his gut in and jut his chest out even though he was sitting down. If he didn't manage to let his belt out a couple of notches by the time they got to the crem, he'd be speared with indigestion all day and probably all fucking night as well.

The CC eased himself back into the squishy grunting leather. 'It does that,' he said, 'because it's old.' He laid his left arm beside DCI Barnard's right on the double armrest. The DCI noticed the Chief Constable was wearing an ordinary stainless steel Timex. 'Not often we see you in uniform, Barney.' Their two sleeves lay side by side; compared to the CC's, Barnard's had a very faint greenish tinge. 'Not often your uniform sees you either, by the look.'

'No sir.'

'We all put weight on, Barney. I've put seven pounds on since I joined. Seven pounds in forty years. You?'

'Couple of stone.' Then airily, 'What they call different metabolisms, sir.'

The CC shot a glance at Barney. 'Heart in order?'

'So the quack says.'

'Mrs Barnard,' said the CC. 'She well?'

'Yes sir. Off on a course, sir. Headteachers' conference, Harrogate.'

'Enjoying her promotion then.'

'Loves it sir.' What the fuck was this all about?

The CC said, 'You make Super, get yourself some new kit.'

Barney felt his job horizons expanding. 'Yes sir.'

'Should that glorious day ever dawn,' said the CC curtly, 'buy yourself something that fits.' He tapped his baton on the smoked glass partition. It slid open with a satisfying hiss. 'Driver.'

'Yes sir?'

'Where do we RV the cortège?'

'At the house, sir.'

'Good. Now when we do, I want you to slip yourself in immediately behind the family. Hearse, family, us. Got that?'

'Yes sir.'

'That's all.'

'Thank you sir.' The partition hissed shut and the driver's gloved hand reached for the radio mic.

'Now then, Barney, run me through the rest of the arrangements. Vehicles?'

'Four sir.'

'Black?'

'No sir.' Christ, what did he expect, the fucking Mafia? 'Two Carlton unmarkeds sir, two Mondeo patrols.'

'Motorcycles?'

'Two sir.' Traffic were playing bloody hell as it was. Any accident or incident during the service and they'd all be stuck carless in the sodding crem. Best not to mention that.

'Total bodies?'

'With us, sir, fourteen.'

'Rank?'

'Inspector and above sir.'

The CC tapped his baton against his gloved palm. 'I want there to be enough to fill the back row, end to end. You follow me, Barney? The back row full, show our respect and support of course, but making a presence.'

'I'll have a word with the ushers.'

'You should have done that. Bearers?'

'Six, sir. Lads from Inspector Webber's station, sir.'

'Going to leave Thornbury very thin on the ground.'

'Yate have agreed to cover for half an hour.'

'Hm.'

'Makes twenty altogether, sir.'

'Women officers?'

'No sir.'

'Fair enough. Anything else?'

'TV'll be there, sir.'

'What?' Turning sharply to face Barney.

'I had a call from Maggi Reed, sir. Interviewed Inspector Webber shortly before the shit hit the fan.'

Swearing. Endemic in the CID. Disregard it or you'd learn nothing. Another damned compromise. 'So you told her what?'

'Tried to persuade her, said she should wait for the memorial service—'

'When's that?'

'Talking about mid-Jan. She said that was PR, this was news.'

'Pushy.'

'What I thought, sir.'

The CC gazed at the students milling about the University Tower at the top of Park Street. Only the overseas blacks in suits. The rest looked as if they'd been tipped out of an Oxfam skip. Skinny, badly nourished and underdressed. Hopeless. He turned back to DCI Barnard. 'I trust you said no interviews? On or off the record. Say it's out of respect for the family.'

'We discussed that, sir. They're looking at general news-item cover plus voice-over. Second lead on the local news.'

'Comprising what?'

'Arrival, coffin going in, the widow, family, other

mourners, our chaps—'

'I want those bearers' uniforms immaculate.'

'Yes sir.' The DCI made a note on one of his Xeroxed sheets.

The CC remained silent until they had passed the BBC buildings on Whiteladies Road. Television. He knew they should have had four black cars. At least four—

'D'you want to deal with the rest of it now, sir?'

'What's that, Barney?'

'The death, sir. Inspector Webber's death.'

The DCI started with the official timetable of events on the day in question:

'Approximately twelve noon, Nigel Evens, twenty-one, a traveller, does black twenty-four-year-old bar manager Ellard Wesley Atkins: blinds him with oven cleaner, strangles him with steel guitar string.

'14.15 hrs, Evens does Inspector Frank Webber, thirty-two, in Bristol Maternity Hospital: severs trachea and jugular with surgical instrument or instruments.

'15.30 hrs, Evens arrested by DC John Cromer, twenty-three, in Montpelier, Bristol.

'16.00 hrs, Evens tops self in cell: found hanging from second steel guitar string concealed in waistband of army surplus trousers.'

'Timewise, of course,' said the CC, carefully examining the stitching between the fingers of his left-hand glove, 'it all coheres.'

'Yes sir,' said the DCI. 'Timewise, we're solid.'

'Pity about the rest of it. Is that it?'

'Yes sir.' DCI Barnard offered the CC the second Xeroxed sheet. 'Detective Sergeant Hallam's report.'

The CC shook his head, waved it away. 'No glasses,' he said. 'You'll have to read it.'

The DCI glanced up at the driver. He was still talking on the radio mic. No sound penetrated the partition. '"The circumstances were—"'

'God's sake, Barney! Is he making an on-the-record statement?'

'No sir.'

'Then why start off "the circumstances were"?'

'I think it's Sergeant Hallam's way of taking the piss, sir.'

'Is it?' The CC snatched the sheet of paper, glanced at the even singled-spaced print and handed it back. 'He do this on a word processor?'

'Yes sir.'

'Do we know he's got a copy?'

'Be a fool not to, sir.'

'He's not left it on, what they call it, hard drive, has he?'

'Not to my knowledge, sir.'

'What's that supposed to mean, Barney? "Not to my knowledge"? We don't want some civilian secretary in the back of beyond keying it in and circulating the entire Force, do we?'

'No sir. According to my information, it went straight to disk.'

'What information?'

'DC Cromer, sir. He typed it up owing to Vic Hallam only having the use of one arm at the time.'

'And where's the disk now?'

'My safe, sir.'

'Have it put in mine.'

'Is that wise, sir?'

'Wise?'

'At the moment, it's only a departmental matter, for the CID, sir.'

'I see.' Breathing out through his nostrils. 'You're saying the CID is used to bending the rules.'

'No sir.' DCI Barnard maintained eye contact. 'What I'm saying, sir, is that the CID is used to that kind of accusation. Entirely different thing, sir, if you don't mind me saying so.' Then, to push the point home: 'It's the sort of situation we're used to managing, sir.'

The CC was having none of it. 'Barney.'

'Sir?'

'I'm where the buck stops. My safe, this afternoon.'

'Yes sir.'

'Carry on.'

DCI Barnard held the paper up to the intermittent sunlight and read the report out loud in a flat courtroom monotone.

'"This report by Detective Sergant V. Hallam, Bristol Central CID. The circumstances were that on the day in question, acting upon suspicion as a result of information gathered during investigations into allegations of rape laid by Senior Staff Nurse Eleanor Wilcox of Cornwallis Crescent, Clifton, I entered the examination room of Doctor Chaudhury, gynaecologist at Bristol Maternity Hospital. I found him lying unconscious on the floor. I also discovered Nurse Wilcox. She was lying upon the examination couch with both legs in stirrups. I saw that she was about to be sexually assaulted by a male figure wearing a surgical mask and hospital greens. The assailant was holding a chisel at her throat and fiddling with the front of his trousers. His intentions appeared to me to involve a second rape of Nurse Wilcox which would, in my opinion, have been closely followed by her death. During the struggle that followed, I was stabbed in the left shoulder by the assailant. Considering my life to be at risk, I fought back and was fortunate enough to chance upon a bundle of surgical instruments which had fallen from an autoclave, or high-pressure steam sterilising tank, tipped over during the aforementioned struggle. I lunged out at the assailant, who was on top of me and lying across me at the time, and by a combination of chance, luck and desperation, was able to drive a scalpel into his windpipe and jugular, as a result of which he expired. It was only afterwards, when Nurse Wilcox opened a window to let the fog of escaping steam clear, that I discovered the identity of the assailant to be that of Inspector Frank Webber, a fellow police officer."'

The CC said, 'Chance, luck and what?'

Barney said, 'Desperation, sir.'

'On.'

'"Later, after having the stab wounds in my shoulder attended to, I was called to a meeting at Bristol Central

CID. I was informed that the purpose of the meeting was to be an informal discussion of the issues involved. During this meeting, in the presence of DC Cromer and three senior officers, I allowed myself to be persuaded by arguments in favour of Mrs Rae Webber, her unborn child, her pension rights and the name of the Force in general, that the blame for Inspector Webber's death should be placed on the suspect Nigel Evens. At this time, Evens, having confessed to the murder of bar manager Ellard Wesley Atkins, was already dead by his own hand. My own future career within the Force came into the discussion. As a result, although I ultimately agreed to the course of action proposed, I did so with serious misgivings, and wish to record those misgivings here in this report. I should add that at the beginning of the meeting the Chief Constable was present but left soon after offering his congratulations and took no part in the discussion that followed. Nevertheless, I have no doubt in my mind that he was aware of what was about to take place. The other officers present were Detective Superintendent Richardson, Detective Chief Inspector Barnard, Detective Inspector Parnes. Signed, in the presence of Detective Constable J. Cromer, V. Hallam.'"

The Daimler, released from the traffic snarl-up at the top of Blackboy Hill, lunged silently across the sunlit Downs towards Westbury and Henleaze. It was quarter to eleven; outside the shadow of the Water Tower and its small copse of evergreens, the entire carpet of frost had melted and the grass shone wet and green.

The CC said, 'He's right, of course.'

The DCI, who hated Vic Hallam's idle, inconsiderate, smartass guts, said nothing.

'But then again,' said the CC, 'so are we.'

'Absolutely.'

'Have you spoken to the widow, Mrs Webber?'

Shifting in his seat. 'Yes sir. A very upset young woman.'

'Naturally. Who wouldn't be?' Then more sharply, 'How did you play it?'

'How d'you mean, sir?'

'Talk to her on the phone or what?'

There was no point in telling the CC about lunch. 'I asked if there was anything we could do, advised her of the facilities for victim counselling, then I went round to see her and her parents, offered the usual condolences, support of the Force, talked about pension arrangements, that sort of thing.'

'You gave yourself that authority, did you?'

'Only when they asked, sir. The old chap, the father's got an engineering and fabrication business. Small generators, Brislington Industrial Estate. More or less retired now.'

'But not short of a bob or two?'

'Comfortable, I'd say, from the house – his wife's a very tidy woman—'

'And how did she strike you?'

'The wife, sir?'

'Daughter.'

'Quiet, subdued, pale. Possibly still in shock. That sort of submerged, underwater thing, as if she's not coming out of it and doesn't really want to. She's still on tranquillisers, of course.' The DCI plucked at a stray nose hair. 'She used to be quite a lively young woman.'

Were her tits white under the bra or pale gold all over—

'You know her, do you?'

Drawing back, sounding convincingly neutral. 'I've met her, with her husband, at the occasional function.'

'She ask you about him?'

'I said what a good fist he made of that TV business at the conference, promotion, prospects, all that, what a fine young officer he was, so on and so forth.'

'He certainly fooled us all there.'

'Yes sir.'

The CC tapped his gloved left hand with his baton. 'As I recall, the original intention was, after a suitable interval, to tell Mrs Webber the truth. About her husband.'

'I can't see that happening much before the child is born, sir.'

'If then.' Turning to look directly at Barney: 'She get

chance to tell Webber she was pregnant?'

'No sir.'

The CC weighed this information, then dismissed it. 'Meanwhile, we've got three loose cannon rolling round the deck.' Counting them off with his baton on his gloved fingers, 'DC Cromer, Hallam, the nurse.'

'Cromer'll keep his mouth shut.'

'Where's Hallam now?'

'On leave, sir, with his shoulder.'

'The nurse?'

'No idea, sir.'

'Best find out,' said the CC, 'before the Press do.'

'Will do.'

The CC watched him scribble another note to himself. 'It's the same old business, Barney, two wrongs not making a right, but not making anything else either.'

'Sit on it?'

'Have to,' said the CC. 'Don't get too involved with Mrs Webber.'

DCI Barnard felt his prick shrivel. 'In what way, sir?'

'Pensions,' said the CC. 'Bloody minefield.'

The Daimler swung right, down into Westbury. The CC sank back into the leather. When you finally got to the end of the road, you suddenly discovered it was all uphill. Time to stick it to Barney again. 'How's the St Pauls thing going?'

'Still under obbo, sir, but it's all there, all set.'

'Meaning what?' said the CC.

'Looking for a result by the end of the week, hopefully.'

'Hopefully,' echoed the CC. His bony face grew even bleaker. 'Tomorrow is the end of the week, Barney.'

'Yes sir, I'm aware of that.'

'So?'

'Sweating on one last phone call, sir.'

'From?'

'Chingola, sir. As soon as the goods are in place and the drop is confirmed, we'll be in.'

'Chingola,' said the CC sourly.

'Place in Africa, sir.'

'I thought you said this chap was white.'

'He is, sir. You do get white men in Africa, sir. Chingola's where he comes from. Place in Zambia.'

'Is it?' said the CC. 'And does this Chingola person know what these people are bringing in?'

'Yes sir. Between two and five keys of top-quality cocaine.'

'Keys?'

'Kilos, sir.'

'Worth?'

'On the street, sir, forty to fifty grand apiece.'

The CC breathed in, and then out. 'Good.'

A police BMW motorcycle swept past, swung in, signalled them to follow.

4

Downtown, three miles south-east, two angry young women walked into Trinity Road Police Station, St Pauls. Both were single mothers and reluctant occasional prostitutes and both had come to lay a complaint: Bristol, like all big cities, had its front line, and Trinity Road Police Station stood like a referee between mainly black St Pauls and mainly white Easton, bang in the middle of the action.

To the south was the city centre with its tower blocks, chain stores and churches; to the west the sprawling mass of old and new buildings that comprised the university and the Bristol Royal Infirmary, casualty clearing station for the front line. North lay the hilly streets of partially gentrified Montpelier, and east the long tarmac dagger of the M32 motorway, the link to the M4/M5 interchange and the outside world.

In shape, and some would say nature, St Pauls was a rough diamond, an area of big, seedy houses, run-down Victorian terraces and seventies pastel-panelled council flats. It had a population which floated between ten and seventeen thousand of whom thirty to sixty per cent, depending on which set of statistics you needed to deploy, were young, black and out of work. Either way, despite the efforts of liberals, reformers and social workers to introduce degrees of tolerance and political correctness, St Pauls was known to the average unreconstructed cop or villain as the Jungle.

Like any inner city area, it was a lively place to live and work and complaints to the constabulary were not uncommon. Inspector Caroline Coombes, a slight fair-haired woman in her early thirties with a nicely curved mouth, sharp little nose and hooded humorous eyes, took the young women into an interview room out of earshot of the deadbeats in the lobby.

Neither Maelee Thomas, who was big and black, nor Nova Perrott, who was skinny and white, liked being in the interview room, which was another reason Caroline Coombes had taken them there. Nor did they like being told to be quiet while she made a note of the time, the date, their names, ages and addresses. Caroline knew both girls, and liked them for what they appeared to be doing to stay off the game and out of the massage parlours. Even so, she knew that either one would lie as soon as look at her, and it made her all the more determined not to be messed about. They might lead their chaotic lives out there on the street; in here, in the station, they had to learn there was law and order. And that law and order came in the well-groomed, tightly uniformed, Estée Lauder-fragranced person of Caroline Coombes, Community Beat Inspector.

'Now,' she said. 'You, Maelee.'

'Why her? She's straight off the banana boat.' Nova stuck her pointed chin out. 'It's because she's black, innit?'

'You'll get your turn, Nova.' Caroline glanced down at her blotter. Nova was seventeen, born in Eastville: Maelee was a year older, from Jamaica, over here since she was fifteen. Sometimes Caroline felt more like a deputy headmistress than a copper.

'Typical—'

'Shut up.'

'Yeah,' said Maelee, pretending to side with Caroline, 'show respec'.'

Nova gave Maelee a bitten-down finger and turned her thin profile away. Caroline let her fake a quick sulk, then asked Maelee what happened.

'They messed on we Pampers,' said Maelee, 'and everythin' else.'

'Messed?' said Caroline.

'Deffickated,' said Maelee.

'Crapped,' said Nova.

'And urinate and rip everythin' up and mek a royal rumpus everywhere—'

'Pissed all over everything, chucked cartons a tampons and ST's about all over, then wiped shit down the walls, it's disgustin', Miss Coombes.'

'All because we tryin' to help ourselves, y' know?'

'Bastards,' said Nova. 'All they are, little bastards.'

'And this was at the Westminster Road Community Centre?' said Caroline.

'Yeah, the old school, yeah.'

'Was anything taken?'

'Only five poun',' said Maelee, 'in small change in a bank bag, for a day's float.'

'It's because we're women see, Miss Coombes.' Nova pulled herself up and stuck her small high breasts out. She was wearing a red bra under a thin yellow T-shirt that read FUCK ART LET'S DANCE. 'They hates us doing anything for ourselves or our kiddies, they only wants us pulling fat old geezers down City Road lights, giving 'em rub-ups down the front-room massage shops—'

'What sort of bank bag, Maelee?'

'Allied Irish, I got it out meself.'

'She won't have British banks—'

'You get a better rate of hinterest,' said Maelee.

Allied Irish. It could be worth something. Caroline made a note. 'When d'you think this happened, Nova?'

'What?' Nova immediately looked to Maelee for help.

'Was done when we got there,' said Maelee.

'Yeah,' said Nova, 'quarter to nine.'

Caroline glanced at the interview room clock. Five to eleven. 'Why didn't you come here straightaway?'

'Had to clean a place up,' said Maelee.

'Yeah,' said Nova defensively, 'you can't have a crèche and go selling stuff with shit all over the walls, can you?'

'No,' said Caroline, 'I suppose not. But you could have called the station first.'

'No fucking phone is there, Maelee?'

'Not no more there fuckin' ain't,' said Maelee.

The three women looked at one another, silently agreeing it was hopeless. It was men, and it was hopeless. Men were hopeless. In fact they were worse than fucking hopeless.

'They vindictive you see, Miss Coombes,' said Maelee. 'They tryin' to drive us outta that place.'

'They hate us,' said Nova. 'Hate the whole fucking idea.'

Maelee and Nova were part of a recently started women's self-help group. They went round the streets and flats collecting a pound or fifty pence a week from each member. The fund was used for small loans of up to three times what the member had paid in, and for buying non-perishable goods such as nappies on discount from a Cash and Carry. There was also a Christmas Club. At the same time they ran a crèche and advice centre twice a week. Community workers had helped set it up, but the idea was for the women to run it themselves. They were nearly all single mothers, all on benefit, some on the game, and most had been battered. The plan was to learn what was called 'empowerment'. It had taken three months to set up and was coming apart in weeks.

'How many break-ins is this?' asked Caroline.

'T'ree,' said Maelee.

'It's not just the break-ins, Miss Coombes, it's the gauntlet of fucking abuse you have to walk through to get there. Can't you put a bloke on the door or something?'

'Tek more than one,' said Maelee, 'an' it only mek matters worse.'

Caroline was inclined to agree and didn't have the resources anyway. 'Either of you have any idea who it might be?'

'Kids, innit?' said Nova, looking at Maelee for confirmation.

'The men don't stop 'em,' said Maelee. 'They stand around laughin', y' know, and puttin' 'em up to all kind a mischievousness and recklessness.'

'Kids, men, it don't fucking matter, they want us out of there,' said Nova, 'and they don't care how they do it, do they, Maelee? They just don't want women in there, they think it's their fuckin' place and it's not, is it?' Nova's black-rimmed eyes welled with outrage. 'It's not is it, Miss Coombes, it's ours as well, the rotten fucking bastards.' She sniffed, blew her nose on a ragged peach tissue.

'Trouble is,' said Maelee. 'They don' know how to share, and I don' think they ever will. You hear me now, Miss Coombes?'

Caroline nodded, chose her words carefully. 'Which ethnic group d'you think might be responsible?'

'Blacks,' said Nova.

'Whites,' said Maelee.

'Well, that's one thing clear,' said Caroline.

'To be honest, Miss Coombes, who gives a fuck?' said Nova. 'Kids' gangs all run together now.'

'Right,' said Maelee, 'they all what they call hintegrated.'

After they had gone, Caroline typed up a report and read through the whole file on the Westminster Road Community Centre. She had promised Maelee and Nova to send someone round, but knew she wouldn't. Not yet anyway. There were two reasons: first, there would be no one to charge, and even if there were, any kid under fourteen would walk in one door and out the other, glazed with boredom, deaf to all bollockings. Undetainable, therefore untouchable – and they knew it.

The second reason was the 'concerted action' scheduled but on hold pending the final tip-off. Caroline had already expressed her opposition to the projected raid on the grounds that it would make her patch virtually ungovernable for days, if not weeks.

As she expected, given the macho potential of a gung-ho drugs bust just before Christmas, she had been ignored. After reviewing her report and the file on the Community Centre, she decided to fax the lot to DCI Barnard at the Well. His pigeon – let him deal with it.

As the pages were jerking through, she dialled his

direct line. After a dozen rings there was a crash of plastic and a rushed voice on the line:

'Bristol Central CID Bridewell – Detective Constable John Cromer speaking—'

'Is the DCI there? This is Inspector Coombes, Trinity Road.'

'No ma'am, he's at the funeral.'

'What funeral's that, John?'

'Inspector Webber's ma'am.'

'Oh right.' After a fortnight of twelve hours on, twelve hours off you lost track of the real world. 'My fax coming through OK?'

'Yes ma'am.'

'I remember you don't I, John?'

'Er, yes ma'am.'

Caroline could see his anxious choirboy look as clearly as if he were standing in front of her. She could sense him colouring up, waiting for his next reprimand. John Cromer, fresh-faced, a flop of soft brown hair hanging over one eye like a girl's, solidly built in the way that fat kids are when they grow up tall, but clumsy with his hands and feet. 'How long have you been a DC, John?'

'Two weeks, ma'am.'

'Well, I suppose they'll teach you how to pick up a phone in the end.'

'In a bit of a rush, ma'am.'

'Always were, John.'

'I mean I'm practically the only one here at the moment.'

'All gone to the funeral, have they?'

'That's right, ma'am.'

'Should be quite a piss-up,' said Caroline. 'Stick my fax where Barney can see it, will you?'

'I will, ma'am.'

'Thanks John, and good luck.'

'Thank you ma'am.'

'Who have they put you with anyway?'

'Detective Sergeant Hallam, ma'am.'

'Vic Hallam? For six months? You'll need more than

good luck, John.'

A pause. 'He's all right when you get to know him.'

Caroline lit a Rothmans. 'Is he?' She blew smoke out. 'How's his arm?'

'Coming on. He's still off sick though.'

'He'll be lowering a few after the funeral then, arm or no arm.'

Another pause – Cromer's voice became guarded and official. 'I don't think so, ma'am.'

She made herself sound casual. 'Not on the wagon, is he?'

'No, ma'am.' Cromer seemed to have run out of words. She decided not to push it.

'Give him my love when you see him.'

'Very well, ma'am.'

'Very well'? A bit stiff and strained, wasn't he? Caroline put the phone down and waited to tear the confirmation slip off the fax. STATUS OK, it said, NO FAILURES. She blew out another long, smoke-laden breath. That's what you think, sunshine.

Years ago, when she was still a probationer, Detective Sergeant Vic Hallam had spent a long time trying to get her knickers off. And would have bloody well succeeded, too, if it hadn't been for probationers' rules. Fuck the rules, he had said. She could still hear him saying it, still hear that rough, gravelly voice. *Fuck the rules.* Ye Gods, he had said it often enough, even then. But she wouldn't, and after that he drifted off and married someone else. Some civilian. All legs, big hair and IKEA furniture. Then all that had fallen apart, furniture included, or so she'd heard.

Now he was still a DS and she was an Inspector. Oh fuck it. More muddy water not quite under the bridge. Fuck it, fuck it, fuck it. She stabbed out the Rothmans, picked up a sheaf of beat reports and timesheets, and wondered what the old bastard was up to.

Vic Hallam, six foot, thirteen and a half stone with pale grey eyes and dark straight hair, was watching a washed-out video of an old Kirkland Laing fight. He was thirty-seven years old and had spent almost twenty years in the Force, the last fourteen as Detective Sergeant. The life had left its marks, the odd dent here and there, but it hadn't – yet – wiped the faint fuck-you grin off his face.

He was wearing a baggy dark-blue suit and had his left arm propped up along the back of the only chair in the room because that was where it felt most comfortable. He had just been to the Bristol Royal Infirmary to have seven stitches taken out of the chisel wound in the ball of tendon and muscle on the top of his left shoulder and it was throbbing like buggery. Tendinitis, the young Indian doctor who had examined him said, and asked him what he did for a living. When he told her she said to avoid driving or wrenching it in any way and to stick to light duties for a month, but there was no way Vic was going to sit in the Well typing and answering the phone with DCI fucking Barnard just up the corridor.

Apart from the black rental TV and video the only other furniture in the room was a figured charcoal grey carpet. You could see where the rest of the stuff had been – settee, chair, sideboard, bookcase – from the dark untrodden rectangles exposed to the sun for the first time since the carpet-fitters left.

Vic's soon-to-be-ex-wife Pat, or Trish as she called herself in her new Cricklewood incarnation, apparently incensed by finding him in bed with Ellie, the nurse whose life he had saved, had got the bailiffs in on the grounds that all the furniture was hers, she'd paid for it and she was having it. *So there.*

Then Ellie had gone, and Vic was left with the legal minimum of bed, table and chair, plus half a shelf of Elmore Leonard paperbacks, some sun-faded blue Conrads that had belonged to his father and, thrown on the floor, a VHS triple-pack BBC History of Rock and Roll he'd bought to remind himself how it used to be, and a couple of boxing videos he'd forgotten he'd recorded.

At first Vic told himself he liked the emptiness and echoing space of the Cotham semi-basement he had lived in for the last eight years; it was bigger, simpler, and there was a sense of freedom. Then he began to feel cleaned out, as if the marriage and everything that went with it had been wiped off the tape and it was day one and he was on his own.

The truth of the matter was that Pat, Trish, whoever she thought she was, wanted him out so the place could be sold and she could use her whack to buy her own 'space' up in Cricklewood – and no doubt get that short-arse little prick of an area sales manager to put her shelves up for her.

It didn't feel like that, though; it felt like being five years old and dumped on some cold and rainy station near Manchester somewhere with the carriages receding and the shiny steel rails going straight through your fucking heart.

Pale grey walls. White woodwork. Dark grey carpet pocked with black cigarette holes.

The only splash of colour in the monochrome room was the multicoloured headband Kirkland Laing was wearing to tie back his dreadlocks. He was giving his usual dismaying-to-disastrous display, shuffle-dancing around like some kamikaze Zulu, arms down by his sides, daring the crowd's boos and the ref's any-minute-now disqualification. Showboating they called it but only Muhammad Ali really knew what the point was; Cooper, a compact and competent white welterweight, was clipping Kirkland all round the ring.

The phone and doorbell rang simultaneously. Vic put Kirkland Laing on freeze, set his wineglass of Konstantin Vodka and Buxton Carbonated Natural Mineral Water carefully on the carpet, and coughed his way to the front door. He heard the answerphone cut in on the third ring – and there was Cromer filling the doorframe, fresh-faced and grinning in a fake Barbour jacket and green wellies.

'Fucking hell, John.'
'How you doing, Vic?'

'Where's your fucking shooting stick?'

'Des finally turned up so I'm off to Oldbury, see that cider bloke about putting badgers' heads in the vats.'

'They don't dress like that up the fucking Severn, John. It's all dungarees and Daewoo Tractor baseball caps.'

'Yeah, well,' said Cromer. 'Can I come in a minute?'

When they got in the sitting room the red LED light on the answerphone was blinking, no sound coming out, and Kirkland Laing's headband was flicking between two frames on the video.

'Christ Vic, what happened?'

'Never get married, John.'

'Jesus.'

'Want a drink?'

Cromer glanced at his watch. 11.35. 'Better not.'

'Only vodka.'

'Small one, then.'

'Mug all right?'

'Anything.'

As Vic shambled out, Cromer looked from the video to the curtainless windows to the full ashtray and the blinking answerphone. Place looked and stank like a dosser's squat. 'I called you earlier.'

'I was out.'

'No answerphone.'

'I know. I forgot.' Vic reappeared with an old Bristol Zoo mug with a picture of Alfred the Gorilla on it. 'Fucking rush to get down the BRI.'

'What they say?'

Vic picked up his wineglass. 'Don't do it again, basically. Cheers.'

'Cheers.' Cromer sipped at the cracked mug, expecting tonic, finding water. 'So, when you coming back?'

'Depends on you, John.'

'How?'

'Not sitting in a fucking office for a month,' said Vic. 'So you'll have to do all the donkeywork, driving and all that shit.'

Cromer grinned. 'So what's new?'

'Cunt.'

Now was the time, Cromer decided. 'Where's Ellie anyway?'

'Who?'

'You pissed?'

'Pissed off more like, mate.'

'Why?' Trying to sound innocent, affronted, caring.

Vic slumped in the chair, stretched his left arm along the back and drained his glass. 'Come on, John, don't fuck about. Who sent you?'

After Cromer explained that DCI Barnard had called him from Henleaze on his mobile and said the CC wanted to know the whereabouts of Staff Nurse Wilcox, Vic seemed to relax, get his fuck-you grin back.

'You arsehole.'

'Why?'

'They've left it a bit late to get worried, haven't they? Then they send you.' Vic looked at Cromer and shock his head. 'Tell 'em to stop shitting themselves, she's gone to see her mother. She broke down at work, they said she'd come back too soon and gave her a couple of weeks off. In sunny Birmingham.' Vic leaned forward, jaw jutting. 'Is that all right, or do you want the fucking address?'

Cromer reddened. 'No need to take it out on me—'

'Look John. You work with me. *Me*, right?'

'Yeah—'

'They're using you. Using you against me. Because if you want to know something, you don't piss-arse about with all this tut-tut fucking sympathy, where's the furniture and what happened down the hospital, you come out with it and ask me straight off, Where's Ellie? And I'll tell you she's pissed off, I'm pissed off, we're all pissed off, but don't you worry about her telling her little old grey-haired mother because she won't. She's had enough of all this, poor kid, and that includes me. Right?'

'Sorry, Vic.'

'Yeah, well, next time you feel inclined to use your brains my son, watch this.' Vic picked up the remote and clicked it. For another twenty seconds or so, with the crowd hissing and booing, Kirkland Laing swayed about, not quite out of range, letting Cooper catch him with a series of one-twos to the head and body, sending his sweat spraying through the TV lights. Kirkland Laing backpedalled, suddenly looking flat-footed. The crowd bayed and Cooper lunged forward. Kirkland Laing leaned elegantly back and hit him with a wicked left cross that had 'insane killer' written all over it. Cooper stopped, wobbled to the floor, legs and brains turned to jelly. It was Kirkland Laing's first real punch and the fight was over.

'Suckered,' said Vic. 'Guy's a genius. Wonder where he is now?' He fumbled awkwardly for a Marlboro. 'He used to fuck off after a fight, nobody'd see him for months.' He lit up, stretched back into the chair. 'What I should've done, John.' They watched Kirkland Laing hold up his Lonsdale belt, not smiling much, and then the screen dissed itself into black and white flashes. Vic put his foot on the remote and turned it off.

'Anyway, the point is, some people can do that,' Vic nodded at the blank screen. 'You can't, John.'

Here we go again, thought Cromer. Still the fucking punchbag.

'I don't know whether I can, any more,' Vic continued. Cromer wondered how you could get maudlin at half-past eleven in the morning. 'I don't know whether I want to, and that's what it's all about, even in this game. Being hungry for it. Looking for the next punter to wade in and chance his arm. And then you lead 'em on and on and on, and then smack. End of story. Lights out and they never knew where you were coming from. Good old Kirkland. Best welter we ever had. But erratic.' Vic levered himself out of the chair, went into the kitchen and came back with the Konstantin and Buxton bottles under his arm. He refilled his wineglass half and half, offered the bottles to Cromer, who declined. Vic set the bottles by the right arm of the chair and lowered himself into it. 'Fuck it.'

'I'm game if you are,' said Cromer.

Vic looked up at Cromer over the edge of his wineglass. 'Never kill anybody, John.' For a moment he was dead serious; then he grinned. 'They don't appreciate it. Nobody does.' He sucked at the drink. 'They all think it's your fault.'

'Bollocks,' said Cromer. 'You saved Ellie's life.'

'Yeah, well, you should've seen the way she looked at me yesterday morning just before she left.'

'How?'

'"What's the mad fucking beast going to do now? How soon can I get through that fucking door?"' Vic leaned forward, stubbed his cigarette and shook his head at the overflowing ashtray. 'I don't know who the sodding hero is but I sure as fuck know who's the villain.' Then, leaning back. 'It's bad fucking news, man. The full bag of snot, as friend Billy says, is a lot to carry round.'

Not knowing what else to say, Cromer said, 'Have you thought about counselling at all?'

They looked at each other in dead seriousness for about four seconds, then burst out into loud hysterical laughter.

'You know what I like about you, John?' said Vic, tears in his eyes.

'No, what?'

'You're not just a big silly pink-faced prat are you? You're a world-class fucking arsehole.'

'Only trying to help,' said Cromer. It set them off again.

'Holy shit,' wheezed Vic.

'Fuckin' hell,' said Cromer, shaking and wiping his eyes.

After that they had another drink and talked about work for ten or fifteen minutes, the main thing being the drug bust and what Barney was doing about it.

'Not a lot by the look,' said Cromer.

'Don't you fucking coco,' said Vic. 'He's a bastard but he's a cunning bastard. Look how he's tried to stitch me up over this fucking Webber thing.'

'Yeah, well, you and him, two black dogs isn't it?'

'What?' said Vic.

'Fight on sight,' said Cromer.

'Tell you something for nothing, my son. You don't stick up to him he'll walk all over you, trample you into the fucking shit beneath his chariot wheels.'

'Different with you and him though, isn't it? You actually like all that fucking aggro and argy-bargy.'

'All right,' said Vic, 'you're such a psychological fucking genius, wait till six o'clock tonight.'

'Then what?'

'Then you'll find out it's all weekend leave cancelled, crash-bang-wallop, falling-downstairs time.'

'He's already got fifty OSG blokes on standby.'

'There you are then,' said Vic. 'I'm not saying he's wrong to keep shtumm—'

'What are you saying then?'

'I'm just saying he's a fucking sadist, John.'

Cromer was grinning again. 'Feel better now?'

Then they started figuring out how the hell to get Vic passed fit so he wouldn't be stuck in the Well. Vic thought the police surgeon, Calder, would help. He was a hard enough case, and didn't give a bugger so long as he got his consultation fee on time. Vic would give it a day, then if his arm was anything like, he'd slap some Deep Heat on it, take a couple of paracetamol, see Calder privately and tell him he couldn't feel a thing.

With the warm vodka-driven feeling that contact had been re-established and progress made, Cromer left. At the door, Vic stopped and looked at his watch. Ten to twelve.

'That cunt Webber should be going up in smoke any minute now.' No trace of a smile on Vic's face. 'And if there was any justice in this fucking world, John, that fucker Barnard would be going with him.'

On the answerphone Inspector Caroline Coombes said she'd spoke to Cromer and hoped Vic's arm was getting better. There was a few seconds' silence as if she were going to say something more, but she didn't.

5

The organist stopped. Rae noticed he played in thick grey woollen socks, his creased black shoes parked neatly under his bench. The blue velvet curtains whirred shut, then swung apart half an inch. The vicar motioned her to start leading people out. They passed the curtained niche; Frank's coffin was still on its stainless steel rollers. *Goodbye Frank.*

They left the Chapel through a green baize side door. She could hear feet behind her, her mother sniffing, her father murmuring comfort, people standing in their pews, men clearing their throats. The organ started again. Bach's Toccata and Fugue. Outside a clock was tolling twelve, there was a hum of traffic, and the air was fresh and cold. Rae felt heavy with relief.

They were in the Garden of Remembrance, a brick-walled quadrangle with raised beds of berried shrubs around a central fountain. The roof, raftered and pergola'd, was open to the sky. Vines and creepers had shrivelled round their blackened nails and the wood was green with lichen. The fountain was dry, with a few dead leaves. The vicar said something over his shoulder about frozen pipes. She heard her father say not to worry.

The walls of the quadrangle were perforated like a dovecote at the top, the floor paved with artificially eroded composition slabs. Laid out on a low brick plinth in front of the fountain were the flowers, cloudy and glistening in their cellophane. The vicar indicated she was supposed to stand by them. She moved obediently forward. The vicar turned and smiled, spreading his hands as if he had just performed his usual trick.

Frank's mother, her face as hard and pale as frozen veal, appeared at her side. They stood shoulder to shoulder receiving a double line of people. It was mind-numbingly slow and awful: a bizarre re-run of Rae's wedding reception with Frank's mother standing in as groom. No one else seemed to notice: it was as if they, not she, had all been slugged by librium. Frank's mother smelled of something faded and flowery; it reminded Rae of the potpourri in the office lavatories.

First came the families, the Webber brothers with their wet doggy kisses, their wives consoling their mother-in-law, then eyeing Rae as the enemy who had unforgivably escaped. After them came Frank's rugby-playing mates, thick-necked and embarrassed in blazers and pale grey flannels. Everybody seemed to be looking for their own flowers, to see what they had paid for, what they had said.

Out in the carpark, Maggie Reed was watching her cameraman load his tooled metal boxes into a Channel One VW Polo. She turned towards Rae and for a second their eyes met; Maggi raised half an eyebrow in what Rae construed as sympathy.

Her two bitch neighbours air-kissed her, looking sad, wiping their eyes and saying they shared her loss. She thanked them for their supportiveness and concern. Neighbours, she said, everybody needs good neighbours. One in dark grey, one in dark blue, both in high-heeled boots and fake Georgina von Etzdorf multicolour velvet scarves. Moving on to ogle the packets of the rugby boys and dream of a bedroom afternoon, semi-drunk and sentimentally shagging their arses off for Frank. *In memoriam.*

Finally, after her boss and a couple of account directors from the Queen Square advertising agency where she worked, a dozen or so uniformed policemen. Older, greyer men, led by the CC. He spent a couple of minutes talking seriously to Frank's mother about the sad loss of her son. An officer they could ill afford to lose. A credit to the Force. Who knows the mind of God. Deepest condolences. The CC grimly relishing the occasion, like a prisoner set free for half an hour, while DCI Barnard took Rae's black kid-gloved hand in his and pressed his thumb on the back of hers. Anything I can do, Rae, anything. His nostrils flaring to inhale her warmth, his hard little eyes boring into hers – then turning hurriedly away, trotting out after the CC into the grounds and the carpark.

The old cow was clearly bucked by her chat with the Chief Constable. She watched him go, checked to see her family were waiting, and turned a combative stare on Rae.

'There's to be a memorial service. Had you heard anything about that?'

'No.'

'Well, there is.' Drawing herself up, looking down on Rae. 'Mister Perry's just told me. St Mary Redcliffe, mid-January. It'll be big.'

'Oh.' Thinking, Jesus Christ, is there no fucking end.

Mrs Webber went on staring at her. Then she said, 'His ashes.'

'Yes?'

'I'd like them.'

'I see.'

'He was my son.'

Rae kept her face blank. 'Of course. I'll see you get half.'

Mrs Webber said, 'You never were any good.' Then she said, 'We shan't be coming back to the house,' and stalked off, thin legs stretching her skirt wide apart, to rejoin her family.

Rae moved out of their eyeline to look at the flowers, conscious for the first time in days that she might be beginning to enjoy herself.

The sound of a pair of heels approaching, slowing tentatively, stopping. She turned round. Maggi Reed was standing in the square brick archway. Spiky blonde hair, slanty cat-like eyes, pointy determined chin. She looked shorter than she did on TV.

'Mrs Webber?'

'Yes?'

'Maggi Reed.' She came forward, extending a gloved hand. 'I'm sorry.'

'Thank you.' Rae had always thought they looked alike: Maggie was shorter and more assertive but the similarity was there.

'I only met your husband once.'

'Yes, I know, I saw your interview. Thanks.'

Maggi said, 'Can I talk to you? Not now, obviously, but later. Some time next week possibly? If you feel up to it.'

'What about?'

Maggi handed her a business card with something handwritten on it. 'That's my home number. I'll leave it up to you.' She turned to go.

'Hang on a minute. What d'you want to talk to me about?'

Maggi gave her a straight no-shit big-sister look. 'Your husband,' she said. The cameraman began calling her from the VW Polo, waving a mobile phone. She looked from Rae to the car, back to Rae. 'Something's not right,' she said briefly and hurried off.

Rae stayed in the Garden of Remembrance, needing to be alone to savour the moment, to feel the surge of triumph. She had felt damped down by everybody treating her as a widow, so this was more like it – and if someone like Maggi Reed thought the police were playing funny buggers, there was a chance they could win. What they could win Rae wasn't exactly sure, but it had to be something to do with Frank's death, some sort of cover-up. For a moment inhaling the sickliness of cut freesias in the cold air, she felt quite grateful to Frank for giving her something to do beside soak up fucking sympathy.

Then she had an image of herself as a child going with her father to his fabricating shop, waiting while he finished off some job. It was dark, there was the soft pop of a cutting torch being lit, a roar of gas, her father pulling the black protective mask over his face, looking for a moment more like Darth Vader than her mild old dad, then a tip of flame hissing hard and fierce, and her father holding its diamond-bright spearpoint in his dark gloved hand.

Yes, that was it, how she felt.

Something's not right. Oh boy.

A muffled roar came from the windowless building at the back of the Chapel. It sounded like a massive central heating furnace.

Her father appeared and took her by the elbow, 'You don't want to stay here any more, Rae.'

Rae knew what she'd got to do, and she knew she'd got to be drunk to do it. It didn't take long.

Even without the Webbers, her parents' house was full. Her mother had prepared a cold buffet: ham, rare beef, potato salad, her rice and pea thing, French bread and cheese. By 12.30 it had been demolished, along with a crate and a half of Australian Chardonnay and a litre bottle of Teachers. Everybody agreed the occasion and the cold weather had sharpened their appetites. People admired the garden. Her father showed a couple of grey-haired inspectors his leeks and brassicas. Her mother stayed inside, telling people to smoke if they wanted to, 'Father did', then hovering round them like a hawk when they lit up, plying them with ashtrays, opening the french windows and looking anxiously at the curtains, wondering how she'd get the cigarette smell out.

At quarter to one the CC looked at his watch and said it was time to make a move and give these good people a hard-earned rest. The uniforms immediately began to move towards the door. Rae heard the rugby boys planning to go on to the Dirty Duck in Westbury and saw her bitch neighbours glancing at each other wondering if it would be worth it. Rae's father was talking to DCI Barnard, calling him Barney, and saying he was worried about Frank's old Renault – it was all the transport Rae'd got until she got something smaller, and it was still stuck in the Bridewell. DCI Barnard looked at Rae, said he'd get something sorted and give her a bell. Rae, three glasses in, put her hand on his back, felt the heat coming out of his thick body, leaned against him to let a rugby boy past and said, Thank you. The DCI swallowed the last of his drink and said, No bother. Rae saw perspiration running down his neck behind his long red ear.

By five to one, they were all gone and Rae's mother said she was going upstairs for a change and a rest. Her father started collecting plates and glasses and stacking them in the machine. Rae, feeling buoyant and decisive, followed her mother upstairs.

'Mum.'

Her mother, in her tea-coloured slip, embraced her and closed the bedroom door at the same time. 'Oh Rae, love.'

'I'm all right, honest.'

'Well,' her mother made space to hang her black and navy two-piece on the wardrobe rail, 'I know it's unchristian of me to say so, but thank God the Webbers didn't come.'

'Bloody cheek. I mean, he hadn't even been cremated and there she was asking for his ashes – no, not asking, demanding—'

'To tell you the truth love, I'd let her have them, just be thankful it's all over.'

'Is it though?'

'Rae,' said her mother firmly, 'you've got the baby, and you stood up to her. What's done is done.' She climbed into their high thirties bed and leaned back against the inlaid sunburst headboard. 'Tell Daddy not to put the machine on.'

'Mum.' Rae sat on the edge of the bed.

'Yes, love?'

'I'm going back to Ashton.'

Her mother took her hand. 'Oh love, are you sure?'

'I've got to start sometime haven't I? You and Dad have had enough the last few days.'

'Oh dear,' said her mother. Rae could tell she was already resigning herself to it. 'But what'll you do?'

'Sell it and get a flat. Clifton, if I can afford it.'

Her mother gazed off into the distance. 'You won't want anywhere with stairs, not with a baby.'

It took Rae five minutes to change and pack, then she went downstairs to find her father. He was standing in the garden scratching his head, looking tired, smoking his pipe. He said what about the heating, and she said she'd already put it back on. He nodded, accepting it just as her mother had done, knocked his pipe out on the sundial, gave her a kiss and told her to call if she needed anything doing – and in the meantime he was feeling pretty whacked, what with everything, and thought he'd go up for a quick zizz himself. At the foot of the stairs he said he didn't know how she was off for food, so if there was anything she wanted from the fridge she was to take it.

Rae found an open bottle of Chardonnay and sat down to wait.

Two glasses later, on the dot of two o'clock, DCI Barnard turned up. He had changed into his dark blue Italian suit.

'Hello, Rae,' he said. 'Fit?'

She stood up, swayed, floated to the front door, feeling woozy but all right. 'Fine.'

'I'll drive, shall I?'

'Fine.'

6

'Fucking hell, Baz,' said Rupert, winding the marine-blue Land-Rover out of Heston Services lorry park, 'there's a red-stripe, man.' A Rover 827i motorway patrol sat between two container trailers, obbo-ing the exit slip to the M4.

Baz was building a spliff and watching 'Home and Away' on a two-inch Casio stuck in the ventilator grille. He lowered the spliff between his knees and leaned back against the white cab-side to hide his face. Rupert slammed up through the gears in the close-set gate. One more graunch from second into first instead of third and the fucking gearbox would be a bag of nails. You couldn't accelerate the damn thing either or the 827i would pull them over for exhaust emissions. Fucking diesels. Fucking Land-Rovers. Fucking Baz. He kept his eye on the shivering image in the rear mirror. The 827i nosed forward, then stopped. Bastards. Playing with them.

He ran out of slip road with the Land-Rover doing forty-five and an artic charging up behind him doing sixty. Lights flashing. Air-horns blaring. The Land-Rover pulling over, hammering on the edge of the hard shoulder, steering all over the place, cab rocking and weaving as the artic blasted past, its strutted wing-mirror smacking the cab roof. A woman's face framed in frizzy black hair, leaning out from the artic's passenger seat, shoving the mirror straight, mouthing *You stupid cunt.* Shit. Fucking diesels. Fucking Land-Rovers. Fucking Baz.

'Heh-heh-heh,' said Baz.

'You couldn't fucking wait, could you?' Glancing in the mirror. No red-stripe. 'Fucking bombhead.'

Baz gave him a loose cock-eyed grin. 'Man, you goin' soft in the belly.' Holding the open spliff between two long brown fingers and a delicate thumb, he sprinkled white powder along the mixture of Old Holborn and ganja. A quick twist and a loving lick and there it was: not perfect but with all the vibration not bad either. The Casio screen had gone into white morse so he switched off, lit up, leaned back and inhaled.

Rupert, wrestling with four inches of play in the steering, sneaked a look at his Bangkok Rolex. Five past two. An hour and a half late already. An average of forty was another two and a half hours to go and then arriving in fucking Bristol in the fucking dark. The cab filled with white acrid smoke like a wet bonfire with added chemicals. 'Holy shit, Baz.'

Baz smiled, wreathed in smoke. 'Relax, man. Be 'appy.'

The week before, Rupert, a vicar's son by adoption, had lowered his lanky frame into a mist-blue Naugahyde settee in Baz's British West Hampstead basement and waited for Baz to come out of the shower.

The most striking thing about Rupert was his masses of long, tight, pale-blond corkscrew ringlets. At first glance they made him look like a public schoolboy imitation of a seventies rock star. Second glance, once you got past the hair, you saw the long, thin lips, the bulging forehead, the expressionless slate-coloured eyes and the general boniness and pallor of the facial structure, and Rupert began to look like a death's head, or the Mask, or even the Mekon when young.

Most people, women included, never got past the hair.

Rupert Lang was import and export: Turkish and Afghani rugs and cushions, Indian brassware, Thai solderwire bicycles, Peruvian felt clothing, Colombian Indian silver, Russian dolls and toys, ex-GDR tinware,

Nigerian woodcarvings, Taiwan lacquerwork and, most recently, wholesale aromatherapy oils and perfumes from India and South-East Asia via the Middle East. He was twenty-eight, looked twenty and had been on the street since he was eighteen.

He had spent the last five years more or less continuously abroad: Africa, the Far East, Central and South America, backpacking and campervanning and working tables when he had to, building up his contacts and suppliers when he had amassed enough strap to start putting a load together.

Because he dressed well – linen suits, English hacking jackets, immaculately pressed trousers – always wore well-polished shoes, and had such astonishing innocent-looking semi-aristocratic hair, he had had plenty of offers to go into the drugs scene but had always stayed clean. Until now.

He leaned back, lit a Camel and looked at Baz's pictures. A couple of bright shiny acrylics of tropical plants, a Montego Bay poster, framed, three or four family Enprints with pigtailed girl children in white dresses and a Gauguin repro of a bunch of sullen heavy-duty Tahitian chicks.

The reason Rupert had stayed clean was, just before leaving home forever at the age of eighteen, he had got himself busted for growing hydroponic cannabis in the roof of the grannexe of his adoptive parents' Cotswold vicarage. Where, because of a fondness for foul language from the age of ten – amateur child psychologist friends wondered about Tourette's Syndrome, but the vicar and his wife knew better – he'd been stuck out of the way of their horse-and-labrador set. He collected three months in Leyhill Open where he learned that, far from being what the family lawyer called 'a schoolboy prank' (ignoring the fact that Rupert had been expelled from Bryanston for dealing hash when he was sixteen), his sentence meant his named and coded mugshot would be on every customs hit-list from Reykjavik to Hobart.

Leyhill Open, in Gloucestershire, was also where he met Baz.

'Hey man, how you doing? Is what 'appen, star?' Baz, aged forty and wrapped in a green and gold towel, came through from the shower. He still had a fighter's upper body, the neck and shoulders, even if the midriff had started to thicken. He looked more Spanish-Caribbean than Jamaican: high cheekbones, curved nose, flat black semi-Indio eyes, narrow moustache and scowl. 'Hit me, lion-man.' They touched fists.

'Yo,' said Rupert. 'Sorry to hear about your sister, man.'

Baz shrugged. 'What 'appen, 'appen.'

Basically, Rupert couldn't give a fuck, he'd never met the woman, but bullshit was always necessary so they talked about Baz's sister and the funeral for a while. Everywhere you went in the world this kind of stuff went on, enquiring about each other's health, families, all that shit. It was necessary to get a smell of each other before getting down to business but as far as Rupert was concerned that was it.

'Looking good, Baz.' Rupert tried not to look at Baz's two missing toes.

'You too, man. Nice threads.'

Rupert was wearing a smooth mid-green Lovat with slant pockets and a single vent, narrow tan moleskins and a pair of gleaming half-brogues which looked as if they'd been carved from a single piece of polished yew. 'How's the leg?'

Baz pulled up the green and gold towel. A fourteen-inch scar the colour of charred wood ran diagonally along his right thigh muscle. In shape it was like a long thin canoe with black elongated dots at intervals where the stitches had pulled. Baz looked at it, frowned, made a kissing noise with his tongue against the back of his teeth. 'I should a bit the motherfucker's head off.'

Eighteen years ago, Baz Baxter had been making a promising name for himself as a twenty-two-year-old soldier with a Kingston wrecking crew round Corona where the Jamaicans were making their moves on New York. A Korean grocer, not appreciating the protection he was being offered, hit Baz with a meat cleaver. Baz blew him away with a pumpgun, but it was the end of his career as a soldier, and his carelessness finished him as far as the hierarchy was concerned. Their view was Baz was just too fucking coked-up to fly right, so fuck him.

After lying low in Jamaica, being nursed by his sister Evelyn for a couple of years and nearly losing his leg as well as his middle toes to gangrene, Baz made it on a dead man's passport to North London. As Winston Simmons, he dealt, ran girls, dabbled in sounds and property, made himself as safe as a black male dealer ever is, with this flat here and a house in Brixton where he kept his wife and family. But deep down, as Rupert knew, he remained full of hate, half-mad, bitter as fuck.

Luckily, Rupert fascinated Baz – the hair, the clothes, the whole public school bit – and Baz fascinated Rupert. Partly because he'd killed people but mostly because, like Rupert, he was a dealer. A dealer in an area Rupert needed to get in on. Despite their mutual fascination, which like all such relationships had both sexual and non-sexual components, it was going to be tricky. Rupert's bottom line was that Baz was fucking mad; Baz's bottom line, as Rupert well knew, was that Rupert was fucking white.

What gave Rupert a window into Baz's chaotic black-rage interior was an incident at Leyhill Open. They were both working in the library at the time, with a nice old queer called Clifford Uley. Clifford was a little sherry-drinking red-faced guy, fiftyish, with dyed-black shiny hair parted in the middle and a mincy way of moving his mouth when he spoke. He said he was an Empire Zionist or something and believed the British people were the Lost Tribe of Israel.

For some reason this made black people the spawn of the devil to Clifford's way of thinking, which amused the hell out of Baz, at least on the surface, and he loved to get the old queen frothed up on the subject. Clifford was so convinced he was almost convincing. The Masons were in it somewhere, and the Pyramids, and all sorts of Bible stuff about Blood and Fire and Scarlet Whores which bored the shit out of Rupert.

Nevertheless it was interesting, instructive even, to see Baz working Clifford. He'd go at him verbally, jabbing here, jabbing there, until Clifford projected from his pink and spittly mouth a blast of screaming hysterical obscenity-laced white race-hate straight into Baz's grinning black face.

On the one hand it was like watching one guy jerking off another – it left Clifford shaky and pale and full of apologies and cups of tea for Baz – and on the other hand it seemed to satisfy Baz that this buried mass of high-pressure white race-hate not only existed but could also be tapped. Like some hidden red-hot gas field he somehow needed to know about.

Maybe it mirrored something in Baz, maybe he just liked to humiliate the old bugger, maybe he was showing off to Rupert, telling him something. Any case, it was weird to an eighteen-year-old, but it livened up their wet Wednesday afternoons when all else they had to do was put the books back in alphabetical order, which was another thing that drove Clifford bereft. He was doing three years for conning old ladies out of their lifesavings by offering them matrimony and the spiritual benefits of British Empire Zionism.

'Love an' religion,' said Baz admiringly the afternoon this came out, 'shit, man, it's solid gold. And they never knew you was a homosexualist?'

'Oh no,' said Clifford seriously. 'Things would never get that far. That's what they liked about me, you see. I was decent.'

Baz nodded soberly at Clifford, raised an eyebrow at Rupert. 'Decent,' he said. 'Yah.' He stretched out one arm and buried his hand in Rupert's locks, tugging affectionately. He put his other arm round Clifford's shoulder. 'Now you and me and him, we all still nice, right? Nice and decent, right?'

The winter afternoon wore on, with February rain sluicing down the full-length brown metal windows of the octagonal reading room. Rupert was deep in a pile of stained *National Geographic*s, supposed to be arranging them by date, but really just leafing through from one warmly described tropical turtle-haunted paradise to the next. Cold places never interested him. Gloucestershire with its livid, rolling, over-fertilised green fields was cold enough, for fuck sake.

Emerald green was what he was looking for, and turquoise and jade-coloured sea, and sand pale as his hair and warm as a bed; somewhere he could heal the pain with black faces smiling their big calm melony smiles at him. And nobody telling him he was a failure and a dropout and a damned bare-faced liar who would kill his mother if he went on and after all they'd done for him, all that money down the drain on his education and look at him, he was still a disgrace and a burden and a hopeless financial liability, a useless long-haired maggot of a son rotten to the very core and centre of his don't-care selfish little soul. Good God boy don't you care for anybody or anything?

Well, no, basically, was the answer to that.

In which case there's the door go and stay with the rest of your precious junkie friends and see where it gets you – on the needle, in the gutter and good riddance.

Except it never was good riddance, it just went on and on. Never-ending. Backwards and forwards like a fucking ripsaw across his fucking nerves.

What made it worse was that during these rows, to their eternal credit and Rupert's tight-lipped resentment, the vicar and his wife never once mentioned the fact that he was adopted, even though he had known since the age of ten when some patchouli-smelling, henna-haired, foul-mouthed hippy virago had turned up bombed out of her tree and tried to claim him. Luckily, one phone call and the vicar had her sectioned.

The incident was never spoken of again but from then on Rupert came to see his adoption not as an act of kindness and charity but as the vicious and deliberate corruption of his innocence by three conniving adults.

The yeast of malice entered the thin blue milk of his existence, fermenting and thickening his resolve, and throughout his teenage years finding new ways of provoking, disappointing and physically frightening his so-called parents was his prime motivation: the more they despaired of him, the greater his lacerated satisfaction.

Serve the false fuckers right.

Since then Rupert had not changed one iota. Parents were shit. Families were shit. School was shit. Home was shit.

Tobago looked nice. He wondered if Baz had ever been there. He shoved the magazine inside his dull-blue prison shirt to ask him later.

He could hear Baz and Clifford off in the shelves. Stacks, Clifford called them. Baz chuckling his deep heh-heh-heh and Clifford mincy-giggling. They often did this making up and flirting after Clifford had got his rags off. Rupert listened. There it was, the clink of Clifford's sherry bottle: they were having sherry in their afternoon tea.

As far as Rupert was concerned, sherry was shit, too.

Then Clifford flounced in and asked Rupert if he'd mind going for a bottle of milk from the canteen, they'd just run out.

When Rupert came back, Clifford was lying dead on the reading room floor with his flies open and Baz was standing over him making that sucking noise with his teeth. He looked up at Rupert as he came in, hair dripping from the rain and holding half a bottle of semi-skimmed.

Baz shook his head solemnly over the body. 'Man got himself over-excited an' have a heart attack.' Then came the slow grin and the raised eyebrow. 'Heh-heh-heh-heh.'

Rupert looked down at Clifford. There was a lot of blood on the front of Clifford's trousers and underpants, and in his half-closed mole-like little hand, fawn grave-spots on the back, was a small, bloody, sausagey thing.

'Fucking hell, Baz.'

'Heh-heh-heh.'

By the time it got around that Clifford had had his prick bitten off, Baz and Rupert had put their heads and stories together and Leslie, a beetle-browed epileptic subnormal library cleaner, with whom it was known

Clifford used to mess around when the pressure became too great, got all the credit.

After a couple of hours of quiet, intense reasoning from a sorrowful Baz, with Rupert agreeing that he'd also seen him at it, Leslie came to believe he'd done what he was supposed to have done and went round telling everybody who would listen exactly how it happened. He was giving Clifford a gam for some snout when he had a seizure, blacked out and bit straight through it. An accident, and not funny really because he liked old Cliffy, but it gave Leslie a bit of status for a while, and he was never going to get out of nick anyway.

In one respect, Baz was right. The prison doctors and the coroner all agreed: Clifford Uley, fifty-six, had died of a heart attack.

A couple of weeks later, a big pissed-up midnight roofer called Redfern thought he'd have a go at rogering Rupert in the washroom. Baz came in and took the guy apart, busting two of his ribs, his spleen and smashing his face through a washbasin. All three agreed Redfern had slipped. Rupert had no more trouble after that, and when he thanked Baz, Baz put his hand in Rupert's hair and said, 'Yah, well now we quits, boy.' Gripping hard and shaking. 'Seen?'

'Seen.'

'Heh-heh-heh.'

Blue and white lights punching left-right, left-right the police 827i slammed past, braked, shouldered over to sit in front of them.

'Oh shit, Baz.' The first time, the very first fucking trip, five keys of pharmaceutical cocaine in the fucking toolbox under the passenger seat, so how long were they looking at? Too fucking long. Oh shit. Out of the corner of his eye, Baz preparing to dump the spliff through the rackety gearbox cover – but not quite ready yet—

'For Christ sake Baz!'

Baz, low-voiced, watching the 827i. 'Stick-a-pin, man.'

Rupert, throttled and panicky. 'Never mind fucking stick-a-pin, dump the fucking thing!'

'Jus' hold on you shit now, boy.' He did that, he thought you were fucking up, he called you boy. Oh Christ, five years minimum.

The cop in the passenger seat looking back. But the POLICE STOP display was not coming on. Watching the blue and red rectangular panel. The fucking thing was not coming on—

What the fuck?

The 827i squatted, gathered itself, signalled and sped out across the middle into the fast lane.

Baz withdrawing the spliff from the gearbox cover, examining it. Oily but intact. Making the teeth-sucking noise, taking a drag. Holding it in. Exhaling.

'Close.'

'Close? We've been clocked, man. You fucking spliffed out your fucking brains—'

'Heh-heh-heh.'

'You saw the guy—'

'No problem, man.'

'No fucking problem?'

Baz going all Yard on him: 'Dem ain't find nothing, dem just checking we.' Taking another drag. 'These is legal wheels, man.'

'Terrific. Two hundred grand's worth of coke under your arse but they can't do us for tax or MOT. Great.'

Baz shrugged. 'Way it goes.'

'We're clocked, they can have us anywhere from here to fucking Bristol, you fucking idiot. Pull us whenever they like.'

Baz's scowl darkened. 'You know what? You a little nervous for this kind a work, ain't you? You hear what I'm sayin', boy?'

It was what Baz had said before, when he came back into the sitting room, changed from his bath-towel into a pale grey jogging suit and white socks with a white towel round his neck.

'Yah,' he said, setting down a bottle of Mount Gay Rum and two thick-bottomed shot glasses, 'I got a deal.'

Pouring until the pale gold rimmed the glasses full. 'You got the nerve?'

Rupert lifted his glass. 'Cheers.' Sipping, not spilling a drop.

'Sure,' said Baz. Then looking at him sideways. 'You know what kind a bad-ass black man involved here?'

'I've been offered enough times.'

'Yah, you been offered. Don't mean shit. These man ain't no toy soldiers, Rupert.' Once in a blue moon he used his full name, showing him how serious he was. 'If they can fuck you they will. Fuck you and dus' you, mash up you life, walk away laffin'. Heh-heh-heh. Fack is, is what I would do meself, you or who know.' No smile now. Scratching his stubble. 'So if you don' need it, don' do it. You hear me nah?' Picking up his drink. 'Don' even waste we time talkin' about it. Seen?'

'I do need it.'

'You bizness gone belly-up?'

'No.'

'You owe a man?'

'No.'

'You been bitin' the clouds?'

'What?'

'What the Chinese people say.'

'Oh.'

Baz grinning. 'That it? You got the taste?'

'Fuck me, no.'

'No habit?'

'No fear.'

Leaning forward, face dark and frowning, trying to make Rupert out. 'So what a fuck you lookin' at a lead pension for, man?'

'I need money.'

'Who don't?'

'Big money. Fast money. Cash money.'

'Yah, yah, yah—'

'For a business opportunity.' Now then, see which way the monkey jumps.

Baz scratched himself, looked round the room, and back at Rupert, sucking his teeth, taking the piss. 'You want a tell me about it, star? You want a tell me about this bizness opportunity a yours?'

He wasn't there yet, nowhere near, but even disinterest was a sign of interest: it was time to move the game forward. He pushed both hands back through his hair, and shook it loose like some vacant Aussie surf-boy. Baz, who loved watching him do all that hairdresser shit, leaned back and grinned. 'Come on, baby, you can tell old Baz.'

Rupert fished a box of Swan out of his ticket pocket. Inside, in tissue paper, were a dozen or so stones, blue, green, red, most polished, one or two still dulled with earth, uneven, straight from the digger's riddle. None of them were much bigger than the average 400mg Mandrax.

Baz poked them about in the spread-out tissue paper with his forefinger. 'How much?'

'Five grand.'

'No shit?'

'No shit.'

'Askin' or payin'?'

Rupert started to put the stones away. It was what you did.

'Stick-a-pin, man.'

Rupert started to lay out his stall, line by line, hook by hook. Sri Lanka was one place. Sapphire, ruby, topaz, garnet, amethyst, cinnamon stone, cat's eye and for real money, big money, the teardrop pearl. Baz should see one. Make your heart bleed, man. Colombia was another, but dicier, obviously, but on the other hand one decent fucking emerald, and goodbye Finchley Road. Watching the light come and go in Baz's flat black Indio eyes.

Weight for weight, crack and smack didn't compare. And if a condom bust in some girl carrier's gut she didn't have to die. Unless, Baz grinned, getting enthusiastic, she flush the pan too soon. Plus a better class of customer, a better way to shift money. Baz nodding, then frowning, Yah, yah, yah, so how was it illegal? Rupert telling him. No tax, no government, no middleman. Either end. People got shot, stabbed, drowned, wasted on a regular basis. You do strict cash deals, no credit, right out in the fucking jungle, man, you got a risk factor. Baz relaxing, toking up. Rupert filling in some of the minor detail; similar routes, similar profits. Then moving on to the crossover deal, how the two operations could coincide, sketching a partnership, him and Baz, stones and powders. Sensing Baz back off, the word partnership wrong, dropping it. But telling him all the rest. Except what Baz already knew: the white kid didn't have the money and that was why he was here. Rupert didn't have the start-up, the finance.

'Where you come in, Baz.'

'Yah, I figured.'

The way Baz saw it was, here's this white kid full of shit and shampoo, bought or, more likely, borrowed some stones, trying to blag his way into a dope deal. Maybe Rupert was come from Heaven, maybe not; maybe he had his own ideas. But he was white and he could drive. Yah. So, the thing was, give the kid a hard time, not let him know he was needed, and maybe there was some accommodation to be reached. As ever, it was who needs who, so that's where the edge was. Baz's edge.

The stones were neither here nor there, but don't let the kid know that. Use them against him.

'What d'you think, Baz?'

'Could be nice, man.' Could pigs fly? He offered Rupert the joint. Rupert took it right down. They smiled at each other. One razor looking at another.

Every deal either one of them had ever done, thought Baz, it was a forest, a fucking maze. Two people went in together, they shook hands and they went in together. You an' me spars, man, big buddies. Hansel and Gretel. Yah. And they made it to the middle, and there was the candy, the gain, the profit. Eldorado. The way Baz saw it now, the way he'd seen it ever since Corona when he gave that Korean fucker chance to jump him, was simple: you hit the other guy first and you hit him hard.

Yah. Hit first, hit hard, get out with the loot. Shazam.

Simple. Hansel fucks Gretel. Gretel, fair curly-haired Gretel, born to be fucked. He wondered if Rupert knew that.

'So what d'you say, Baz?' Handing the joint back.

'Sound like a good deal.'

'It is, man.'

'So what you need me for?' Watching Rupert trying not to squirm. 'Say you and me go down the Market, all the Jewish guys with the hats and beards, who they goin' to buy from, you or me?'

'I don't see that as a problem, Baz.'

'Yah, well you ain't me.'

'Fuck sake.' Looking him in the eye.

'Another ting,' said Baz. 'What kind of a split we lookin' at here?'

'Down the middle.'

'And what you puttin' in?'

Rupert tapped the box of stones. 'Half what's here for a chance of earners. All I need is a five grand cut to buy 'em. You sell, you're two and half grand up.'

Now Baz knew the stones weren't Rupert's he cut loose. 'Fuck the stones,' said Baz. 'You knockin' on wood, boy. You don' know shit about this bizness. You don' know how it organise, who the man is, who you see, who you talk to, how much you pay, how much you take, who you come back to, who is up, who is down, who is no fuckin' where, who cuts, who don't, what the word is on the street who the Beast is shakin' down—'

'I can learn.' Rupert didn't even know who the Beast was, but he guessed it was Drug Squads in general.

'Who goin' to tell you?' asked Baz. 'I ain't.' Leaning back. 'Even you can figure that out.'

'Yeah, but—'

'Listen, man, any black kid in school know more'n you'll ever know, and you know why?' Eyes starting to flash. 'Because they got to live it, they got to live it because they got no fuckin' option. You hear what I'm tellin' you? A man can work 'ard all his life, keep his head low, give his woman reg'lar money, keep his kids nice. He can live clean as a whistle *but*—' Baz shot his finger out at Rupert's head, pointing it like a gun, stabbing it at him fast, one-two-three – 'he still got to know *what-goin'-down*. They all got to, an' you know why, boy? Because they got to live in this fuckin' countree, live with the hassle, ride the blow, know where the Man is coming from nex'. Seen?'

'Yeah, but—'

'You beginning to vex me, boy.'

'I really need this one, Baz, it's too good to fucking miss. I need it bad. Please.'

Baz breathed in and out, curved nostrils dilating, shaking his head. 'Man,' he said, 'you got to be the lowest of the fuckin' low.'

Rupert forced a grin. 'Everybody's got to start somewhere.'

'What your mobile?'

Rupert took out a silver pencil, keeping his head down, thinking, Got you, you old bastard. As he wrote out the number, a young woman, lighter than Baz, walked in from the bedroom carrying a baby. Acknowledging neither of them she sat down in front of the TV set.

Baz drawled over the back of his chair, 'Him jus' go. You can watch now, Serena.'

The young black woman switched on the video. Laughter came out of the speakers. Rupert couldn't see the screen but it sounded like *The Cosby Show*.

Baz called him the next day. 'You ever drive a Land-Rover?'

'Only since I was a kid. Why?'

'Man tell me nobody ever get stop in one.'

A mile up the motorway, the low December light blinding off the stream of traffic in front, Rupert saw the artic pulled over, hazard lights flashing, and the 827i parked in front of it. The driver, a big-gutted guy in a white T-shirt, was showing his papers to one of the cops while the other kept the frizzy black-haired woman in the cab. None of them took any notice of the Land-Rover. Baz took another drag on the spliff.

After Reading the traffic thinned out. Rupert began thinking about the deal. It was what he liked doing, fondling it, examining it for flaws, like a stone. He'd had to take a rain check on the stones he'd shown Baz because of lack of strap; Michel, the Lebanese guy he was dealing with, hadn't gone much on hanging about for his money and had sent his guys round. Well, fuck him. And Baz. If this deal came right, with five grand in his strides he'd be up and away, out on his own. Sri Lanka here I come.

Baz had gone into a doze. Good.

On the surface, from a distance, the deal was straightforward, clean, simple: move A from B to C, get paid D. So get close up, prowl round it, poke it, sniff it, see where it could go bad. Because somebody always got to suck the fucking fluffy end. And he, the new kid, the white guy, was favourite. So look at it hard. Turn it over, every bit, piece by piece, see where it could start to turn stinkypoo.

It was a straight mule-and-bagman job, Baz had said. Rupert was the mule, Baz was the bagman. He did the driving, because of Baz's leg, and Baz delivered it, took the shit, as he said, 'if ting go wrong'. For that, Baz got ten grand, Rupert got five. On the street, bagged up, five keys of cocaine, uncut, top quality, which Baz said this was, was worth three-fifty max. Say two hundred minimum. Less even, depending on how much was about: anything down to one-eighty. But call it two hundred. Yeah. Two hundred was nice. Which Rupert figured meant an investment by Baz and the North London brothers of, say, ten grand plus big exes straight from Colombia, anything from twenty to fifty inclusive from Galicia or Kerry. Definitely not silly money – but why straight cocaine, why not washrock, crack? Even Rupert knew that was where the big return was.

So they were working on, say, ninety per cent of the risk, punting the stuff out in the open, cross country, for less than ten per cent of the gross. Call that Point One.

Point Two, all they were doing was the delivery. So

how usual was that? Who was collecting the cash, and when? Plus if Baz was number one dealer, one down from the main man, the North London brothers, why was he operating as bagman?

Point Three, if the Bristol dealers and their sub-dealers and their point-guys on the streets and in the clubs were looking to get their outlay back, plus profit, before paying these – as far as Rupert was concerned – mythical cash collectors, where was Baz's ten and his five coming from? London, Bristol or Timbukfuckingtu?

Not to mention 'When'. Or 'If'.

Fuck you and dus' you, mash up you life, walk away laffin'.

Also, call it Point Three and a Half, he couldn't see Baz operating on less than ten per cent of the gross, so that made it look more like Baz was on fifteen to his five.

On the other hand, you ask for five, five is what you get, cunt. If you get it.

And, hanging over all, not so much a Point as the Million Dollar Fucking Question: was this the way they operated? Was this really What Went Down? Really? Rupert couldn't believe it. Nobody said here's the goods, send the money later. Not in Rupert's world anyway.

So was this a one-off, or a con, Baz setting him up, or what? Yeah, but if so, why? Why offer some guy five grand to drive a Land-Rover to Bristol and back if you weren't going to pay him? To see the look on his face? Teach him a lesson? Too much of a risk, and even Baz wasn't that fucking weird. Was he?

Rupert drumming his fingers on the wheel, getting more and more wound up with every passing mile. You took a deal straight off the shelf, all clean and shiny with its little bar-code and sell-by date, and by the time you get it home, open it up, it's full of fucking worms.

Was that how it was?

It couldn't be. Maybe it was the noise and the driving and the diesel, making his head, back and brain ache.

Fifth or sixth biggest industry in the country, they couldn't operate like this. They couldn't – it was too fucking slipshod-slapdash, man, even for them—

Baz woke up around Junction 17. It was dark, and his mouth felt coated with dried dogshit. 'What time we reach?'

'Twenty odd miles to go.'

They peeled off into Leigh Delamere Services, had sausage egg and chips and Fantas. Baz put three sugars in his. Rupert looked at him, eyes red-rimmed from driving, said, 'What's the real deal, Baz?'

He went through it Point by Point. Sometimes Baz grinned, sometimes he frowned. Most of the time he sat sucking bits of sausage out of his teeth, looking at Rupert as if he'd just landed from Planet Zog.

Then Baz told him some of what the real deal was and it blew Rupert's gaskets. Especially the bit about the guns.

Baz said that Bristol CID had been told to get the place cleaned up for Christmas, and somehow, via some fucking middleman, some fucking musician or other, Baz and the brothers had rowed themselves in on it.

Fucking musicians. Jesus Christ.

It was so fucking risky it wasn't true. It couldn't be. Just listening to Baz made Rupert want to shit himself. 'The Man wanta mek a big raid, mash up all a local deadstock, lock away all dem bad black and white mothers an' mek a big fuss about guns an' all on TV. And that suit the brothers, what is call a community a hinterest.'

'How?'

'It mean now on we supply direct.'

'By selling these Bristol guys down the river?'

'First rule a bizness, man.'

'Fuck me.'

'This life you got to 'radicate the competition, man.'

'Holy shit. What about us, what about the cocaine?'

'You too fuckin' nervous, boy—'

'Baz, we're looking at ten, fifteen years for five k, I got a right to be nervous. We're not going to get away with "It was only for personal use, your honour." Not on five kilos—'

'I tol' you, man. The guy is on our side, he got the

whole a his CID looking out for us – all he want is a bunch a dem local villains, lock 'em up for Christmas—'

'And what happens to the cocaine, Baz? You hear what I'm asking you? What are you going to do, hand it over and say "There you are Inspector, that'll be two hundred grand"? Or is he going to say, "No that's all right, Baz, you've driven it all this way down here, you keep it."'

Baz looking serious. 'Listen, Rupert. What 'appen, appen. All you got a do is be ready for it. Seen?'

'Yeah, seen, but guns, for fuck sake—'

'Hear what I tell you. If the Man try fer cross we, whole deal blow up in his face, press, TV, wherever. He know that. We safe, man.'

'With a bunch of tooled-up doped-up black and white heavies all over the place? Oh yeah—'

Baz grinned. 'Listen boy, you get in bed with the Beast, who know who get fucked?' Shrugging. 'Risk you take.'

'Yeah, but I never fired a gun in my life—'

'Heh-heh-heh. It ain't that hard.'

7

Because he said he hadn't got long, Rae deliberately made DCI Barnard go shopping with her. He took it without a murmur and steered her trolley round the Henleaze Waitrose, heading for the slaughter in his boxy blue suit. She began to grow queasily excited at the prospect. He paused by the poultry counter, auditioning mountainous goose-pimply fat-lady turkeys with their legs tucked up their bums, thinking God-knows-what but obediently waiting to see what she chose. He was trained, obviously, but he was looking round, nervous, worried about being seen, recognised.

Like all men he was hopeless with the trolley.

Surprising her at the checkout he offered to pay.

She smiled, shook her head. Not just yet, thank you.

Back in the car, he drove, jaw up so the double chin didn't show. Queasiness rose, excitement fell. Oh God, the thought of it. That solid red neck, those thick shoulders, that stomach. The weight. A shudder inside her clothes.

He picked up on it straightaway. 'You all right?'

'Fine.'

'Looking a bit pale, my girl.'

'No, I'm fine, really.' Frank used to call her his girl. The car still smelled of him. She felt her hands start to sweat. The old Renault wallowed round on to the fly-over. He was driving too fast, showing off. It was making her sick.

'You don't look it, Rae.' That awful, caring look when both of them knew all he wanted was to rip her clothes off, shove his hot meaty prick up her and stuff her like a turkey.

She forced a smile. 'I just want to pee, that's all. Too much wine, I expect.' She watched him shift in his seat, swallow his saliva, process the information. Oh God, he was just like Frank.

'Not long now, Rae.'

No. Not long now, Detective Chief Inspector Barnard.

She lay in the bath for hours. She had thrown up in the upstairs loo as soon as he had left. Then she had felt shivery and vulnerable, like a child needing to hide, because in her mind there were two grown-up strangers downstairs still monstrously at it.

She locked the door, ran the bath, lashed in the Badedas, stepped out of her contaminated clothes, searched the rapidly clouding mirror. Apart from the underwear creases round her middle her body was as unmarked as it had been this morning. She felt battered, pounded, sick, unsatisfied, scattered and used; did nothing leave a mark?

Apparently not.

She sank through the prickling foam into the soft green water, feeling it warming her, welcoming her. At least there was no come to sully forth, so be thankful for small mercies.

She began to feel better. Time to review the situation, relive it, get it out of her system. See how things had changed. See the funny side, if there was one.

As an experience it didn't register on the Richter scale, the needle didn't even quiver. In fact – thinking of her father's workshop again – it was more like a squirt from a passing oilcan than a fuck. Which was a pity, because she could have done with one. As a tactical move, however, it was masterly. Death's black wing had definitely fanned DCI Barnard's flame, and she'd got him, he was hooked, she could tell.

The only pity was she'd had to make the first move. She slid further down the bath to hide from the fact. She put her knees up, her hands behind her head and let the water fill her ears with the soothing hum of traffic on the Portway.

He'd followed her into the dark hall with the grocery bags, put them down on the floor and pushed his hands through his thick iron-grey hair. They looked at each other. Both knew it was the moment. But he'd stood there, the pillock. The fifty-year-old red-faced pillar-box-bodied pillock. Full of lust but even more full of nerves, twitchy as a pot-bellied little stallion.

'Well,' he said, weakly trying to grin his way out of it. She waited. All he did was pull his mobile phone out.

'What are you doing?'

'Calling up the Well.' Thick fingers dabbing small keypads. 'Get one of the local lads round, give me a lift—'

She laid a hand on his arm. 'Don't go.'

He glanced from her to the front door. It was open about three inches. He looked back at her, swallowed. 'What?'

'Stay with me.'

Lying in the bath, looking at the pearly steam halo round the sealed lamp unit. Yes. Her fault.

You cow, said Frank's voice. She lifted her flat belly out of the water, looked at the foam cresting the crispy hair between her legs, and gave his memory her slyest Buddha smile.

The DCI pulled her to him, his lipless mouth opening to fasten on hers, face squidging sideways to force his tongue into her mouth. She held him off for a moment or two, then let him in. He tasted of stale wine, but she supposed she did too. Then his hands were all over her like paddles, hard flat broad hairy paddles, squeezing her buttocks, her belly, her breasts, feverishly trying to get to know all of her at once. He was making a yumming, quivery noise in his throat, his face was turning puce and his short thick legs were trembling uncontrollably. Then his whole body began shaking. Christ—

'Oh Rae,' he said. 'I'm shaking.'

'I know. So am I. Lock the door.'

She went into the sitting room. Curtains still closed, sunlight outside. She heard him kick into the wine bottles, mutter Fuck and come stumbling up the dark hall, looking for her. 'Rae?'

'Oh Rae.' He held her tight, crushing the breath out of her, and then held her tighter. She couldn't even get her arms to meet round his overheated barrel of a torso. His legs were still shaking, but the erection was there now: she could feel it hardening. She put her hands on his lapels and pushed him off.

'—crushing me.'

'Sorry.'

'Barney—' Forcing herself to say it.

Now he was kissing her neck, his face a rough prickly slab of hot flesh, his mouth making yumming noises. 'Yes love?'

'Be gentle with me.'

In the bath, Rae found herself grinning.

Then he was lifting her over to the sofa, Frank's oatmeal nubble-tweed sofa, a wedding gift from his mother, laying her down on it and kneeling at her feet, his thick fingers fumbling at the dark blue shirt she had changed into, opening her buttons, kissing between her breasts, hands groping madly behind her, pulling her about like a sack to unhook her bra. She felt pissed, her face hot, her head swirling, unable, unwilling to help. Finally freeing her breasts, he gazed down on them in triumph – Oh Rae, you're so beautiful – and then fell upon them, sucking greedily at each one in turn, and twiddling the one he wasn't sucking. Oh God, she thought, what have I done? And then his hands were under her skirt, dragging her steel grey French knickers down her legs and pulling her shoes off. My God he was holding her knickers to his face, sniffing them, and moaning. Then he was hoiking her skirt up – for a moment she thought he was going to throw it over her face – and looking down on her again, unable to believe his luck that she was wearing a suspender belt and stockings. Oh Rae. And then his face was gone, under the skirt, like some comic photographer, Buster Keaton or somebody, and his hot rough hands were lifting up her legs and pushing them apart, thumbs and palms sliding over her inner thighs and spreading her. She looked over the tops of her knees at the ceiling. It swung round the Tiffany-style light-fitting until it was halfway and then it came veering back. When she closed her eyes it was even worse.

She concentrated on raising her legs up further for him, feeling glad and ashamed, wanting it, wanting to get to the point where she would be carried away and not care, not *think*, and simultaneously wanting it to be over, finished with and him out and gone. She pulled her skirt off his head to see what he was doing. He was looking at her flattened bush as if he'd never seen one before, stroking it wonderingly with his thumb. Oh Rae, he was saying, his eyes imploring her for permission, and then sinking his head gratefully between her legs for what looked like the first meal he'd had in ages.

Sucking and mushing and lapping at her, his face rough on her inner thighs, making a droning, mooing, slurping noise. But nothing much was happening to her, she wasn't opening, and he was making her more wet with spit than anything else. And then – Ow! – he was sticking a finger up her, and wobbling it in and out – Jesus Christ! – while he knelt up and tried to drag his trousers down to his knees one-handed. There's no rush, she said, be gentle. Oh Rae you're so lovely, and then, thank God, he pulled his finger out and pushed his trousers down. Marks and Sparks boxers, green with yellow stars, and a big meaty heavy prick poking out. Goody goody gumdrops. It was slightly bent but it would do.

While he was fiddling with the foil on the condom, she reached forward and grabbed it and squeezed it, thinking, Oh yes I do need it and suddenly feeling herself go juicy and saying, Fuck me, lick me, suck me, fuck me, Oh Barney fill me up, fuck me hard, and if I say stop, don't will you? And him saying, What? and biting his lip, and saying, Oh Christ, don't do that, Rae, unpeeling her fingers, *Don't Rae.* He was looking down to roll the condom on right, studiously, like a little boy, fiddling with it and snapping it tight round the base, saying, I'm sorry about this. While a sheet of cold flaming-petrol rage shot up in her mind as she said, Don't worry. Thinking, For Christ sake man stop fucking me about. And then he was at her, sucking her again, and moaning and groaning, blindly seeking her clitoris with his lips and tongue, finding it and losing it, finding it and losing it – damn, damn, damn – while he tried to insert first one then two then three fingers inside her. Jesus Christ! As if she was a cow and he was a vet. She tried to writhe, pull away from him – but he was rearing up wet-faced over her and saying, Oh I want you Rae, I want you so much, and then he was shoving it in.

For about twenty or thirty seconds it was like falling downstairs inside a wardrobe, everything happening at once, with him bunting and shunting and grunting away at her, gritting his teeth and going, Ugh ugh ugh, oh God I'm coming Rae, I'm coming, his voice a mixture of relief and despair, as her head and the back of the sofa went bang bang bang against the wall. Oh Rae, he was gasping, oh Rae, oh Rae. His head fell on her neck, sweating, heavy as lead. Oh Rae.

Then he was climbing on to the sofa with her, the condom dangling until he pulled it off – spluk – and surreptitiously knotted it and stuffed it in his pocket. Oh please God, she prayed, please God let his wife find it.

He lay alongside her, panting, his hairy, pregnant-hard belly pushing her into the crumby gap between seat and backrest. Oh Rae. And then he was kissing her, and cuddling her, slabbering his dirty mouth all over her face, and sliding his hand down between her legs and rubbing at her, trying to get his fingers in again and asking her if she wanted more.

More? she said, coldly. *More what?*

Rae in the bath, remembering the look on his face, shaking with silent laughter.

After that, of course, he was contrite. Contrite and pathetically grateful, but still in a wham-bam hurry, the bastard. Now he was standing up, wiping his dick on a wodge of tissue and opening his wallet at the same time.

'Are you going to pay me?' she said.

'What?' looking for somewhere to put the tissues, shoving them back in his pocket.

'I said are you going to pay me?'

He took her hand, kissed her palm, held it tight, gazed at her with that hopeless wet-eyed spaniel look some men got. 'Rae,' he said seriously, 'nothing could pay for what you've given me today. You don't know how long—'

Oh Christ, she thought, spare me the fucking wife.

He gave her a card. 'My mobile, and that's my direct line. Any time you want me.' He tried a grin. 'For anything.'

She took the card. 'Thanks.' Oh yes I've got you now, DCI Barnard, Bristol Central CID. The question is, Do I want you?

Once again he picked up on it straightaway. 'Can I come back?' He was putting his jacket on – Christ what a nerve.

'When?'

'Tonight. Five, six-ish.' Checking his pockets. 'Got something on at the moment but it could easily get postponed—'

'Call me first, I might have my other lover in.'

'What?' His flinty little eyes boring into hers, filling with suspicion.

'Don't be silly.' She kissed him on the cheek. Jesus. He really was hooked.

But he was still hurrying down to the hall door, the bastard. Any second now, he'd be out, the door would close and he'd be off whistling down the street—

At the door he turned, kissed her on the mouth, cupped her bare breast in his hand. 'Like holding a live bird,' he said solemnly.

'I am a live bird.'

'I mean it, Rae.' Getting even more solemn. 'Never in my whole life have I known a woman like you, as beautiful as you are.'

'Thank you.'

He kissed her again, then didn't seem to know what to say. 'Look, I can do better than that, I was nervous—'

She put her hand up to his mouth. 'We both were. Don't worry.'

Lying in the bath, thinking, After that you deserved to throw up. She attached the rubber shampoo hose to the mixer tap, pulled the spray rose off, turned the flow on full and let the strong jet play between her legs until she floated gracefully free of the whole grisly event.

She was in bed, zipped up in her lovely warm pink dressing gown and fast asleep on half a librium, when the phone rang.

'It's me.'

'Oh.'

'What's the matter?'

'I was asleep.'

A pause. 'Can I come round?'

'When?'

'Fifteen minutes?'

Thinking about it, wondering exactly who had got whom. 'How long for?'

'An hour, an hour or so.' Then, sounding desperate. 'I want to see you, Rae.'

'All right.'

She got up, put some eye make-up on, wondered about moving Frank's silver-framed photograph, decided against it. When he walked in, bringing a draught of cold night air with him, it was the first thing he saw.

She watched him go over to it, pick it up, look at it, set it down. 'Good-looking bloke, wasn't he?'

She said, 'He still is, to me.'

'I'm sorry, love.' He came to her, put his arms gently round her waist and held her to him. 'I'm sorry.'

She wondered if now was the time to ask him, now that she'd got him softened up. No. Better to wait, see what Maggi Reed had to say. Then use that information for the oyster knife, to slit his muscle, prise him open, watch him squirm.

You owe me, you bastard.

'Come to bed.' She let him unzip her dressing-gown top to bottom and gaze at her sweet-smelling body. 'Come on, it's cold.'

They lay in bed naked, spoon-fashion. He stroked her breast. She felt his prick rise and start knocking softly between her buttocks, asking to be let in. 'Tell me what you like,' he whispered.

She did, and it was better without his fingers up her, but she couldn't come. Perhaps it was Frank looking at them fucking in his bed, perhaps she was too relaxed, perhaps it was the child inside her unconsciously sticking up for his father – Christ what a prospect – but more likely it was the fucking librium getting in the way again. Anyway, she faked it well enough for Detective Chief Inspector Barnard to look supremely pleased with himself.

Afterwards, washing his dick, looking at himself bollock-naked in a dead man's bathroom, Barney fell prey to hurried male anxieties. Where had he been? Suppose some neighbour, some friend, Jesus Christ, her fucking parents, called round? Looking at his watch. Shit, fifty minutes. How was he going to account for that? Supposed to be on duty for fuck sake.

Then, back whole in his boxy blue suit, his confidence returned like the sun. He was safe. Safe, and seriously bucked. Two fucks and no convictions. It was two fingers up to the world, the CC and the late Frank Webber included. Fuck 'em, fuck 'em all. He'd scored, he, Barney Barnard, fifty-one years old in February and convinced his days of a bit of fresh were long gone, had scored. Twice. The entire stadium was on its feet cheering and his heart felt as big as a balloon. Fucking great, kid. Moving nimbly on the balls of his feet, he slid back into the bedroom, an old Sinatra number surfacing in his mind. Oh Rae, you make me feel so young; he'd been a good dancer once, ballroom and latin, and now he felt like sweeping her into his arms, showing her—

She was taking her time, and he had chance to feast his eyes on her, heart and prick swelling at his luck. Oh Rae. She had her back to him, fastening her bra, letting her perky little breasts fall into their small black cups, the skin taut across her ribs, pale gold and then white across her buttocks.

Jesus, how good life could be, once you'd bet the lot.

Her bra on, she walked around the bedroom looking at herself in the mirrors, jutting her puss out. He went down on his knees in front of her and licked at it. She was still moist, still sweet and fresh as an oyster. She put her head back for a moment and let him nuzzle away, looking at the tableau in the wardrobe mirror.

Hooked, she thought, well and truly hooked.

'Oh you,' she said, finally pushing him away, her hand gripped hard in his stiff iron-grey hair.

'What?' he looked up, his mouth wet, grinning like a kid.

'Don't men ever get enough?'

He stood up, his knees cracking, and held her against him. 'Not of you, Rae,' he said. 'Not of you.'

Then, when she was stepping into a clean pair of knickers – white, warm, high-waisted, no-nonsense M&S – she saw him sneaking a glance at his watch.

The bastard.

He watched her pull on a black woollen high-necked sweater and a pair of jeans. She flicked her hair out and gave it a few tugging strokes with a brush from the dressing table. Frank's photograph was staring at him in triplicate; Rae was remote and self-absorbed; all at once, with a pain sharp as angina, he saw how it would all end: her pale, cold, immaculate face shutting the door on him forever.

He cleared his throat to drown the panic, reassert his existence. 'Any chance of a lift?' he said.

'I'm not going anywhere.' She picked up a gold tube, spat on its built-in mascara brush and peered myopically at her eyes. 'I always do this.'

'I see.'

'It makes me feel better.'

'Well, thanks a bunch.'

She capped the tube and turned to face him. 'Why don't you call up one of your "lads"?'

'You think that's wise?'

She looked at him coldly, saying nothing.

'Just to the Mariners,' he said. 'You know, that caff under the flyover? Come on, Rae. It'll only take you five minutes. I'm fifteen minutes late already.'

Men. Always leaning on you. Never saying fucking please.

Looking at his watch again, the bastard.

In the car, he was better, almost human. He started asking her about herself, not like Frank – a relentless wall of questions and suspicions that made her feel worn down and worthless even when she'd done nothing – but like a friend, somebody older who liked her, a father even. Some men were like that, she thought: once they got their way, they were happy. Then she thought, Make that all men.

He was saying he wanted to go on seeing her. On a regular basis. She said, You mean you want to fuck me twice a day and then go home for din-dins? He said, No, more than that, Rae, a lot more. There was something pent-up about him, like a thunderstorm waiting to burst, something he couldn't, wouldn't, admit to. She wondered what would happen if she said, Yes, all right, you can.

Instead, she said nothing but thought maybe what happened was that in some ways one man wiped out another.

It didn't wipe out the fucking debt, though, did it?

Now he was on a new tack, asking her what she was going to do, saying he envied her, how she was young enough to start again, and not even 'all this business' would last forever.

When she mentioned wanting to get a flat in Clifton, but doubting whether she would be able to – because of the price differential and the negative equity hanging over the house in Ashton – he fell abruptly silent and looked sideways out of the window, thinking how fucking suddenly five kilos of coke were going to change his life.

The Renault's tyres thudded over the separated concrete sections of the flyover. As they turned off down into Brunel Lock Road he turned back to her. 'Suppose I said I might be able to help you.'

'How?'

'I may be able to, that's all.'

'You know somewhere?'

He shook his head.

'You're not talking money, are you?' A quick rush of adrenalin, hope, delight. Was he offering her a deal? Oh boy. Somebody she could use, as well as somebody she could hurt. Perfect – unless he was setting her up. Better to make him say it, get it straight, right now. '*Are* you talking money?'

'That depends.'

'Don't mess me about, Barney.'

'I'm not.'

'Because I can always get any topping-up I might happen to need off my parents.'

'I know.'

'No strings attached.'

'Tell you the truth, Rae—'

'What?'

'I don't know who I want to help, you or me. All fucking mad, anyway.'

'What's fucking mad?'

'Plus, it could all turn to shit.' He pulled the passenger visor down, looked at himself in the vanity mirror, pushed both hands through his hair. 'It usually does.'

'Barney, if you're going to tell me, tell me. If not, not. Just don't mess me about, that's all. I don't need it. Especially now.'

'Yeah. Sorry. Fair enough.' More silence, then: 'It's just, you know, complicated, everything depending on everything else, a lot of things, all hanging together.'

'What sort of things?'

'Imponderables. Variables.'

Jesus Christ, he was *worse* than Frank. Blood out of a stone. 'Such as?'

'Tonight, for a start. You and me, for another.'

'In what way you and me?'

'I want to go on seeing you.'

'So you keep telling me.'

'Rae, the reason I was shaking like a leaf this afternoon is that everything else in my life is a walking fucking death—'

'I don't want to know. I don't want to know about your fucking wife, Barney. Or the rest of your fucking awful life, your piles, cancer, varicose veins or why your kids hate you – I don't want to know. It's nothing to do with me. If that sounds hard, tough.'

'I haven't got any kids—'

'I don't want to fucking *know*!'

'Stop the car here.'

Thinking she'd pushed him too far, she said, 'I'm sorry.'

He was staring straight past her, scanning the prussian-blue frontage of the Mariners Transport Café.

Built directly under the flyover and fenced round by a dozen metre-thick cylindrical concrete supports, the café lay trapped under the roadway like an oversized Portakabin. At one end a galvanised ventilation stack all but touched the concrete above. A flight of concrete steps led to a door which, like the windows, was covered in a heavy metal grid so close-meshed scarcely any light escaped. Separate sheets of card hung like washing, spelling out C-A-F-E and A-M-U-S-E-M-E-N-T-S. On three sides the Mariners was surrounded by debris-laden parking bays; on the fourth, across the Brunel Lock Road, lay the Cumberland Basin, its choppy black waters riddled with orangeade reflections from the quadruple sodium lighting towers. Because it looked like a place nobody in their right mind would ever wish to enter, it was popular with truck-drivers, dodgy shaven-headed characters covered in tattoos, and members of Bristol Central CID who needed to talk to them publicly but in private.

The café door opened, smoke rolled out into the cold air like steam, a figure was silhouetted for a second, then the door shut again.

Barney fingered his ear and said, 'If things pan out right tonight, we could be a hundred thousand pounds better off by tomorrow.'

This time, when he kissed her, it was as if she was trying to suck his tongue out by the roots.

Off in the shadows between a Volvo and an Iveco, Baz sat in the Land-Rover and chuckled to himself.

'What?' said Rupert, hunched against the cold.

'Man don't kiss his wife like that.'

Rupert saw the shapes separate and part, then the Renault passenger door opened and a stocky figure got out, hitching up the trousers of his dark blue suit. The figure bent for a final kiss.

Baz wasn't chuckling now: he was alert, thinking hard, watching, getting into the Man's mind, waiting, willing him to turn, show his face—

All the time situations change. Fights, talks, deals. Run this way, run that, like a shoal of fry. You had to be there, ready, waiting for them to run your way. It was beautiful when they did that, come to you, a thousand little slips of silver, all turning flick, as one, out the blue – but you had to be fast, you had to be there, get in their mind before they knew themselves—

The man turned. Yah, it was him. The musician kid was right. The old guy, looking older now. The one who'd had him cuffed up, fitted up, slammed in the fucking cage. 'Rupert.'

'What?'

'See where she go.'

'What about you?'

'I'm here, man.' Baz slid out of the door without a sound. 'Talkin' to the Beast.' Then he was gone and the Renault was driving off towards the Swing Bridge over Cumberland Basin. Rupert crashed the gearbox into first and lumbered after it.

When Rae got home she opened a bottle of Chilean

Merlot and proceeded to get drunk for the second time that day.

If things pan out right we could be a hundred thousand pounds better off by tomorrow.

We. Oh boy.

After the third glass the euphoria moderated and she began to feel very wise. Men were very simple machines really; what made them dangerous was they didn't have any brakes.

Yes, that was it.

Basically. Totally. Absolutely.

Oh please dear God don't let me die alone.

Her eyes slurred over to the kitchen clock. Quarter to six. She put her glass in the sink, took a deep breath and rang Maggi Reed. She wasn't in. Rae left a message on her answerphone and hoped it made sense.

8

Barney eased himself into the Mariners. He felt alert, confident, sharper than he'd felt in ages. He was up for it, going for it and – quick roll of the shoulders inside the suit – to hell with it.

He had spent the last thirty-two years in the Force, twenty of them married. His wife Rhona, a big sandy-haired Welsh girl with a strong-willed lower jaw, had been a student teacher when he met her. Now in her middle forties, she was head of one of the rough comprehensives on the outskirts of Avonmouth. In the second year of their marriage she'd had an ectopic pregnancy; it had knocked all chance of kids on the head. He felt even further cheated when he discovered she had been having an affair with a young Welsh PE teacher at the time.

Later, Rhona had a much longer affair with the sixty-year-old head whose job she finally speared. By then Barney didn't give a fuck: they'd only stayed together for the sake of their joint careers and, in one sense, he admired the long-term cold-eyed way she'd gone in for the kill. And that was about it: he liked her nerve, but didn't go a lot on her otherwise, and love had gone down the tubes along with the rest of her reproductive equipment.

Now, despite HRT, which had made her big freckly breasts rock-solid, sex, apart from the odd perfunctory fuck to keep the peace, was off the menu, and work, work-work-work, was on it.

As far as Barney was concerned, listening nightly to her parade of bad homes, battered slaggy mothers, violent absent fathers and drug-crazed pregnant teenagers was a kingsized pain in the arse – one he knew about on a daily basis without her vomiting on all fucking night. And so, since in his long-held opinion teachers were a bunch of useless fakes and wankers, whatever Rhona had coming she richly deserved. Any case, she'd pissed off to her poncy three-day conference in Harrogate so there was nothing to worry about in that direction. In fact, looked at realistically, there wasn't enough of their relationship left to be worth bothering about anyway.

The only thing that had stopped him up to now was that he was fucked if he'd give her a divorce and lose the house and possibly half his pension rights when to his way of thinking he was the innocent fucking party. But now it appeared there might be a way round that, and whatever happened with Rae and her kid, at least he'd got himself a springboard. All he had to do now was fucking jump.

Barney had never considered himself a bent copper. He had kept his nose clean and had refrained from shitting on his own doorstep, either sexually or financially, inside or outside the Force. At the same time, he'd investigated a lot of bent coppers who didn't consider themselves bent coppers either. They all blamed it on force of circumstances, stress, lack of time for family life, or – the most bizarre fucking excuse he'd ever heard – being fitted up by some criminal fucking mastermind. Do me a favour, John. Funny thing was, they all said it was just the one fucking lapse, what the defence called an exemplary career ruined by a single moment of weakness.

Bollocks, they were on the take, on the grab, until they'd got their arms so fucking far down their victims' throats they couldn't help but get caught. Look at that cunt Webber, or all the shit Hallam was still in over the nurse. You don't go round fucking the chief witness, not before the case is over anyway. That was the difference between him and Rae and Hallam and the nurse.

Not such a fucking smartass after all, are you, Hallam?

What irritated the fuck out of him about Hallam was the guy was continually and deliberately pushing up against the rules, two-fingering his superiors and generally pissing people off.

You're so fucking clever, Hallam – why you still only a sergeant?

The point was you had to keep your nose clean, know where the job stopped and the funny stuff started. Not the bunce, the odd drink here, meal there, that was all part of it, in return for information, if not at the time then later, something to be called in, made to count. The only rule was, never fit up a totally innocent punter. If it was some hard case like that Simmons guy who deserved to go down and simply needed his memory jogged round the cell walls that was different. But he'd got to have done *something*, otherwise he'd start screaming blue murder and writing to the fucking *Guardian*. The same with all blacks: if you planted gear on them you had to be moderately sure they were dealing; on the other hand, if they weren't, they shouldn't be so fucking stroppy, should they, and they shouldn't fucking bite—

The way Barney saw it, either all coppers were bent, or none were, and if you followed the logic of that through, to be bent you had to get caught. No proof meant no crime, and no case to answer. It was as simple as that, black and white.

All the same, for God knows how many years, the greyness had been seeping into his life like damp into a back room, and until today, it had been looking pretty bleak, pretty black round the edges. Now, he had chance to let a little sunshine in so fuck it, fuck the risks. Risks were risks, and if you took them one at a time, and never thought about the rewards before the possible falls, you could piss it. As far as this job, this raid, was concerned, everything was channelled through him anyway, all the reins were in his hands, so fuck 'em all. In Technicolor.

After the raw cold outside, the Mariners was like a sauna, a thick fug of steam, chip fat and Golden Virginia. Banked rows of slots flashed, chunked and played insane snatches of electronic tunes. Barney walked through a double line of drivers feeding fistfuls of pound coins into the machines, their faces expressionless, the road still rolling behind their eyes. More drivers lay slumped over the tables. Clocking the suit and immediately avoiding eye-contact. 'Country Roads' played on the wall-mounted two-hundred selection CD player: it was too early for the long-haired heavy-metal mob.

He got to the counter, registered the hiss of bacon frying in big black pans and realised he was fucking starving. He ordered bacon, egg, chips and tomato, tea and a packet of Garibaldis, walleted the till receipt and looked round.

Chingola Bell was sitting in the far corner, at the window by the rear door. A pale, slight, thin-faced kid in his mid-twenties, with lank Jesus-length hair, bad skin and a wispy minge of beard – he looked like a disciple with Aids. In fact, as Barney knew well, Chingola had a degree from the Royal College of Music, playing the church organ of all fucking things, but all that had gone out the window once he discovered the highway to heroin. He had ditched his Danish wife, two kids, his flat, car and fifteen-hundred-quid Yamaha Clavinola. Now, on the increasingly infrequent occasions he managed to get his head together, he played borrowed keyboards with Junk City Rollers, a mixed black and white pick-up band at a club on the edge of St Pauls called The Moonglow. Basically, all Chingola Bell had left to sell was information.

He grinned up at Barney: inward-sloping teeth, and a smile so weak it kept sliding off his face. One way or another, Barney couldn't see him lasting much longer. He squeezed into the seat opposite and looked round. For a smackhead, Chingola had picked a good place: by the rear door and the view blocked off from the rest of the café by the backs of the slots.

'Your bloke ring yet?'

'Yeah, once.' Chingola scratched the scabby red backs of his long-fingered hands. 'He rang once.' He looked nervous and his soft accentless voice was dry, despite the constant sips of Diet Coke. He wasn't sweating yet, but he would be soon.

'He say where from?'

Chingola squirmed forward in his chair. 'I need one, Mister Barnard.'

'Can you get one here?'

'Not inside. They're banned, estate skins are banned.'

'Waiting for you in the carpark, are they?'

'I fucking hope so.' The weak grin came and went. The kid's face was so thin you could see the ligaments working the bones.

'You'll have to be patient then, won't you?' If he slipped him a fifty now, chances were he wouldn't see him again. 'This bloke say where he was ringing from?'

'Yeah, the M32. He said the M32.'

'When?'

'What?' Chingola was peering out through the close-set mesh of the gridded window.

'When did he ring you?'

'Thirty, thirty-five minutes. I thought—'

'You thought what?'

'I thought you said you'd, you know, be here.' Apologising for the fact Barney was late.

'Well I got delayed, didn't I?'

A nod and the weak smile again, the kid accepting anything he was told because he had no option, no interest, no strength to think any different.

'Was he on a mobile?'

'Yeah, a mobile.'

'Carphone or portable?'

'I don't fucking know, do I?' His forehead beginning to sweat now, but even his belligerence was weak, and he lapsed into moping over his Diet Coke. 'Fuck's it matter, anyway?'

'On a carphone, you hear the vehicle moving, and the signal's better. On a portable you get more break-up.'

'Oh. Yeah. Right.' Even the words were an effort now. 'Yeah, there was traffic. Yeah, you know, traffic going past. Trucks and stuff. Whush.' The grin slid across his face and he made his voice deeper. 'Black tarmac, white noise, Kimo Sabe.'

Barney stabbed three chips together and shovelled them into his mouth. Whoever this bloke of Chingola's was, he was either a fucking idiot or he didn't give a shit. Probably both. Probably fucking stoned. What a fucking cowboy, pulling up on a motorway to make a fucking phone call. Any patrol going past and the whole shoot would have been shit before they started.

'What did he sound like?'

'Black.'

'That explains it then,' said Barney.

Chingola looked up wearily. 'Fuck off, Inspector.'

'What kind of black?'

'He wasn't African. Definitely not African.'

'West Indian, then?'

'Yeah. Right.' Sweating now, losing interest.

'He say a name?'

'Fucking joking.' Then, defiance fading: 'Please Mister Barnard, I'm shaking to fucking bits—'

'No, you're not.'

Getting up now. 'Fuck you then.'

Barney took hold of his wrist, and with no more effort than pulling a lavatory chain, hauled him back down into his seat. The kid's wrist was all bone and slimy wet.

'Fucking freezing—'

'No you're not, you're warm as toast.' Barney kept hold of his wrist and held out a fifty with the other hand. 'Now then, son, you give me every fucking word and you can go out and play with your friends.'

Chingola nodded, stared at the fifty and held his jaw in his hand to stop his teeth chattering. 'He said he'd check the school and then the church—'

'Church! What fucking church?'

'Lion of Judah.'

'You never told me about any fucking church!'

'He only just told me—'

'Holy shit—'

'How they work. Leave it to the last minute, change the whole fucking gig.'

'Fuck.'

'Don't worry—'

'Don't worry? You little cunt!' Twisting his wrist, wanting to snap it, snap it right off—

Calmly, looking at Barney with contempt, Chingola said, 'I can't afford to have my hands hurt, Mister Barnard.' When Barney let go, he said, 'He won't be able to use it, I checked. It's their wino night. You know, night shelter. It'll be full of deros.'

'Better fucking be. What else?'

Now the kid had both hands to his face, elbows on the table, trying to keep his whole head from shaking. 'He said, "When we check 'em out, we call you back."'

'We?'

'That's right, Mister Barnard.'

'When? He say when?'

'Any time now, should be.'

Barney looked at him. The kid was shivering head to foot. Too fucked to be of any use unless he shot up straightaway. Barney held out the fifty, and said, 'Give me your mobile.'

'You said two fifty, Mister Barnard—'

'Then you'll have to come back, won't you? Fast as you fucking can.'

Chingola took his battered taped-up Nokio out of his inside pocket, exchanged it for the fifty, and pushed himself painfully to his feet. The weak grin came briefly back. 'Thanks, Mister Barnard, you're a star.'

When Rupert heaved the Land-Rover back into the parking bay after following the woman in the Renault home, the close-set headlamps picked up a movement against the far wall. In a three foot deep rectangular hole waiting for a liquid gas tank to be installed, there was a guy on his knees with his trousers down, looking for the vein in his leg.

Baz slid into the passenger seat from behind the Iveco.

'You see that, Baz?'

'Yah.'

'I thought at first he was having a tom tit.'

'Heh-heh-heh. Man shootin' up in a hole in a road.' Baz began to stick four Rizla Greens together. 'Is like I tell you back there.' He tapped cocaine delicately over the mixture of ganja and Old Holborn. 'We in the land of the Beast.'

It was an hour or so earlier, when they had just come off the M4 on to the M32, that Baz had said to pull over.

'We're still on a fucking motorway, Baz.'

'No we ain't. The lights is changed colour.'

'Still a fucking motorway—'

'Pull over anyway. I got a take a leak and make a call.'

'Holy shit, Baz—'

'You hear me, boy?'

Rupert coasted up to an emergency telephone point. Baz said to keep the engine running, got out and stood facing away from Rupert to piss against the telephone point. Then, back still to Rupert, he made a short call on his mobile. He got back in smiling. 'It's good to talk, man.'

It irritated the shit out of Rupert. 'What the fuck's going on, Baz?'

'We goin' in,' said Baz. 'We check out a couple places, then we party.'

'Fucking hell.'

'Heh-heh-heh.' Then, harder: 'What a matter with you, white boy?'

'I don't get it, Baz. Why all the fucking secrecy? I thought this was a fucking team—'

'Well now you know. It ain't.'

'What is it then?'

'You workin' for me, Rupert.'

'Yeah, OK, right.' Trying to stay patient, but failing. 'So why stop in the middle of a fucking motorway, why piss all over the phone box? Fucking mad—'

Baz's punch only travelled six inches. It hit Rupert just above the bicep and slammed him up against the cab door. 'Ow—'

'You see that place there?' said Baz as if nothing had happened.

'Fucking hurt, Baz.'

'Jus' look where I'm telling you.'

Rupert looked. Across the opposite lane of the M32, on a conical hillock surrounded by bare trees and lit from below against the orange night sky by construction workers' flat white halogen floods, stood a massive grey Victorian pile. Built like a keep, four-square with a turreted tower jutting from each corner, it was three storeys high from the roof to the terrace and then two more rows of blank stone windows to its buttressed foot. Below, by the side of the opposite lane, a bus-sized sign read 'Hillside Home Developments'. To Rupert, the building had insane asylum written all over it. Now it looked as if they were turning it into sheltered accommodation.

'Where they put me, man.' Baz lit the spliff. Without taking his eyes off the place he motioned Rupert to drive on.

Two years ago, apparently, on a 'bizness trip' to St Pauls, Baz said he'd been gripped and fitted up by Bristol Central CID. While he was on remand in Horfield Jail some white guys on the same landing kept bugging and dissing him about his leg and he snapped. Two white guys ended up in the prison hospital.

'They sent me out that place for tests, man. Tests, they ain't no tests, they just fill you full a pills and shit six times a day. Place is full a fuckin' zombies, so I keep all that stuff in my cheek, spit it out down the toilet. Yah.' Baz glowered at the memory. 'They got beds in there worse'n the fuckin' Chair, man: strap you down, pump you so full a volts sparks fly out you black ass. They only give that to me once. Nex' time I was ready for 'em.'

'What'd you do, Baz?' Humouring him.

Baz sucked his teeth, shook his head. 'Was six of 'em, an' a big black bitch with a needle. They put me in the chicken run, in the fuckin' basement, man, no light, no heat, no fuckin' clothes, no fuckin' air, and they put me in a fuckin' cage. In a fuckin' iron-bar cage two feet square by five feet long. You can't stand up, sit down, lie down, you can't even shit right.'

'Fucking hell, Baz. How long for?'

Baz shook his head and opened the sliding window to let the smoke out. He remained silent until they came to the M'WAY END signs painted on the road, and then he said, 'I fooled 'em, man. I stuck the fucker out till they said I was cured. They said I was sane. Heh-heh-heh.'

Rupert saw his arm coming over and flinched away. Instead, Baz grabbed a handful of Rupert's hair. 'How I come to Leyhill, how I come to meet you, babe.' He shook Rupert's head gently. 'Now you mek a leff then a right.'

As they were cruising Easton and St Pauls, checking the street system round Westminster Road, Trinity Road and the Church of the Lion of Judah, Rupert, thinking over what Baz had told him about the chicken run, said, 'You really bite that guy Clifford's dick off?'

'Heh-heh-heh.'

'Did you?'

'You think I put a white homo dick in my black mout'?'

'No,' said Rupert, 'No I don't. So what did you do?'

'I cut it off with a breadsaw, man.'

'Oh, right.' Then, thinking back: 'What breadsaw?'

'Course I bit the fucker off,' Baz said. 'Nyah,' he said. 'Like that,' he said. 'Why you think they sent me that place?'

Rupert thought about it, swallowed before he spoke. 'But they didn't, Baz.'

'Was after, after you leff.'

'You said it was when the CID guys fitted you up.'

Baz shook his head irritably. 'What 'appen, 'appen.' He drew on the last of the spliff and dropped it out of the window. 'Fuckin' place. They put you in a fuckin' cage, y' know?'

'Yeah, right,' said Rupert. Baz wasn't only blitzed out of his brains, he was puddled to fuck. Also, he was sitting on five kilograms of cocaine, carrying at least one gun, and they were driving straight into a face-off between God knows how many police and a mob of armed villains.

Rupert looked at the pinched white faces hurrying past the sullen black faces on the harsh-lit streets. Neither lot seeming to see the other. Terrific. Welcome to Bristol.

Now, sitting in the parking bay, Rupert watched the thin long-haired guy in the hole pull blood up into the syringe before injecting. Baz was rolling another spliff.

'You see where the woman go?'

'Yeah, some place over the flyover, mile, mile and a half.' Rupert picked up an address scrawled on the back of an NCP ticket. 'Twenty-three Churchwood.'

'Nice?'

'Is it fuck. Backs on to some allotments by the river.'

Baz unfolded the Bristol A–Z and held it up to the dim orange streetlighting. 'Yah, by a railway line. Nice.'

'Is it?'

Baz lit the spliff and considered the glowing feathery end for some time. 'You ever get busted?'

Rambling again, thought Rupert. 'Yeah. That fucking grass in the attic.'

'How they come in?'

'Who?'

'The Beast, man. How they come in?'

'Fucking lunatics,' said Rupert. 'Four o'clock in the morning, they're smashing the fucking door down.'

Baz grinning, encouraging.

Some reason, it annoyed Rupert. 'No, man, I mean, this isn't some inner city fucking shithole, this is the Cotswolds, this is a fucking vicarage, man, and they're hammering seven shades of shit out of it with a fucking great mallet.'

'Heh-heh-heh.'

'Bunch of fucking arseholes.'

'Right. The Beast gettin' excited.'

'Fucking maniacs.'

'No, man,' said Baz. 'They fuckin' heroes. In they own mind they fuckin' heroes.'

'Fucking Georgian doors, man.'

'Is all a same,' said Baz, drawing on the spliff. 'The Man go out on a raid, he get excited, smash some place down, beat some fucker up, he feel good, he don' wanta go home, he feel like a fuckin' hero, he wanta get pissed, he wanta get fucked. He don' wanta go back to his ol' misery-face wife moanin' and groanin' about bein' woke up and laid like a bag of shit.' Blowing the smoke out in a thin stream. 'Specially if he got some nice new piece a pussy round the corner.'

'You reckon?'

Baz shrugged. 'What 'appen, 'appen. Is what I'd do. Deal like this, fish can go all ways, you got to be ready.'

'Fuck are you talking about?'

'Heh-heh-heh. You don' get it, do you, Rupert?' Leaning back, giving him that cockeyed sideways look. 'Could be you never will. Heh-heh-heh.'

Rupert decided it was all fucking dope-talk. He went back to watching the long-haired kid. He was pulling his trousers up, looking round, knotting the length of fuchsia-coloured chiffon he'd used for a tourniquet into a cravat round his neck. Then he was clambering out of the hole and walking unsteadily on stick-thin legs that didn't seem to know where the ground was. Shit, he was coming straight for them.

'Fucking hell, Baz—'

'Stick-a-pin.'

The guy wavered round to where Baz was, grinned loosely and said, 'Thanks man, I needed that, Jesus Christ, I needed it. I was really fucking strung out.' Laughing and showing his bad teeth. 'Saved my fucking life, man.'

'You welcome,' said Baz. 'You tell the Man where you get it?'

'Did I fuck. I said white skins. White skins off the estates.'

'Seen,' said Baz. 'After we had a talk let the Man leave first.'

'Yeah, right. Got it.' Still grinning, he wobble-legged his way back to the café.

'You carrying smack as well now?'

'Yah,' said Baz, laying the spliff carefully on the gearbox cover and taking out his mobile. 'You want some?'

'All I want is to know what the fuck is going on.'

'You do?'

'Yeah. Why have we got to be so fucking close? Why don't we just go in there and talk to the cunt?'

'That for me to know and you to figure,' said Baz. 'Now shut the fuck up.'

Rupert listened to Baz negotiating times and places and amounts with the long-haired kid. The kid was clearly taking instructions from the Man. After five minutes or so, Rupert's disbelief had turned to despair. Baz was getting walked all over. What made it worse was him looking so doped-up fucking happy while they were cutting him to pieces.

Baz lazily closed down the phone, drew on the spliff and gave Rupert his cock-eyed grin. 'Is all set.'

'All set? The worst fucking deal I've ever heard, man.'

'Heh-heh-heh. You ain't seen nothin' yet.'

'Given 'em everything, man, and you got nothing. *Nothing.* You've given 'em the time, the place, how much we're carrying – and for what, what do we get out of it?'

'Heh-heh-heh.'

'Don't give me that black dude shit, Baz, this isn't what-goes-down this is what-fucks-up – I'm out of it.' Opening the cab door. 'I'm serious, man.'

'Stick-a-pin now, stick-a-pin.'

'Fuck stick-a-pin. You're out your fucking tree, man, you screwed up, you blew it, so what's the fucking point?'

Baz opened the sliding window and spat into the night. 'We see how hungry the Man is.'

'Baz. You just offered him two hundred grand's worth of coke for nothing.'

'Not for nothin'. For evidence. Man got to have evidence.'

'Fuck evidence. You just offered him a hundred grand to buy the fucking stuff back.'

'Right.'

'Then, Baz, then, you let him walk you up to a hundred and twenty.'

'Him greedier than I thought, man.' Baz grinned.

Rupert found himself wanting to smash the grin off his fucking black face, smash it to a fucking pulp. Instead, he said, 'And this is the clincher, Baz, this is your final fucking masterstroke: this guy tells the kid to tell us – and these are his very fucking words, man, I couldn't believe they were coming out of the phone – we should prepare ourselves to get arrested and he'll do what he can to get us out ASAP.' Rupert thumped his fist against the steering wheel. '*ASA-fucking-P!*'

'Yah.'

'What he said, right?'

'Right.'

'Fucking worst deal I ever heard.'

Baz, still giving him the doped-up sleepy-eyed grin, said, 'We ain't buyin' the coke, we buyin' the cop.' He stopped, dropped the spliff and stamped his foot on it. Reflections of flashing blue light bounced round the concrete boles and a small white Fiesta with traffic cones in the back pulled up in Brunel Lock Road. Facing them, diagonally opposite, no more than twenty yards away.

'Holy fuck, Baz.'

'Hold on you shit, boy.'

A stocky grey-haired figure in a blue suit trotted confidently down the café steps and across the tarmac. Rupert saw Baz's hand go deep inside his jacket.

The Man leaned in to speak to the uniform guy, giving him directions with the flat of his hand. The Fiesta's map light shone up into flinty grey eyes and iron-grey hair.

'That him, man.' Baz eased something out of the waistband of his trousers.

'Who?'

'Man fit me up, put me in a fuckin' cage.' There was a snick of metal. Baz's eyes were brown-bloodshot with dope, staring hard and wild at the stocky figure bent over the Fiesta.

'Fucking joking.' Rupert's mouth was dry as paper.

The Man bundled himself into the passenger seat. The Fiesta drove straight past them, the loom of its headlights filling the cab. Baz watched the tail-lights all the way to the Swing Bridge, then he relaxed and leaned back in his seat. There was another snick of metal.

'Was him for sure.'

'Fucking hell, Baz.'

'Him a badmouth fucker, man.'

'I thought you were going to shoot the cunt.'

'Heh-heh-heh. You grey as a sheet, boy.'

'Fucking scared me to death, Baz.'

'Yah.' Baz looked at him. 'Well now you seen it.'

'What?'

'Face of the Beast.'

The long-haired kid came loping up. 'Yo, man, how she burn?' Grinning and smacking Baz's hands, down and then up.

Baz said to Rupert, 'We met a Horfield Jail one time.' Then to Chingola, 'Name a Rupert, he our drive.'

A nod, then taking fuck-all notice of Rupert, Chingola said, 'He's going for it, he's really going for it.'

'What you tell 'im?'

'I told him it's tonight, and I told him it's the school.'

'What else?'

'I don't know anything else, do I?'

The laugh, then a sudden change of tone. 'You tell 'im we met before, me and 'im?'

'Take me for, Baz? He knows you're black, that's all.'

'OK.' Baz leaned forward so the kid could climb in the back. 'Where you wanna reach?'

'The Moonglow, I got a gig at The Moonglow.'

'OK. We go there, an' you tell me about the Man, this little widow he got.'

'I could smell her on him.' Shaking his head, grinning, leaning on Baz's shoulder. 'Pussy and chips, man.'

'Where the fuck's The Moonglow?' said Rupert.

9

Vic had taken two of the eight red and white Tylex painkillers the Indian doctor had given him and he slept dreamlessly all afternoon and into the evening. When he woke the daylight had gone from the uncurtained bedroom window and the green figures on the clock radio read 19:32. For the first few seconds, his left arm felt fine, no pain at all. Then he leaned on it to get out of bed, felt the muscle tissues pull, and the throbbing came sharply back.

There were three messages on his answerphone.

'Vic, this is Caroline.' Pause. 'Caroline Coombes, Trinity Road. I know you're off sick but do you know anything about this do tonight? I'll tell you why I'm asking. One, because your boss Barney Barnard has apparently gone AWOL, nobody else knows when the briefing is and they can't even get him on his mobile. Two, I'm trying to juggle my evening beat schedules so I don't end up with an eighteen-year-old probationer in sole charge of the desk on what could be a pig of a night. Three, as of now, nineteen hundred hours and the tail-end of the rush hour, my lot are telling me the blacks in St Pauls and the whites in Easton are taking their girls off the street. Now I know it's nearly Christmas but this is ridiculous.' Then, in a different voice, 'The streets are empty, Vic, it's weird, and I'd like to talk to you.' Another gap. 'You can still talk, can you?' Click, whirr, hiss.

Vic poured himself a warm vodka and mineral water. He was still thinking about Caroline, her sweet mouth and bloody stubborn nature, when the second call clicked on. 'Oh hi, this is Maggi Reed. We have met on the odd occasion.' Vic remembered her from the County Court, working for the *Evening Post*. She was pretty cool and career-focused even then, but with long brown hair and not nearly so full of herself. 'I've just done a piece on Inspector Webber's funeral. I don't know whether you saw it, but something's come up as a result. I'd like to talk to you. I'll be at The Moonglow at nine if that's any good. Otherwise ring me back at Channel One.'

Something's come up as a result.

It could mean she was really on to something as far as Webber was concerned; or it could mean that she was hoping Vic would open his mouth and put his foot in it. It was a chance to blow the gaff on the Webber thing, get it off his back once and for all—

But then what? You'd be out of a job, Hallam.

To cover himself, Vic phoned the Well, reported the contact, asked for Cromer to get in touch and went back to the last message. 'Vic. It's me. Ellie.' *Midlands Today* was loud on the telly. 'Hang on a minute.' He heard her voice go up in pitch, become impatiently Brummie. 'No it's all right Mom, don't switch it off, I'm going in the kitchen.' A door banged, and then Ellie said, 'We've got one of these walkabout phones, but she doesn't believe in it – she's going deaf in her old age, but she won't have it, just shouts at the television to speak up.' Vic found himself starting to smile, then her voice became jerky and awkward, as if she were thinking what to say and what not to say at the same time.

'Well Vic. How are you? Are you all right? . . . I know you've had your stitches out because I rang the hospital . . . The M5 was dug up all round Bromsgrove, took me nearly three hours . . . Sorry I haven't rung before but I've been asleep nearly all day. Whacked . . . If you want to ring me can you make it after half ten or tomorrow morning? . . . I'm taking Mom to see *The Jungle Book* tonight. She hasn't been out at night since Dad died.' A long pause. 'Oh Vic.' Another pause, then a sniff and her voice raw and breaking. 'Oh Vic, I don't want it to stop now, but I don't know if I can go on with it. Tarrah love—' The tape clicked and whirred itself back to the start.

Vic looked round the bare room. Again he had the sensation of things rushing away from him: of being dumped, five years old, on the cold and rainy station, the ugly black arse-end of the train rocking, jeering, lumbering away from him; the other passengers hurrying off the platform, heads down against the rain, leaving him, alone, abandoned, nothing but dim electric light on pitiless steel rails.

He picked up the phone, dialled and hoped it wouldn't be her mother. Ellie's voice saying hello, sounding rushed.

'It's me.'

An exasperated breath. 'Vic, I've got Mom on the loo and the taxi's waiting—'

His own voice, sounding harsh, uncontrolled. 'You don't want it to stop but you don't know if you can go on.'

'Are you all right, Vic?'

'Wonderful.'

'You don't sound it.'

'Not drunk if that's what you mean.'

'Look, love, phone me later. We'll be back by half-ten—'

The sound of a lavatory flushing, her mother calling. 'Ellie.'

He tried to keep the self-pity down to let the anger through. 'What's more important, me or the fucking *Jungle Book*?'

'In a minute, Mom!' Then her voice, lower, faster. 'Vic, I want to talk to you—'

'Go on then.'

'I don't know who's the bigger kid, you or her—'

'She must manage when she's on her own.'

'More than I can say for you—'

'Are you coming back or not?' He felt better for saying it, even if it left him wide open. 'All I want to know.'

Pause. He wondered if the next thing would be the phone crashing down. 'Vic, I *want* to talk to you, I *want* you to ring me, I want to hear your voice—' He heard her take another breath. Her mother was shouting something about the taxi. 'Vic, I don't know whether I can face seeing you yet.'

'Why?' His throat feeling hard and swollen.

'Vic, it's too soon. It's too soon. It's all still there. Oh, I don't bloody know, one minute I'm out shopping, watching telly, and the next he's there. It's like it just comes up and he jumps in, still there, between us. All of it, Vic, the chisel, everything—'

'For Christ sake woman it wasn't me holding the fucking chisel, was it?'

A longer pause. 'I don't know, Vic.' Then: 'Call me later, if you're not too drunk.'

The phone went dead. He clenched on to it, wanting to crush it, strangle it. What was the matter with the woman? It was Webber who'd attacked her and now the cunt was dead. Dead, burned, and crushed to a pound and a half of fucking Bonio. So what was the point? He dropped the receiver back on its base and set the machine to 'Record'.

Now the call was over he felt he'd made a prat of himself. He thought he'd let himself down. So why did he feel relieved?

Oh fuck it, maybe she was right, and it was all part of the echo, the aftershock: to her, as they struggled and crashed about on the examination room floor, lashing out and trying to kill each other, he and Webber must have looked equally fucking insane.

Yeah, he could see that, if that was what she meant.

To him, the whole thing, the fight, the killing, all that shit afterwards, was like having a big, cold, undigested lump inside him. Something foreign and obscene, like a cyst, a growth – cancer, big and hard as a grapefruit—

He looked round the living room again. Pale grey walls, dark grey carpet, dusty black TV, ashtray full of dog-ends, two empty bottles, no curtains and one bare 150W bulb. The place looked even worse in bright electric light.

Time to get out.

See Caroline first, find out what Barnard was up to. Then see what Maggi Reed had got to say.

He walked into Trinity Road, showed his warrant card to the young WPC on the desk and said that Inspector Coombes was expecting him. She told him to wait. He said to give her a ring and tell her it was Vic Hallam. She thought about it for a few seconds, taking her time to check through a couple of rosters and then dialled an internal number. There wasn't much love lost between Trinity Road and Central CID – never had been . . .

Two uniformed sergeants dressed for the street were coming out of Caroline's office as he walked down the corridor.

She looked peakier than he remembered her. Her hooded blue eyes looked worn, tired, lined, less amused by life; her nose was sharper, her whole body thinner. Only her mouth, small and curved and shapely, remained unchanged.

'Hello, Vic.'

'Good evening, Inspector.'

She opened the door wide to let him through. 'I'll be with you in a minute.' He caught a hint of her perfume as he moved sideways past her: the same mild, faintly cloying, middle-class English fragrance.

The door closed behind him. He heard her talking to the two sergeants, a brisk list of streets and times, and moved out of earshot. There was a rubber plant and a fern on the windowsill, and two small terracotta pots of African violets on a shelf above the radiator. One of them was trying to bloom: small yellow-centred flowers so dark velvet blue they looked rusty-black in the middle, sitting on a mount of thick fleshy pale green leaves. The other plant seemed dead, and dry.

Caroline stepped back in and shut the door with the heel of her shoe. They stood less than a couple of feet apart and for a few seconds watched each other trying to gauge the effect of the past on the present.

'Ah, well,' said Caroline. She moved briskly past him, sat down behind her desk and waved a hand at the chair opposite.

'You said you wanted to talk to me,' said Vic.

'You don't have to call me Inspector, Vic.'

'Right. What's the problem?'

She lit a Rothman's and then offered him one. He took it to see if she would light it for him; she didn't. Instead she said, 'I finally got through to Barney.'

'When?'

'About forty minutes after I phoned you. He was on his way back to the Well.'

'So I've come down here for nothing. Thanks for calling me back.'

'I did. The line was engaged.' She blew out a cloud of smoke and wafted it away from her. Her fingernails, he noticed, were cut shorter than before and clear-varnished. She hadn't smoked when he had known her. Her mouth had tasted of raspberries or cachous or whatever, but always luscious and sweet; he wondered what it would taste like now.

'I see.' It must have been while he was talking to Ellie. 'What did the old bastard have to say for himself anyway?'

'He said he'd been talking to his contacts.'

'So what's the problem?'

'For four hours?'

Vic shrugged. 'That's the job, hanging about.'

'Vic, he's got a mobile, he's got a pager—'

'You can't have those things going off all the time. Like a walking fucking alarm clock.'

'I get it.'

'What d'you mean, you get it?'

'It's still CID versus the rest of the world, isn't it? The same old *esprit de corps*. Isn't it Vic?'

'Not as far as me and Barney fucking Barnard are concerned. Man's an enema.'

'But you still wouldn't drop him in it, would you?'

'How do you drop an enema in the shit?'

She leaned back, relaxing slightly. 'How much d'you know about this operation tonight?'

'Only what John Cromer's told me. I've been off for a week.'

'How is your arm?'

'Could be worse. Thanks for ringing by the way.'

A shrug. 'I was . . . concerned.'

'Yeah. Well, if you've spoken to Barnard—'

'Oh, I've spoken to him, and a fat lot of good it's done me.' She waved a hand at the large-scale map of Easton and St Pauls. 'This is my patch, Vic. It's no rose garden now, but it's taken three and a half years hard graft to get it this far and now, for the sake of one stupid macho drugs bust, all that could go out the window and we're back to Day One in the black and white war zone. With my lot in the middle. The Thin Blue Line.'

To Vic, it sounded like something she'd rehearsed. 'You mention that?'

She wasn't listening. 'All so Barney Barnard and the CC can get their faces on TV with a bunch of guns and a bag of cocaine and say they've "Kept Bristol Clean, Operation Clean Sweep has been a Big Success, so Merry Christmas and Evening All". Meanwhile war breaks out and nobody gives a fuck—'

Vic tried again. 'And you told them that?'

'Till I was blue in the face. CC, supers, commanders—'

'What did they say?'

'"See Barney, it's his pigeon." He won't tell anybody, and nobody else wants to know. It's the Manuel Defence, Vic. I'm from Barcelona, I know nothing.'

'Could be a lot of people are waiting for him to fuck up.'

'Could be a lot more people are waiting for a certain female inspector to fuck up.'

'When you finally got through to him—'

'What?'

'He said cocaine, did he?'

'Yes. Why?'

'Well,' said Vic, 'it's E kids are looking for at Christmas. Cocaine is more your sex and dinner party shit.'

'I must get some.'

'What else did he say?'

He listened while Caroline went through it on the map. Main target, Westminster Road Community Centre, the old school, the Lion of Judah secondary. School under obbo ten days, since a delivery was first rumoured. Barney was getting four twelve-man OSGs in unmarked vans to roadblock and cordon the four corners of the school, and going in on a pre-arranged signal with an armed squad of eight. Full breathing kit so they could swamp the place with CS gas. Caroline was to keep Trinity Road on standby for an arrest overspill, and her people on the street were to look after the Lion of Judah. Any luck, Barney had told Caroline, she shouldn't have any more to do than the average Friday night. If it turned into a street party, she was to keep her people back and let the OSGs deal with it.

Vic looked at the map. The old school was easy to isolate: with its flanking tarmac play areas, now used as carparks, and its strip of grass at the back, it formed a rectangular block with streets on each side. A chainlink fence ran round the perimeter so only the front and the adjoining caretaker's flat were left open. If anything, the Lion of Judah looked even easier. There were four doors, one in each wall, but except for the double doors in the entrance, they all led into narrow alleys backed by blank house walls. There was nothing wrong with Barney's plan, as far as Vic could see, but either venue was a dumb place for a drop.

Caroline said, 'When I complained about not being able to reach him and not being told until the last minute, he told me to Stop bloody whingeing, woman, had I never heard of fucking security.'

'Sounds like Barney.'

She perched herself on the edge of the desk. There was a ladder stopped with clear nail varnish on the knee of one of her black stockings. 'You drive down here?'

'No,' said Vic. 'Taxi.'

'You saw the streets, Vic. There's nobody about.'

'Not many, no, but it's early yet.'

'Two young women came in here this morning,' said Caroline, reaching for a copy of the fax she'd sent to the

Well. 'Maelee Thomas, black, Nova Perrott, white. Names mean anything?'

Vic shook his head.

'They said they were deliberately being kept out of the old school. They run a crèche and mother's group. All their stuff's being vandalised, and they're getting a lot of harassment and aggravation.'

'Who from?'

'Kids, mostly, but older guys looking on.'

'So?'

'That was this morning, Vic. This evening the girls are being taken off the streets.'

'Yeah,' said Vic. 'So much for fucking security.' He offered her a Marlboro and lit it for her. They stared at the map and listened to the sound of traffic. 'You tell him?'

'And faxed him,' she said. 'A girl's got to watch her arse.'

'As I recall,' Vic said, 'you were quite good at that.'

'Ha-fucking-ha and no thanks to you.'

'How did he take it?'

'He was very pleasant if you can call slime pleasant.'

Vic felt himself warming towards her: the edge was still there. Then he felt protective. 'Don't end up like me.'

'I'm not likely to, don't you worry.'

'But you told him you thought there was a leak?'

'He said it had to be the punters, the organisers, gearing up for the drop, keeping the lid on the streets. Anyway, he said, it wasn't as if it was a random sweep, the target was well-defined, and there was no reason it should spill over into the streets.'

'The kids round here,' said Vic, 'they see a cop they pick up a brick.'

'Exactly.'

'Chuck it for the hell of it.'

The wound started to throb, and then his whole arm. It was time to take a couple more shiny red and white Tylex but he didn't want her to see him doing it. It was stupid, but there it was. 'Either way it's a leak,' he said, 'punters or contacts. Any idea who?'

A bleak stare. 'CID tell us everything don't they?'

Vic felt a familiar early-evening hopelessness begin to seep in. Nothing to do but wait for the train to come off the rails and into the crowd. 'I tell you what we should do, you and me.'

'What?'

'Pinch a canoe and fuck off up the Orinoco.' He got up to leave, and she pushed herself off the edge of the desk to stand facing him. She smoothed down her skirt, and gave him an abrupt, searching look.

'Have you got anybody, Vic?'

'I thought I had,' he said. 'But you know what Thought did, don't you?'

'What?'

'Shit himself, thinking about it.' He felt a wave of betrayal drench through him over Ellie. Oh fuck it. 'What about you?'

'Not even a thought. It must be the uniform putting them off.'

'Don't kid yourself.' It was hopeless – now he was going, he'd started chatting her up.

'Maybe you and I should just up-sticks and go and get pissed witless somewhere.'

'Yeah,' he said. 'Then what would we do?' He wasn't only hopeless, he was helpless, not knowing whether he was chatting her up or being sucked into it. Jesus Christ, he thought, how do women do it? Or was it dick waking up and taking over, still after what it couldn't get last time? He looked at her mouth – one move – and then she was holding her hand out.

'Goodbye, Vic, nice to talk to you.' A warm grip, and then she let go and became Inspector Caroline Coombes again.

Women did that – her, Ellie, anybody. Somehow they were that vital, cunning fraction of a second ahead. So that even if you were forced into that first move, they could still say Yes or No. If they said No, you'd lost; if they said Yes, somehow they'd still won. How could they surrender and still win? Whatever it was that warmed or flooded them, sex or desire or even simple wicked fucking curiosity, they were still one step ahead, amused, watchful, protective of themselves. It was weird and it was getting fucking weirder, every passing year; he was fucked if he knew why or how, but the balance was definitely swinging the other way, if it hadn't already fucking swung.

'Yeah,' he said, feeling stupid. 'Nice to talk to you too.'

'I can get you a lift home if you like.'

'No thanks,' he said, lying, knowing he was going to The Moonglow. 'I'll wander back towards civilisation, get a cab in Old Market.' Lying made it better somehow: they didn't know everything, not yet anyway.

In the lobby he passed a skinny white girl and a big nice-looking black girl with a baby. Maybe that was it, maybe they were protecting the kid they were programmed to expect from the first move to the moment the sperm socked home. If that was what it did. Did it swim or was it sucked? My God, Hallam, he thought, what a failed fucking chauvinist you've turned out to be.

'Sergeant Hallam,' said Caroline in her crisp no-nonsense station officer's voice. 'This is Nova Perrott and Maelee Thomas, the young women I told you about.'

'They keepin' a dance up there, Miss Coombes,' said Maelee, completely ignoring Vic. 'Up in the school.'

'Funny fucking dance,' said Nova, eyeing Vic belligerently, 'with no fucking girls.'

'I'll be in touch,' said Vic to Caroline. He left sensing three sets of lasers trained on his back.

Then, as he swung the heavy metal-faced door open, he heard Nova say, 'Here, you fancy him, don'cha, Miss Coombes?'

'No, she don'.'

'Course she does, see the way she's looking at his arse.'

He missed Caroline's reply, but heard the raucous female laughter that followed him all the way out through the door and into the street. Fucking nerve, he thought, taking the piss.

Then, walking along in the sharp night air, he found

himself grinning to himself, and feeling better.

What really grated on Rupert was being treated like a no-no by a fucking junkie.

All the way up through Clifton and down through Cotham on to the Gloucester Road this Chingola plonker was kneeling behind Baz whispering and muttering The Man this and The Man that and Baz going Yah, Right, but Rupert couldn't hear what the fuck was going down because on Radio Bristol an urgent voice called Roger was telling the people that every year in Britain an area the size of Bristol was being bricked or concreted or tarmac'd over and what did the callers on the phone-in think of that? Most of them were listening for tomorrow's roadworks and didn't give a rat's left knacker.

All Rupert got was when Chingola started talking about keeping a dance in the old school. 'Keeping a dance.' Jesus Christ, thought Rupert, the cunt's born in Africa, he thinks he's fucking black.

Chingola tapped Rupert's shoulder and said, 'This is me, man.' Then he turned straight back to Baz and said The Moonglow was off the end of Picton Street on the edge of St Pauls and because he was known it was better for him to be seen walking there. Fucking known, thought Rupert. You fucking scrunter.

'Seen,' said Baz. 'Take care.'

'You too, man.'

'Nex' time you talk to the Man you ask 'im if he remember a piss-stain' black reptile call' Winston Simmons.'

'Piss-stained black reptile?'

'Right.'

'That what he called you?'

Baz getting that heavy, clouded look. 'Ask 'im.'

'I will, man. Stay safe.'

Not a fucking word to Rupert.

He watched Chingola cross Gloucester Road and move down into Picton Street. The Chinese and

Jamaican foodshops were still wide open and the pavements were bushy with Christmas trees. Half an hour ago Chingola was a shivering wreck shooting up in a hole in a parking bay, now he was stick-legging his way down the road, high-fiving the fucking shopkeepers, not a care in the world.

'Cunt.' Rupert jammed the gear-lever into first and drove north up Gloucester Road.

'Who?'

'Him. What a fuckwit.'

'Heh-heh-heh.'

'What?'

'You white guys.'

'What?'

'Always puttin' a man down.'

'So?'

'Don't know a man from shit, you put 'im down.'

'Fucking junkie.'

'Guy's a musician.'

'Grey fucking shoes, man. He's out of it.'

'Yah, out of it is right,' said Baz. 'Why they fuck themselves for music?'

'Fucked before he started,' said Rupert.

'Hey man, you fuckin' jealous—'

'Fuck off.'

'Yeah man, you jealous as fuck—'

'Bollocks.' Rupert shifted savagely into third. 'What d'you give him that fucking name for?'

'Was a name I use.' Suddenly glowering at Rupert. 'So the Man know. So nex' time him an' his assholes know.'

Holy shit, I'm riding round with King Kong.

'What's all this keeping a dance crap?'

'We keepin' a dance, is all. Up at the school.'

'Nobody told me.'

Baz shrugged and sucked his teeth.

'Why a fucking dance for Christ sake?'

'What you want?' said Baz. 'A load a guys, black guys, white guys, turnin' up dead a night in a empty buildin'?'

'Oh yeah,' said Rupert. 'Fucking room full of people,

fucking guns, fucking dope everywhere, fucking cops come piling in. Fucking mayhem. Great. And now we've got a smackhead running the fucking show.'

'Him just tellin' we.'

'Not me he fucking wasn't.' Rupert thought about it. 'Telling us what?'

'What goin' down,' said Baz. 'What goin' down on the street, what goin' down with the Man.'

'He's been up that cop's arse all afternoon, now he's up yours. First he's all strung out and suddenly he's a mine of fucking information. How does he know anything?'

They were passing a place called The Promenade. All it was, a stretch of extra-wide pavement lined with snack-bars, dry cleaners and boarded-up shops. Some Promenade.

Fuck it, thought Rupert, go for it. 'So far, Baz, so far, all we've done is carried five K of coke all the way down here so we can go to a fucking dance, hand it over to a fucking copper and get ourselves arrested.' He glanced at Baz. He was staring out of the cab window, head moving left-right, left-right, checking every house and shopfront. The shops were thinning out, a lot more were boarded up, and the rest were the sort that had clutch parts and brake pads hanging off a blank piece of pegboard. 'Then, when this copper decides to let us out, we give him a hundred and twenty grand to get the coke back, all so we can get a few toerags put away for Christmas. Who we working for, Baz, fucking *Crimewatch*?'

'You know what?' said Baz. 'You brain goin' buzz like a bee in a bottle. You nervous, boy.'

'Nervous? I'm fucking confused, Baz. Confused to fuck.'

They were going uphill now, and a thin rain was starting to fall. Rupert rowed the Land-Rover up and down through the gears. All the wipers did was smear the windscreen. They passed a Good News tobacconist's.

'Mek a leff,' said Baz.

They came to a long featureless red-brick wall and then, on the corner, a set of high double doors. Rupert could barely see through the smeared windscreen.
'What the fuck?'
'Horfield Jail, man,' said Baz. 'Where I was before they put me in the fuckin' cage.'
'Fucking hell, Baz. You gone fucking mad?'
Baz stared at him. For a long moment Rupert was sure he was going to kill him.
Very softly, Baz said, 'You don't get it, do you, boy?'
'Well, no, actually—'
'Deal like this don't just fuckin' 'appen, y'know.'
Deal like this don't just fuckin' 'appen, y' know. What the fuck was that supposed to mean? It was *planned*? Giving cocaine away, bunging coppers, shelling out a hundred-odd grand for the sake of a few pissy-arsed Bristol dealers? Come on, even the brothers couldn't be that fucking dozy. 'All I'm saying, Baz—'
Baz gestured him to shut up and went on staring at the long brick wall. The road swung round to the left. Rupert followed it. The wall continued to move past on the right. Millions of dull-red bricks, too high to see the top, too long to see the end. Baz said, 'Some ting change, some ting don't. Where they put me in a cage, man.'
Rupert decided Baz had lost it, same way he had before, outside that other place, Hillside. So humour him. 'That's right, Baz.'
Now the wall veered off to the right and, Jesus Christ, it was even longer. It ended in what looked like a road block topped with rolls of glittering harsh-lit razor wire.
'Pull up a minute.'
Rupert looked in the mirror, held the Land-Rover on clutch and handbrake. Baz's gaze travelled all the way down to the wire, and then came back to Rupert's face.
Baz said, 'If the Man get us in there, you tink he goin' to let us out?'
Rupert shifted, tried to shrug his way out of it.
'He ain't that stupid,' said Baz. 'I ain't that stupid. But you, Rupert, I ain't so fuckin' sure.'
'Talking about?'

'Why we come here,' said Baz. 'They ain't just walls you lookin' at, boy. They got lifers in there, boy, big black ugly fuckers like me, but they mean, man, they *fuckin'* mean, and they love white boys like you, and they get you in there you ain't never goin' to get you tongue out a their black ass. You hear me, boy? You get the message? You got that firm fix in your mind now?'

Wearily, 'Yeah, I got it, Baz.'

'You keep it there. Now get the fuck out.'

Checking all three mirrors for cops or passing screws, Rupert heaved the Land-Rover out across the junction away from the jail and back down the hill. Every time he tried to figure where Baz was at, the guy moved, shifted, shot off in some direction he didn't fucking expect. Oh shit. He made one last stab at getting a grip on it. 'What about the money?'

'What fuckin' money?' Baz was looking at him as if he couldn't believe anybody could be so dumb.

There was nothing to do but plough on, shit or bust. 'The cop's money – if we get banged up, how does he get his fucking money?'

Baz's expression did not change. 'What fuckin' money?'

Everything started to slide. 'All right,' he said, swallowing hard. 'What about the cocaine?' All Baz had to say now was that there was no fucking cocaine, or it all belonged to the Wizard of Oz, or some fucking thing, and he would drive the Land-Rover through the nearest fucking plate glass window—

The grin again. 'Is all fix, man.'

'Is it? I mean, it *is* cocaine, not Johnson's fucking Baby Powder?'

'Heh-heh-heh.' Then, voice hardening: 'Now listen. Reason you don' know shit is because I don' want you to know shit. I don' want nobody to know shit about this deal but me. When you need to know shit, I fuckin' tell you. Seen?'

'Yeah, all right. Seen.'

'Deal like this, closer you get, more ways the fish swim, more fuckers get they own ideas. You with me nah?'

'Yeah—'

'You, me, the Man, the musician kid, who know. All get they own ideas. Well, fuck 'em. Some bad mothers out there think we Father Christmas. Fuck them too. We ain't. We bad fuckers.'

'*Bad fuckers*?' Rupert made the mistake of grinning.

'You fuckin' vex me, man, you vexin' me raw. Fuckin' question-question-question. You got to stop all this cheap bitchin' shit, and you got to stop now, you hear me? You worse'n a fuckin' woman, boy. You know when you got to *know*, not before. You got that, Rupert? Seen?'

'Seen.'

'Right now only one ting you got to do and that is drive. Seen?'

'Seen.'

'An' when we reach a school, only one ting you got to do and that is watch my back. You got that fix? Stay on my black ass. Where I go, you go. My eye this way, you eye that. You got that? All you got to do, so don' fuck up.'

'No. Right.' Rupert wanted to ask about guns.

'Seen?'

'Seen.' Maybe he'd get a chance later.

'OK. Pull in now.'

'What?'

Baz slammed his fist down on the gearbox cover. 'Just PULL the FUCK in, you white piece a SHIT!'

Rupert pulled in. They were close to the Promenade again. Baz said calmly, 'Right, now we can eat.'

As he got out, Rupert could feel the muscles in his left leg quivering uncontrollably. He told himself it was the heavy clutch action on the Land-Rover.

The Taj Mahal was a big red and gold place with thick white tablecloths, nightlights floating in saucers, scarlet napkins and thickly padded gold-painted chairs. Baz ordered raita and chicken biriani with a side order of bombay duck and pickles and Rupert had lager, steak and chips, mixed salad. Neither spoke.

Baz started figuring his plan of action. Time to stop

going with the flow and get ready for go – make some decisions and make 'em stick. First off was Chingola. The kid was too close to that fucker Barnard, so he had to go. The only question there was when.

Next thing was bagging up a little coke. The baggies would keep the dealers happy and give him a chance to park the rest before that fucker Barnard sent the raid in. The dealers would be caught in poss and that fucker Barnard would think he was five K up so that was cool.

Third and most important was to organise a diversion so that he and Rupert could get out as the raid came in. After that he'd already got a plan for that fucker Barnard so that only left Rupert. He looked up at Rupert and grinned.

Rupert went on sawing away at his steak, wondering whether the loose shivery feeling in his bowels was due to flat lager or something else.

Baz asked the waiter for a biro and some paper and started making out his shopping list.

10

Vic walked into The Moonglow looking for Maggi Reed around quarter to nine. He had strolled past the front of the old school, and a bunch of black guys with tam o' shanters pulled down over their ears were loading in amps and turntables. Across the street four white skins were sitting in a black D-reg Sierra with a detachable phone aerial. They were off the estates, and called themselves point-men because they were dumb enough to be the first guys in on the other man's patch. And to show how important they were, even though they had nothing to do but wait around in the cold, they were all wearing black overcoats and white silk miners' scarves. During his half-mile walk Vic saw no girls patrolling the street lamps and the only police presence was a PC and WPC chatting to the old winos and the young homeless lining up outside the Lion of Judah. There was a smell of chilli-peppered goat curry in the cold air and it sharpened Vic's appetite.

The last time he had seen Billy Jewel's hair it was curly gold like brass waste from a lathe. Now it was David Gower white. He was leaning against the bar of The Moonglow having a mid-evening livener. Although he was on the skids since his wife Mandy had pulled the lease out from under him at the Kit Kat, Billy was still looking sharp in his waisted blue chalk-stripe and red bow tie. But his face, once boyishly handsome, was now puffy from drink and sun-bed yellow. Billy was a friend who occasionally helped Vic out rather than a straight informer, and Vic had been swapping favours with him ever since Billy had run black clubs back in the seventies.

In those days, The Moonglow had been a back-street car showroom with a paint-shop on the side. Now it had crushed raspberry carpeting, pale green Lloyd Loom furniture with glass-topped tables and black ceiling fans. On the walls, sandwiched in frameless perspex, were black and white posters of Bogart and Dietrich, Swanson, Cagney and the young Judy Garland. The curved art deco bar had a bleached lime top, pinkish mirrors with concealed lighting and hotel-silver ice buckets. The restaurant seated about sixty in the main showroom area, and where the paint-shop used to be there was a small bandstand and waxed parquet dance floor. It was an airy, relaxing kind of place, and its light camp edge made you feel you were there to party not to fight.

The couple who ran it, Michael and Georges, were standing chatting to Billy as Vic came in. Michael, who did the greeting and ran the bar, was a black-haired Kinsale Irishman with a beefy face and a thick moustache. His partner, who did the cooking and later schmoozed the tables, was a neat, smooth-skinned, nut-brown Tunisian who smiled a lot and flirted shamelessly with the lady punters. The couple had survived a year on the edge of St Pauls, but so far tonight there were no takers and the chat was lively on the surface, tense underneath. It was coming up to Christmas and the office-party Titanics were failing to materialise through the fog.

It was, so Billy was saying, the same all over town.

'Even Vic's takings are rockbottom, isn't that right, Vic?'

'Hallo Billy.'

Georges stood on tiptoe to kiss Vic on the cheek and said *Ça va*? Michael asked him what he would take for it.

'Low flyer?' said Billy, pulling a lone tenner from a silver clip stuffed with fifties.

'Both wings, Vic?' Michael shovelled ice into a tall glass and held it expectantly under the Grouse optic.

'Why not?' said Vic. There could only be one reason Billy was flush. He drew him aside. 'Thought you were boracic?'

'I had a little touch, little investment opportunity—'

'Billy, if you're in on this deal tonight in any way, shape or form, don't tell me, right?'

'What deal's that, Vic?'

'I don't know what you're talking about,' said Vic. 'How's Mand?'

'Don't ask,' said Billy. He was still telling Vic how Mandy had stuffed and basted him financially when Maggi Reed arrived. Georges went into immediate hand-fluttering air-kissing action and, although Maggi deliberately did not acknowledge either Vic or the other two, within seconds they were all made aware that the thigh-length red jacket was this designer, the black glitter dress was that, and the perfume was the other. Even Vic, who was in his second-best baggy black suit and didn't go a lot on eating with women who smelled noticeably of perfume, could see that Maggi Reed was dressed to kill.

Billy, who was looking gobsmacked, leaned over to Vic's ear. 'You're punching outside your weight, mush.'

'Business, my son.'

'And the other one.'

Georges seated them well away from the bar, one row back from the dance floor, at a table for two where anyone sticking their head through the door could see that Maggi Reed was in tonight. Michael came over and said the first bottle was on the house so what would it be? Maggi automatically took the wine list, flashed her millisecond smile and said, 'The rest is on Channel One – if that's all right with you, Sergeant?'

'No problem,' said Vic. 'I'm off duty.'

'Is white all right?'

'Fine by me.'

Maggi ordered a bottle of Jurançon Sec and asked Michael for another glass. Michael swept the whole place-setting off an adjoining table, laid it in a glittering flash, bowed, said, 'Enjoy yourselves now,' and melted away.

Maggie said flatly, 'It's good here.'

'They're a nice pair.'

'No, I meant here, away from the bar. Who's your friend?'

'You mean Billy?'

'You always answer a question with a question?'

'Don't you?'

Another camera-flash smile and she put her hand out. It was warm and she had a good no-nonsense grip.

'Hi.'

'Hi.'

Vic decided it was her way of saying quits. The timing was good, too: any earlier and she would have been shaking hands all round, there would have been conversation and drinks at the bar, and Billy would have elbowed himself in on the action. The obvious question was who the third place was for, but that wasn't the way Vic worked.

'So who is he?'

'My friend?'

'Are you always this cautious?'

'How you get,' said Vic, 'dealing with the media.'

'Cheers Vic!' It was Billy, calling from the bar, slipping on his black trenchcoat and turning the collar up. 'Let me know if you need any help.'

'Cheers Billy.'

Billy tipped his wide-brimmed black velour at Maggi. She inclined her head in reply.

Vic said, 'Billy Jewel. Used to run the Kit Kat.'

'The Kit Kat?' She was about to say something else when the wine arrived.

They were being looked after by a waitress now. It was the big nice-looking young black woman from Trinity Road. Maelee. She showed no sign of recognising either him or Maggi. Sensible girl. She poured half an inch into Maggi's glass. Maggi said No that's fine, flashed her the smile and Maelee filled up both glasses and looked enquiringly at the third.

'Not yet, thank you.'

'OK,' said Maelee. 'Enjoy.'

Maggi lifted her glass to Vic. He did the same. The wine was almost colourless and so fresh and crisp it felt as if you could drink a bucketful and still imagine you were talking sense. Vic wondered if that was the idea.

'The Kit Kat,' said Maggi. 'Wasn't that where that black guy was murdered? Luard or something?'

'Ellard,' said Vic. 'He wasn't murdered there, he worked there.'

'Oh, right.'

'As if you didn't know.'

'What's that supposed to mean?'

'Look,' said Vic, 'you've just done Webber's funeral, you say something's come up, you say you want to see me, well here I am. Just don't come on you don't know the case – all right?' Vic waited. She looked at him, then deliberately away, towards the door. He followed her glance. A middle-aged couple had come in with their daughter. She was wearing a striped medical faculty scarf with a fawn duffel coat. All that fifties stuff was back in with the better-off kids. Michael moved forward to take their coats and asked them if they would like a drink first. The father looked doubtfully at the mother. The mother thought perhaps something at the table. Georges arrived and said how nice to see the daughter again. The father looked even more doubtful. The daughter insisted on introducing Michael and Georges to her parents. Daddy's a doctor, and look, Mummy, I know gay people by their first names. Georges led them to a table near the window and made a fuss of seating the mother. The father coughed into his fist and said he didn't know about anybody else but he'd like a small gin and water.

Vic picked up the third glass, gave it an offhand twirl. 'Expecting someone?'

'It doesn't matter.'

Vic set the glass down. 'If you want to talk to me about the Webber case you must have read up on the facts and background. That's all I'm saying.'

A smile like shit wrapped in silk. 'What facts are we talking about exactly?'

'You tell me.'

'Fair enough.'

She told Vic that when she first started as a graduate trainee on the *Evening Post* they put her on what they called the bangers-and-mash run: car accidents and emergencies, punch-ups and muggings, going round the hospitals, interviewing old-lady burglary victims.

'It was one of the tests.'

'To see if you could stand the sight of blood?'

'Something to do with that,' she said. 'And something to do with being a woman and a graduate with a law degree.'

'It's called equality,' said Vic. 'But you could handle it?'

She nodded. 'Except for children. I couldn't handle that.'

'Neither can I,' said Vic. 'But some of us have to.'

'Yes, I know.' She leaned her elbows on the table and looked into his eyes. It was one of those points where warmth was supposed to flow between them. Vic decided to ignore it and lit a Marlboro. She drew back from the smoke. 'Anyway, the point is, I still have a few contacts.'

'And you contacted them.'

'That's right.'

'What did they say?'

'Nigel Evens was wearing combat jacket and trousers, wasn't he?'

'He was when he was arrested, yes.'

'None of the people I spoke to has any recollection of seeing a young man of that description in the Gynae reception area. Or anywhere else in the Maternity Hospital.'

'I see,' said Vic. 'Who did you speak to?'

'On the other hand,' said Maggi, 'all three of them have a distinct recollection of you being there.'

'All three?'

'Doctor Chaudhury's secretary said you burst in and asked her about Nurse Wilcox's appointment. Then you barged past an orderly in the corridor and when Doctor Chaudhury's assistant tried to stop you entering the examination room you said "Sorry", shoved her out of the way and charged in.'

'I said "Sorry" did I?'

'Apparently.'

Vic could remember nothing between asking the secretary and seeing Webber with the chisel and Ellie with her legs in the stirrups. Time to be careful.

'You don't deny it then?' said Maggi. 'You don't deny being there?'

'Course I don't,' said Vic. 'I was chasing a bloody rapist.'

'When you caught him—'

'I didn't catch him, DC Cromer did. I wasn't there.'

'But you work with DC Cromer, don't you?'

'He works with me, yes.'

'When DC Cromer caught him, was Nigel Evens wearing his combat jacket and trousers?'

'I've already told you that. As far as I know, yes.'

Maggi took a sip of wine and looked at the lipstick smear on the edge of the glass. 'Were they covered in blood?'

Fucked.

'Well, Sergeant?'

'I can't tell you, Miss Reed. As I said, I wasn't there.'

'No,' she said. 'By the way, how is your arm? Doctor Chaudhury's assistant said you had a fairly serious chisel wound, in your shoulder.'

Double-fucked.

'Excuse me a moment,' said Maggi. She stood up and went to the door. Vic turned his head. A young woman in an ankle-length camel coat and a long black mohair scarf had just entered. She was swaying slightly and had her hand to her eyes, peering through the cones of light over each table. Apart from her hair, which was pale blonde and cut close to her jawline, she looked like Maggi's taller younger sister. Michael was following Maggi to the door. A few words were exchanged, and then, as Maggi brought the young woman to the table, Michael caught Vic's eye and shrugged.

'This is Rae Webber, Sergeant Hallam,' said Maggi.

'We think there's been a cover-up over Inspector Webber's death.'
Triple-fucked. In spades.
Rae Webber smiled loosely at him. She was paralytic.

11

DCI Barnard was in the showers at the Well, lathering his prick and thinking about Rae and wondering whether he should give himself one to calm his nerves when the shower room door banged and the CC's voice rasped, 'Barney, you in there?'

Barney closed his eyes, gave his half-swollen prick a farewell squeeze, thumbed the chrome lever into the blue section and shuddered as the high-pressure cold jets hit him simultaneously in the neck and groin. 'Yes sir!'

'Quick as you can now.' The CC's eye took in the state of the grey-tiled shower room. It was clean but stank of Barney's toilet requisites; the CC had his own cubicle and used nothing but small tablets of Imperial Leather. Barney's suit hung from one peg, his shoes on the bench underneath, tubes of shower gel and shampoo in one, a can of deodorant in the other. On the next peg there were a set of black coveralls, rubber-soled boots slung from their laces, and a black flak-jacket.

Barney appeared clutching a towel to his groin, hair plastered down his face. With his patchy black body-hair, the man looked like an Italian chef. His legs were too short for a start and the fact that he was carrying at least a stone and a half of flab didn't help. The CC threw him another towel and turned his back. There was a hiss and squirt of deodorant and the room filled with a smell like cat piss. The CC opened the door and breathed the air from the corridor.

'When's the briefing?'
'Fifteen minutes, sir.'

'This part of the ritual?'

'I find it freshens you up, sir. Gets the circulation going.'

'No doubt.' The CC turned round as Barney, with his back to him, was pulling on a pair of baggy green boxer shorts covered in small yellow stars. He was thinking how strange the habits of one's fellow creatures were, when – God in Heaven – the man had a row of four water-reddened scratch-marks down the left side of his back. The CC, who wore nothing but crisply ironed Y-fronts and whose relations with his wife had terminated to their mutual agreement and satisfaction several years ago, thrust the knowledge to the back of his mind. The man's wife was a headmistress for God's sake.

'This briefing. You don't want me there—'

'Well, sir, as you wish—'

'Your show, Barney.'

'Right, sir.' He began to struggle into a set of shiny, dark blue thermals.

'Nylon?'

'No sir. Silk.'

'Good Lord.'

'Tog ten, sir. Gets pretty nippy hanging about. Silk stretches, makes it easier to move.'

'Not issue, are they?'

'No sir.'

'Good,' said the CC shortly. 'The thing is, Barney, at some point you and I are going to have to talk to the media.'

'Right, sir.' He was into his black coveralls now.

'It's important they see this as an ongoing part of Operation Clean Sweep, not just another bloody-minded raid on the blacks.'

'Quite agree, sir.' Barney had been at the launch of Operation Clean Sweep nine days ago; it had been followed almost immediately by riot and murder. First that black guy Ellard, then Webber.

For an instant he was back in bed with Rae, her nails digging in his back . . . Oh shit – Oh Rae—

The CC was saying, 'We've got considerable ground

to make up here.'

'Absolutely, sir.'

'Now what I want to get across is something like this . . .' He flicked through his notebook until he came to a few pencilled lines: 'This operation must be seen by blacks and whites alike as a powerful and positive statement of police intent. Giving clear notice to those criminal elements who continue to profit from this trade in human misery, wrecking the lives of young men, women and, yes, even children, that this threat, this scourge, this plague of drugs, will no longer be tolerated in this great city of ours. *Drugs Must Go*.'

'Excellent, sir.' Anything like the last time, the press and TV guys would use 'Drugs Must Go' and ditch the rest.

'If you bog up, you're on your own. Is that understood?'

'Absolutely, sir.'

The CC gave Barney's bulky, black-clad figure a critical look and consulted his watch. 'You've got ten minutes to run me through essentials.'

'Right sir.' Barney picked up his flak-jacket.

DC Cromer and DI Parnes were in the briefing room. They were standing on grey metal tables adjusting the relative heights of the pull-down screen at the front of the room and the slide projector at the back. The DI, a compact, dark-haired man with a broad backside, was in his shirtsleeves; Cromer was wearing a black studded biker's jacket, black jeans and trainers, and had his hair gelled back.

'Problem, Parnesy?' said Barney, entering with the CC.

'Not really, Chief. It's just that we're going to have to fit so many bodies in here some of them are going to have to stand up. All we'll get on screen is the backs of their heads.'

'Later, Parnes,' said the CC.

'Yes sir,' said DI Parnes. 'Cromer.'

'Yes, Inspector?'

'Leave that.'

Cromer looked up from fiddling with the wingnuts that were supposed to hold the frame rigid, saw the CC and DCI, and leaped smartly off the table. The three-legged screen wobbled but stood firm. The CC stared at the back of Cromer's retreating jacket. A triple row of riveted studs read 'F.T.P.'

'Cromer in on this?'

'Outside surveillance, sir. Why he's dressed like that.'

'F-T-P?'

'Fuck The Pigs, sir.'

'Carry on Barney.'

The first slide showed the streets round the perimeter of Westminster Road Community Centre. The sixteen-man OSG vehicles at each corner were solid blue rectangles; Barney's eight-man minivan was a smaller red rectangle blocking the flight of steps to the front entrance.

'You going in, are you?'

'Yes sir.'

'You don't think you're too old?'

'Question of morale, sir.'

'Your funeral.'

'Thank you, sir.'

'Your pigeon, I meant.'

'Yes sir.'

'Don't go mad will you, Barney?'

'No sir.'

The next slide showed the interior of the old school: a central hall the size of a badminton court with classrooms on each side, now used as activity rooms, cloakrooms and toilets. There was a stage, and beside it, a small band-room.

'The old headmaster's study, sir, where we're counting on the divvy-up.'

'Information from?'

'Obbo reports of small-time dealing, and Chingola, sir.'

'How would he know?'

'It's small, it's secure, there's an old safe in there.'

'On.'

The plan was, said Barney, at a given signal, to fill hall and band-room simultaneously with CS gas from the launchers and then, armed, masked and carrying CS sprays, the eight-man team would wade in. The OSG squads would deploy half their strength inside the perimeter fence to detain and search, and the rest outside to maintain public order. Barney estimated the whole operation at twenty minutes, start to finish.

'Who's giving the signal?'

'Chingola, sir.'

'Chingola?' Fingering his chin. 'How?'

'On a mobile, sir. Dealing starts, he calls me, we're in.'

The CC stared bleakly at the screen. 'One more question.'

'Yes sir?'

'Guns. They necessary? As well as all this CS?'

'Let me put it like this, sir—'

'Why not a stand-off and loudhailers?'

'I considered that, sir.'

'And?'

'One, they'll never hear us, the volume of bloody noise they pump out. Two, they'd have time to conceal or dispose of the evidence.' And fuck that for a game of soldiers.

'I'm not convinced, Barney.'

'Why's that, sir?'

'Public safety. We can't assume that everyone inside that building is a villain.'

'I understand that, sir. Why the bastards are doing it.'

'I don't consider that sufficient cause. Not to issue weapons. I'm sorry, Barney—'

'Can I just say one thing, sir?'

'One single solitary shooting of some unmarried mother or child and there'll be absolute hell to pay.'

'Can I just say one thing, sir?'

'Never get them off our backs. Media, official inquiries, civil suits – absolute bloody nightmare. And not only your head – mine, too.' The CC gazed at the plan of the old school. 'Quite rightly so, of course.'

'Can I just say one thing, sir?'

'Yes?'

'Safety of our own men, sir. Some of these fuckers will be coming tooled up. Most of 'em, in fact. Blinded or not they'll be banging away like fuck. What the little bastards are like. Sorry, sir.'

The CC shook his head. Barney's effing and blinding was neither here nor there, and it certainly didn't matter now. He was right, that *was* what the little bastards were like. The safety of our own men. Chief Constable Royston Perry sighed. Guns there would have to be. Two years to go, and all uphill. Oh Lord, I am weary and sick at heart.

'What time you calling the conference?'

'I thought 0800 tomorrow.'

'You'll lose the *Western Daily Press* and all the mornings.'

'Get the TV people all day, sir, *Evening Post* from about eleven.'

'Right,' said the CC. '0800 it is. I hope to see you then.'

'I hope so too, sir.'

'As I said before – bog up and you'll be doing it on your own.' Looking him in the eye. 'You clear on that?'

'No problem, sir.'

After briefing the sixty-odd men and women involved in the operation Barney went back to his office and strapped on two pounds of leather and metal under his body armour. He stood in front of the small mirror and checked that the Smith & Wesson .38 slid easily in and out of its shoulder holster. It did.

When they came out of the Taj Mahal, Baz told Rupert to find a garage. 'One a them big motorway places sell everyting, run by Indian people.'

Rupert, who was still pissed off over being called a white piece a shit, not to mention all the rest of the bollocks he was being forced to put up with, all the fucking lectures and secrecy and slaggings-off, sullenly fished out the motorway map. Don' fuck up this, don' fuck up that. Give him a gun and two pins he'd shoot the black cunt in the back.

'What a fuckin' matter now?'

'Can't fucking see, can I?'

Baz pulled out a pencil torch and switched it on. A bluish fluorescence moved over the paper.

'What the fuck?'

'Call' black light, man.'

'Why, because it's fucking blue?'

'Heh-heh-heh, you still vex, ain't you?'

'Bollocks.'

Baz put his hand in Rupert's hair and tugged. 'You and me still nice now, ain't we, star?' His breath smelled of bombay duck and biriani.

'How would you like being called a white piece a shit?'

'I ain't white, baby.'

'Black piece a shit then.'

'It 'appen,' said Baz. 'Several time.'

'Well, it's not very fucking nice, Baz.'

'No it ain't,' said Baz. 'Ain't meant to be.'

Rupert turned and let him have it straight. 'I'm fucking pissed off, man. I'm seriously fucking pissed off. Not just the fucking insults, all of it. Deal's a crock of shit, start to finish. I've had it. Fuck it.' He took the keys out of the ignition and held them out to Baz.

Baz looked at the keys, looked at Rupert, went tsssssss through his teeth. A length of time passed. Rupert continued to hold out the keys. He could feel his mouth starting to quiver and clenched his teeth to stop it. Some reason, it reminded him of watching his so-called parents arguing over who was going to drive the Honda back from Bryanston Open Day, both half-pissed but neither giving way and the summer holiday stuffed before it started.

Well, fuck it, he wasn't giving way either. Cars passed, their headlamps glinting off the keys. He didn't move. Baz didn't move. His hand started to tremble. The keys clinked. He wondered how much longer he could keep his arm up.

'OK,' said Baz, seeming to give in, but figuring that if Rupert hadn't let go of the keys by now he wasn't going to – all it was, the kid acting womanish again. 'You want me to tek it back, I tek it back. You ain't a white piece a shit, Rupert, you me bruddah. Seen?'

'Yes, thank you. Seen.'

'Now where the fuckin' garage, you white piece a shit?'

'On the fucking map, you black piece a shit.'

'Heh-heh-heh.'

There was one on the Severn Bridge to the north, and another, Gordano Services, just over the motorway bridge from Avonmouth.

'Yah,' said Baz. 'That the one. Avonmout'.'

'Avonmouth?'

'Yah, Avonmout'.' Then, 'OK, you white piece a shit, let's fuckin' move it.'

They went on calling each other. You white piece a shit and You black piece a shit all the way out along the Portway. It was mostly dual carriageway and followed the line of the river from Ashton Flyover to Avonmouth Docks. At quarter to ten it was still low tide and the Avon was no more than a trickle winding its way through big curved banks of slug-coloured mud.

As far as Rupert could see, Avonmouth was another arsehole of a place, all sheds, container depots and factories pluming out red and black smoke from massive ribbed silver stacks. For some fucking reason, Baz insisted on being driven round the dock approaches. Rupert didn't bother to ask why; now he'd made the black bastard apologise there was no point in starting the whole thing off again.

When they came to a big Edwardian pub called The King of Prussia, Baz told Rupert to stop. The pub was isolated on a patch of waste ground a hundred yards or so from the dock gates. Every building round it had been knocked down and its elaborate brickwork façade was blackened by carbon and sulphur. The upstairs windows were boarded up or hung with grey rags of sheet; those in the bars showed a cheerless nicotine-yellow light. The few minutes they were there no one went in or out.

'Looks like a fucking rough old gaff to me, Baz.'

'Yah,' said Baz. 'Don' it?' Then he said, 'Where we switch, man.'

Rupert looked out over the waste ground, nodded. 'Yeah. Good place.'

'You sure how we reach?'

'No problem.' Baz hadn't said anything about switching cars, but it made sense. He drove out noting the street names and thinking, That was how you worked it with Baz. You waited and waited and when the time was right you got it out of him. Rupert began to feel warm and secure and back on track with the deal.

'I tell you one thing, Baz.'

'Yah?'

'I'm fucking glad about this switch.'

'Yah?'

'Because as a getaway car this fucking Land-Rover's a complete non-fucking-starter.'

'Heh-heh-heh.' Baz watched Rupert smiling to himself as he drove. The kid looked to have his shit back together. Good. Because what Rupert meant by switch was one thing. What Baz meant was another.

On the way to Gordano Services, he had Rupert check out the new road that led off Junction 18 to the Second Severn Crossing. When Rupert said that if Baz was thinking of a route out they'd have all kinds of security shit on the new bridge, Baz said Yah, right, and Rupert felt even more useful.

After Rupert had filled up with diesel at the service pumps, Baz gave him a fifty off his roll and told him to go in the shop and buy a load of things. A couple of five-litre plastic petrol cans, five packs of filler compound, freezer bags, butane gas-lighter tubes, sealing and masking tape and bottles of fizzy water. Rupert felt all right about doing Baz's fetching and carrying until Baz mentioned a small pack of Lil-lets.

'Lil-lets?'

'Yah. You know, one a them little cellophane packs ladies keep in their purses.'

'I'm not buying fucking Tampax, man.'

'I didn' say Tampax, Rupert, I said Lil-lets.'

Ten minutes later Rupert came back and dumped three heavy plastic bags behind the front seats. 'You should have seen the fucking look I got.' Climbing in, panting for breath. 'Off the checkout woman.'

'Yah?' Baz was deep in the Bristol *A–Z*.

'Yeah.' In fact the sari'd Indian lady hadn't looked at him at all, just packed the stuff in the bags and held out her hand for the money.

'OK, now we go to the Centre. Prince Street multi-storey.'

They parked right at one end on the top floor, well away from the lifts. Nobody else was up there and it gave them fifty yards of clear space between them and any car coming up the ramp. Boats and ferry launches moored opposite lit up the water with sliding bars of yellow light and people moved around inside the glass-boxed galleries of the Media Centre. Now and again, as Baz and Rupert used plastic motorway teaspoons to measure approximately a gram of cocaine into each one of the hundred resealable freezer bags, organ carol music and kids' voices drifted out across the water.

They were finished before half-ten. Half a dozen cars had arrived, each one making Rupert jumpy, but they had all parked near the ramp and the lifts. Baz had carried on without a flinch. Rupert was thinking if each baggie held about fifty to sixty quids' worth of cocaine they were giving away well over five grand. Which was as much as he was getting for the entire fucking trip.

When he mentioned this, Baz said, 'You hope.'

'Fucking better be.'

'Heh-heh-heh,' said Baz. 'You got to give people a taster, man. Keep you customers 'appy.'

'Fucking mad, start to finish.'

'Also,' said Baz, 'when Chingola give that fucker Barnard the signal and the bust come in, all a dealers goin' to be caught red 'anded, in possession, man.

Seen?'

'Oh, right,' said Rupert.

Baz pulled the Nike sports holdall out from under his seat and loaded the baggies on top of the rest of the cocaine. 'Now,' he said. 'School. Reach there, see how we start we moves.'

En route, he told Rupert to stop off in Picton Street while he went into the Chinese grocers. He came out holding a brown paper bag full of fireworks, smiling all over his face.

'Chinese nice people, man. Not like them fuckin' Koreans.'

They drove past the Community Centre. All the lights were on, feedback shrieked and howled from the crew setting up inside, and on the flight of steps to the entrance three tall black youths were passing a fat five-inch joint round.

'Fucking idiots,' said Rupert.

'They ain't doin' no harm,' said Baz.

Across the street, the skins in the black Sierra were watching the blacks and pretending to take no notice.

Rupert parked a couple of streets away. Baz hefted the holdall up under his arm and slid out of the cab. He held up his palm, fingers spread wide. 'Five minutes.'

Twenty minutes passed. Rupert convinced himself he had seen the last of Baz and the cocaine. Then the rear door flung open, the three black youths were clambering in, and Baz was stuffing the holdall back under the seat. 'OK,' he said, 'now we go some place quiet.' One of the black kids directed Rupert to a cobbled alley full of lock-up garages. He drove in.

The father of the university student took a dim view of Cromer walking in dressed like a biker and so did Michael until he saw who it was.

'Your man's over there,' Michael pointed out the table.

'Cheers, Michael.'

'Love the jacket, now.'

Self-conscious about having his bum watched, Cromer moved quickly through the tables. The place was about a third full, two tables of blacks, young and noisy and dressed for a night's clubbing, and the rest quiet and white. Vic was sitting on his own near the bandstand, watching a long-haired guy in a scruffy maroon tux fuss about with mic stands and amp leads.

There were two other glasses on the table.

'Sit down, John.'

'Supposed to be on the street by quarter to—'

'Sit down, John.'

'Only just got out of the briefing—'

'This won't take long.' Vic stubbed his cigarette out. 'How's it looking?'

'Could be worse. I'm outside the school.'

'How was Barney?'

'Full of himself.'

'Yeah,' said Vic. 'I thought he might be. Fancy a drink?'

'No thanks.' Cromer pushed a lipsticked glass away from him. 'What's all this about Maggi Reed?'

'She's in the Ladies.'

'Oh right—'

'With Rae Webber.'

'*Rae Webber?*'

'Yeah. She passed out.'

'What?' said Cromer. Vic watched him struggling to take it in. Twenty-three years old, two weeks as a detcon, a practising Methodist engaged to be married – and a career about to be fucked up the arse.

'Passed out cold. Where you're sitting.'

'I don't get it, Vic.' Brow wrinkling. 'She's only just buried her husband.'

'Yeah, too much excitement for one day.'

Cromer looked at the bottle. 'How much have you had?'

'Not enough, John.'

'Why, what's happened?'

'Maggi Reed thinks there's been a cover-up in the Webber case.'

Seconds passed. 'Fuck,' said Cromer.
'What I thought.' Vic lit another Marlboro. 'Rae Webber was out of it when she got here.'
'What, pissed?'
'Stressed, John, stressed.'
'Was she here?'
'When?'
'When Maggi said there was a cover-up?'
'Yeah, she was here.'
Leaning forward, his whole body tense with anxiety. 'What did she say?'
Vic decided it was too soon to tell Cromer everything, and did a quick mental edit. 'Not a lot, John. One minute she was here, the next she'd gone. That nobody-at-home look and then wham, face down on the table.'
Cromer, looking worried: 'Bloody hell, Vic.'
'Mixture of librium and booze apparently. Michael and Georges were very good, they had her out in seconds.'
Cromer stared at the table top, pushed his hands through his gelled-back hair a couple of times, then looked up uneasily. 'Did you say anything?'
'What are you getting at, John?'
'After they took her out, did you say anything to Maggi Reed?'
'I said what you're supposed to say, John. I said that if they had any evidence of interference or possible malpractice they should refer the case to the Police Complaints Authority. I said their complaints would be fully investigated, and I said the results would be corroborated by senior officers from another force and an independent inquiry. All that bollocks.'
'And what did she say?'
'She said they weren't going to be fucked about by a bunch of Masons and had I ever heard of investigative television.'
'Cow.'
'Yeah, she's quite sharp.'
'She got any evidence?'
'Some.'

'Such as?'

'Ask her.'

Maggi was coming towards them, the light rivering up and down the glittery material of her dress. She had a nice compact figure and moved well for a small woman, arms swinging, chin up, but there was something about her strutting bantam self-confidence that made Vic want to fuck her out of spite. Then he realised it was probably what she wanted him to think. How she worked. Sexual aggression and barely concealed female contempt. If a bloke tried it he'd be up for harassment.

'How is Mrs Webber?'

'Much better. She sends her apologies.'

'No need.'

'That's what I said.'

'This is Detective Constable John Cromer.'

Maggi looked from Cromer to Vic and back at Cromer. 'Has Sergeant Hallam told you about this?'

Cromer glanced at his watch. 'Actually, Miss Reed, I've got to go—'

'Can I ask you just one question?'

'I'm sorry, Miss Reed—'

'When you arrested Nigel Evens, can you remember what state his jacket was in?'

'His jacket?'

'Yes. His camouflage jacket.'

'Well,' said Cromer, looking at Vic, 'it was dirty.'

'Dirty?' said Maggi.

'Yes. He'd been lying on the ground for a couple of hours—'

'Nothing else, just dirty?'

'Well, it was damp, covered in earth, dead leaves—'

'Damp with what?'

'Water.'

'Water?'

'Yes, where his body heat had melted the ground frost—'

'Not blood?'

'Blood?'

Fucked, my son. Just like I was.

A minute or so after Cromer had left, Rae came out of the Ladies. She had re-done her eyes, but she still looked wiped out. 'Oh God,' she said.

'I'll get you a taxi,' said Maggi.

While Maggi was with Michael at the bar, Rae said, 'Look, what I said about—'

'Don't worry about it, Mrs Webber,' said Vic.

'I was out of it, completely gone.'

'You should see me sometimes,' said Vic.

'Really?'

'Oh Christ yes. Now and again you got to get out of it to get on with it. What they call letting the rat out.'

She touched the back of his hand lightly and stood up. 'Thanks.'

'No problem.' Hearing his boss described as 'that useless fucking wanker with a prick like a banana' was the best thing Vic had heard all day.

The bit about the money was something else. Where was Barney going to get a hundred grand to set her up in a flat? Maybe when you got cuntstruck at that age it was one of the things you said.

On the other hand, maybe it wasn't.

And if it wasn't, and Barney was organising a raid involving large amounts of highly saleable cocaine, it would explain why the old bastard was playing it very close to his chest and not letting anybody else in on it.

Whatever the truth of the matter, there was no point in telling Cromer. Or anybody else. Not yet. But when the shit hit the fan, as it was bound to – and sooner rather than later – it was going to be a weapon.

In fact, it was going to be *the* weapon.

Vic drew in a long satisfied breath and imagined himself putting it to the old bastard in private and watching him react. Watching DCI Barnard struggling and wriggling on the end of that particular hook. Especially when he realised he'd been suckered by Rae. He tried to imagine Barney on the job. It was impossible. No wonder Rae had thrown up.

Maggi came back from seeing Rae to the taxi. 'Well,' she said brightly, 'shall we order or have another bottle?'

'How did you guess?' said Vic.

Chingola shambled up to his borrowed keyboards and started with a straight Bach improvisation that slowly turned into 'A Whiter Shade of Pale'. The drummer and bass player joined him, and then, as two more guitar players, sax, trumpet and three big smiling women dressed in African costume came on stage, they segued into 'Wimoweh' and the young black kids got up to dance.

Halfway through the second bottle, Vic and Maggi moved on to the floor. They danced without touching.

12

Quarter past midnight, during the band break, Chingola told Michael he couldn't do the second half, he'd got another gig. When Michael asked him why the holy fuck he hadn't bothered to tell him before, Chingola grinned weakly and said he meant to but what with one thing and another, he'd got so much on, worried to fuck about this and that and his kids and Christmas and everything, man, and somehow it had just slipped his mind and he'd forgot. He was really fucking sorry, he said, wiping the sweat off his jaw and neck, but that's the way it was. Michael, who knew exactly how it was with Chingola, pulled two tens and a fiver out of the till and told him he was a useless Zambian gobshite. Chingola grinned and said Thanks, man, you're a star, and Michael said Fuck off and don't come back now. Chingola told him not to worry, he fucking wasn't because Michael wasn't only a miserable Irish git he was a mean cunt to boot. Then he stick-legged his way off the bandstand, and when Georges asked Michael what all that was about, Michael said he figured Chingola had got smack money in his pocket and wouldn't be back before Wednesday, probably.

By twenty to one Chingola was dead and The Moonglow had been firebombed.
   The raid on the school went in, not exactly as planned, at 0041. One reason was, DC Cromer, on the corner by the school and 150 yards from The Moonglow, saw a mass of yellow-white flame ballooning out of The

Moonglow's doorway. Then two petrol bombs went end over end through the plate glass and three rangy blacks came running and yipping and laughing like fuck straight at him. He caught one of them round the neck but the young black's speed carried him on and left Cromer spun against the wall. By the time he recovered, red and yellow flames were licking out of The Moonglow so he called up the nearest OSG squad just as the raid was going in.

It was well past midnight when Vic and Maggi finally got round to eating. Vic had grilled sardines and Maggi half a dozen rock oysters. Michael said the oysters had been flown in from Galway that morning. When Vic asked where the sardines came from, Georges said Abergavenny.

Vic watched her tip back the last and biggest oyster. She didn't so much eat as perform eating: fingers angled, neck back, pink tongue out, eager lips sucking the oyster and its juices off the shell. As it went down he saw the swallowing action of her stretched white throat, and instead of speculating about acts of oral sex with her, as he was clearly supposed to, he thought about Frank Webber dying.

She dipped and wiped her fingers and said, 'I didn't want to say this in front of Rae.'

'No.'

'The state she was in.'

'Obviously.'

She rested her breasts on the table, squashing them up into the vee of her dress, and reached out a hand to him. Vic watched her glittery black arm slide across the table. Her still-damp fingers rested on his. 'You killed him, didn't you?'

Her eyes, her mouth, her whole expression breathing and smiling *You tell me, you can fuck me*. The skin of her throat above her pushed-up breasts was mottling with excitement. Vic wondered what was wrong with the fucking woman. Her hand closed round his first two fingers like a vagina. 'You killed her husband, didn't you, Vic?'

Vic felt the great weight of the last ten days lift off his chest and fly away. All he had to do was say yes. Then for a variety of reasons, mostly to do with the avid little smirk on her face, he thought fuck it. At that point the firebomb went off. First the shock wave, then the blast, then the fireball, and the air inside the restaurant was compressed, filled with needles of flying glass, and ignited.

Half a second later two flaming half-gallon jugs full of petrol and polystyrene came hurtling through the windows and smashed against the wall. He pulled her arm and they fell sideways to the floor. Her face was in his left shoulder, her body under his and even while shards of glass and ceiling fragments were showering down all over them, part of his mind was registering how pliable and soft and treacherous it felt – one of those bodies some women had that seemed to be all warm flesh and no bone – and then the place was full of rushes of hot air, cold air, smoke, breaking glass and screams.

—Oh God, she was shouting, burying and wriggling her head into his shoulder, My face, my face—

After debris had stopped falling Vic rolled off her. Her face was flushed pink from the flash but otherwise unmarked. He got up to see who else was screaming. The Moonglow was a rough and still-breaking sea of flame; tongues of it were spraying off the tables, streaming across the floor. Michael was struggling with an extinguisher and near the window bits of melting, burning polystyrene had set the student's mother's hair on fire.

Two hours later Vic was still helping reassemble the smashed kaleidoscope of the night's events. The fact that he wasn't officially back on duty was neither here nor there: DI Parnes had co-opted him to work with Cromer – they'd been assigned The Moonglow and that was that. The main action was up at the school, with

Chingola dead and several other shootings. Retaliatory outbreaks of car-burning and looting were still going on in the streets, nothing major so far, it was too cold and too late, but from what Parnesy said it sounded as if there had been one or two fuck-ups, so Vic was glad to stay out of it.

The restaurant was a sodden, smoke-blackened wreck. The façade was hidden from the street by a draped tarpaulin lashed with fluttering POLICE INCIDENT tape, and the interior was lit by naked bulbs in wire inspection cages and filled with bluish fumes from the emergency generator. Overall there was a smell of wet burnt wood, carpeting and plastic; after a while it got into your eyes, lungs, clothes and skin.

Thanks to Cromer calling up the OSG squad they had managed to get most of the customers out and the fire partially under control by the time the Fire Brigade turned up. The sprinklers had worked, for which Michael said he was going to offer up a dozen Hail Marys because getting insurance in St Pauls was a terrible fucking pain. Even so, the Fire Brigade, who were also on a hiding to nothing insurance-wise, got Michael to sign the indemnities, and drenched it down again. Then the appliances roared off to deal with a string of incidents caused by the raid on the school. The chief fire officer told Vic an OSG vehicle had been rammed and the guys inside were trapped by their own steel window grilles because some joker had superglued the locks.

Before the ambulances arrived, the medical student and her father got stuck in to treating burns and cuts. Vic and Cromer followed them round taking names, addresses, basic details. No two people had the same version of events and one table of four were convinced there'd been some sort of explosion in the kitchen and were talking about suing. The doctor had put his wife's hair out by pouring a whole jug of water over her and seemed to be considerably bucked by the night's events. Most of the rest were in shock and either sat dumbly where they happened to be or wandered round looking for things like spectacles. Vic noticed that all the musicians had legged it, probably because they were all on benefit, and the only thing left on stage was Chingola's burnt-out borrowed keyboard.

The ambulances came and went, and the customers who didn't need treatment trooped off home. Around quarter to three, Forensic arrived straight from the Community Centre. All Vic and Cromer could do was make sure Michael and Georges did not start clearing up until Forensic had finished.

Vic slid himself into a stool at the bar. The ash-blond wooden surface was pocked with what looked like cigarette burns but were in fact marks left by burning polystyrene nuggets. He saw one floating unburnt in an ice bucket and dropped it in an evidence bag – it was about the size and shape of an old-fashioned humbug, the sort of stuff they used for packing glass and electrical goods. Michael pushed a couple of scotches across the bar. He and Georges were drinking brandy. Cromer was out on his feet and just stared at his glass. Now the excitement was over, they were all so done-in that the idea of going home, going anywhere, seemed impossible. Contemplating the wrecked restaurant bound them together like men at a wake. Even the boiler-suited Forensic guys were moving about as if they were underwater. Vic sniffed his scotch. It smelled of smoke.

'Well,' said Michael, 'if this doesn't get us on the television nothing will.'

'Not funny,' said Georges mildly.

Michael broke. A wild swing of his arm, hurling the glass against the wall, voice bellowing with pain. 'Oh fuck – endless fucking years – to end up in shite like this—' He sank his head on the bar, thick shoulders heaving.

An embarrassed silence, the Forensic guys looking round. Georges put a slim brown arm round Michael. 'What you think, Vic?'

Vic was thinking there was no way it could be a

coincidence the place had been firebombed just as the raid went in. But if it was supposed to be a deliberate diversion, why hadn't it happened sooner? Ten, twenty minutes earlier and they could have screwed the whole raid. He turned to ask Cromer about the three black kids. Cromer was staring at Georges kissing the side of Michael's beefy face over and over again.

'Michael,' said Vic.

The head lifting. 'Yes?'

'You keep a staff list, a rota?'

'Ah, right.' Trying to sound normal. 'Wait till I look now. Excuse me, Georges.' He lifted Georges' arm from his shoulders, moved to the till and took a piece of paper from the drawer. 'It's all casual, cash in hand on the night, no surnames, no addresses. They don't go a lot on that round here.'

Georges said, 'They do it for spliff money, you see, Vic. They get enough, they don't come back.'

'Kids,' said Michael, 'they're just kids, all they are.'

'The trouble is, Vic, they don't know what it is to work for a living.'

Vic thought about it. 'Yeah,' he said, 'you could be right there.'

The Forensic team leader came crunching through the glass and cinders. 'Just about finished, Vic.'

'Anything?'

'Bits and pieces. Know more by morning.'

As they watched them carrying out sacks of labelled rubbish, Georges said, 'Miss Reed, was she all right?'

'Yeah,' said Vic. 'She fucked off to find a working phone.'

'She'll be lucky,' said Michael.

The Forensic guys left. Georges picked up a dustpan and brush. 'Come on, Michael.'

Michael shook out a bin-liner and Georges shoaled glass into it. It was like watching a pair of refugees. Vic looked for Cromer's reaction. Cromer's head was on the bar, his eyes shut, his mouth wide open.

*

Billy Jewel's statement was taken down at the Well:

> Earlier in the evening I had been having a drink with my friend Detective Sergeant Vic Hallam whom I have known for over twenty years. He can confirm this. Later, in the region eleven to eleven-thirty, I arrived at the Westminster Road Community Centre. As a person who has run and managed clubs in St Pauls and elsewhere for many years I have long had an interest in the music and cultural activities of the area and my purpose in visiting the Community Centre was in connection with my connections in the recording industry. My intention in particular was to scout the potential of local drum and bass groups.
>
> By twelve the hall was, I would say, ninety-per-cent capacity, mostly young black and white males, but there was no trouble at that time. Shortly after, a group of young women tried to gain access but were told the place was full. I did not see much but believe there was a slight fracas. It must have been half-past twelve or later when there was a sound of breaking glass, doors being kicked in and shouting. It was then that what I now know to be CS gas canisters began to burst and fill the hall with smoke. Shortly afterwards, I believe armed police came in but by then I was blinded and choked and the lights had gone out. There was a lot of screaming and panicking and what sounded like gunshots. It was chaos. I was hit across the back by what felt like a heavy club and, still blind and incapacitated, I was dragged across the floor out of the hall down the steps and manhandled into a van. It was full of sick and retching people some of whom were still being hit and sworn at in a racist fashion.
>
> When I arrived at Trinity Road Station and my sight was restored I found my clothing was ruined beyond repair, my wallet containing £470 was missing and that what is called a 'baggie' had been planted on my person. This baggie consisted of a small resealable

plastic pouch which I was then informed contained a quantity of cocaine. This is a clear case of a fit-up since, as a club manager whose licence depends on it, my opposition to all forms of drugs is well known, as I hope DS Hallam will confirm, and I consequently deny all charges.

William Herbert Jewel was detained overnight.

Nova Perrott was recorded by Inspector Caroline Coombes in Trinity Road Police Station:

'After we left you, Miss Coombes, I walked Maelee down The Moonglow where she does waitressing Thursdays and Fridays while our Ma looks after both our kiddies and I goes down Old Market, the hotels and pubs and that, to see if there's any bar-work going. It's only picking up glasses and that or stacking the washer but it's a few quid in your hand and drinks for free – well, it usually is this time a year but it's been bloody quiet about so far I can tell you. Anyway, I generally turns up to walk her back because she's got her night's wages and a bag a goodies if the chef Georges is in the mood, and Friday nights there's usually some party on or something and neither of us can get out Saturdays because that's when our Ma goes out. So we're walking down there round about eight, and I goes, I don't know about you, kid, but I'm not fucking having it, being kept out of our own fucking gaff – this is what we were talking about earlier, Miss Coombes, the aggravation and then the dance and all that.

'Anyway, we went. I'm finished at twenty-to, and she gets off at twelve so we got there about ten-past. Place is only about three-quarters full, and there's women in there, but they won't let us in, will they? Said we was troublemakers. Well, we played fuck didn't we? Screaming we'd been assaulted and going for the police and all like that so finally they let us in.

To shut us up really. Now I wish they fucking hadn't.

'I didn't recognise any of the other women, they was off the estates mostly, white girls with blokes in white scarves, but they didn't bother us and we didn't bother them and we got some tabs and Es and that was cool when, bang, all the lights go out, bang-crash, and they're fucking gassing us. I thought the fucking aliens had landed I really did, Miss Coombes, all these blokes in black helmets and goggles and tubes and things sticking out their chests. Mind you I was well tabbed up by then. So I goes to Maelee, Come on kid, leg it, no fucking Martian's fucking me.

'Anyway, I gets out, and she's nowhere, she's gone, and I can hardly see by now and then there's two other blokes in black hoods coming out of the ground so I just lay down on the steps and howled my fucking eyes out. I think I went hysterical but by then everybody was hysterical.

'Oh, and there was an orange minibus at the bottom of the steps so you couldn't get in or out. And that's it, really. You haven't heard anything of Maelee have you, only I haven't seen her since and our Ma's got her kid.'

Caroline switched off the twin-track recorder. She had already spoken to the Infirmary and they had advised her not to tell Nova yet that Maelee had been shot through the stomach and the bullet had lodged near her spine. She was still in emergency theatre, there was no news so far and no names were being released. She established with Admissions that Nova and her mother were to be telephoned as next of kin – Maelee had no one else and they had Maelee's baby – and got on with the rest of the night's interviews.

Statement from Neville Alen Hart, twenty-four, self-employed security operative, Knowle:

I was operating door security and admissions from half-past nine to eleven and later I was positioned between stage and band-room to prevent equipment damage or pilfering. We had no trouble from skins or blacks or nobody until the police come in. My opinion is that the trouble started with them and their heavy-handed way of going about. I was definitely not aware cocaine was being dealt on the premises and had I been I would have ejected those responsible. Personally I respect my body and I do not contaminate it with drugs or even alcohol and also my job depends on it. Nor was I involved in the shooting or any other trouble. I would be out of a job if I was caught messing about like that. All I did was find this gun on the floor, and when I put it in my belt to be secure until I handed it in, I was arrested. That is all I wish to say at this time.

Statement from Maurice Perreira, fifty-six, caretaker, St Pauls:

I have been caretaker at Westminster Road Community Centre five and a half years. Before that I was caretaker at St Luke's Primary. I have never had any trouble until tonight, although there have been recent complaints from the Women's Self Help Group that uses the hall. On the night in question I had to supervise the installation of the equipment. That is, the sound equipment. I do not want to get into trouble but I am bound to say that the dance was arranged late over my head because it is local council policy to maximise income in respect of the Centre. I had to supervise the equipment because I know these boys of old and they will try and get in up to ten kilowatts of amplification when the system is only capable of taking three. Also it is against the Noise Act.

When I returned to my flat, which abuts on to the school, at 10.35 pm I discovered that my spare set of keys was gone missing. That is, my spare set of keys to the Community Centre which are kept in the locked box inside my front door for emergencies. The fireproof glass was smashed and the keys were gone. No one in charge at the hall knew anything about it needless to say. I reported the loss by telephone to Trinity Road at 10.40 pm. There was another disturbance around 12 midnight involving two women known to me as Nova Perrott and Maelee Thomas but by then I had had enough and told them to get on with it. I am not a well man, I have a bad stomach condition known as pre-ulcerative colitis, and I live on my own.

By the time I reported the keys, I had been on duty from 8 in the morning until after 10.30 at night, which is against the terms of my employment unless advance notice is given which in this case it was not. In my opinion the lights failed because as I suspected the system had been overloaded. I was given no advance notice of the police operation, which if I had been would have saved much trouble in the matter of access and broken windows and such. As a result the building is no longer secure, which means more trouble and work for everybody, including myself, in sorting it out, which could all have been avoided. 12.45 I was woke up by noise and screaming and banging and that, and shortly after I was dragged out of my bed by armed policemen. It is now after 3.00 in the morning and I wish to state I have still not been allowed to my bed. This has been the worst and most troubled night of my life.

In all, taking The Moonglow and related incidents into account, there were 157 witnesses interviewed. This meant that at least one third of those thought to be at the Community Centre had avoided being detained by the OSG squads.

Of those interviewed, twenty-nine were charged with

possession of cocaine; seventeen with firearms offences; fourteen had been injured and were being kept in hospital overnight; four patients, one of whom was Maelee Thomas, were sufficiently ill to be described as serious.

Antony Christopher Bell, twenty-five, was dead, believed murdered.

Twenty handguns and sixty-eight grams of cocaine were recovered.

13

Half-past three in the morning and they should have been halfway back up the M4 but instead they were stuck in the bushes by the side of the Bristol–Portishead railway line and Baz had gone sullen. He had been high before, after the killing, but then, after the phone call, he had gone sullen.

Some guy called Riad, sounded Lebanese or Saudi, some fucking Arab anyway, could hardly speak fucking English, and him and Baz shouting all sorts of shit at each other about some fucking storm in the Bristol Channel and Swansea – fucking Swansea of all arse-end places – and Baz shouting back, We in fuckin' Bristol, man, and they *ain't* no fuckin' storm. And then when Rupert tried to tell Baz Bristol and the Bristol Channel were two separate things, Baz swinging round, spit flying, and telling Rupert to shut the fuck up, you fuckin' bloodclot piece a shit. And then when Riad said the whole collection deal would have to be delayed until the ship could fucking dock, Baz went berserk and said didn't Riad realise they couldn't hang about Bristol Avonmout' for fuckin' ever because four thousand policemens looking for them. Riad said talk to Shabba-somebody and rang off. Baz said fuck you and tried to dial back but there was no reply. Shouting and screaming blue fucking murder at the phone . . .

And then going sullen. And then trying to read the Bristol *A–Z* with that fucking stupid blue torch jammed in his mouth. And then making Rupert drive the fucking Land-Rover up over the railway track and down into the cutting at the back of the allotments, no fucking lights and the bloody thing rearing and nosediving into thin sheets of ice like white glass and full of black mud a foot deep – the Land-Rover dipping into it like a fucking barge and great splats of black shit coming up over the windscreen and the wipers dozy as fuck. On and on, looking for the bank to get lower, level out, the Land-Rover bucking and wallowing and twisting until the steering wheel spun out of his hands – the fucking thing was designed to break people's wrists – crabbing sideways up the bank, the whole thing lurching and scrabbling, threatening to tip over and roll back down, wheels in the air – then what, call the fucking AA?

After all that, getting stuck. Stuck in a stretch of hawthorn hedge, ancient mangy fungus-ridden spindly things, ticking and scratching at the cab sides. Jesus Christ. He switched the engine off.

'Baz.'

'Turn to shit.'

'Where the fuck—'

'We off the fuckin' map, man. Fuckin' maps.' Baz threw the *A–Z* on the cab floor and stomped on it.

'Shine the fucking torch over here.'

'Shine it you fuckin' self.'

Rupert took the torch, wiped Baz's spit off it, and twisted himself upside down and sideways to find the black and silver plate fixed to the bulkhead. He read the instructions and put the Land-Rover into what he hoped was four-wheel-drive. When he started the engine again the gearbox rattled like a cement mixer full of bricks. He switched off rapidly and jerked and heaved at the stubby drive lever. Nothing. 'What a bollocks.'

Baz started building himself a spliff. 'Everyting goin' nice till you fuck up, Rupert.' There was no accusation: Baz's voice was dry, resigned, matter of fact.

Rupert remembered the last time Baz had sounded like that and felt his guts go shivery. A thin swollen-jointed twig tapped its claws against the windscreen. What a place to fucking die.

'Talking about?'

'What 'appen, 'appen.' Baz licked the spliff.

'Not my fucking fault, was it?'

'Wasn' it?'

'No. Not in my opinion.'

'Is in mine, Rupert. You fucked up.'

'How?'

Baz went tssssss through his teeth. 'I tol' you to stick on 'im.'

'I fucking stuck on him, didn't I?'

'You followin' me roun' like a loss sheep, man.'

'Jesus Christ – you said stay on your fucking back – I don't even get a fucking gun—'

'No, because you fuck up.'

'Fuck off.'

'An' you know why?' said Baz.

'Yeah,' said Rupert. 'Because you were skunked out of your fucking skull.'

'No, Rupert, because you don' know what to fuckin' do, man. You think I goin' to give you a fuckin' matic and you ain't never shot one before? You know shit, Rupert, an' you don' even know you know shit.'

Rupert shifted his ground. 'All right,' he said, 'who am I following, you or him?'

'You stay *on* 'im, you stay *with* me.'

'Fucking hell, Baz—'

Baz dabbed a wetted finger on the spliff to stop it burning down one-sided. 'That's how it is, Rupert, and that's how you ain't. Only you can be the judge, baby.'

Rupert thought about it.

Chingola had turned up at the old school about twenty-past twelve. He was wearing a creased red tux that came right over his arse with shoulderpads drooping down his arms. Rupert, in the too-small hooded black sweatshirt Baz had given him, watched Chingola grinning and high-fiving people.

He seemed known, accepted, liked even. Rupert wondered the fuck why. Now Baz was asking him something and Chingola was bending his head to have a word in Baz's ear. Baz pointed out the three black kids who had jumped in the back of the Land-Rover and gestured them over. Rupert couldn't hear a word Baz or Chingola said to them even though he was only six inches away. The bass was like being hit by a punchbag, the same slow chug-a-lug rhythm from start to finish, overlaid every eight bars by a drum break that clattered you round the head, and from time to time, at no recognisable interval, a disembodied black voice shouted 'Ring my number'.

Now the three blacks were leaving. Kids on the floor were jerking and shaking their sweat off through a mesh of lasers that stabbed and clashed like falling pick-a-sticks. Rupert couldn't see what was so great about it, but even Baz was grinning and wagging his arse.

As directed, he stayed back-to-back on Baz, but since for some reason Baz hadn't seen fit to tool him up, Rupert didn't see what good it would do, except possibly to stop Baz getting shot in the back by stopping one himself.

Terrific.

Baz and Chingola were weaving through the crush to the small band-room. The stage was a semi-circular Stonehenge stacked with black amps six to eight feet high. The noise level was close to concussion until you got behind them.

A neckless massively built white guy in a bouncer's DJ walled off the door to the band-room. He let Baz and Chingola through and stopped Rupert.

'Where you think you're going, Curly?' The bouncer was a good head taller than Rupert and had the dull steroidal glower of a man so far denied the pleasure of inflicting pain. There was a half-empty crate of Two Dogs at his feet and a bottle hidden in his cauliflower-sized fist.

Chingola turned back and rested his scabby hand on the bouncer's shoulder. 'It's all right, Nev, he's the drive.'

You prick, thought Rupert.

Grudgingly, the bouncer turned his body sideways and let Rupert squeeze through into the band-room. It was crammed. Fifteen to twenty black and white guys in suits were bent over the desk, the coffee table, the window-ledges, even the top of the old safe, examining the baggies he and Baz had made up in the multi-storey. For some reason the only stuff to drink was small bottles of fizzy mineral water. One or two suits already had their mirrors and rolled-up twenties out. The others had the same blue glims as Baz, spreading the white powder with ballpoints, shining the UV light up close, checking for impurities.

Chingola was moving easily between blacks and whites, taking a pinch here, a pinch there, introducing Baz and his notebook. The talk was brisk, low-voiced, serious: dates, times and prices, deals sealed on an up-and-down handslap. Rupert tailed along behind. Nudging and squeezing his way through, he could feel hard blunt metal bagging down the suits. He considered Baz hadn't tooled him up purely out of spite, because he knew for a fact that Baz had one stuck in the back of his trousers and another in the pouch of his sweatshirt.

One good thing was, dealwise, Baz was taking no shit from these guys. He wasn't going below sixty a gram on a full kilo, and lesser amounts were going in the book up to seventy-five. The payments system was still a fucking mystery though. Most of the suits had big wads, but only one, a white-haired guy with a hepatitis tan who seemed known to Baz, wanted to deal cash.

So where was his five grand coming from?

The rest of the deals, collection agents seemed to be involved. Chingola had obviously rowed himself in as contact man and looked to be on a percentage from Baz which, as far as Rupert could tell, Chingola was taking in heroin.

What was going to happen later tonight when the whole thing blew up in their faces was an even bigger fucking mystery, but from what Baz said to the three black kids when they were assembling all that stuff in the lock-up, he and Rupert and Chingola wouldn't be there when the bust rolled in at 1 am so he must have figured some way out.

You hope.

Right now, Baz and Chingola were still moving and

dealing. It was all far too fucking slow for Rupert's liking. Apart from the white-haired guy the rest of the punters were due to pay in what Chingola called 'smellies', used notes of twenty or under, in fifteen or thirty days' time according to the amount booked down to them. After that something called 'the vig' started ticking away at a daily rate of interest that Rupert figured would double the original debt in a week. Fail that, and Men Would Call: you and the debt would be wiped out simultaneously.

He looked at his Bangkok Rolex. 'Baz.'

'Is what 'appen, star?'

'After half-past, Baz.'

'So?' Baz turned his back, dismissing him.

He saw Chingola grin, and pocket a paper screw of heroin.

Arseholes, both of them. He turned away, looking for something to drink and found an unopened bottle of mineral water. The small room was layered in smoke, the bass shuddering through it, one drum and bass number mixing into the next. This one had a maddening two-bar telephone loop:

My name's Tracy   how can I help you
My name's Tracy   how can I help you
My name's Tracy   how can I help you
My name's Tracy   how can I help you
My name's Tracy   how can I help you
My name's Tracy   how can I help you
My name's Tracy—

The noise grew suddenly louder. The band-room door was opening and smoke was being sucked out—

Where the fuck was Chingola?

Baz, notebook in hand, was head to head with two black guys.

Now what the fuck? Rupert shoved his way to the door.

My name's Tracy   how can I help you

My name's Tracy   how can I help you
My name's Tracy   how can I help you
My name's Tracy   how can I help you

The bouncer's back filled the doorway.
'Excuse me, man—'
'What you want, Curly?'
'Was that Chingola?'
'Yeah. Gone for a piss, hasn't he?'
'Shit—'
'Why, you going to hold it for him, was you?'

My name's Tracy   how can I help you
My name's Tracy   how can I help you
My name's Tracy   how can I help you

Rupert struggled his way back. When he told Baz Chingola had gone for a piss, Baz went coldly berserk.

My name's Tracy   how can I help you
My name's Tracy   how can I help you
My name's Tracy   how can I help you
My name's Tracy   how can I help you
My name's Tracy   how can I help you

The Gent's cloakroom was at the far end of the hall, converted from one of the classrooms. There was a wooden table with a set of raffle tickets on it and rows of silver-painted pegs along the walls. No coats hung from them.

A second door led to the urinals and lavatories. The urinals were vandal-proof stainless steel and the lavatory doors were aluminium-faced. Only one of the doors was completely shut and Baz kicked it in. Rupert saw the lock fly across the cubicle and dink off the white-tiled wall on to the composite stone floor.

Chingola was sitting on the stainless steel pan, fuchsia scarf knotted round his thigh, mobile phone angled into his neck so he had both hands free to get the syringe into the vein. A man's tinny voice was shouting *What the fuck* out of the mobile. Chingola removed one hand and switched it off.

Baz said, 'You said one a clock, man.'

Chingola said, 'One o'clock, twenty-to, what's the difference?' Even Rupert knew it was the coke talking. Chingola bent over the syringe and pulled blood up into it.

Baz waited as Chingola slowly plunged blood and heroin back in. 'That nice?'

Chingola looked up, spread his hands, raised his eyebrows and grinned. 'Heaven, I'm in heaven—'

'You are now,' said Baz, dry and matter of fact, and shot him twice in the face.

'Go!' shouted Barney. 'Go-go-go fucking go!'

Van tyres squealed, adrenalin roared. Parnesy was relaying orders to the other vans and the guys with the launchers, and then with a bang and a jerk that threw Barney and the eight-man crew forward and back, the van was up the pavement and skewing to a halt right alongside the school steps. Excellent—

'Get the fuckers!'

Barney leaped out the back, knees staggering after the confinement of the van, and led the eight-man charge up the steps. CS launchers socked canisters spinning trails of gas through the windows. Barney shoved his men through the double doors two by two, checking masks and respirators. Most had long rubber torches rather than the new-style batons – they were easier to account for and lose, if necessary—

'Go! Go! Go-fucking-go! Get the fuckers!'

When Parnesy and the driver were out of the van and on the steps, Barney pulled on the respirator mask and shouldered through the double doors. Smoke. Noise. Lasers flailing, CS sprays coming out, screams starting.

Then the lights went out and the sound system went down with a noise like a dying cow.

Barney flicked on his torch and charged straight for the band-room and safe. Thick greyish smoke was pouring off the stage and out of the classrooms on each side of the hall. Bodies were heaving, smashing, fighting to get out. He saw a flash and stab of gunshot – the crack and shock of it seeming to come later. Then everybody was screaming, the grey CS smoke was swirling up to head height, and there was more stabbing red gunfire. Zzip, and something hit him in the chest like running into a wall. He staggered and was knocked back breathless against a classroom door. Fucking hell – he put his gloved finger in the hole of his flak-jacket – some cunt's shot me. He looked down. The black fabric was ripped and the mesh was smoking. Fucking hell. Reality fled. He began crawling forward, .38 in one gloved hand, rubber torch in the other. His breathing was harsh inside his respirator and helmet and he was yelling *Police, stop or I fire*. They couldn't hear him and he couldn't see them but what the fuck, some cunt had shot at him so he was shooting back. *Self defence, sir*. Pulling the trigger one-handed and feeling the narrow heavy butt kick and try to leap out of his glove. Someone screamed but he couldn't see and he couldn't stop anyway. His blood was up and pounding and it was imperative he drive forward. He felt charged and invulnerable, locked inside his black helmet and body armour like some gigantic fucking uncrushable cockroach.

Shapes loomed up out of the fog, choking, clawing at their blinded faces, cursing, falling. He lunged and smashed his way through heads and bodies into the band-room.

Now then. Calm yourself. He stood up. His heart was hammering, shaking his body like a diesel engine with a lumpy tickover. Calm yourself. Two canisters were casually spinning, belching gas. He picked them up, tossed them through into the hall and slammed the band-room door. Sweeping the torch round the room. No bodies, just baggies everywhere. He removed a glove, dipped a finger in the spilt powder, shoved it inside the respirator and sucked. Coke. The Real Thing. Grinning to himself. Manic. He'd been shot at for fuck sake. Apart from that first slamming impact he'd never felt a thing. He wondered if there'd be a bruise, hoped there would be. To show Rae—

The torch wavered over the safe door, picking out the lettering on the oval brass plate:

J.A. HARVEY
DEFIANCE SAFE WORKS
LATE WITH CHUBBS
AGENT BRISTOL

Jesus Christ. Trying the handle. The fucking thing was locked. Wrenching at it. The fucking *fucking* thing—

Staggering out, shouting for Parnesy through the fucking stupid respirator.

In the hall, all the doors and windows open, torches lancing, CS gas clearing. A couple of dozen people on the floor, some moaning and screaming, others lying immobile, some still being walloped flat. He pulled the mask aside a second. Gas immediately rasped his throat.

'Anybody hurt?'

'No sir.'

'No sir.'

'One over here.'

'And here.'

'One here sir.'

'Parncsy – where the fuck's Parnesy?' His throat drying, blundering towards the double doors. 'Parnesy!'

A black-clad figure, unrecognisable, bent over the body of a young black woman.

Oh shit.

'Parnesy?'

'She's been shot, Chief.'

'Get the fucking caretaker!'

'She's been fucking shot!' Parnesy shouting back. Not like Parnesy, not like Parnesy at all. He wanted to hit the stupid bastard.

'Then get the fucking ambulance, tell the fucking driver! But get the fucking caretaker!'

The caretaker was a thin brown-faced man with a lot of wild greying black hair and a gaunt, frightened face. He looked more Indian or Portuguese than West Indian. He was in his dressing gown, shivering and coughing a lot and holding his stomach. Parnesy held him by the arm until he had shut the band-room door.

'Mister Maurice Perreira, sir.'

'How do you do, Mister Perreira?' Barney produced his warrant card, gave him the flat, professional smile. 'I'm Detective Chief Inspector Barnard, in charge of this operation. Sorry to get you out of bed.'

Maurice Perreira's eyes were red and streaming from the CS and he had long yellow teeth like a horse. 'I am not a well man, Chief Inspector. Not well at all.'

'This won't take long, Mister Perreira. Do you have the keys to this safe?'

Because you fucking better had.

'I told this gentleman here, the other set has been stolen. From my flat earlier this evening. The other set, in case of fires and such . . .'

What was the stupid bastard on about?

'The fire and emergency box was broken into, sir,' said Parnes. 'Mister Perreira says he reported it to Trinity Road.'

'What time was that, Mister Perreira?'

'After half past ten, the ITV news had just finished—'

'Then you're in the clear, aren't you, Mister Perreira?'

'I can go?'

'Once you produce the keys, yes.' Jesus, give me strength.

Maurice Perreira dug the keys out of his dressing gown pocket. A fist-sized bunch, all plastic-labelled, on a brass snake-chain with a leather button-hole. 'But how am I to make all secure?'

'Not your problem, Mister Perreira. My officers will be here some considerable time. You'll get the keys back when we leave.'

'I see. Then I can go to my bed?'

'We'll need a statement, Parnesy.'

'Yes sir.'

'And send somebody in here, evidence bags and tape, will you, get this lot sorted for Forensic.'

'Will do, sir.'

'Oh, Mister Perreira—'

A scared look. 'Yes?'

'See if you can get the lights back on for us, will you?'

They left. Barney picked out the band-room key and locked the door. There was only one key for the safe, a big iron thing, the lever-ends worn silver with use.

The lights came back on as he swung open the thick iron door. Two old black-enamelled cash-boxes, a newer one in bluish metal with rounded corners and a pile of red and green ledgers with marbled edges. Nothing else.

Barney felt sweat flash out all over him.

He jerked at the galvanised lower compartment. Fucking locked.

The fucking thing's fucking locked.

He went through the keys again. Nothing.

Fucking fucking hell—

Nothing in the cash-boxes. Nothing in the ledgers. Flinging them across the room. *Shit and corruption—*

Then, on the bottom of the blue cash-box, a two-inch square of masking tape. He ripped it off. A small chromed key fell on the parquet.

On his knees. A lump in his throat as big as a toad. Fumbling the key in.

If it didn't fucking fit, he'd shoot the fucker open—

His gloved hand twisting the slippery metal. It turned. Once, twice, and the drawer slid smoothly forward. Inside, ten long flat plastic packages of firm-packed fine white powder.

Hallefuckinglujah.

Now all he had to do was grip that black cunt. Simmons or whatever Chingola said he called himself now. Baxter. Shoot the fucker if necessary.

But as for now—

He couldn't wait to show Rae.

Oh Rae—

'You finish?' said Baz.

'What?'

'You figure out where you fuck up?'

Rupert nodded. Five seconds, looking for something

to drink. Jesus Christ. 'Least I didn't shoot the fucker in the face.'

'Guy try fer dus' we,' said Baz shortly. 'Had it comin'.' He tossed the roach out of the cab window and gave Rupert the loose cock-eyed grin. 'Fack is, he had it comin' a long time.'

'How?'

'Was part the deal. Nobody trus' the fucker.'

What had surprised Rupert was the lack of mess. Just two black holes above the eyebrows, Chingola still grinning and his head clonking back against the stainless steel cistern. Sliding sideways, leaving a reddish-grey slime trail down the steel. Falling at Baz's feet, the needle still lodged in the skinny thigh, blood starting to pool out of his head. Baz taking a couple of finicky steps back to keep it off his trainers. Saying, *We out a here, out-out-out!*

After that it was run-shout-bang-crash but all Rupert could remember was Chingola's face. Now he was stuck in the fucking bushes with a killer who was blaming him for everything.

Baz glaring at Rupert. 'You goin' to back this fucker up or we goin' to sit here all night?'

'Where we looking for anyway?'

Baz picked up the NCP ticket. '23 Churchwood.'

'What the fuck for?'

'Hinsurance.'

'Insurance for what? We've already delivered.'

Baz said, 'We ain't here to deliver, Rupert, we here to collect.'

This time, Rupert found the right transfer-box position and as the four-wheel-drive clunked in, he backed the Land-Rover up and began to inch it forward through the splintering hawthorn. Crushing a chestnut paling fence flat, and moving through into the frost-whitened lane servicing the allotments which backed on to Churchwood.

We ain't here to deliver, Rupert, we here to collect.

Grinding over and over in his mind.

14

Rae's phone wasn't answering yet but otherwise Barney was as happy as a dog with two dicks. Gunning the red Fiesta round the race-track oval of the Centre, 03:50 on the digital, 'Silent Night' on tape, grass and pavements white, tarmac slick, water black and silver, the sixty-foot-gift-from-Norway Christmas spruce looped with red and gold light – half a million people and not a soul to be seen. Alone and King of the City.

All is calm, all is bright.

Grinning at his masterstroke, replaying it. Watching himself slide four of the ten flat packets inside his coveralls. Telling himself no need to be greedy, then pocketing the loose baggies on top of the safe. Relocking the drawer, sticking the key back under the masking tape and shouting for Parnesy. Telling Parnesy the drawer was locked and the key was missing and where was the fucking caretaker? Parnesy coming back, saying according to Mister Perreira the key was under the blue cash-box. Picking up the blue cash-box, saying, I don't see no fucking key.

Letting Parnesy find it. Letting Parnesy open the drawer. Letting Parnesy show him the six flat packets full of fine white powder. Backslapping Parnesy. Letting him take the credit.

Fuck me. Brilliant.

Back at the Well, changing, checking in his Smith & Wesson, five shots fired; his body armour, two impacts received. Christ, he hadn't even noticed the second, a .357 angled down, the copper-clad slug still stuck in the tailpiece. He spent five minutes shooting the shit with the Weapons blokes over copper-jacketed constipation and the possible consequences to his wedding tackle and then, feeling a bigger hero than ever, said if he was ever going to get to this 0800 press call he'd better get some fucking beauty sleep. Then off, out, free.

Behold yon virgin mother and mild.

Oh Rae. What a fucking Christmas present you ever are.

Up past the cathedral, hard-on bulging and heart as light as a helium balloon. He took a couple more pinches from the open baggie in the ashtray. Accelerating along Hotwells, the spars and rigging of the *Great Britain* stark with frost. Magic. A phone clattered and her voice came on.

'Hello?' She sounded smaller, younger, dazed. 'Who is it?'

'Me.'

'Oh God.'

'Why, what's the matter?'

'Barney, I'm not well.'

'What's happened?'

'I'm sick, I feel awful.'

'Why?'

'I think I had too much to drink.'

'When?'

Pause. 'After you left.'

'What, on your own?'

'Yes.'

'Shouldn't drink on your own, Rae.'

'Don't nag me.'

'You have anything to eat?'

'No.'

'Well that's it, isn't it? Drinking on an empty stomach.'

'Barney.'

'What?'

'Please leave me alone.'

Rage firing up. Rage born of fear. 'Rae, listen.'

'Just let me go to sleep, will you?'

'Listen, Rae. What I've done, I've done for you.'

'Always bullying me, badgering me—'
'I'm serious, Rae.'
'What?'
'I've done it, Rae. What I said.' Give it time to sink in. 'What I said I'd do, I've done.' Then, unable to keep the triumph out of his voice, 'I've fucking done it, Rae.'
Now then. See what she says to that.
'Barney, I've been throwing up all night.'
'What?'
'Throwing up. Being sick.'
Another pinch from the baggie in the ashtray. 'Listen. I've got just the stuff to perk you up.' Three lines of this and you'll shag like a rabbit. A rattlesnake. A polecat.
'Barney, I'm wiped out.'
'Come on, Rae love. I need to see you. Just for a minute, love. I won't stay if you're poorly.' Waiting. Come on, woman.
Her voice, giving way. 'Don't expect anything, will you?'
'I just want to be with you, love.' And shove my red-hot prick right up you. 'Leave the door on the latch, all right?'
'Barney, are you sure?'
Just do it, woman. Just do it. 'Rae, I love you.'
'Do you?' Doubtful and hopeful at the same time.
'Rae, I swear to God.' Sounding so convincing it had to be the coke.
Everything was so fucking clear – the road was as wide as a runway – pull back on the steering column now and he'd take off like a fucking Phantom, afterburners and all—
'Barney.'
'Yes, love?'
'Don't park too close.'
'Don't worry, love. See you soon.' Closing down the mobile before she could change her mind.
Sleep in Heavenly peace.
He swung up towards the Flyover. Five minutes, less, and he'd be there. He began to think seriously about fucking her. The coke lit up his imaginings in minute

and savage detail. He saw himself fucking her in the mouth, up the arse, in her sleep, everywhere. The way he felt, Jesus Christ, anything was possible. The red Fiesta shot up the slipway and blinding white chrysanthemums of street-lighting burst on the windscreen. Every single object was crystal clear, every move perfectly coordinated. He was a brass hammer in a glass city. He was invincible, all-powerful and totally fucking bullet-proof.

All was calm, all was bright.
And he was fucking King.

The way Baz saw the deal, it was still nice, just. What had happened, had happened, but the basic direction was still there. Everybody think you going one way, all the time you going another. So they were still on track, still on target.

We ain't here to deliver, Rupert, we here to collect.

That was all the kid needed to know so fuck him. Now add up the rest. Chingola was deadstock, the dealers were deadstock, the coke was delivered, so all that was nice. What was rass, they got to wait another day. Fucking Riad. Fucking weather. But what happen, happen. The cop come, he come. If not, not. What happen, happen. Baz laid out his makings on the gearbox cover and licked up four Rizla Greens.

'Baz.'
'What?'
'Listen.'

Baz slid the side window back. Cold air, then car noise. A loom of headlights crossing the end of the allotment track.

Rupert drew back from the wheel. 'Shit, he's not going to park down here, is he?'

'Heh-heh-heh.'

The loom of light shifting the other way as the car reversed into the cul-de-sac next to Churchwood. Lights and engine were switched off. A door softly closed. Door and boot locks clunked. Then the sound of shoes slithering about on the icy pavement and a muffled curse.

A bulky grey-haired figure hurried past the end of the track, treading on the soles of his shoes, trying not to slip. There was a patch of white on the back of his jacket.

'Look at him stumpy little legs.'

'He fell on his fucking arse, Baz.'

Holding on to each other not to burst out laughing.

The creak of a gate. A front door snicked open and closed.

'Oh shit, Baz.' Rupert wiped his eyes. 'Now what?'

Baz lit his spliff. 'Now we give him time to get comfortable.'

It was like no ride he'd ever had.

She wasn't up to much at first – in fact, she wasn't into it at all. She was half-asleep, her skin felt clammy and her breath was dank with wine. Then he got her on the coke – not for the first time either, the way she hoovered it up.

After that it was as if the bottom part of her was possessed by a different animal. One second she was writhing under him like a giant conger, the next she was on top of him, teeth and skin shining, contemptuous and triumphant, tantalising herself with his dick, her eyes closing, her back arching and biting her lip and saying, Fuck me, fuck me, fuck the fucking arse off me if you can, you fucking pig. And then switching on him and burying his cock in her mouth while he looked up at her pretty little puckered rosy-pink arsehole and lapped and sucked at her plump and swollen lips. Barney, she was saying, in between slithery gobfuls, put your tongue up me. He tried to but he couldn't, the angle was wrong or something, and then she was sitting down hard on him and for a moment he saw himself dying of asphyxiation, smothered by cunt. Then somehow, because he certainly wouldn't have thought of it by himself, as he dragged his head up to breathe, he found himself with his nose in her cunt and his tongue licking fairly tentatively round the puckered skin of her arsehole and she was shuddering somewhere on top of him saying, Oh God, give it to me, give it to me, so he did. To his surprise, one hole tasted much the same as another. Maybe slightly saltier. When that game was over – and it was already crossing his mind that he was the one getting his arse fucked off – she made him stand up by the edge of the bed, wrapped her legs round his waist, took him right inside her and fell backwards on the bed. Oh God, she grunted, oh God, you've got me. For a few moments she lay passive, star-shaped and impaled, groaning as if she'd pigged out on lunch. Then, her appetite recovering, her top half lay gleaming and smiling at him while, seemingly of its own accord, her pelvis began revolving like a piston picking up speed. He could feel her vaginal muscles dragging up the underside of his prick on one stroke and bearing down on his knob on the other. In fact, his knob was getting quite sore, and wonder-fuck though it was, it began to get through to him he was in the grip of a runaway machine. Her face was staring and grimacing at him, she was biting her mouth and screwing up her eyes and then looking at him, pleading with him to put her out of her agony. It came to him that neither was in charge of what was going on. He couldn't understand why he hadn't come, except of course he had twice already, and he couldn't understand why she hadn't either. She had before, hadn't she? And a lot quicker than this, too. It was as if his prick was engorged with a life of its own, drawn from her cunt and its mad and desperate striving, and the two of them, cock and cunt, conspiring against their owners to show what they were really capable of once they were well and truly off the leash. It had to be the cocaine, had to be. Meanwhile her groin was roller-coastering up and down against him, up and down, mashing their hair and sweat together until his whole pelvic area felt like one large bruise. All the ligaments in her neck were stretched, and her chest and sternum blotched red, and in her eyes, when they weren't clenched tight shut, was a look of incandescent blue hate. Fuck me, she was gasping, fuck me you cunt, fuck me, work your fucking arse, you bastard. He duly pounded away, gritting his teeth and thinking, I am fucking you, you cow. Panting and grunting, a red mist rising before his eyes, thinking, Christ, here comes the coronary – hurry up and come, you fucking cow—

Looking down, he expected to see their loins lathered and steaming like a pair of racehorses – and then her mouth went all loose and smiley and she was going, Oh yes! Oh God! Oh yes! and making a long high-pitched keening squeal right off the fucking scale like a tortured chinchilla. Then there was a warm enveloping gush around his dick which seemed to melt and milk the come out of him in a series of long ocean swells rather than his usual jerks and spasms. When it was over he crashed down to one side of her, face bloated and agape against hers.

Her eyes had gone glassy and she was smiling at the ceiling. It felt as if they were lying in a pool of warm come, soldered together with it, and their skin, their hair, the whole room and, for all he knew, the whole world smelling of it.

He craned his head to see the top of his dick. It was rubbed red-raw and wrinkled like the sunburnt head of some bald old fucker who had forgotten his four-knotted handkerchief.

'Oh God,' she said, 'that's more like it.' She turned to look at him with eyes as mild and blue and innocent as a baby.

Barney lay there fucked mindless and appalled.

Baz removed the cover and spinner from the yellowing plastic Ventaxia in the window of the downstairs loo, slipped his arm through the hole and lifted the grey metal strut off its pin. They had been outside the back of the house for twenty minutes and for the last ten there had been no noise whatsoever.

'Bend you back, white boy.'

Rupert felt one trainer dig into his neck, the other

push down on his kidneys and then Baz's body and legs were slithering through the propped-open window. Seconds later he was at the back door, grinning at Rupert.

'Come on in, man.'

Barney was lying across her, fast asleep. The first thing he felt was the oval muzzle of the Browning ice-cold against his coccyx. His eyes opened to see Rae's face squirming under a black-gloved hand. Then warm breath on the back of his neck and a voice saying, 'One move, you bacon.'

15

'Where is he, Parnes?'

The CC was striding out so fast DI Parnes had to skid corners to keep up.

'The latest we've got, he's not at home – nor his wife – it's a Neighbourhood Watch area, sir—'

'Is it?' A sour look.

'Yes sir. The neighbours showed a couple of WPCs round. Bed hadn't been slept in—'

'Parnes.'

'Sir?'

'I don't want to know where DCI Barnard isn't.'

'No sir.'

Long black legs scissoring up the corridor. 'Not my job to clean up CID mess.'

'No sir.'

'Because that's what this is.' Turning on him. 'A bloody mess. He could have had an accident, a run-in with these jokers, anything.'

'Yes sir.'

They came to the briefing room door. The CC stopped, throttled his tie up. 'I've decided to tell the press we picked up the whole drop in last night's raid.'

Parnes, who would sooner sit things out than make a decision, and often missed lunch as a result, immediately began to cavil: 'But we don't know that, sir. Intelligence suggested it could be anything between two and five kilos. All we've picked up so far is three – and we shan't know how pure that is until it goes to Forensic—'

'I don't give a bugger about any of that. My job is to

reassure the public and that's what I'm going to do.'
'Yes sir.'
'Your job is to get this bloody mess cleared up.'
'Yes sir.'
'Right. As soon as this shambles is over you're going to tell me who you're putting on Barnard.'
'Yes sir.' DI Parnes opened the door and followed CC Royston Perry into the briefing room. It was exactly 0800.

The CC told a dozen reporters and two camera crews that he would give them the basics and that would be that. He hoped they would understand but if they didn't there was nothing he could do about it. Yes – a murder investigation was underway. No – further details were *not* being released at this stage.

However, what he could tell them was that over fifty people had been arrested on drugs, firearms and public order charges; the entire cache of cocaine intended for the city had been seized and a major drug catastrophe averted. No – it was not his policy to discuss so-called street values. Why add false glamour to a filthy life-destroying business? The officer responsible for discovering the cache was DI Parnes here. Camera-flash flickered and TV cameramen began to prowl round the knives, guns and flat white packages laid out on the green baize table. The CC asked them brusquely if they would mind saving all that until the end.

Meanwhile, unfortunately, fourteen people were still in hospital, three of whom were police officers. Four of them, including two women, had fairly serious injuries. Hospitals would be releasing details once relatives had been informed. He confirmed there had been a number of shooting incidents but refused to speculate whether officers were involved. All police weapons were being checked. When further pressed, he said there would be updates through the day and he hoped all questions would be answered more fully at those times.

Overall, he said, and he wanted to stress this, Clean Sweep had been an extremely satisfactory and successful operation which spelled out loud and clear the message *Drugs Must Go*.

Now they must forgive him: he had a murder enquiry, a street situation not yet fully under control and large-scale criminal investigations to pursue.

DI Parnes followed the CC out. As he walked past Vic and Cromer, he said, 'Hallam, CC's office. Now. And you, Cromer.'

Maggi Reed stopped Vic at the briefing room door. 'I need to talk to you.'

'What about?'

'Lover Boy.'

'Never heard of him,' said Vic. 'Where's he running?'

'You tell me.' Maggi handed Vic a Channel One card with a number scribbled on the back. 'My mobile.'

DI Parnes swung round on them. 'I said *now*, Hallam.'

'I'll be in touch,' said Vic.

'Do that,' said Maggi.

Vic and Cromer followed DI Parnes' neat dark head and big bustling backside up the corridor. Cromer's look was asking what was that all about, so Vic pocketed the card and said, 'I think she fancies me, John.'

Up ahead, the CC slowed for Parnes to catch up. 'Hallam and Cromer?'

'Yes sir.'

'They the best you can do?'

'Nobody else, sir.'

'Are you sure, Parnes?'

'Absolutely, sir. All out on murder-and-drug-relateds.'

'I'm thinking about that bloody Webber business.'

'I considered that, sir.'

'Did you?'

'If I can just put this to you, sir. Nobody knows the DCI better, plus it's what Hallam's good at.'

The CC looked down at Parnes' round dark head and mild brown eyes and decided that DI Parnes wasn't the dogsbody DCI Barnard thought he was. Just as well.

All the way up the CC's corridor phones were ringing. There were four secretaries in his outer office, all fielding calls. The CC kept Vic and Cromer standing, nodded

Parnes to a seat.

'Last night, Hallam,' said the CC.

'Yes sir?'

'I gather you weren't on duty?'

'No sir. Not passed fit yet, sir.'

'In that case well done.'

'Thank you sir.'

'When do you get passed fit?'

'Today, sir, if I get time to see Mr Calder.'

'Take it as read. I'll have a word with him.'

'Thank you sir.'

'Now then. I'm taking you off The Malibu.'

Vic managed to stop himself saying, Moonglow sir.

'I'm putting you on DCI Barnard. Parnes . . .'

DI Parnes told them DCI Barnard had stayed at the SOC until 0320 or thereabouts, checked in at the Well and left around 0345 saying he was going to get some shut-eye before the 0800 conference. Since then, he had not reported in and attempts to contact him by radio, bleeper and mobile had proved negative. Details of the DCI's car had been circulated, and the house searched. It transpired from neighbours that Mrs Barnard had left the previous morning for a three-day headteachers' conference in Harrogate. To avoid undue alarm, she had not as yet been informed.

But what worried DI Parnes, and he was sure he also spoke for the CC here, was that the DCI had been shot in the chest during the raid, and although the body armour had prevented penetration or direct wounding, there was a possibility of delayed shock given the adrenalin and stress levels generated, so therefore it was a matter of some urgency.

The CC decided that DI Parnes was overplaying the heart thing and held up a big raw-knuckled hand. 'He's not been home, and he's not called in. He's your first priority. Everything else secondary. Got that?'

'Yes sir.'

'And you, Cromer.'

'Sir.'

'Now, this chap Chingola. He one of yours?'

'No sir.'

'He's not the Drug squad's either.' The CC rat-tat-tatted a rubber-ended pencil on a buff file, then he shoved it across to Vic. 'It appears only DCI Barnard used him, or knew about him.'

'I thought you did, sir.'

A glacial, irritated look. 'You haven't changed, have you Hallam? It doesn't do you any good, you know.'

'Sorry sir, I meant in connection with the raid, sir.'

'Did you?' The CC pushed a sheet torn from a notebook towards Vic. There was nothing on it but telephone numbers. 'His notes. You CID people don't write much down, do you?'

Neither Vic nor Cromer spoke.

'Anyway, find him, that's all. I need to speak to him, get this bloody mess sorted.'

'Yes sir.'

'Any ideas where he might be?'

In Rae Webber's bed, sir, overfucked and overslept—

'No sir.'

Parnes handed the CC a contact form. The CC glanced down at it, up at Vic. 'This call from the Reed woman?'

'She wanted to talk about Nigel Evens, sir.'

'Say why?'

'I think she wanted to do a piece on him, sir.' Vic could feel Cromer heating up beside him.

'And your response?'

'I declined, sir,' said Vic. 'As per our agreement.'

DI Parnes leaned deferentially close to the CC's ear. 'She approached him again, sir. Straight after the conference.'

'You hear that, Hallam?'

'Yes sir.'

'Well?'

Cromer had gone bright red.

'I'm asking you a question, Hallam.'

'Yes sir. She noticed DCI Barnard wasn't there, sir. Asked me where he was. I said I didn't know.'

'I see.' The CC listened to the phones ringing in the outer office. 'Any further contacts, report to DI Parnes.'

'Yes sir.'
'Parnes, you come straight to me.'
'Yes sir.'
'Bad enough already, without bloody television.'
'Yes sir.'
'That's all.' The CC waited until Vic and Cromer reached the door. 'Hallam.'
'Yes sir?'
'I don't want this Webber thing getting in the way.'

Cromer drove. Vic argued with himself.

He could have blown the gaff on Barnard there and then in the CC's office. So why hadn't he? The answer was the usual plate of cold spaghetti.

One, it was nothing to do with him what DCI Barnard did with his dick, who he went over the side for. Two, the old bastard could easily turn up late, deny the whole thing, where he'd been, everything, and then any leverage Vic might have would be out the window. Three, Vic wanted to stick it to him personally and watch the blood drain out of that big red meaty face. Four, Vic didn't like admitting even to himself: what it came down to – yet again – was esprit de fucking corps. Even with an arsehole like Barnard, all the shit he'd put Vic through, Vic couldn't go behind his back, shove the knife in cold.

That's why he's a DCI and you're still a fucking sergeant, Hallam.

Cromer said, 'What did you say that for?'
'Say what for?'
'"As per our agreement",' said Cromer. 'Always getting up their noses. Why do it?'
'Why not?'
'Because it's bloody dumb, you're in enough shit already – yet you're still doing it, deliberately.'

Nagging at him. Time to get things sorted with Cromer.

'Look, John. You can't be on my side and their side over this Webber shit, so what's it going to be?'

Cromer turned left into Rupert Street, and left again round the back of the Well. Traffic into the Horsefair was jammed solid. 'They're going to know soon enough if Maggi Reed has her way.'

'What's it going to be, John?'

Cromer plodding on, working through it, step by step. Jesus Christ—

'If she knows Nigel didn't do Webber, you want her to find out who did?'

'What's it going to be, John?'

'It's your arse they're protecting, Vic. In the final analysis.'

'Never mind the final fucking analysis. What's it going to be, John? Me or them?'

Cromer turned left again into Nelson Street. 'What I can't understand is why you want to get yourself lumbered—'

Vic's temper, already bar-taut, stripped its threads. 'Because Webber was a fucking killer! Because all the rest of it, this fucking cover-up, is a pack of fucking lies! Because I need to get it off my fucking back! What I did was fucking *right*—'

'Nobody's saying it wasn't, Vic—'

'Yes they are! Now *you're* fucking denying it! Next thing you'll be saying is Webber's dead, Nigel's dead, so what the fuck's it matter? Well, it matters to me, John, *me*! I'm not a fucking murderer, I saved that fucking girl's life, and if I fucked her afterwards, so what?'

'Nothing to do with it—'

'Isn't it? I tell you what, John, you don't forget. You don't forget what's happened, either of you. It's there, John, like the fucking chisel. It's fucking her up, it's fucking me up, it's fucking everything up! And all the rest of this shit, you, her, Maggi Reed, Rae Webber, all the rest of the fucking wankers – Barney, the CC, fucking Parnesy – you're all making *me* feel like a fucking murderer!'

He pulled out a Marlboro, lit the wrong end, said shit, threw it out the window, lit another one and watched his hand shaking.

He'd gone too far, said too much. Fuck it. It was true. He *had* felt like a murderer. For days, weeks, it felt like. Now he'd got it off his chest, suddenly he didn't. He dragged the smoke down.

'That answer your question?'

'Yeah,' said Cromer. 'You all right?'

'Am I fuck. What's it going to be, John?'

Cromer heading down to Union Street, still chewing it over, worrying at it like a dog with a bloody great knuckle-bone.

'For fuck sake, John, *yes* or *no*?'

Cromer frowning through the windscreen, slowly, reluctantly, coming to the point. Turning to face Vic. 'You're right. It is a fucking lie. All of it. So bollocks to it.' He stuck out an awkward right hand and went on driving with his left. 'I'm with you, Vic. You take it to court, say Webber was a rapist, Barney organised the fucking cover-up, I'll back you. All the fucking way.'

Vic took his hand. All the fucking way. Terrific.

'Thank Christ for that. Now turn this fucker round and head for the Flyover.'

Great. No more pussyfooting, calculating this against that, what if the other. They'd been told to find DCI Barnard and that was it, that was what they were going to do. Simple. Like everything else in life. Simple when you got down to it, got on with it. Fucking thinking about it was the paralyser—

'Why?' said Cromer. 'Where we going?'

'23 Churchwood. Rae Webber's place.'

There it was. Simple as that.

Vic told him the full story. They drove down Hotwells. Opposite, imprisoned in its dry dock, lay the *Great Britain*, spars and rigging white with frost.

Cromer said, 'I didn't think blokes like him did things like that.'

'All led by our dicks, John. You get any last night?'

'I could have done with some.'

'And me.'

When they got to the Swing Bridge over Cumberland Basin, the information on the phone numbers came through. There were two for Chingola, home and mobile, two for the Mariners Transport Cafe, one staff, one a public payphone, and two for Rae Webber, her parents' and her home number.

'We could check out the Mariners first,' said Vic.

'Fuck him,' said Cromer, accelerating hard up the slope to the Flyover. 'Wasn't for him, we could be getting a result on The Moonglow.' He cut in between a pair of gravel trucks. 'I shall know that black kid again. The one I got round the neck. And that's Arson with Intent to Endanger Life. So fuck Chief Inspector Barnard. He's old enough to know what he's doing.'

One way or another, Vic thought, Cromer was developing the requisite hard streak.

'Yeah. If he's there.'

'If he is,' said Cromer, 'we're walking into another cover-up. You realise that?'

'Yeah.'

They zipped past the big white South West sign and zoomed into the underpass. Even if they caught him on the nest it would still be Detective Chief Inspector Barnard's word against theirs and he'd fight like a cat in a coalsack.

Every time things started going right, they turned to shit.

You should be used to that by now, Hallam.

'Turn right down towards the old art school, John.'

'I know.'

As they drove into Churchwood, Vic got a radio message to call Maggi Reed. Control said it was urgent and understood Vic had her number.

'Nine four two two, thanks over.'

'You going to report it?' said Cromer.

'Fuck it.'

He and Cromer walked round the frozen dogshit by the gate and up to the front door. It had a leaded oval light with a picture of a yacht in it. When Cromer had moved down the side alley to the back garden Vic rang the bell.

Door chimes went ding-dong.

16

Cromer answered the door with a yellowing plastic Ventaxia cover in his hand.

'Back was open. This was outside the downstairs toilet.' The cover was newly split round the screwholes.

'Break-in?'

'Window was propped open.'

'What else?'

'Nothing downstairs. Or in the garden.'

Vic glanced past Cromer. A short dark hall led past the sitting room to the kitchen-diner at the back. The kitchen door was open. So was the back door to the garden. The Ventaxia spinner was on the edge of the stainless steel sink. The door to the downstairs lavatory was under the stairs on the right. It, too, was wide open.

He moved to the foot of the stairs. The last but one wooden stair-rod had been kicked loose. A gold-framed watercolour of cornflowers and yellow poppies hung askew halfway up the stairs. Near his feet a Waitrose bag spilled out its empty bottles: a couple of two-litre plastic Volvics, a Californian Zinfandel and a Chilean Merlot.

No lights, no sound, all doors open.

'Police!'

Nothing.

'Right, John, let's give it a whirl.'

The main bedroom and bathroom doors were open. The bedroom was a mess but empty. No Rae. No Barney. No sweaty-desperate junkie toerags. The tension evaporated and Vic's shoulder started to ache. They moved down the landing. The second bedroom had a page from a notebook stuck on the door with Blu-Tack: WET PAINT DO NOT ENTER. H.N. HAMMOND. Cromer flung the door open, stepped to one side, waited, stuck his head round. Vic moved in behind him.

A bare, narrow, empty room. The woodwork had been painted sunshine yellow and there was a frieze of Beatrix Potter characters laid out on a folding wallpaper trestle.

'Who's H. N. Hammond?' said Cromer.

'Rae's dad,' said Vic. 'He's been coming round to keep an eye on the place. She didn't mention decorating.'

'Looks like a kid's room.'

'Yeah.' Vic closed the door, checked the hatch to the loft. An anodised aluminium bolt, still fastened.

Going downstairs, he mulled over the possibilities. Barney had broken in. Rae had lost her keys. Toerags thought the house was empty. None of it fitted. Time to go by the book, give the place a thorough going-over.

'Get the gloves and bags, John. Got a camera?'

'In the car. You want me to radio in?'

'Not yet.'

Cromer left and Vic moved down the dark carpeted hall towards the kitchen. There was something about the feel of the place. He couldn't put his finger on it but it was somewhere he'd been fairly recently. The same look, the same smells. Polish. Cleaning stuff. Cooking. Perfume, very faint.

The kitchen was clammy-cold even with the muffled intermittent rumble of the central heating; the back door had to have been open for hours. No open drawers, no cutlery on the floor, no sign of anything being turned over. He sniffed the cold air. Traces of spices, washing-up liquid, wastebins. A single wine glass in the sink, a crust of red in the bottom.

No cosy dinners for two, then.

He moved back up the hall, looked into the sitting room. The carpet: charcoal-grey, and figured; not just in the sitting room, but in the hall and up the stairs. He should have noticed it before. It was the same carpet he had all over his place.

Even the sitting room furniture looked familiar. Not that he'd got any now, thanks to that cow, but it was similar. The same low, chunky, deep-padded, squared-off shapes.

The only difference was, where he and his ex-to-be had gone for black leather and iroko, the Webbers had gone for something lighter. Oatmeal, and what looked like ash or sycamore. But the shapes were the same. They'd probably got the same police discount at the same time in the same IKEA.

For the first time Vic felt remorse – Webber wasn't much more of a berk than you are, Hallam.

There certainly wasn't that much of a difference in their domestic lives. One ending in divorce, the other ending in death. He moved into the darkened room. At least Rae Webber had still got her curtains.

There was a wedding photograph on the sideboard. Rae looking demure in ivory silk and a circlet of flowers, Webber in a grey morning suit holding a grey topper, pretending to smile.

You poor bastard. You probably liked all this furniture, didn't you, Frank? It made you feel good, feel safe, feel at home, it was yours, you'd paid for it, and you could fuck all over it.

Just like we used to, on ours.

Vic moved back to the doorway and stood on the threshold. The telly was still in place, and the video. There were no other signs of disturbance. For a moment, looking at all that remained of Frank Webber's existence, Vic didn't know who to feel sorry for most.

He closed the sitting room door, and the shallow wash of remorse receded. He took a deep breath, in and out, and felt better. Maybe that was what happened, part of the process. The guy could be the biggest fucking arsehole in the world, but once he was dead you could start to feel sorry for him.

Because he's dead and you're not; so what does all that add up to? Only that remorse is yet another luxury, yet another way of feeling fucking superior. Fucking carpets.

Come on, Hallam, get a fucking grip—

Cromer came back with the SOC kit and an Olympus twin-lens compact. 'Vic.'

'What?'

'He drive a red Fiesta from the pool?'

'When he can't get anything else.'

'One parked across the road in the cul-de-sac.'

'Sure it's a pool car?'

Cromer nodded. 'I checked.'

'Locked?'

'Yeah. He doesn't smoke, does he?'

'Why?'

'Ashtray's open, that's all.'

'Anybody about?'

'Bathroom light on next door.'

'Give 'em a knock, tell 'em we're here, ask if they heard anything.'

'Right.'

'Then we'll get the gear on, have a look round.'

Vic pulled on a pair of black plastic overshoes and snapped the elastic round his trousers. By the time he'd got the latex gloves on, Cromer was back, grinning.

'She said did I want a cup of tea. Or anything.'

'What else did she say?'

'What a good bloke Frank Webber was. How awful it all was. How she and her friend went to the funeral.'

'Terrific. She hear anything?'

'Said they were too busy drowning their sorrows. She went out like a light and she thinks her friend probably did too.'

'Put these on,' said Vic.

Cromer photographed the bottles, the stair-rod, the picture and the inside of the downstairs lavatory. Then they went upstairs. Cromer took a couple of wide-angle shots from the door and they moved in.

Bedclothes lay strew across the floor. It looked as if somebody had heaved the whole lot off in one. But once again, no drawers or cupboards ransacked. Tangled in amongst the blue and white coverlet and duvet, a set of shiny dark blue thermals and a pair of green boxer shorts covered in small yellow stars. Vic pulled them free, held them up.

'Somebody's been here.'

Cromer was focusing on a large damp patch in the middle of the bottom sheet. 'You're telling me.'

Vic edged round the bedding to the built-in headboard table. Another IKEA self-assembly special. Rae Webber's handbag stood on the coffee-ringed glass top, and beside it her purse and compact mirror. He breathed on the glass top – fingerprints everywhere.

In the purse, credit cards, a fifty, two tens and a receipt from Henleaze Waitrose. Ten freezer-pack Lean Cuisines, six bottles of Merlot. He picked up the compact by the lid. There was a trace of white powder in the bevel where the mirror met the frame. More underneath, on the glass top. He bent down and put his tongue to it. Cocaine. The bedside phone rang. Vic walked over to the dressing table and windowsill. A black and white portrait of Webber in his peaked cap. A set of ten small prints in the thin layer of dust on the paintwork. The phone stopped on the fourteenth ring. Cromer's camera flashed. Vic picked up the phone by its cord and dialled 1471.

It was a mobile number. Vic checked it against the Channel One card in his pocket.

'Fuck me.'

'What?'

'Maggi Reed.'

He bipped in the number.

Her voice came through a swish of noise like air-conditioning. 'Maggi Reed.'

'This is Vic Hallam. Why did you ring this number?'

'What?' Then, confused, 'What are you doing there?'

'I'm asking you why you rang this number, Miss Reed.'

A pause. 'I see. We're being official, are we?'

'That's right.'

'I've been ringing her on and off since half-past seven.'

'Any reply?'

'I wouldn't be ringing her now, would I?'
'Why were you ringing her?'
'What's happened for God sake?'
'Why were you ringing Mrs Webber?'
'Oh God. To see how she was of course.'
'That all?'
No reply.
'I said, was that all.'
'Look, *Sergeant*, if something's happened to her—'
'When was the last time you called?'
'Can I speak to her, please?'
'Not at the moment.'
'Why? Why can't I speak to her?'
'Just tell me the last time you called.'
'After the press conference.'
'And before that?'
'Before the press conference.'
'When you put her in the taxi last night, what address did she give?'
'What?'
'At The Moonglow. You put her in a taxi.'
'Oh, right. Churchwood. She said Churchwood.'
'Thank you, Miss Reed.'
'For God sake, Vic, what's happened?'
'You've been ringing this number from seven-thirty to now,' Vic checked his watch, 'eight-forty-five. Is that right?'

Exasperated, giving up. 'Yes.'
'How many times, would you say?'
'Oh God, I don't know. Half a dozen.'
'Why didn't you mention it, at the conference?'
'Why should I?'
'It's called obstruction.'

Traffic noise. 'Actually, it's called concealment, you have to prove intent, and I've been trying to ring you about her.'

'Have you?' He remembered the radio call.

'Not only that,' getting her sass back, 'I am perfectly within my rights as a journalist, associate and friend of Rae Webber to ask you where she is and what's happened—'

It was time to cut her off. 'Miss Reed, I have to caution you that this conversation will be reported and in consequence legal action may be taken—'

'Sergeant Hallam.'

'Yes, Miss Reed?'

'Fuck off and die, will you?'

Click. Vic handed the receiver to Cromer. 'Call Forensic, see if they've got anybody free.'

'What about Parnesy?'

'He can wait.'

'Forensic won't come round for a bloody break-in.'

'Make something up. Tell 'em they get their arses in gear, they can get themselves on television.'

'Why?'

'Maggi Reed'll be here,' said Vic. 'But we won't.'

Leaving Cromer to work it out for himself, Vic went through every drawer and cupboard in the bedroom. Finding nothing, he moved across the landing into the bathroom. In the airing cupboard, under a stack of thick Habitat bath-towels, he found four flat packets of fine white powder.

'Vic.' Cromer was standing in the bedroom doorway, his gloved hand over the mouthpiece.

'What?'

'They want to know what the fuck it's all about.'

'Tell 'em it's last night's cocaine.'

'What?'

'Two kilos. Get a couple of shots now.'

Cromer took a wide angle and a close-up. 'What else?'

'Tell 'em we want a DNA on a pair of green underpants and blue silk thermals.'

'Right.' Cromer went back into the bedroom.

Vic took the packets out of the airing cupboard, laid them flat on the bathroom floor and measured them with the SOC tape. They were all intact, exactly the same as those at the Well.

The more he looked at them, the more he began to smell fuck-up.

He found a chromed Boots toenail clipper-nailfile in

the bathroom cabinet and cut a half-inch curved slit in one of the packets. He looked up and saw Cromer watching him.

'They're sending a couple of blokes round.'

'Good.' Vic dabbed his latexed forefinger in the white powder and tasted it.

'Fucking hell, Vic—'

The stuff tasked chalky. He spat it out and wiped his mouth. 'Your turn, John.'

'What?'

'Taste it.' Cromer was backing off, looking reluctant. 'Come on, John, for Christ sake taste the fucking stuff. It won't kill you and I guarantee you won't get addicted.'

'Not the point is it?'

'What is, then?'

'Tampering with the evidence.'

'Jesus Christ, John, if I'm going to say I found what I believed to be two K of cocaine, you've got to corroborate it, you've got to back me up, mate – "all the fucking way" – because otherwise they're going to make mincemeat of the pair of us.'

'Who's they?'

'Them. Parnesy, the CC, Barney's fucking brief in court. Everybody—'

'Everybody?'

'Yes John.'

'You're getting fucking paranoid, you know that?'

'Not getting, John. Am.'

'Why?'

'Just stick your fucking finger in, you'll find out.'

Cromer did so, gagged, tried to spit and went to the washbasin to rinse his mouth out.

'What's that remind you of, John?'

'Polyfilla?'

'Builders' filler of some sort. Now you come with me.' Vic led the way into the bedroom. He showed Cromer the powder on the headboard table. 'Now try that – not the same finger, you dickhead—'

Cromer touched a fraction of the powder to his lips. 'Makes your lips tingle then go numb.'

'If you say so, John. Get a wire coathanger.'

As Cromer rattled around in the wardrobe, Vic perched himself on the edge of Rae's bed. He looked at the wet patch. It was a big patch, the shape of the Isle of Wight. There was a faint lingering smell.

Jesus Christ, what a way to make a living, sniffing people's sheets, and then telling yourself there was plenty for Forensic to get their teeth into.

Filler. It was either a fuck-up or a cover-up or, most likely, seeing what had happened already, a combination of the two. Either way, somebody's arse was definitely heading for the bacon-slicer.

Barney's for one.

17

It took Vic about twenty seconds to open up the Fiesta. He gave the mangled coathanger back to Cromer who immediately started straightening it. By the time Vic had disabled the alarm two women in housecoats had appeared from the front doors on either side of number 23. They stood together, arms folded tightly under their breasts against the cold, making sure Vic and Cromer knew they were being watched.

'Get in, John.'

A dusting of white powder on the lip of the black plastic ashtray, more on the centre console and carpet. They tasted it. Vic asked Cromer what he thought this time.

'Same as the stuff in the bedroom.'

'Not the same as the stuff in the bathroom?'

'No.'

'So we're agreed then?'

'What?'

'We found what we believe to be cocaine in what we believe to be a red police Fiesta last driven by Detective Chief Inspector Barnard.'

'I suppose so.'

'Yes or no, John?'

'Yeah.' But still not happy about being pinned down.

The only other thing in the Fiesta was a tape of Christmas Music recorded by the Choir and Organ of Salisbury Cathedral. Vic slotted the cassette back in its case and slipped it into an evidence bag.

One of the women was waving to them, mouthing something.

'That the woman you spoke to?'

'Mrs Taylor.'

'See what the other one's got to say.'

Coathanger in hand, Cromer walked across to the two women. He was still wearing his latex gloves and black overshoes.

Vic sat in the red Fiesta and tried to imagine how Barney must have felt. Four am. Shagged out but charged up. Cocaine in the ashtray. Rae in the bedroom. Tall, blonde, slim. Naked.

He thought of how she'd walked into The Moonglow and stood inside the door, swaying slightly, peering into the cones of light. Waiting for someone to rush up and look after her. And they had.

She'd managed to keep it together for a while. Loud and slurred and glittery-eyed but still looking good and in control. Some women could do that. Hold themselves together by a defiant act of will. Some kids had it, too: you can hit me but you can't hurt me. A lot of villains were the same. Exhibitionist but on the edge.

So what does that tell you?

It wasn't just a question of guts or nerve, because when she was dishing the dirt on Barney and she and Maggi were snorting and cackling at men and their deluded, filthy little ways, all the time she was watching him, challenging him, waiting to see if he was going to stop her, boss her, shut her up.

Look at me, fuck you, listen to me, fuck you. Help me, fuck you. Help me.

Then she'd passed out. After that she looked rough. He'd liked her more when she looked rough. Then, when she'd touched the back of his hand and smiled at him and gratitude seemed to flow out of her – yeah, he'd had that instant male thing of wondering whether there was a fuck in it.

But not now, not at ten to nine on a frosty morning. She was too twitchy, lost, neurotic without knowing it. It wasn't her fault exactly, considering what she'd been through, but there had to be a vicious self-destructive streak in there somewhere. In Vic's experience most people were most dangerous when most vulnerable. Especially women. Help me. Help me scratch your eyes out, cut your balls off, and then I'll show your wife. What you're really like. But at least Rae did it with a nice line in fuck-you smiles.

And Barney had gone for it.

In Barney's position, Vic could see himself taking the stairs to her bedroom three at a time—

Fucking hell, Hallam, she's your enemy's wife. Widow. Mistress.

It was enough, perversely, to stir the prick. Even more perversely, to arouse his sympathy for the pair of them. Rae, because she didn't know what kind of emotional washing cycle she was going through; Barney, because he was, as she said, well and truly hooked.

Hooked. Staring through a frost-crazed windscreen at a street full of dead suburban semis, Vic tried to remember what it was like. It wasn't how it was with Ellie – well, it was at the moment, because things were fucking desperate – but there was something else going on there, some hope of coming home.

This was the full kamikaze, straight down the runway and no coming back. Banzai. That insane, bright, hopeless focus you got on the one and only, shutting out everything and everybody else, sense and reason not so much gone as bloody-mindedly ignored.

Like watching yourself as a kid burning your hand with a magnifying glass and not being able to stop until you smell the skin and pale gold hairs burning like pork and the pain really *bites*.

You think you know someone, he thought, you think you understand someone, know their weaknesses, their need to put you down at any price – and then they come up with a new one, a gap in the armour so big you can slip your hand in and squeeze their soft black heart until it stops – and what happens? You start to feel sorry for the bastards. First Webber. Now Barnard.

He looked in the ashtray. To spill all that, Barney must have been sniffing and driving at the same time. Fucking mad. Crazy. You poor old bastard. It's not the cocaine that drives you insane, it's love and desperation. He had a sudden flash of himself and Ellie in bed together. Yeah, love and desperation, that was about it. The same thing, really, hope or no hope.

Cromer came back over. He was still carrying the coathanger. 'The other one, Mrs Osbourne, thinks she may have heard something about four-ish.'

'Such as what?'

'She said it sounded like an old van starting up in the allotments.'

'She see anything?'

'No. She said it was too cold to get out of bed.'

'Yeah,' said Vic, 'it nearly always is.'

They found some fresh-looking oil on the frozen ground about ten yards back along the alley that led to the allotments. The ground was too hard to show up tracks so Vic told Cromer to tape it off and leave it for Forensic.

He made his way back to number 23 working out how much he was going to have to tell Parnes. The two women were standing outside Rae's gate, looking at her open front door.

One said, 'Excuse me. Is Rae in there?'

The other one looked down at his overshoes and said, 'She thinks you only wear those for bodies.'

Vic said there was no sign of Mrs Webber and at the moment they were treating it as a break-in.

The two women seemed disappointed.

He was sitting on the kitchen table waiting for Parnes to answer the phone when Cromer came in still working away at the wire coathanger. 'Vic.'

'Hallo.'

'If that stuff in the bathroom is filler, then the stuff at the Well was filler.'

'That's right, John.'

'The CC said Parnesy discovered the whole cache.'

'That's right, John.'

'So what's two K of it doing here?'

'Well, Parnesy didn't bring it, did he?'

'No.'
'Rae?'
'No.'
'And your average gasmeter-buster wouldn't leave two K of cocaine behind, would he?'
'No.'
'How much is two K worth?'
'A hundred grand?'
'And who told Rae Webber they could be that much better off in the morning?'
'Barney.'
'That's right, John.'
'But it's not cocaine, is it?'
'That's right, John.'
'It's filler.'
'That's right, John.'
'But Barney didn't know that.'
'That's right, John.'
'So Forensic must have tested it after he left.'
'That's right, John.'
'Why wait?'
'Murder, woundings, shootings, arson. They all come first.'
'Nevertheless,' said Cromer, 'Barney's in the shit isn't he?'
'That's right, John.'
Cromer twisted away at the wire neck. Vic watching, thinking, Jesus Christ you can see the wheels going round, grinding away. Maybe that was what was good about the kid: once he'd got his teeth in, he'd never give up until he'd shaken the bloody rat to death. If only he was a bit quicker about it.
'If Forensic knew it was filler, the CC and Parnesy knew it was filler.'
'That's right, John.'
'So why tell everybody it's cocaine?'
'What do you think?'
Cromer put a final twist in the neck of the coathanger. 'I'd say there's been a fuck-up and somebody's aiming to cover their arse.'

'That's right, John.'

Cromer squinted at the coathanger, turning it this way and that, decided there was nothing more he could do for it and laid it on the kitchen table.

'Where does that leave us?'

'We're the pigs in the middle, John.'

Cromer thought about it, and picked up the coathanger again. 'I think I'll just stick this back in the wardrobe.'

While Cromer was out, Parnes came on. Vic told him about the Ventaxia, the break-in and the red Fiesta. Parnes sounded pleased about the mess Barney had got himself into and said No shit?

Cromer came back in and sat close enough to the wall-phone to hear what Parnes was saying.

When Vic told him about Maggi's phone-call and the flat packs of fine white powder in the airing cupboard and how the powder tasted like builder's filler, Parnes sounded less pleased and told Vic to hang on.

'Hallam? Perry here.'

Holy shit. Here we go—

'What's going on, Hallam?'

Vic told him.

The CC asked him for an exact description of the packs of white powder. Vic gave him the measurements and said in his opinion the stuff was some kind of filler.

A brief silence. 'We are aware of that, Hallam.' He went on to say the strategy was two-fold: first, to reassure the public, and second, to use the news of Chingola's murder, coupled with the story of the cocaine haul, to extract a few confessions. 'The thing is, Hallam, once they realise they're not only on to a loser but facing ten years accessory to murder, they'll come swarming and buzzing out of the woodwork like flies—' The CC coughed, seemed to be thumping his chest.

Vic waited. 'Then what, sir?'

'*Then*, Hallam, we use that evidence to nail the source. And the cocaine. Which is the way we see it at the moment.'

The way Vic saw it, far from swarming out of the

woodwork, any self-respecting villain would be long-dogging it down to Malaga as fast as his bandy legs could carry him. Even the toerags would vanish into the undergrowth.

Cromer was right. The CC was trying to save his arse. Trying to avoid carrying the can for an operation which had caused massive disruption and had so far resulted in murder, arson and just about every other kind of mayhem for eleven pounds of filler. Well, fair enough, up to a point: it wasn't the CC's operation, it was Barney's. But after Webber, that was no reason to let either of them off the hook—

He said, 'Have you ever seen a brick of cocaine, sir?'

'A brick?'

'Yes sir. They tend to wrap them up in parcel tape, sir.'

'Meaning what?'

'Well, sir, I think the average villain might know the difference between a brick of cocaine and a pack of filler, sir. When he sees it on television.'

This time, the silence was prolonged. Then, sour and threatening: 'Why not mention this before, Hallam?'

'Forensic said it was cocaine, you said it was cocaine. I saw no reason to doubt anyone's word, sir.' Cromer closed his eyes in disbelief and put his head in his hands.

'That's enough, Hallam.'

'Sir.'

'Parnes says you called Forensic.'

'Yes sir.'

'You tell them all this?'

'No sir.'

'What did you say?'

'I said it was to do with last night's cocaine. But that was before I tasted it.'

'Anything else?'

'A DNA on some clothing, sir.'

'What clothing?'

'A set of dark blue thermals and a pair of underpants.'

'Underpants?'

'Green boxer shorts with small yellow stars, sir.'

Another silence.

Then, in a voice that sounded tired and glacially depressed, the CC said, 'Hallam. Tell Forensic not to bother with the clothing. It's Barnard.'

'Is that a positive ident, sir?'

'*Yes.*'

'Thank you sir.'

'Hang on a minute, Hallam.' A clatter of plastic, as if the phone was being stuffed in a drawer, then mutterings. The CC's voice. Parnes' voice. Both indecipherable. Cromer looking at him, What the fuck? Another clatter. 'Hallam.' The snap and crackle was back. 'You're supposed to be the man on the ground. What's your assessment?'

'Back doors and window left open, nothing stolen. Bedclothes ripped off, thrown all over the floor, traces of cocaine on Mrs Webber's compact and bedside table—'

'Jesus God.'

'More traces in the car, a cassette and cassette case should provide evidence of prints there. Glass surfaces in the bedroom, table tops, photographs, compact mirror, should show up more—'

'Get on with it.'

'Yes sir. What look like semen stains on the sheets, sir.'

A dismissive sniff. 'And you've searched the house?'

'Yes sir. No sign of DCI Barnard or Mrs Webber but indications they could have been hustled downstairs.'

'What indications?'

'Picture, stair-rod dislodged, bottles knocked over.'

'Abduction?'

'Either that or they've done a runner.'

'Without this so-called cocaine?'

'Exactly sir.'

'Thank you, Webber.'

'Hallam sir.'

'Quite.' The line went dead.

Vic replaced the receiver. 'The CC thinks abduction, John. What about you?'

'I think you fucked it – you're pushing it too far—'

'You're the one that said all the fucking way, John.'
'Yeah, I know—'
'Well, this is what it's like.'

Cromer eased himself off the table and went to the kitchen window. When he turned back he was grinning. 'How come he knew what underpants Barney was wearing, anyway?'

'Fucked if I know.'

Door chimes went ding-dong. It was Forensic.

On the way to the Mariners they passed a blue and white Channel One Polo stuck in traffic in the opposite lane. Her cameraman was driving and Maggi was looking in the sunblind vanity mirror, fiddling with her spiky blonde fringe.

'Maggi Reed,' said Cromer.

'Yeah.' If she didn't get anything out of Forensic, she would out of the neighbours.

As they pulled into Brunel Lock Road, they got an all units missing persons call. Descriptions were given of a tall slim woman in her late twenties with short blonde hair, and of a grey-haired man in his fifties, five-ten, stocky build, believed to be wearing a dark blue suit. Neither was named.

'They're getting their fingers out,' said Cromer.

'Not far enough,' said Vic. 'Or fast enough.'

He got out of the Escort on the Cumberland Basin side of the road and turned to survey the prussian-blue frontage of the Mariners. Because it was roofed by the Flyover and trapped inside a dozen concrete boles, it got no sun and the fluorescent lighting strips lit the place up like a cage.

'You wait here. When I wave, call me on the mobile.'

Cromer put the radio on stand-by. The missing persons call was repeated. This time it said wanted in connection with last night's operations in St Pauls. Vic's head appeared behind the 'U' of A-M-U-S-E-M-E-N-T-S.

'Vic.'

'Right. He was here with Chingola last night. Chingola was on his mobile.'

'I'll get the Well on to suppliers and billing.'

'Before you do that, go to the Nova Scotia and call me again.'

The Nova Scotia was a couple of hundred yards away on the other side of the Swing Bridge. It was an old dockside pub with seating outside. Half the slatted pine tables were still covered in frost. The others, where the low morning sun had reached them, gleamed and dripped.

Cromer took his mobile and went to look at the stretch of broad wind-flattened water that ran right into the heart of the city. Half a dozen bright red Mirror dinghies from the Docks Sailing School were tacking and reaching in a fluky northerly. When he tried Vic's number all he got was OUT OF RANGE.

Vic was waiting outside the Mariners. 'It's line of sight, John, and not much of that. You practically have to be in the carpark to get through. All this concrete kills the signal. Traffic doesn't help either.'

'How d'you work that out?'

'I didn't. Hazel told me.'

'Hazel?'

'Lady who runs the place. Says the drivers moan about it all the time. She does a mean egg and bacon buttie though.'

Cromer looked aggrieved. 'Where's mine then?'

Vic pulled a greasily translucent paper bag out of his jacket pocket and watched Cromer wolf down a thick steaming doorstep. 'You call the Well?'

'Not yet.' Cromer wiped bacon grease off his chin.

'When you do, tell them we want a carpark search as well.'

'What I can't understand,' said Cromer, 'is why you can never get a decent egg and bacon buttie at home.'

'Wait till you get divorced, my son.'

En route to the basement flat which was Chingola's last-known address, Vic skimmed through the file the CC had given him. 'Antony Christopher Bell, born Chingola, Zambia, March 17th, 1972. Father mining engineer, mother teacher. Studied organ and piano Royal College of Music, '89 to '93. Moved to Bristol '94.

Married, two children two and four. Profession, musician. Two possessions cannabis, fined. One possession heroin with intent to supply, conditional discharge.'

'Joking,' said Cromer.

'When Barney got hold of him.'

'Oh, right.'

Flat 5A Beaufort Road, Clifton, wasn't the sort of dark and dripping rathole Vic expected. It was a big, bright, airy place with its own door on to a back garden whose well-kept lawn sloped gently down to a herringbone brick patio. Marika Bell wasn't what he was expecting either. She was small and slightly built with tied-back oat-pale hair and a face more like that of a worn fourteen-year-old than a woman in her mid-twenties. She wore jeans and a long roll-neck seaman's sweater. She had no make-up and her eyes were red.

Vic held out his warrant card. 'We're police officers, Mrs Bell. I'm Detective Sergeant Hallam, this is Detective Constable Cromer, Bristol Central CID. May we have a word?'

'Of course. You wish to come in?' As with many Scandinavians, her English was formal, her accent vaguely mid-Atlantic.

The living room was warmed by a big-bellied Jotul stove, children's bricks, toys and books were scattered across a dark-green needlecord carpet. There was a Christmas tree, undecorated as yet, with a few presents underneath. Behind it was a bookcase filled with seven-inch tape-reels and hundreds of cassettes.

'The children are with their friends.' She turned to face them. 'More police officers. What do they want this time, I wonder?'

'We're sorry to hear about your husband, Mrs Bell.'

'You knew him, perhaps?'

'I've heard him play, that's all.'

She nodded a tight, twisted little smile, more to herself than to them, waved negligently to a couple of chairs and sat on the edge of a settee, leaning forward, her hands clasped between her knees. She looked straight at Vic. 'You know he was sick?'

'Was your husband ever a registered addict, Mrs Bell?'

'No. He said all that was too much hassle, for him. He was just sick. Too sick for me to cope with him as well as two small children.' She glanced over her shoulder at the bright, airy room. 'He sold everything, you know? Everything that was here, he sold, except for those tapes.' She rubbed her small hands together and held them out towards the stove. There was a pale space where her wedding ring had been. Vic wondered whether Chingola had sold that too, or whether she had taken it off. 'But we have a year's lease on this place, so - we survive.' She shrugged, and looked into the ashes of the fire behind the glass. 'It was hard to dislike him, you know.' Vic watched her small, set expression as she considered what to say next. 'Not impossible, just hard. He was just too weak. Too weak for this world. He left us November, the end of November.'

'You have any idea why, Mrs Bell?'

She reached up and repositioned the painted wooden comb in her hair. 'You must understand, Sergeant, that I could not have him shooting up in front of the children.'

'Did he tell you where he was living?'

'People's floors. Half the time he was not knowing where he was.' It was the first time her English had slipped. 'I told him he was killing himself. Now he has, that's all.'

She took a tissue from her sleeve and roughly dabbed at her nose. She tilted her head back to show them there were no tears.

'Mrs Bell,' said Vic carefully. 'Were you told how your husband died?'

'Yes. He was shot. They think it was murder, I am to identify him later.' She sat back and folded her arms. 'You can be murdered and still kill yourself, Sergeant.'

Vic nodded. 'Did he ever mention a man called Barnard?'

'Barnard? No.'

'Did he ever talk about a police officer, inspector, chief

inspector, in connection with his heroin charge?'

'No. All he said was, between them, the police and CPS had messed up.'

'"Messed up"?'

'It happens, as I am sure you both know.'

'Any other names, contacts, people he spoke to on the phone, came to the house?'

'My husband may have been a junkie, Sergeant, but he was not so stupid as all that.'

'I'm sorry to have bothered you, Mrs Bell,' Vic stood up. 'Thank you for talking to us.'

'No problem.'

As if it had just crossed his mind, Vic said, 'Those tapes. Are they all your husband's?'

'Yes.' The tight little downturned smile returned. 'He thought he could write songs. But they are all, as you might say, junk.'

At the door, she wished them Merry Christmas.

In the car, Cromer said, 'She was a hard case.'

Vic said, 'Some people have to be.'

It was the last thing he said until they reached St Pauls.

18

Sirens nervously crisscrossed each other and white cars and sixteen-man vans slewed up over pavements and blocked off alleys. Headlamps stayed on and blue and orange beacons blitzed off walls and windows into rooms and faces. Van doors opened, men jumped down, ran and shouted without reason. St Pauls was being swamped by saturation policing. It was heavy, deliberate, intimidatory, and in part, it worked. Within minutes the streets were cleared. Then, minutes later, people – kids, shoppers, rubberneckers – came drifting out again.

As Cromer and Vic drove in, uniformed helmets and flatcaps were overlapping in pairs from house to house. Traffic intersections were being shut down and manned by motorcycle cops. Burned-out wrecks were being levered up on to hired flatbeds. Tapes fluttered. Crowd barriers were clanged and tied across every main junction from Picton Street to Trinity Road. Plainclothes with clipboards were stopping every other vehicle, questioning every young black adult they could lay hands on.

Knots of kids watched and shoved and shouted in the side streets behind the barriers, all of them bunked off school for the day. Older people, black and white, laden with Christmas shopping, waddled past each other, eyeing each other and then, in passing, stared down at the pavement or swapped bags around to leave them one hand free. Talking and gesticulating to the stationed policemen and women, explaining who they were, where they lived, and only then being allowed to duck under the tapes or through the galvanised barriers.

Cromer felt like a probationer walking into a rough pub for the first time, not knowing whether his uniform would stop a fight or start one. There was a pretence of order, no more, and an equal pretence of submission, neither side seeing the other except in terms of threat. It was tense and unreal, even from inside the car, and Cromer could see everyone was feeling it: the kids rollerblading outside the old school waiting to get their amps and turntables back; the riot cops watching motionless from the school steps; the people threading between them, heads down, determined to ignore what was clearly on the cards. The only thing they had in common was that all of them, even the kids, looked grey, drained, worn out.

He drove slowly from block to block heading for Trinity Road. Every barrier passed was another layer of safety stripped away. From the old school on, there were no neutrals: you were exposed, the gap was clear, and before long there would almost certainly be bricks and bottles to prove it. A dull and constant friction existed, not just between the baseball-capped kids and the vizored cops, but the people shopping too; each lot waiting patiently, like cattle under rain, for the spark, the stampede.

Vic said, 'The job's fucked, John.'

What Vic said, and the matter of fact way he said it, had the effect of clearing Cromer's mind. It certainly was at this level: this wasn't community policing, it was community control. It was a big ugly bully of a concept and it shoved itself right in Cromer's face: if you lived on the bottom, as these people did, black or white, young or old, then sooner or later, through no fault of your own, you were bound to hit the bump stops and come slam-bang up against the police state and, intentional or not, provoked or not, the chaos that followed was still chaos.

And all anybody outside all this would say was, Yeah, well, you know, tough shit.

A burning car tyre bounced out of one of the alleys

alongside the Lion of Judah, orange petrol flames whorling round inside the rim.

Vic said, 'Fuck sake don't stop now.'

Cromer accelerated and felt the tyre thud off the Escort's rear wing. 'You see anybody?'

'No,' said Vic. 'You?'

'No. Fucking hell, Vic.'

'Yeah, that's about it.'

'They looking for Barney or dealers or what?'

'Name of the game, John.'

'What is?'

'We shouldn't be here. It's a mistake. Our blokes know it's a mistake. The kids know it's a mistake. The old people know it's a mistake. Everybody knows it's a mistake and we all go on doing it. It could all have been avoided. None of this need ever have happened, but they had to go and shoot him, didn't they?'

'Who, Chingola?'

'No,' said Vic. 'Martin Luther King.'

Cromer glanced across at Vic to see if he was taking the piss. It didn't look like it but you never knew with Vic. 'Jesus Christ, Vic,' he said cautiously, 'I didn't know you were like that.'

'We're all fucking liberals until we start work, my son. Then what happens?' Vic's eyes were flicking from side to side across the road and pavements, up into his mirrors and back to the road again. 'What happens then is, you find out the boss man's idea of fun is shitting on you from a great height and when you answer back, you're a fucking troublemaker, you get all the shitty jobs and when he gets tired of fucking you about it's the order of the boot.' Vic pulled out a crumpled pack of Marlboro and counted how many he'd got left: three, and nowhere to stop and buy another pack. 'All you can do, John, is either wait for the arsehole to die, chewing the sheets when he's eighty years old, or you can dream about sticking one on the bastard. Well, dream on, my son, because that's all you can fucking do. People's lives are full of dreams of revenge. That's why we're here.' He lit one of the bent fags. 'Not very fucking liberal though, is it?'

Cromer drove on. Everything he'd ever learned told him Vic was wrong, but what he was seeing now made him wonder.

Vic wound the window down half an inch to let the smoke out. 'I was watching a video last night. Half pissed, couldn't sleep, nearest fuck's a hundred miles up the M5, turn on the vid and watch the history of rock and roll. In the middle of it they shoot Martin Luther King. You know what it's like, four in the morning and you're a complete sodden fucking blur with eyes like pissholes and guts like a fucking volcano and then, fuck me, holy shit, suddenly the interior light goes on and everything becomes miraculously fucking clear—'

A bottle arced across the road and burst on the opposite wall.

'Where was I?'

Cromer said, 'Everything becomes fucking clear.'

'Yeah. Watching this video. Anyway, first we had Fats, and Little Richard, and James Brown, and the Supremes, and Otis, and Wilson Pickett, and the Four Tops and "Reach Out", and "River Deep"—'

'Yeah.' Cromer nodding then looking puzzled. 'So?'

'And after,' said Vic, 'we had rap.'

'After what?' said Cromer.

'Martin Luther King,' said Vic. 'They shot him, they shot it all away.' He put his finger and thumb round the place where the bent cigarette had broken. 'And there's me thinking, Yeah it could've worked, yeah, it *was* working, yeah, fuck me, Vic, that's why they shot him. They don't like things starting from the bottom. What we're for, mate. The jam in the fucking sandwich.'

'Bloody hell, Vic.'

'What?'

'You must've been arseholed.'

'Stressed, John, stressed,' said Vic. 'Fucking video was still going when I woke up. Got as far as punk and glam rock.'

There was another galvanised barrier, unmanned, knocked flat and run over so it was bent in the middle. There was no one about but the shop on the corner was newly boarded up and a thick shoal of broken glass spread across the pavement and into the roadway. Cromer decided to take the next street down.

'Now it's the same here,' said Vic.

'How?'

'Fucking looking at it. We asked these people over here. We went to Brum once when I was a nipper, see Rovers play City in the Cup. I thought all the bus drivers up there had been issued with brown suede gloves.'

'Joking.'

'True. They still had hand signals then. You'd look up, their faces were brown as well.' Vic pushed the broken cigarette through the window, shut it and pushed down the door latch. 'You invite somebody into your house and then you kick them in the teeth and up the arse and tell them to fuck off back to Monkeyland, what are they going to think? Fuck it, that's what they're going to think. Then some great bloke comes along, tells them he's got a dream, and we shoot the fucker.'

Cromer saw his chance. 'Or put him on the cross.'

'Fuck off, John.'

'Merry Christmas to you and all—'

'Jesus Christ! *Look out*!'

A half-gallon plastic jug came rolling out of an alley of lock-up garages. It had a butane lighter-gas tube stuck in its neck with a wick and fizzing thunderflash taped to it. The jug vanished between the Escort's front wheels. They felt it thud against the sump, drag and lodge against the exhaust.

'Put your fucking foot down, John, the cunts are trying to kill us!'

'Fuck it, I'm having the bastards!'

Cromer handbraked the Escort through ninety degrees. A double bang and a blast of heat shot up through the car floor. For a second, their faces shining like oranges, they were wrapped inside a rolling ball of flame and smoke. Then – *slam, slam* – they were up the kerb and into the alley. Smoke, thick and oily, was pouring out of the footwell heater vents. Flames were leaping and ballooning after them. Vic wrenched the extinguisher off its brackets. The interior filled with its white, gassy smoke.

'Fucking hell—'

'Bastards!'

Two black youths were haring along the alley to the wall at the end. Cromer broadsided the smoke-filled Escort against the wall and slammed his door open into a pair of trainered jeans. One black youth fell on top of him across the door. The other put his foot on his friend's back, leaped for the top of the wall and scissor-kicked over it.

Clutching his throbbing shoulder, Vic piled out of the Escort. Cromer and the black youth were rolling around in a flailing tangle of arms and legs among the weeds and cobbles between the car and the wall. The black youth seemed to be laughing his head off. Then Cromer hauled him up and slammed him against the car. The black youth screamed it was fucking hot, man, and one hand went for his bomber jacket pocket. Cromer swung him round and hit him in the face with a forearm smash. The youth buckled and put his arms over his head. Vic thought it was clumsy but at least Cromer had got his weight behind it. It was a million miles from all that rabbit in the car, but what the fuck.

Cromer was kneeling on the kid's back handcuffing him. Blood and snot was coming out of the kid's nose and he was yelling into the cobblestones it wasn't fucking me, man. In one of his cuffed hands there was a piece of plastic like a credit card. Cromer drew it out of his fingers. It had a passport photo heatsealed on to it, and a name and signature: Benjamin Ray Foley. It was an ID card issued by the Avon and Somerset Police Campaign Against Underage Drinking and certified that the Holder was over eighteen.

'I know you don't I, Benjamin?' said Cromer.

'Wasn't me, man, I was trying to catch him.'

Cromer pulled a wad of tissue from the door panel pocket and wiped the kid's face clean. 'No, Benjamin. What I mean is, I know you from last night.'

The youth looked at Cromer. 'Oh shit.'

One of the lock-ups was open. While Cromer was cautioning Benjamin, Vic had a look round the garage. He found two five-gallon jerricans, a box of polystyrene granules, a brown paper bag of Chinese thunderflashes, two half-gallon jugs fitted with butane containers and wicks and a cellophane Lil-lets pack.

Inspector Caroline Coombes was standing by the desk when Vic and Cromer walked in with Benjamin. 'We're full,' she said. 'No room at the inn.' She turned her back and walked away. Vic nodded Cromer and Benjamin over to the desk, and followed her into the corridor leading to her office.

'Caroline.'

'What?' She'd been up all night booking and interviewing. Her hair was lank, her eyes creased and blinking from too much VDU-gazing, and the back of her uniform skirt was bagged and shiny. It made Vic want to take her tired naked body in his arms and rock her to sleep.

Whether it got through to her or not, all he got back was an irritated glance. 'I should warn you I've been on my feet for the last twenty-four hours, I'm feeling extremely ratty and I've forgotten what bed looks like.'

'It's oblong,' said Vic, 'and it goes up and down if you're lucky.'

A flat icy stare. 'You CID blokes make me sick, you know that?' Turning her back on him. 'Not content with last night's bollocks, you're back with another brigade this morning.'

'Not our idea.'

Roused now, and with a focus for her anger, she swung back on Vic. 'Not a word to me, Vic, not a fucking word. Last night was a shambles, this is ten times worse. It's put the job back ten years. Maelee Thomas has been shot – all sorts of people are going to end up getting killed. *They* don't care. They don't have to live here, work here. They're bastards, deliberate ham-fisted bastards. Not just Barney, it's Parnes, the CC, the commanders, the whole pack: middle-aged middle-class white fucking males – none of them give a shit about these people.'

She walked over to a window and looked at the plants on the sill. She felt the soil and turned back to Vic, resolution back in place. 'They're not getting away with it. They think they are, they can bloody well think again. I've had it. I've had enough. Enough of being bloody well doormatted thank you very much. This is going to full inquiry and they're going to find themselves facing charges of harassment, sexual discrimination, interference in community relations policy – anything I can drag up.' Anger burned out and exhaustion returned. She leaned against him a moment, then rapidly withdrew. 'Oh shit, what's the use?'

Vic said, 'Barney's gone missing.'

'Good.' Then looking at him.

Vic told her. Barney, Rae, cocaine, Parnes and the CC.

Caroline considered the situation. 'So they're all in the shit together – that's what this is about.'

'Yeah,' said Vic. 'And Cromer and I get stuck with it. We come down here, and suddenly there's OSGs all over the place. Nobody told us either.'

'Panic,' said Caroline shortly. 'Panic time.'

'Yeah,' said Vic. 'So don't do anything rash.'

Nodding. 'You could be right.'

'Always a first time.'

Cromer appeared with Benjamin at the end of the corridor. Caroline drew herself up. 'What d'you want, exactly?'

'A room with a dual-track and a Sony portable,' said Vic. 'Twenty minutes.'

'What have you been doing now, Benjamin?'

'I ain't been doing nothing, Miss Coombes.'

'Attempted murder,' read out Cromer, 'riot, resisting arrest, possession of bomb-making equipment, destruction of police property, arson with intent to endanger life. Twice.'

Caroline sighed. 'Use my office.'

Cromer and a uniformed PC brought in a table and dual-track recorder. Cromer already had the Sony portable in his shirt pocket. Vic plugged the dual-track in, wound both tapes past the clear plastic leaders.

'This interview 0935, conducted by DS Hallam, Bristol Central CID. Also present, DC Cromer, Bristol Central CID. That all right, Benjamin? That OK so far?'

'Yeah.'

'And you have been informed of your rights under the Police and Criminal Evidence Act?'

'Yeah.'

'And you have expressed no wish for any legal representative to be present at this juncture. Is that correct?'

'Correct.'

Vic leaned back, checked Cromer's position – standing, almost at right angles to Benjamin, so the kid would have to move his head to see what Cromer was up to – and said, 'Tell us about it, Benjamin.'

'You got a cigarette, then?'

Vic chucked the crumpled packet of Marlboro across.

Benjamin opened it, looked at the two bent cigarettes. 'These all you got?'

'I can get some more, Benjamin. There's a machine in the canteen.' He leaned across with his lighter. 'But you can't.'

'What d'you mean?'

'You're not going anywhere, son. So you better make those two last.'

Benjamin drew on the cigarette, looked at it, looked at Vic. 'Thanks, man.' He jerked his head at Cromer. 'I already told him. I saw this other kid throwing something, and I went to catch him, that's all.'

'Right,' said Vic. 'You went to catch him?'

'That's right. Yeah.'

'Now tell us about last night. You went to catch them as well, did you?'

'Don't know what you're talking about. Don't know anything about last night.' He tried to pull the anodised red tin ashtray towards him. It was screwed to the centre of the plywood table.

'Where were you last night, Benjamin?'

'Home. Watching telly.'

'All night?'

'Yeah.'

'Who with?'

'Mates. I had some mates round.'

'What was on?'

'Crap.' The kid smiled at Vic, then at Cromer. He had a nice smile. They smiled back at him.

Vic said, 'What sort of crap?'

Benjamin went on smiling. 'Shit horror movies. White crap.'

'Right. How long did you and your mates watch this white crap?'

'Well, all night, really. Two, three.'

'Half-past two?'

'Yeah, about then.'

'You hear anything, see anything, while you and your mates were watching the telly?'

'No, we're watching it, aren't we?'

'What, even though it's white crap?'

'Yeah. You get used to it, you know?' He looked from one to the other, grinning, challenging them.

'Right,' Vic leaned back. 'Last night you were watching television with witnesses until at least half-past two in the morning and as far as you know none of you saw or heard anything unusual going on outside?'

'No.'

'Where d'you live, Benjamin?'

'Whittier Street.'

'One street away from where you were arrested.'

'Yeah.'

'Two streets away from the old school, from Westminster Road Community Centre.'

'Yeah.'

'A hundred, hundred and fifty yards away?'

'Yeah. About that.'

'And you still didn't hear or see anything?'

'No.'

'Right. Thanks very much. This interview terminated at 0941, DS Hallam, Bristol Central CID.'

Vic switched off, flipped out the two tapes and passed

one to Benjamin. 'there you are, Benjamin. You show that to your mates, they'll know you haven't grassed them up, won't they?'

'What, I can go now?' He pocketed the tape, and scraped his chair back to stand up. Cromer moved a step closer. Benjamin froze, then sullenly sat down again.

'You're not going anywhere, Benjamin,' said Vic. 'I told you that at the start. The only place you'll be going for the next fifteen years, my son, is up and down staircases and through steel doors. Clang-bash, clang-bash, you're in the cell. The first lock turns, the second lock turns, the third lock turns. Boots clattering away, keys jingling, and the bastard's whistling, Benjamin. He couldn't give a fuck about you, Benjamin. Nobody could. Then it goes quiet. And apart from the odd scream, moan or thump, that's it. Now and then a little shutter slides back, some screw eyes you up, you can't even gob back at them. That's what you're looking at. That, no snout, and arse bandits. There's old guys in there, creeping round in manky old Dunlopillo slippers, Benjamin, look as if they've had the horrors all their lives. And they have.'

Vic reached for the crumpled pack and lit the last cigarette. 'On the other hand, you cooperate and you could be out in as little as eighteen months.' He drew deeply on the cigarette and held it out, tip first, to Benjamin. 'Fancy a drag?'

Cromer turned away, put his hand inside his jacket pocket, and pressed the red record button on the Sony portable. Then he took another step closer to Benjamin.

Benjamin said him and his mates had been approached by this tall thin curly haired blond kiddy, mate of Chingy Bell. Chingy was looking out for him, greasing the wheels, and this blond kiddy, never said his name but he had this Toyota Landcruiser, big metallic-brown four-litre, he said how did they fancy a big drink for not much, and they said how big, and he said five but if they fucked up they'd be fucked in spades, if they saw what he meant. Because he had some very serious spars, man, and he was carrying himself, one of them short-barrel Smith & Wessons, so Benjamin looks at Dash and Dash looks at Griffin and they go yeah, don't they? The blond kiddy had all the gear, all ready, all they had to do was chuck it, so at the dance Chingy comes up and says it's The Moonglow because he's pissed off with the guys there and anyway it's dead right for what they want, so the blond kiddy goes, Cool, be there at twenty to one, dead on, because by one the raid was coming in and The Moonglow would screw that, give them chance to fuck off out of it. So that's what they did, God's honour, Mister Hallam.

'Five?'

'Yeah, that's right.'

'Hundred?'

'Yeah.'

'Between you or each?'

'Come on, man. Between us.'

'Up front?'

'Yeah.'

'All of it?'

'Yeah.'

'In cash?'

'Not taking cheques, are we?'

'What cash? Twenties, fifties?'

'Fifties. He had this wad as thick as your fist—'

'Why didn't you and your mates roll him, Benjamin?'

'He was carrying, wasn't he, and he was connected.'

'How d'you know that?'

'He was talking to the hard cases off the estates and the big bad-ass geezers from round here and they was all giving him R-E-S-P-E-C-T, you know?'

'Then what?'

'Then your mucker here gets me round the neck, and Dash, he's going shitless we're all tabbed, and then, today, just, he sees you coming through in the Escort, and he goes, Fuck it, burn the fuckers, and I'm going, No Dash don't be a cunt, but he does anyway, and that's it, Mister Hallam, God's honest truth I drop dead on this spot.'

They waited, but nothing happened.

Cromer went to the door, found a PC he'd worked

with when he'd been at Trinity Road and got Benjamin squeezed on the next van going to the Well. When he came back he was buzzing the Sony tape back to the start. He replayed Benjamin's first few words to check for clarity, pressed REW/REVIEW, flipped the tape out, and laid the Sony portable on Caroline's blotter.

'Fucking great, Vic.'

'What?'

Cromer, grinning all over his face, flushed to the neck with pleasure. 'We got a result on The Moonglow. Fuckers tried to stop us, take us off it and we fucked 'em. We got it.' He spun the cassette in the air, caught it and slipped it inside his jacket. 'Plus all this stuff at the school besides.'

'Yeah, well done, John.'

'It was that prison shit of yours tipped him—'

'John, when it's over, I'll see you get the credit. Your show, you'll make sergeant on it. That's a promise. Deal?'

'Well, yeah, thanks Vic—'

'Now just shut up about it, will you?'

'Why?' The wind suddenly taken out of his sails. 'What's the matter?'

'I've run out of fags for one thing. For another, how d'you divide five hundred by three?'

'What?'

'You've got three blokes, you either offer them four-fifty or six. That's how these guys are, you deal in fifties, you deal in fifties, you don't carry a bag of fucking change about do you? And if he's pissing us about on that, what else is he pissing us about on?'

'Oh. Right.'

Vic switched Caroline's PC on. 'Now then, statements. How many prelims we got listed?'

Cromer sat down, dit-datted about on the keyboard, entered TOTAL ALL. 'Hundred and fifty-seven.'

'Fucking hell,' said Vic. 'I'm going to get some fags.' He stood up.

'We could keyword it,' said Cromer. 'That'd cut it down.'

'Yeah, if we knew what we were looking for.'
Both fell silent.

'What we want, John,' Vic screwed up his gaze, trying to visualise what he needed to see, 'is to be in that band-room from the time this blond kiddy gets there to the time Barney leaves.'

'The dealers. Guy on the door. Parnes. This caretaker bloke.'

'Still doesn't give us a link between Barney and this blond kiddy.'

'The only link is Chingola. And he's dead.'

'Yeah.' Vic stared at the green screen. 'What's a tall thin blond kiddy doing on his own, in St Pauls, setting up a major drugs deal with a terminal junkie for a minder? Ninety-nine per cent of these guys don't even trust their own fucking mothers.'

'Got to start somewhere,' said Cromer. 'Give me a word.'

'Barnard,' said Vic. 'Any officer-statements in there?'

Cromer tapped about and ran TOTAL ALL: SUB. 'Zero.'

'No,' said Vic. 'There fucking wouldn't be, would there? All waiting to see what everybody else says.'

'Like us,' said Cromer.

'Fuck it,' said Vic. 'I'm going to get some fags. Want anything?'

'Coffee and a Twix or a Mars Bar.'

'Try Barnard, Cocaine, Band-room, Chingola, Tall Thin Curly Haired Blond Kiddy and Toyota.'

'Only trawls single words.'

'Try blond then.'

Vic found Caroline in the canteen. She was sitting at one of the yellow and grey formica-topped tables handing over to the day-shift inspector. He was a solid, broad-backed uniformed black guy in his mid-forties. Their heads were close together over a pile of reports and they obviously got on well. Vic had a twinge of wondering how well, and then told himself, None of your business.

'Vic, this is Trevor Hughes. From now on you're sitting in his office, not mine.'

'We can push off whenever you like, Inspector.'

'No problem. I'm off to see what's happening on the ground.'

'It's not the greatest piece of policing in the world.'

A pause while Inspector Hughes took Vic's measure. 'So I'm told.' He shuffled the reports quickly together and stood up. 'Caroline thinks you might support any internals we might institute.'

'Be a pleasure, sir.'

Inspector Hughes stuck out a hand. 'Thanks, Sergeant.'

They watched him leave. 'Cautious sort of bloke.'

'Has to be,' said Caroline. 'Down from Swindon, been here about a month.'

They went on looking at each other, talking about the job, Inspector Hughes, his family, the trouble they were having finding a house. She'd washed her face and brushed her hair, and from the peppermint smell of her breath she'd cleaned her teeth. Her eyes were still tired, but her mouth looked young and fresh again. He offered her a Marlboro from his new pack. She half-reached for it and then stopped. Her eyes started doing that face-searching thing.

He said, 'You ought to go to bed.'

She stared at him evenly, then shook her head as if to get rid of something bothering her and put her face in her hands. 'Oh God.'

'What?' He touched the back of one of her hands with his.

She lifted her head, and sat up, straight-backed. 'Yes. That's what I ought to do. Go to bed.'

'You're done in, girl.' Again he saw himself with her naked body in his arms.

Their eyes held. First, she looked wounded; then she seemed to be hating herself and him equally; finally she gave up, exhausted.

'Vic.'

'What?'

'Come and see me, will you?'

'If I can.'

She got up, shook her head, and left, walking quickly.

Vic put the lid back on his spongy styrofoam mug, slipped Cromer's chocolate bars into his pocket and lit a cigarette. In one part of him a fanfare was blaring, and in another a voice was saying, You bastard.

Come and see me, will you?

The demand twisting into the question. What did they call it in court? Beseeching. Yeah. The order that was only a request, the promise that wasn't exactly a promise. The battle that wasn't, the surrender that could be ignored, cancelled, or even reversed. The invitation to play cunty, wrapped in all kinds of tissue-paper possibilities of refusal. The only game you were bound to lose, whatever you did.

Telling himself wait, leave it to events, let the job make it impossible. In any case, it was only that randiness brought on by fatigue: that itch, that tired loss of control, that orphan feeling of being all alone in the world so fuck me please, anyone, please. It was how he'd felt the night before, if the truth be known. Telling himself that as soon as she hit the sack she'd be fast asleep all day and the last thing she'd want to see was Vic Hallam with a hard-on. Even if he were such a rotten bastard as to turn up. Yeah, rotten to her and rotten to himself. Not to mention Ellie: every time he got near Caroline, his prick started Tippexing Ellie out. Telling himself all this and knowing in his balls he was going to see the woman even though he was hoping in his heart he wouldn't.

He picked up the two styrofoam mugs, pushed through the double canteen doors, squashed one, squirted hot coffee up his arm and told himself, Serve you right you bastard.

When he got back to Cromer, he was starting to feel safe and sane again. He told himself he was going to get so stuck into the work there could be no possible excuse, no possible time left free—

Cromer said, 'What the fuck are you grinning about?'

19

Cromer really liked zipping the smoke-blackened Escort through St Pauls. It said street-fighting, battle-scars; the adrenalin from the bust on Benjamin and cracking The Moonglow was making him feel like some gung-ho Israeli tank-driver. One minute you were being firebombed to fuck, the next you'd smashed the bastards and the Holy City was back where it belonged: in your grip.

You were young, you were tough, you were unstoppable. Yeah – Cromer began to think that, actually, he would have made a bloody good tankie—

Vic said, 'Park in Picton Street.'

'Picton Street? Fucking miles away—'

'Park in fucking Picton Street.'

Vic got out and walked into a Jamaican grocers carrying the brown paper bag he'd found in the lock-up garage.

Cromer waited. Now they weren't on the move, the adrenalin rush evaporated and left him beached. The Escort clock read 12.09. They had spent two hours on Trinity Road terminal, not getting anywhere much, except filling in details, because cocaine was only mentioned in a negative sense – 'I was fitted up, never saw none, not me Officer' – and neither Chingola nor the blond kid featured at all. All the same he'd gone on trawling through while Vic talked to Surveillance. They had no record of a brown Toyota Landcruiser – during the whole ten days' operation the only big four-wheel drive vehicle they'd got on tape was a Series 3 Land-Rover registered to some construction hire firm in

Willesden, north-west London. Vic took the number and said they should put a call out. Surveillance said they already had thirty calls out on Wrecked or Stolen but they'd get the information down the line. When Vic asked who to, Surveillance said they had instructions to channel everything through Command and Control at the Well. They said the point was to avoid duplication of effort. Vic said Is that a fact, and put the phone down.

'Fucking Parnesy. And the CC.'

'What?'

'Keeping it all up their chuff so they don't get fucking lumbered. We're wasting our time, John. We're looking for a straight line and they're knitting a fucking rats' nest. We should never have come down here.'

'We cracked The Moonglow.'

'Fuck The Moonglow.'

Cromer's opinion was Vic had changed since he'd come back from the canteen with that big grin on his face. He'd got progressively rattier, gone back to the way he was the night before, fucking paranoid, arguing with himself and lashing out at everybody else. Maybe it was his arm, but Cromer's bet was it was something else bugging Vic, something he wasn't going to tell Cromer about until he had to.

When he got like this it was a real pain in the arse working with him. Like waiting for a boil to burst. Oh well, fuck it, Cromer told himself, I've still got The Moonglow. *You'll make Sergeant on this.* He kept his head down and went on trawling through the statements while Vic swore at the phone, the job, and life in fucking general.

The only thing cheered Vic up was when Cromer dug out Billy Jewel.

'Fuck me, Vic.'

'What?'

'Billy Jewel's been lifted.'

'Where?'

'The school.'

'Stupid bastard. I told the silly cunt to stay away. What's he say?'

Cromer read it out. '"Earlier in the evening I had been having a drink with my friend Detective Sergeant Vic Hallam whom I have known for twenty years."'

'Fucking typical. Billy's in the shit, all his mates get invited. What else?'

Cromer scrolled down through the statement. Vic scraped his chair towards the screen, but from his angle the sun was blinding off it. 'I can't see the fucking thing, John.'

Cromer said, 'He says he was only there for the music.'

'Bollocks. Supposed to be cleaned out, he's flashing five or six hundred sheets.' Vic thought for a moment. 'He say he was in the band-room?'

'No.'

'No he wouldn't, would he?' Making an exasperated, hissing noise, breathing out through his teeth. 'Stupid bastard, thinks he's hard, he's soft as shit. Mention anybody else?'

'Only you, so far.'

'Good old Billy. Go on.'

'Then it's the raid, blah blah blah, and he's "manhandled into a van".'

'Read that bit. I still can't see.'

Cromer swivelled the screen round. '"It was full of sick and retching people some of whom were still being hit and sworn at in a racist fashion."'

'Billy the fucking liberal. All we need.'

'"When I arrived at Trinity Road Station and my sight was restored I found my clothing was ruined beyond repair, my wallet containing four hundred and seventy pounds was missing and that what is called a 'baggie' had been planted on my person."' Cromer scrolled on to the end. 'Then he mentions you again.'

Vic leaned forward, pulled the monitor round. '"My opposition to all forms of drugs is well known as I hope DS Hallam will confirm." What an arsehole. Time I sorted the fucker out.' Pushing his chair back. 'Cunt's never had a wallet in his life. Likes to feel it raw. Let's go.'

'Why?' Cromer was happy enough sitting at the desk, playing the computer. 'What good will it do?'

'He's a mate, John.'

'Fucking hell.'

Vic looked at him. 'Something wrong with that?'

Cromer pressed RESET and said nothing.

'Billy hates being banged up. He can't stand it. Twist his testicles, he'll spill his guts. That sound any better?'

Cromer thought No it fucking doesn't, then said Yeah, it fucking did.

Now in Picton Street, Cromer was still trying to work out what was going through Vic's mind. What had Billy got to do with Picton Street? Or anything else? No matter how Vic slagged Billy off, Cromer was convinced it was still all that same old mate shit.

He watched Vic come out of the Jamaican place, go into the Chinese place a few doors down. Not a word, not even a fucking glance.

12.12. Forced to sit and wait and listen to the fucking radio. There was a tailback on the M4/M5 Almondsbury interchange. A lorry had shed a load of timber. The vans were being ordered to pull out of St Pauls. Thanks to Vic he was going to end up on his own. Thanks to Vic he'd become a sitting target. Even old ladies towing shopping trollies were waddling past and smirking—

There was a blur across his side window and a kid about ten in a Rasta tammy ran past banging on the roof. A soft black-skinned banana slapped into the screen and slimed it. Something else soft hit the back. A happy-ugly mood was developing now they knew the vans were pulling out. Cromer wondered how they knew. It had only just come over the radio. Did they all have hand-held fucking scanners now? Even ten-year-olds? He considered putting the wash-wipe on to clear the screen, and then he considered getting out of the car. Anything he did would only make it worse. It was what they were waiting for. More bad fruit thudded against the car. There they were, picking it out of broken Spanish pallets in the gutter. Four or five of them hiding, nipping out, chucking stuff, then dipping back behind the shoppers. You little bastards. But it would be bricks and wrecking bars and ripping out the radios if he got out and went for them. Best do nothing. Ignore it. It made him vicious and sullen towards Vic. Fuck you Sergeant Hallam. What would you do if I suddenly just pissed off out of it. You'd be fucked then, wouldn't you? Serve you fucking right. You don't tell me, I don't tell you—

Vic came out of the Chinese grocers, holding his left shoulder and rotating his arm. He winced as he ducked into the passenger seat. A rattle of rocksalt and gravel out of a yellow road-gritting bunker scattered off his side window.

'Time to go.'

'Telling me,' said Cromer.

When they got on to the Gloucester Road, Vic straightened the brown paper bag, unlocked the glovebox, put the thunderflashes back in the bag and relocked the glovebox. 'All going out now, John.'

'What are?'

'Brown paper bags,' said Vic. 'Some black bloke bought twenty three quids' worth of Mighty Dragons half-ten last night. Paid Mrs Lee with a fifty. Genuine, apparently.' He dug his right hand into his jacket pocket and pulled out a transparent plastic evidence bag with a fifty-pound note inside. 'She thinks this is it. Cleaned me right out, so stop at the next hole in the wall will you?'

Cromer said, 'What black bloke?'

'Hooded sweatshirt, jeans and trainers,' said Vic. 'Land-Rover driven by a blond kiddy. Take the next left into City Road.'

'I thought we were going to see Billy in the Well.'

'We are. We're just going to see Mister Perreira first.' Giving him a look. 'If that's all right with you, John.'

Outside the Community Centre, the older black kids were still waiting to get their amps back. Eight of them, standing on the pavement side of the DO NOT CROSS tape, not rollerblading now, just punching their mittened fists together and shuffle-dancing round each other to keep warm in the chill north-easter. Vic and Cromer showed their IDs and the line of half a dozen vizored cops parted to let them through and closed again behind them. Nobody said anything: the cops and older black kids were too busy eyeballing each other.

Vic and Cromer walked through the old school first because Vic wanted to see where Chingola had been blown away. Inside the front doors was a thick white outline of a woman's body. There was a name written inside the ghost-shape: M. Thomas. On the dance floor were three other body outlines, also named.

The floors, walls, internal windows and two of the amps were ringed in white chalk to show where spent ammunition, slugs and ejected shells, had been located. The Forensic team, in fluorescent yellow-patched boiler suits, were still measuring, recording, digging away.

There was a doghandler in the cleaned-up band-room with a tail-stump-wagging liver-and-white springer.

'Hallo, Steve,' said Vic, 'how's Buster?'

'Confused,' said the handler. 'Trails everywhere. He thinks he's in dope heaven.'

'He pick up anything big?'

'Only baggies. Forensic have got the glory on this one.'

'Thanks, Steve.' There was no point in saying anything else.

Chingola was outlined next to the toilet bowl. There were two ringed holes in the stainless steel cistern. The way Chingola had fallen, together with the long hair and the skewed legs, made it look as if he was a thin girl dancing. Vic thought about him hunched and sweating over the keyboards in The Moonglow. Now he was just a shape on a toilet floor.

He waited for the wave of blackness to pass over. It was an animal thing, the presence of death, even dogs and cats had it. Even fucking seagulls, when they lost one of their own. A feeling of being cut off the stem, vague and amorphous, like losing your breath for a few seconds. It didn't always happen, but when it did you had to wait for it to fade. There but for the grace of God. Some fucking grace.

'Anything on the weapon yet?' said Vic.

One of the Forensics was holding a portable sun-gun over the top of the cistern while his mate measured the inside. 'Smith & Wesson,' said the one with the sun-gun. 'Thirty-eight Special. Could be a two-inch, could be a four, but it's probably a two, the slugs were still inside the cistern and a four's inclined to go straight through.'

'How close?'

'Enough for flash and grain burns.'

'Any struggle?'

'No marks, apart from needles. He was shooting up. Hypo was still hanging out his leg.'

'Door was kicked open,' said the guy with the tape.

Vic thought about it, picturing it in his mind.

'He's sitting there, quietly shooting up, the door bangs open, there's no struggle and he's still sitting there when he cops it.' He glanced at Cromer. 'What d'you think, John?'

Cromer shrugged. 'Either he knew who it was or he was already out of it.'

The two Forensics grinned at each other. The one with the sun-gun said, 'He is now, son.'

Vic said, 'Anything else we should know?'

'Trainer print where the door was kicked in. Eight and a half Nike Air, traces of talc.'

'Talc?'

'Off the dance floor.'

Mister Perreira was in his carpet slippers talking to Steve the doghandler on his doorstep. He didn't look too happy about Buster snuffling and bustling round his feet and legs. Beside the slippers, he was wearing a pair of thick old ginger tweed trousers with the pyjama legs showing underneath. He had his plaid dressing gown wrapped round him against the cold and both dark-veined hands were pressed into his stomach. He had combed his greying hair into a series of ridged finger-waves off his forehead but he hadn't got around to shaving and white stubble showed on his bony mahogany face.

Vic showed his ID. 'Good morning, Mister Perreira, we're police officers.'

'You don't say?' Big yellow teeth showing in a grin that wasn't a grin, then the mouth curving down, pulling the skin creases into deep black lines. He had one of those precise, lilted accents: it sounded more Indian than West Indian.

'I understand you're not a well man, Mister Perreira.'

'You do? Well, thank God somebody does.'

'Can we come inside, have a quick word?'

'I was just explaining to this officer here that I do not consider the private property of my apartment to be within the scope of this investigation.'

'I'm sure you're right, Mister Perreira.'

'Also I have an allergy against animal hair, especially cat fur.'

Steve gave him a pissed-off look. 'Buster's not a cat, Mister Perreira.'

Backing off from Buster to the safety of the door. 'All I can say is you talk to my GP, Doctor Johnson of Health Centre, and you will see what he says.' Starting to close the door.

'Mister Perreira,' said Vic, 'we all understand what you've had to put up with—'

'Do you? I wonder.' Glaring at Steve, making to poke his slipper out at Buster, then thinking better of it.

'If you prefer, we can wait until you're dressed, take you down to Trinity Road and talk to you there.'

'How can I leave here, tell me that? You policemen, you are not the only ones on duty, let me tell you.'

Cueing Steve in, Vic said, 'I can't speak for my colleague here—'

Steve said, 'I was just giving Buster a walk, clear his head, he came dragging over here and next thing this gentleman's out on his step giving me a mouthful about dogfouling.'

'Is that right, Mister Perreira?'

'There is too much of it. Children play in this yard. Even police dogs have holes, Sergeant.'

Vic said, 'Can't argue with that, Steve.'

Steve shook his head and turned away.

Vic said, 'Mister Perreira, you said in your statement your spare keys had been stolen from a secure box inside your front door. All I need to do is see the box, ask you a couple of questions.'

Perreira looked at the dog, at Vic, at Cromer. 'Let me just shut the inside door, stop all the heat going out of this damn place.'

Inside, there was a small red-tiled hall with two doors leading off at right angles. One was glassed, the other was planked, painted dull corporation green.

'This is the box.' Perreira pointed to a red metal box with a smashed safety-glass door. White lettering read IN EMERGENCY BREAK GLASS. The inside was varnished and had a row of brass hooks for keys. Crumbs of safety glass like the irregular cubes from old car windscreens lay scattered on the bottom of the box.

Vic turned an evidence bag inside out, stuck his hand in and opened the glass door. Inside, in brown faded copperplate on lined exercise-book labels:

SCHOOL   YARD   COALS   B'HOUSE

'What's "B'house",' Mister Perreira?'

Perreira nodded at the green-painted door. 'Boilerhouse. It is no longer in use since the new oil-fired system was installed in the main building.'

Vic nodded. 'How many keys altogether?'

'Thirty-six.'

'Lot of keys for a small school.'

'All voluntary groups have different cupboards and all cupboards have to be checked and locked every day for purpose of insurance.'

'I see.' Vic picked up a few glass crumbs, peeled the evidence bag off his hand and shook the crumbs to the bottom. 'Tell me, Mister Perreira, d'you remember speaking to Detective Chief Inspector Barnard or

Detective Inspector Parnes?'

'Yes. Yes I do. Both of them.'

'Like to tell us what happened?'

'First Inspector Parnes comes and fetches me for the keys. Then Chief Inspector Barnard takes them from me and says they will be returned. I have to tell you, Sergeant, so far they have not been.'

'They will be, Mister Perreira.'

'So you say. So he said. You understand I cannot do my work without keys?'

'I'll see what I can do.'

'Thank you.'

'When Chief Inspector Barnard took your keys, did you see, did you witness, Mister Perreira, either the Chief Inspector or Inspector Parnes open the safe in the band-room?'

'No.'

'Are you sure?'

'Positively.'

'What did you see?'

'Look, Sergeant, all I know is what I'm saying to you now. I gave them the keys, I came back here for some rest, then Inspector Parnes comes to me again and says the bottom safe drawer is locked shut, and I tell him the key is stuck under the blue cash-box.'

'And that was it, was it?'

'Yes.'

'Thanks Mister Perreira. You've been most helpful.'

He followed Vic and Cromer out to the front doorstep, reminding them about the keys, and once again Buster went straight for his trousers. He shook his leg at the dog and bits of glass flew out of his trouser turn-up. Vic picked them up and looked at them.

'Were you wearing those trousers yesterday, Mister Perreira?'

'Yes.' Showing his long yellow horse's teeth. 'Some of the damn stuff must have got in when I was cleaning up the mess.'

'Yeah,' said Vic. 'Gets everywhere, doesn't it?'

When Mister Perreira had gone back inside Vic led

the way across the tarmac yard to the main school building. He looked up at the panelled classroom windows. They were some seven feet off the ground, and a few shards of window glass lay where the CS canisters had gone in.

'Most of the glass is on the inside,' said Steve. 'Why we can't get the dogs in until Forensic have finished.'

Vic said, 'Can you do me a favour, Steve?'

'Such as?'

'Get your Super to get a warrant out on Perreira's place while we're down the Well?'

'Be a pleasure.'

'Have to be watertight. You know what he's like.'

'Don't I just.'

Vic watched Steve go, Buster to heel, his flaggy tail-stump wagging with eagerness. 'Best job in the world, John.'

'What? *Dog*handling?' Cromer still sounding sullen.

'Yeah. You've always got someone to talk to,' said Vic. 'And they don't fucking sulk.'

Cromer said, 'Wasn't me going Fuck-it-fuck-it-fuck-it in the car, was it?'

Vic said nothing. They moved down the side of the building. On the corner, by the steps, there was a large cast-iron grating. Vic figured it was the coal-hole for the old boilerhouse. There were bits of moss and black earth round the edges as if somebody had been cleaning it out with a knife.

'Hang on a minute, John.'

'What?'

'That young woman, Nova something, Perrott.'

'The tabbed-up kiddy?'

'Yeah, what did she say?'

'"No Martian's fucking me", that one?'

'After that.'

'Some fucking horror-story about things in black hoods coming out the ground—'

'Got a torch?'

'No.'

Vic grunted, took out his Imco, put it on full burn, and

pointed the six-inch gas flame through the grating. Before the lighter got too hot they saw a scattering of Phurnacite at the bottom of the delivery slope and, in amongst the black egg-shaped lumps, a galvanised padlock.

'One way out, John.'

'Yeah. Could be.'

Vic glanced at Cromer to show he was registering his lack of enthusiasm. 'Thing is, how'd they know where to get in?'

In the car, when Cromer wanted to know why they hadn't booked Perreira, Vic said he wanted to let him stew. 'We need the warrant, John, to worry him. We rush in now, he'll fuck us about. That's what he's like. We get a warrant, he's worried, we sit back and watch him dig his grave with his teeth.'

'You hope.'

After a pause, Vic said, 'No, John, I *know*.' Then he said, 'One more thing, while we're on the subject.'

'What's that?'

'When I started this job you were still getting your arse wiped by your mother.'

Nothing else was said until they pulled into the Well. Vic heaved himself, wincing, out of the Escort. 'Nag him,' he said.

'Who?'

'Benjamin. Nag the poor bastard.'

'What about?'

'Anything. The Toyota, his mates, Perreira, anything.' Vic took an alloy container out of his inside pocket and swallowed a couple of red and white Tylex. 'It's called being a detective.'

Billy was sitting in his holding cell looking at his wrist where his Rolex used to dangle. 'What's the time, Vic?'

'Quarter to one.'

'Stroll on,' said Billy. 'It feels like fucking February.'

12:48 on the big flip-over digital in Channel One

reception and Maggi was leading the CC and DI Parnes through soft pink and beige corridors into a venetian-blinded room with all four walls packed from floor to ceiling with grey metal racks of black electronic machinery winking with red and green LEDs.

Parnes had taken Maggi's call. Maggi had said she understood that all her contacts were being reported, that she considered this undue interference but nevertheless if they were so concerned about the extent of her involvement, perhaps they should meet.

The fireproof door closed behind them.

A boyish, smiling young man with shiny black hair cut like a World One lieutenant swung round on his five-wheeled pump-up stool. 'Hi,' he said. He didn't get up.

'This is our editor,' said Maggi. 'His name's Jonathan.'

'Nice to meet you, sir.' He put his hand out to the CC. His handshake was very soft, and fingers only. He put his other hand out to DI Parnes. 'And you sir.' For a moment all three of them were holding hands. 'It's not often we get such distinguished visitors.' Blair-like, his smile widened to his ears. He had very good teeth, no visible fillings, and the CC reckoned he couldn't be a day over twenty-five.

'What we'd like to do,' said Maggi, 'is show you what we've put together so far, and get your reaction, see what you think. Right, Jonathan?'

'Right.' Jonathan spun his stool back to the wall. 'Don't worry about the black bits, gentlemen, this is only a first assembly – although I should warn you we are looking at a 13.35 transmission.'

'In forty-five minutes?' said the CC.

'Right, but we should all be hunky by then. All bona on the tube come trans.' An arch look at Maggi. 'As they used to say when Madam started.'

'Balls,' said Maggi. 'Roll them.'

A very tall young man appeared with two more five-wheeled backless stools. He had the same brisk haircut as Jonathan but his hair was ginger.

'Thanks, Miles.'

Miles nodded, backed out through the door and put the overhead light out. Three screens lit up simultaneously. The middle one was black and white, the other two high-definition colour. The picture, of Maggi in a green costume with her lips pressed together, was pin-sharp. Unlike domestic screens, the edges of the rectilinear image were clearly defined against cyan blue; white numerical codes blinked top to bottom.

'It may take you a while to get used to,' said Maggi from the semi-dark, 'we don't work with domestic cut-off.'

The CC cleared his throat. 'No problems so far.' His voice sounded self-conscious, even to him. He consoled himself with the thought that back in the days of National Service they had called this sort of thing being blinded by science. They also called it Bullshit Baffles Brains.

The white numbers started to spin faster than the eye could follow and Maggi's lips began to move. Her voice came in husky sibilant clarity from several speakers at once. 'Maggi Reed, Channel One, Bridewell.' She waited a moment, glancing off camera for what the CC was pleased to recognise as a sound-check, and then her image swelled to fill the screen and stared directly at him. All he could see was slanted greenish cat's eyes – even though in real life they were pale grey-blue – spiky blonde hair and a livid scarlet mouth. Her stare was unblinkingly severe; it was impossible not to watch her.

'In the early hours of this morning armed police carried out a massive drugs raid in the St Pauls area of Bristol. Cocaine with a street value estimated to be in excess of half a million pounds has been seized.'

Now the pictures began changing every three seconds with quick intercuts to black. A shot of the flat white packages, guns and knives. A shot of the CC, hatless, silently miming Drugs Must Go, Jonathan murmuring about synching later. Night shots of ambulances and fire engines howling – shots the CC was certain he had seen before – then another night shot of a man on a stretcher - burning cars – the drenched and blackened interior of

The Moonglow at dawn.

And Maggi's voice, dramatic and staccato, cut to fit the clips. 'Together with quantities of knives, guns and ammunition. Chief Constable Royston Perry claimed a "major drugs catastrophe" had been averted. But confirmed a murder investigation was under way. Several other people, including women and teenagers have been injured. Some seriously. No names of victims are being released as yet. Rioting and looting have been raging through the night. The Moonglow, a popular multi-ethnic restaurant and nightspot, has been firebombed. And is now a wrecked and gutted shell—'

The screens went black, white squiggles writhed speedily across, the numbers jerked, vanished and restarted – and there was Maggi again, this time in a red plaid designer-tough jacket, long black riding skirt and knee boots.

She was standing with her hand on the roof of a small red car. 'Nine thirty-five Saturday morning in a quiet residential cul-de-sac in Ashton, Bristol. This is Maggi Reed for Channel One on a surprising new development in connection with last night's violence in St Pauls.'

The camera zoomed slowly to show Maggi standing beside a red Fiesta with the Churchwood road sign clearly visible in the background. There was a slight tremor in mid-pullback and Jonathan said, 'Oh bloody hell, Adrian.'

Maggi said, 'Only one we've got.'

Jonathan said, 'Plonker couldn't pull his prick out of a blancmange.'

The CC cleared his throat.

On screen, Maggi was saying, 'Detective Chief Inspector Barnard, who planned and led the raid on the Westminster Road Community Centre in St Pauls, has not been seen since he left Bridewell CID headquarters after the raid. Fears are also being expressed for Mrs Rae Webber, tragic pregnant widow of Inspector Frank Webber—'

The screens went black. 'Pic of her in there,' said Jonathan, 'and you're not having tragic *and* pregnant—'

'Why not? It's factual—'

'Grounds of taste,' said Jonathan.

'Taste my arse,' said Maggi.

'Mmm,' said Jonathan.

Jesus God, thought the CC.

'Inspector Webber, who was buried yesterday, was the victim of a savage attack ten days ago which was also investigated by DCI Barnard. It is thought in some quarters that the two events may be related.'

After that, as far as the CC was concerned, it couldn't get worse. He felt himself flushing and sweating into his interlocks and heavily suppressed anger raced and thudded through his chest. God he was hot. Felt like bloody flu—

Shots of the Webbers' house and garden. Shots of Forensic carrying bedding out. Jesus God, they'd be in the damned bedroom next. No, thank the Lord. Two dull inconclusive interviews with badly dressed neighbours, then a mass of badly shot footage of that morning's police operations in St Pauls with a white typewritten caption AMATEUR VIDEO flashing on and off throughout. The St Pauls coverage ended with blurry shots of the sixteen-man police vans withdrawing and being pelted by gangs of youths and children. Maggi's voice-over was saying that the house-to-house search had produced no further information regarding the whereabouts of DCI Barnard or Mrs Webber, and that informed local opinion in St Pauls considered the police intervention to have been 'unnecessary, unproductive, obstructive and unwise in the extreme'.

The screens went blank, the door opened, and Miles moved in to put the overhead light on, then moved out again. The CC wondered distractedly if that was all his job consisted of. Maggi and Jonathan were discussing how to get the 5.20 running-time down to 5.00 dead. Parnes was looking at his fingernails.

Finally, Jonathan swivelled his stool round to face them and gave them his gleaming Blairite smile. 'Well, gentlemen?'

The CC, noticing Maggi had her shorthand notebook

and Rotring ready, struggled to keep his self-control in the heat. Probably all that damned humming machinery. The other two were obviously used to it. Odd that Parnes hadn't noticed it. Fingering the dampness inside his collar, he said, 'Have you had your lawyers look at this?'

'Actually,' said Maggi, 'I am a lawyer.'

More bullshit. Call her bluff. 'In what sense, Miss Reed?'

'I specialised in Media Law at Strathclyde University, Mister Perry.'

'But you don't practise, do you, Miss Reed?'

'Daily, Mister Perry.'

'Maggi,' said Jonathan.

'Yes?'

'I don't think confrontation is really going to get us where we want to be on this one.' He turned his smile on the CC and pushed his shiny black hair back off his forehead with what the CC considered to be an extremely girlish gesture. God, it was bloody boiling in here.

'D'you mind if I have the window open?'

'Not at all,' said Jonathan. 'Absolutely.' Neither he nor Maggi moved, but after a second Miles came in, drew up the venetian blind, opened a centre-hinged window a couple of inches and moved noiselessly out.

'Thank you.'

'No problem.' Jonathan shot an anxious glance at the racked machinery, then at Maggi. She had folded her arms under her breasts. 'If the Chief Constable has any reservations, objections, points to make, as I'm sure you have, Chief Constable, then we should hear them, consider them, see what accommodation, compromise, solution, can be reached between us. It is, after all, why we're all here. Why you were invited, Chief Constable. And you, too, of course, Inspector Parnes.' Parnes nodded, coughed into his fist. Jonathan panned the smile back to Maggi. 'If that's OK with you, Maggs.'

'Fine,' said Maggi curtly. 'Fine.'

'Right. Great. Carry on, Chief Constable.' Jonathan

leaned forward. For a moment the CC thought he was going to touch him on the knee. The smile became little-boy mischievous. 'I'm sorry, sir, I've always wanted to say that.'

You oleaginous little bugger.

The CC stroked the bridge of his nose and said, 'You are aware that this investigation, in fact several investigations, are still continuing?'

'Of course.'

'Then you must also be aware that this report is highly prejudicial to those inquiries.'

'I think we can discuss that, as an issue.' Jonathan steepled his fingers. 'As far as questions of balance are concerned, I think I can say here and now that both Maggi and I would agree that it's only fair to offer you right of reply, in an equal-length interview. Right, Maggs?'

'Fine. Fine by me.'

The CC felt himself go into overheat. The greasy little bugger was trying to suck him in and fob him off. All in the hope, no doubt, that this bloody woman would chivvy him into making a bloody fool of himself on television. He stood up, opened the window a good six inches. There. That was better. He remained standing to show them who was who. The dizziness and thumping began to clear. 'You are aware that Mrs Barnard has not yet been informed?' It wasn't strictly true; but neither was it untrue: it was all in the hands of the Harrogate CID.

'Ah,' said Jonathan. 'Maggs?'

Maggi gave him a cold stare. 'All I can say is I find that extremely difficult to believe.'

'Nevertheless, it happens to be the case, Miss Reed. Parnes?'

Parnes straightened himself up, rising a couple of inches on his pump-up stool. 'Messages have been left. They have not so far been confirmed.'

'In addition,' said the CC, more relaxed now he was on his feet and breathing cold fresh air, 'it is clear to me, from the material you have assembled and the interpretation you have chosen to place on it, that you are also aware that a man's life, that of a senior serving police officer, may be in considerable jeopardy.'

Maggi leaned forward, eyes lasering into him. 'What about the woman?'

The CC ignored her. 'A jeopardy this news item—'

'What about the *woman*?'

'A jeopardy this news item—'

'*Jesus Christ*!'

'Does nothing to alleviate!' The CC leaned on the edge of Jonathan's desk and waited for this new attack of heat, this sudden, irregular thumping rage, to subside.

When it had, he clasped his hands behind his back and addressed them with firm, fatherly regret. 'I can't believe, I sincerely cannot believe, that responsible professional people such as yourselves, as I truly believe you both to be, intend to go ahead with this dangerous nonsense. You are aware of the guidelines, you must be aware of the reason for last night's operation, the reason for this morning's operation, and the reason why we have not yet released DCI Barnard's name. *Are* you aware of these things?'

'What about the woman?' said Maggi. 'What about Rae Webber?'

'As I am sure you are aware, Miss Reed—'

'Aware! Aware aware aware! Fuck aware!'

The CC felt like striking her. He gripped on to the edge of the desk. 'As I am sure you are *aware*, Miss Reed, Mrs Webber too may be in danger—'

Maggi stood to face him. 'And are you *aware*, Chief Constable, that Rae Webber and DCI Barnard are having what is commonly known as an affair?'

Silence.

Damn the woman. 'No, Miss Reed, I was not aware of that.' He glanced at Parnes. Parnes was studying his toecaps. 'May I ask where you came by this information?'

'Rae Webber,' said Maggi. 'Rae Webber told me.'

'I see.'

'She also told Detective Sergeant Hallam. In my presence.'

'I see.' Bloody Hallam again. He glared at Parnes – this is your bloody fault. 'Anything else, Miss Reed?'

'Yes,' said Maggi. 'There is. Something else did come up. I believe I can prove it to be true, in a court of law if necessary, that you were *aware*, Chief Constable, *you* were *aware* Detective Chief Inspector Barnard had engineered a cover-up of the facts surrounding Inspector Webber's death.'

The CC gazed out of the window. Sunlight. Traffic noise. The nearest slope of Arno's Vale Cemetery had been deconsecrated and greened over now. Part of it was the TV company carpark. An ambulance wailed in the distance. The machinery hummed. The other three sat and waited. He turned to face them.

'Never in all my thirty-seven years with this Force have I had occasion to deploy this procedure but you should know that it is within my capacity as Chief Constable to request the Home Office to impose a D notice on any press or programme material deemed to be not in the public interest. May I use your phone?'

'Ah.' A long pause as Jonathan swerved his stool this way and that. 'Right. Yes. I think we get the message. You, Maggs?'

Maggi gave the faintest of shrugs, stood up and walked out.

Jonathan waited a moment, raised his eyebrows conspiratorially – Women – and gave the CC a hesitant smile. 'If you'd allow me, sir, I'd like to show you Plan B.' The smile widened. 'One, as they say, I prepared earlier.'

The CC and Parnes left through the back door of the Channel One block. The CC felt mauled, fingered, warmly sucked, thoroughly abused and smilingly discarded by someone who wouldn't be his age until a third of the way through the 21st century. Boys. The CC thought of them all as boys, Jonathan, Miles, and the other slim young men he'd been introduced to afterwards. Boys with the haircuts of the dead.

The brave, foolish, patriotic, ignorant, idealistic dead: the blood, the bone, the loam of England, to whom the CC, who had never fought in any war, felt indissolubly linked.

This lot, this latest generation, were neither brave nor foolish. His England and theirs were, quite simply, divorced. Perhaps it wasn't their fault, but in his heart, in his soul – a soul the CC felt Jonathan had done his best to turn into a pair of soiled underpants – the CC knew it was. They didn't give a toss. Not a toss. Any of them. And that way evil lay.

Given Plan B had been worked out in advance, the CC wondered whether Maggi Reed knew about it – and decided on the evidence available she did. Pity. It meant that her sharpness, her severity, her cold lasering indignation were all faked; they were no more than the heartless female equivalent of Jonathan's slimy persistence. A front, a lever, a means of triumphing over those you despised. Career poses, no more, no less.

At the death, just before Miles showed up to usher them out, Jonathan had given the CC his card. It had his picture on. Smiling. The CC took it out of his buttoned top uniform pocket, tore it in half twice and dropped it in a wire litter bin full of soft drink cans and greasy pizza boxes.

'What did you think of Plan B, Parnes?'

'Well.' Parnes hesitated, calculating his options. Then he said, 'I think it'll suit our purposes, sir.'

The CC glanced at him. Parnes, he decided, was another one who tried to keep a foot in both camps. As a result, as far as the CC was concerned, DI Parnes had just split his personal integrity right up the arse. At least you knew where you were with Hallam, even if the man was an absolute pain. Perhaps it had to do with how much you had to lose, or, to be more accurate, how much you thought you had to lose. Hallam had convinced himself he had nothing to lose; Parnes, on the other hand, thought he'd got a lot.

For a moment, the CC wanted everything to stop, just stop – but knew that he had to go on to the bitter end, even with Parnes for company.

'In what way will it suit us, Parnes?'

'Well, sir. Better than the alternative, sir.'

Plan B was a plain 3.00 piece, voice-overed but not fronted by Maggi, centring on the press conference. It reported the raid, the murder, the casualties, but all within the context of the display of flat white packets, knives and guns, and featured a large chunk of the CC's 'Drugs Must Go' speech.

It ended with a clip of DCI Barnard from the previous conference, neatly held in freeze-frame, and managed to give the impression that he may have been injured or concussed during the raid and that his colleagues were anxious to contact him. Crimewatch-style, the public were given two numbers to call. Rae Webber was not mentioned.

In return, Jonathan had asked for and received the CC's guarantee of exclusivity, access and full cooperation, if and when both parties agreed that the full story, starting with Inspector Webber's death, could be told. Jonathan said it was important: important to him; important to Maggi; important to the public. And above all, Jonathan said, important to the image and reputation of the Force.

The CC had shaken Jonathan's peculiarly soft pink fingers thinking to himself, Over my dead body. Two can play at your game, my boy, and there is no way that report or anything like it is going out while I am Chief Constable of this city.

What he said was that he had always believed it was important, indeed essential, to reach a satisfactory compromise in such matters and he was glad agreements had been reached so amicably. Then he had clapped Jonathan on the shoulder and called him a good chap.

Their black Carlton was in the RESERVED carpark. On the freshly rock-salted gravel beside it was a used condom. Parnes kicked it aside. 'Sorry about that, sir.'

'Not your fault, Parnes.' The CC sank himself into the passenger seat. He could still see the condom, draped across the kerb where Parnes had kicked it. Ah, well.

Another small failure. It was all relative, of course. What was ten minutes of feeling used and abused compared to thirty-seven years of striving and hard-worked-for success? On the other hand, it was always those same ten minutes that stayed in the mind and came back to nauseate a man in the middle of the night . . .

The car felt hot, sweaty and uncomfortable. The CC put it down to the fact that it had been standing in the sun. Rocksalt crunched satisfyingly under thick tyres on full lock. They drove out on to the Bath Road. As the air-con started to kick in, the CC's spirits revived. They would win this one. Easily. Go to the top, talk to the chairman of the holding company, members of the board, bring a bit of pressure to bear, and, lo and behold, young Jonathan and Maggi Reed would never work in the West Country again. Excellent.

By the time they reached the main Bath Road traffic lights by Temple Meads, he was thinking pleasurably of seeing the great red lump of Ayers Rock at sunrise, when he felt a dull, heavy ache in his left arm, a spreading pain like sudden indigestion in his chest – and then the sweaty sick-making jolt of a serious heart attack.

He heard Parnes put the emergency siren on and felt the big car surge forward, but that was all. By the time Parnes swung into BRI Casualty and the green-clad emergency team began running forward, Chief Constable Royston Perry had joined the dead.

20

Parnes took the 1400 briefing. 'I hope we all agree – a minute's silence?'

Fourteen officers, CID and uniformed, sitting at pushed-together tables in the briefing room, each thinking his or her own thoughts, some with heads bowed and eyes closed, others, like Vic, watching the red second-hand jerk round.

Shock, loss and simple incomprehension had jarred them all; Vic felt he had run down a flight of stairs to find no floor beneath his feet – weird but on the other hand reasonable . . .

For all his faults, Royston Perry had been the Old Man, the fixed point: abrupt, awkward, an out-of-touch old nitpicker with more prejudices than a hedgehog had spines – but wrong as he was, religious as he was, authoritarian as he was, he was still the Old Man, the hard-faced, bloody-minded father they had all got used to. It was good to have a bit of weight, pressure, on top, if only to push and kick back at.

And he had *looked* like a CC, tall, erect, skin scrubbed red raw, impossible to imagine out of uniform.

God bless you, you old bastard, and good luck.

Now he was gone it was as if the Well itself had cracked from top to bottom. Everything had become unstable. There was an undercurrent of guilty excitement – what would happen next, would the promotion be from inside or out – but on top of that, Vic thought, a stubborn determination to stick together, close ranks, staunch the wound: *esprit de corps* all over again.

Only Parnes, with no Barney, and now no CC to hide

behind, looked to be in any sort of a panic – that shifty-arsed look.

As soon as death had been confirmed, Parnes had got straight on to Detective Chief Superintendent Sam Richardson. Sam, a heavy-jawed pale-eyebrowed northerner who was head of the Murder Squad, had been in on the Webber cover-up. Parnes needed to talk to him, not least about this poxy television business.

Basically, Sam Richardson owed his series of promotions to his intimidating physical presence: he was built like a lock forward and witnesses and suspects alike felt they were in the presence of some glowering Saxon gorilla who could go berserk at any moment. In his younger days, he had. Now, he had learned to control himself, to smile and bully at the same time, and to some extent it had made him the CC's blue-eyed boy.

DCS Richardson and DI Parnes went to see the CC's wife together.

On the way back, both felt they had got over the worst of it. Emily Perry was a slight, worn-looking woman who had long ago accepted that she was always going to play second fiddle to the Force as far as her husband was concerned. She had, they agreed, taken it as well as any woman could be expected. After making them a cup of tea, she said, quietly, the next day was Sunday and asked to be left in peace until Monday, so that she would have time to speak to her children. One was in Canada, the other Australia. They said they would do their best to keep the press off. It was, after all, in everybody's interests.

Within ten minutes of the black Carlton's arrival, the next-door couple came round to be with her; luckily, they agreed to drive her to the BRI.

Parking the Carlton in the CC's space at the Well, Parnes said, 'I don't know – first Barney, now the CC.'

Sam said, 'Oh no you bloody don't, Parnesy.'

'You're the next in line, Sam.'

'Only on the murder, son. Rest of the cock-up's all yours.'

'You're the senior officer, Sam—'

'I know I bloody am,' said Sam. 'That's why you're taking this bloody briefing.'

The red second-hand ticked over the 12. Parnes coughed into his fist and looked up. 'Well, ladies and gentlemen – the last thing he'd want us to do is hang around. What I propose to do is go round the table and as far as possible keep it chronological so we all get the same picture. That all right with you, Sam?'

'Your meeting, Parnesy.'

'Right. Since I was one of the last people to see DCI Barnard, I'll kick off. He left the Westminster Road SOC approximately 0320. Firearms at the Well tell us he checked out of there 0345. Anybody?'

Vic had his notebook open. 'A Mrs Osbourne, 25 Churchwood, thought she heard a van start up in the allotments behind Churchwood. She said that was about four-ish.'

Parnes said, 'Reliable?'

'Not much use from our point of view—'

Parnes said, 'Why tell us then, Hallam? Wasting everybody's time—'

'What I was going to say, Inspector Parnes, was that it wasn't much use on its own – but when we located DCI Barnard's red Fiesta in the cul-de-sac opposite Rae Webber's house—'

Parnes said to the two secretaries, 'Delete that.'

Vic took a breath and said, 'When we located DCI Barnard's red Fiesta in the cul-de-sac opposite 23 Churchwood, the windows and bodywork were covered in thick frost—'

'Meaning what?'

'Meaning it had been there some time. Four or five hours at least. And as you know, Inspector, a definite ID on clothing—'

'All right, Hallam. Next?'

A guy from Forensic 2 read his notes: 'Two sets of footprints outside the downstairs cloakroom, ground too hard for pattern ID. Clearer sole-imprint on toilet-bowl lid. Eight to eight-and-half Nike Air similar to one at school SOC. No handprints. Oil-leak from vehicle in lane to allotments. Traced back, paling fence to embankment demolished. Deep-ploughed tracks and turns in culvert below confirm Land-Rover 88 Series 3. Defaced tracks at the Mariners possibly same vehicle.'

Parnes said, 'Anything from Surveillance?'

The Surveillance Super pushed a pile of tapes forward. 'Two sightings of a marine-blue white-cab short-wheelbase Series 3 cruising the Westminster Road area Friday night, 1758 and 1807. Third possible sighting turning into Whittier Street 2238.'

Parnes said, 'You get a reg?'

'On the board.' All eyes turned to the white melamine display board. On it, in blue laundry marker, a W registration number. 'Hired from Wil-Con Hire, Willesden, north-west London, name of hirer Robert Long, International Driving License number incomplete, false insurance company details. M4 motorway patrol logs show the vehicle seen leaving Heston Services westbound 1403, NFA.'

Parnes put his hand to his ear. 'Sorry?'

'No further action.'

'Pity,' said Parnes. 'Anybody else?'

Vic said, 'Mrs Lee, Picton Street, St Pauls, said a black guy got out of a Land-Rover driven by a white guy with long blond hair, walked into her shop, bought twenty-three quids' worth of bangers round half-ten last night.'

'Bangers?' said Parnes. 'What's that got to do with the price of fish?'

Vic shrugged. 'Ask Forensic.'

The guy from Forensic 1 said, 'The fragments we picked up at The Moonglow SOC included plastic, granulated polystyrene, small pieces of alloy from a butane gas-lighter tube, bits of thunderflash cartouche and a partially burned Lil-lets tampon.'

Parnes said, 'Explain.' Trying to sound like the CC.

'It's what's known as a Brixton Mortar, Inspector. You light the petrol-soaked tampon, that ignites the thunderflash, the thunderflash blows the butane tube, the gas and petrol go up in a ball of flame and the polystyrene sticks like napalm.'

Parnes said, 'Thank you for that. On.'

Forensic 1 said, 'The gear found in the lock-up behind Whittier Street corresponded to the fragments found at the SOC.' Forensic 1 glanced at a uniformed Traffic Super.

The Super said, 'In response to this information one of our motorway patrols called at Gordano Services. Bar codes from the articles found in the lock-up were consistent with service station stock, and a copy of the relevant till-roll was obtained.'

Vic wondered how long you had to be in Traffic to get to speak like that.

'The goods listed were confirmed as being purchased by a tall thin Caucasian in his twenties with long fair hair who tended a fifty-pound note to the till operative, a Mrs Amin. All goods subsequently traced with the exception of five one-kilo packs of builders' filler compound.'

Vic glanced round the table. Parnes, Sam Richardson and the Forensic 1 guy all had their heads down, studying their notes. Vic scribbled WOT, NO COKE? on his pad and put it where Cromer could see. Cromer nodded.

The Forensic lab girl was saying, 'We tested the notes from Mrs Lee and Gordano. Both had traces of cocaine hydrochloride.'

Parnes shifted in his seat and said, 'All very well and good, but let's not get off-road, shall we? Can I bring you in here, Sam?'

Sam Richardson said, 'Only as far as the murder, Parnesy. As I understand it, matey was DCI Barnard's informant. We know he was on the phone to Barney because your lot heard him.'

Parnesy said, 'That's right, 0040. Go on, Sam.'

Vic thought, You've rigged this fucking meeting.

Sam Richardson said, 'The phone's cut off, Barney calls the raid in, matey, Chingola, Antony Christopher Bell, is shot twice in the face with a short-haired Smith & Wesson Special. No struggle, no weapon found, so my assumption is whoever shot him knew him, and is still tooled up.' Sam Richardson stared belligerently round the table and ended up looking at Vic sitting next to him. Vic shrugged, nodded his agreement. Sam leaned back and relaxed. 'Other than that, my lads and myself interviewed a certain Neville Alen Hart who describes himself as a security operative from Knowle, if that's not a contradiction in terms.'

Vic noticed Parnes and one or two others grinning. They loved this in-yer-face-fuck-the-toerags stuff.

'He's a big lad is Neville, but he's quite amenable when spoken to as he deserves to be.'

The grins froze.

'After a short but fruitful in-cell discussion he volunteered the information that he had seen matey, Chingola, in the band-room in the company of a man about forty of Afro-Caribbean extraction, and a tall thin blond kiddy with curly hair. Chingola tells Neville this blond kiddy with the curly hair is "the drive". Shortly after Chingola left the band-room, the blond kiddy comes looking for him. Neville tells him Chingola's gone to the urinals. The blond kiddy goes back in the band-room and seconds later comes back out with the man of Afro-Caribbean extraction, who is, to coin a phrase, looking extremely black.'

Relieved, the grins spread round the table. One or two of the older officers made chuckling noises.

'So there we are,' said Sam. 'One black one, one white one.' He shuffled his papers together and eyed Vic. 'As DS Hallam has already mentioned.'

Parnes said, 'Thanks, Sam. Any more from you, Hallam?'

Vic decided to play it straight until Parnes and Richardson showed further signs of bending it. 'Only to confirm and add to what the Chief Super says.'

Parnes said, 'Add what exactly?'

'Two witness statements. Benjamin Ray Foley, William Herbert Jewel.'

Parnes said, 'This isn't *Billy* Jewel, is it?'

Knowing full well it was.

Vic said, 'Yeah. Why?'

Parnes said, 'He's your mucker, Hallam.'

Vic said, 'He's also a contact. As Chingola was Barnard's—'

'Not the same at all—'

'Parnesy,' said Sam Richardson. 'Let's hear what DS Hallam's got first.'

Now everyone knew who was running the meeting.

In the holding cell, Billy had said, 'Fucking terrible claustrophobia in here. Stretch your arms you can touch the walls.'

'Cosy, yeah.'

'Worse than the fucking box.'

'How's that?'

'Fucking dead then, aren't you?'

'You in the band-room?'

'What?'

'You get claustrophobia in there? Hot sweaty bodies. Noise. CS dinging in. Must've been dead rough. Was it Billy?'

Billy shook his head, sat down on the tiled shelf of the holding cell and looked up at the inch-thick armoured-glass ventilator near the ceiling. 'You sit here and you think, poor bloody Irishmen. They dig the fucking holes, they build the fucking walls, one Friday night piss-up and they're back in the fucking place.'

'You want to get out, tell me about the band-room.'

'Eleven and a quarter fucking hours I've been here, Vic. I mention your name, and nothing. Nothing-nothing-*nothing*-nothing-nothing. Suddenly you're the invisible fucking man. I'm sorry, Vic, but bollocks. No can do.'

'You've been got at, right?'

'Some heavy metal out there, Vic.'

'This rate, you'll end up inside with 'em.'

'No fucking fear.' Billy felt for his tie. It wasn't there. 'We've all got fucking rights, and twelve hours, that's it, long as they can hold you. Forty-five minutes and I'm out—'

'Only if I say so, Billy.'

'You what?'

'You're a material witness, my son.'

'All right,' said Billy, nodding to himself, thinking he was going to tough this one out. 'If you want me to stand up in court and tell 'em I was gassed, shot at, spat on and had the shit kicked out of me, I'm there, I'm up for it. Fucking right I am.' Giving Vic everything but two fingers. 'Anything else, sorry, mate, no can do.'

'Anybody tell you Barney Barnard's gone missing?'

'Hooray fuck.'

'Officer's life at risk, Billy. Force don't like it.'

'Always told me you hated the bastard.'

'Nothing to do with it. Look at it from my point of view. You're a material witness, you're my contact, and I'm supposed to let you go? Last time you ended up in Stoke-on-fucking-Trent.'

'That was different.'

'This is worse.' Time to wind the old bugger up. 'I tell you what I'm supposed to do – and what I'm *going* to do if I can't get any sense through your thick fucking skull – I'm going to go down to our number one tame fucking magistrate and I'm going to get you held for twenty-four hours, then another twenty-four hours, then another twenty-four hours after that. Right into the middle of next week, Billy, and in all that time your feet won't touch the floor and your eyes won't fucking close. You'll be questioned in fucking relays, and not by me either, because they, Billy, *they*, think I'm too fucking soft on you.'

Silence, then Billy said, 'You cunt.'

'I know.' Vic decided to wing it. 'And after that you'll be on remand in Horfield, free association with these heavy geezers because you've been caught in possession and we'll have witnesses to swear they saw you handing over five or six hundred quid in smellies for an imprisonable amount of a Class A prohibited drug. You'll be in Horfield Rec playing ping-pong with a bat up your backside, Billy, wide end first. Then you'll go down the steps for several years and you'll have arseholes for breakfast on a fucking daily basis. You want to be loyal to your fellow dickheads, that's your privilege, but don't yack on to me about your fucking rights.'

After a while Billy said, 'What's an imprisonable amount?'

'In practice, anything over five is Intent to Supply.'

'Fuck my old boots.'

'Why, how much you front up for?'

'Twenty-five.'

'Goodbye, Billy.'

'Don't be like that, Vic.'

Billy was wobbling. Vic stopped to think. 'Twenty-five grams for six hundred quid?'

'Five.'

'*Five*? How come you get such a good deal?'

'I'm Mister Clean, aren't I?'

'Yeah? Tell me about it.'

'I fucking *am*, man. I don't touch the fucking stuff.' Billy's head and neck twitched first, then his shoulders. 'Well, not usually.'

'You're not a regular punter, you're flashing cash, and you get a rock-bottom deal for five hundred fucking quid? What are you, his long-lost fucking uncle?'

Billy's head, neck and shoulders twitched again.

Vic grinned at him. 'You old bugger.' No point in pushing now, best to ease it out of him. 'What d'you do, Billy? Get it for twenty, cut it, sell it on for seventy quid a pop?'

Billy shrugged. 'Yeah, well, you know. Life's a problem.'

'Tell me about it.'

'How can I?'

'I'm your mate, Billy. Only one you've got.'

Billy put his elbows on his knees. His chest heaved in and out and he stared at his creased black Oxfords. They had no shoelaces in. He looked up defiantly at Vic. 'It's fucking Christmas, isn't it, and I'm fucking skinned and boneless, aren't I? This guy comes up to me in the Clifton Wine Vaults.' He shook his head at the memory.

'He said everybody was fucking panting and was there anything I could do. Fucking Clifton, fucking dinner pwarties, fucking architects, fucking barristers, fucking antique dealers, fucking luvvies, they're all fucking cokeheads-for-Christmas, aren't they? Let alone the fucking musicians.'

'Then what?'

'They had a fucking whip-round didn't they? Five hundred and forty-five fucking quid, the mean fuckers.'

'You got a cheap deal for that load of wankers?'

'Look, mate, life is fucking hard everywhere, but up in Clifton you could be drowning in the fucking river and all that lot'd do is piss on you off the fucking Suspension Bridge.'

'Where would you sooner hang your stocking up, Billy, Horfield or Clifton?'

Billy was on the verge now. The trouble was, he couldn't admit it, even to himself. 'I can't, Vic. I'm known.'

'So was Chingola.'

'Whole fucking point, isn't it?' Another deep sigh, his upper body crumpling over his knees on the tiled bench. 'I daren't go inside and I daren't stay fucking out.' He hauled himself up, leaned his head back against the cell wall and looked helplessly at Vic.

Vic said, 'You know this cunt, don't you, Billy?'

Billy's eyes stayed on Vic's face, his expression unchanged. 'And you say you're a fucking mate.'

Billy was so close it was worth winging it again. 'How does protective custody sound?'

'What?'

'Witness protection.'

'Do I get a drink?'

'Bottle of Grouse a day if you like.'

'No, a real drink. I'm talking about a real drink. I'm B, D and O, Vic, broke, down and out. I need something to get me back on my feet again.'

Vic got out his Marlboros. 'We can but try.'

Billy's hand was steady enough, but when he put the cigarette in his mouth and waited for Vic to light it, the end was quivering all over the place. 'Fuck me, Vic. I'm in a right two-and-eight here.'

'Nerves.'

'Thank you, Doctor.' He took a heavy drag and closed his eyes. When he opened them, tears ran down his face, but he didn't seem to notice them or try to wipe them away.

Time to lead him gently through it. Very gently. Make it look as if he was just poking around for information; even though they both knew he wasn't, it would make Billy feel better. 'How did it work?'

'What?'

'The system.'

Billy got out a paisley handkerchief and wiped his eyes, nose and face. 'All goes in the book, doesn't it? Nothing there only baggies. I was the only one paying cash and I was told I should look on that as a fucking favour.'

Vic wanted to ask who from. Instead he said, 'Then what?'

'Then, in a few days, nobody was saying when, you get a tinkle on the mobile, the time for a meet and that'll be the drop. You got to have a mobile and you got to be where they say when they say or tough shit, no deal, and in my case the candidate's lost his deposit. They got it all sewn up, Vic.'

'Wouldn't you?'

'They must be employing half St Pauls.'

'One good thing.'

'Yeah,' said Billy. 'Oh, and the guys buying weight got either fourteen or twenty-eight days' credit. Depending. After that,' Billy took another long shuddering drag, 'the men from Rentokil turn up. Something like that, anyway. I mean, I'm not bothered, am I? I'm dealing cash up front.'

'Because it's a favour?'

'Yeah.'

'Because you know the guy?'

More silence as Billy finally, reluctantly, heaved himself over the hump. 'Yeah, I do. And he knows you. So what's it worth?'

And he knows you?

Vic ignored it and said, 'I told you. You get out and we watch your arse.'

'Oh yeah,' said Billy, 'and what am I supposed to do for a fucking living? Write fucking fairy stories? I'm talking over and above that, Vic, I'm talking ten large ones.'

Vic thought, Dream on, my son. Billy might get his five hundred quid back out of the Police Fund, and a bit of *ex gratia* on top but that was about it. He said he'd see what he could do, and then he said, 'Who is he, Billy?'

Billy said, 'Who, the black guy?'

'Who is he, Billy?'

Billy did something he'd never done before. He reached out his left hand and gripped Vic's right. It was the sort of thing your mother did, telling you to be careful. 'He's a fucking killer, Vic. Right fucking maniac.'

Vic pulled his hand out of Billy's grasp. 'Who says?'

'Everybody. Fucking band-room full of tooled-up six-foot-six shavehead GBHers and there's this middling-size guy with a gammy leg and they're all falling over themselves to get out of his fucking way.'

'The black guy?'

'Yeah. Used to call himself Winston Summers, something like that. That guy with the leg, Vic. You know him.'

Oh yeah, I know him. 'Simmons?'

'Yeah, him. But this kid he had with him called him Baz.'

'Baz?'

'Yeah, Baz.'

'And the kid?'

'Nobody called him anything. Chingola said he was the drive. More like the fucking dogsbody to me. Nervous as a whippet bitch, trying to come on he wasn't, you know, all that me-I'm-dead-cool-I'm-from-public-school crap.'

'What'd he look like?'

'Tall, thin, shoulders up. Hair like that Led Zeppelin

mush. Face like a skull.'
'What'd he say?'
'Who?'
'Baz, Winston.'
'He said, "How's your friend?"'
'Meaning who?'
'Meaning you.'
Oh fuck. 'Anything else?'
'He said, "He still got a punch on him or he gone soft in the belly?"'
Vic remembered the fight. Outside the Palm Grove, the other end of St Pauls. The kerb. The guy pasting and clipping him all over the place saying he was going to stick him on the fucking railings. Coming for him but not seeing the kerb and his bad leg going down it. Vic, knowing he was getting hammered, tried a right cross, but as the guy dropped his head to get his footing the cross turned into an accidental rabbit punch and the guy went down and Barney sat on him and banged his head against the kerb and the guy bit him so Barney put his stick between his jaws and said he'd shove it down his fucking throat but it still took Vic and Barney and two hefty uniform guys to get him in the van. When it turned out the guy was clean Barney planted him and told Vic to search him and charge the fucker.
Charge the fucking piss-stained black reptile, Hallam.
The bite-marks in Barney's stick were a quarter-inch deep.

Parnes said, 'And as usual, Hallam, I suppose you believed every word Billy Jewel said?'
Vic, still up from reliving the fight, took a deep breath. 'He's scared witless, why's he going to lie?'
Parnes said, 'Billy Jewel would sell his mother's false teeth to stay out of nick and you know it.'
Holy shit – suddenly losing it. 'Look, *Parnesy*, I haven't said a word about cocaine or any of these other bloody cover-ups so far—'
Cromer under his breath going, 'Oh Christ—'

Sam Richardson laying a heavy hand on Vic's bad shoulder, saying, 'That's enough, Vic.'

'Bollocks,' Vic threw his hand off, then said, 'Sorry ladies,' to the secretaries and two plainclothes WPCs at the far end of the table. The WPCs were trying not to show they were enjoying it. He turned to Cromer, 'You better take it, John.'

Parnes saying, 'Have we quite finished?' and Cromer opening his notebook and clearing his throat.

'Statement from Benjamin Ray Foley, eighteen, Whittier Street, St Pauls. Statement confirms Detective Chief Superintendent Richardson and DS Hallam's descriptions. One black male about forty years of age, medium height, stocky build. One white male, twenties, tall, thin, long blond curly hair. The black male was referred to as Baz, the witness has no recollection of the white male's name. Witness claimed to have been threatened by the black male, but later confirmed that the vehicle was not a Toyota Landcruiser as he first maintained but the Series 3 Land-Rover as previously recorded by Surveillance.'

Parnes said, 'Thank you, DC Cromer. Have we all got that?'

A general murmur and rustle of notebooks and pads.

Parnes said, 'When was this?'

Cromer said, 'What?'

'Don't say what to me, son.'

Cromer reddened. Flicked and fumbled through his notebook.

'Come on, Cromer, when was it?'

Cromer, puce, saying, 'When we cracked The Moonglow, Inspector.' Finding the page. 'Interview timed at 0935—'

Parnes saying, 'When *who* cracked The Moonglow?'

'Me and DS Hallam—'

Vic read it out from his notebook to get it right, 'I'd like to say that DS Cromer, by his personal bravery, skill and quick thinking, made the arrest leading to confession on the firebombing of The Moonglow. He acted on his own initiative, at considerable risk, and he deserves full and sole credit. All I did was be there. I'd like that recorded at this meeting.'

Parnes waited sourly for the secretaries to finish. When they looked up, he said, 'Put this down, if you will: "In view of DS Hallam's hostile and disruptive attitude he was asked to remain silent for the rest of the meeting. He was told if he declined he would face the consequences at an internal disciplinary hearing. Given his conduct in relation to events of the last two weeks those consequences could well be severe." Do I make myself clear, Hallam?'

'Yes, Inspector. Apologies for the interruption.' And fuck you.

After Cromer it was agreed that descriptions of the two chief suspects and vehicle should be circulated as of now. One of the two secretaries left the briefing room, her heels clacking on the parquet.

Then it was the turn of Surveillance and Communications. The Surveillance Super, given his head, went for it. He said that, assuming the suspects had a mobile phone and were stupid enough to use it, then it was possible that, if the officers leading the investigation could persuade the company operating the network through which the call had been made that the incident was sufficiently major – which, by the way, he didn't doubt for a minute, but he had to stress that in these circs the cooperation of what was in effect an entirely private and profit-orientated company was entirely voluntary – then, yes, it was, in theory, possible to track down the point of origin of a mobile phone call to a particular cell. That was the upside.

The downside was that in the inner city or a suburb where mobiles were at very high-use levels, a cell was several hundred metres across, and calls were constantly being switched from frequency to frequency – even if the user was standing still – so the upshot was that direct pinpointing of an *individual* within the city was virtually impossible. On the other hand, he went on, it had been known, he understood, that three or more network engineers, working in conjunction, using hand-held or, better, vehicle-mounted scanners had succeeded in triangulating a particular call to, for example, a particular car. But he must stress that this was very rare and the engineers only usually did it for fun.

Parnes said, 'Fun?'

'That's right,' said the Surveillance Super. 'To demonstrate their technical expertise. As when, for example, a chap may be phoning another chap's wife with a view to, say, a bit of rumpy-pumpy, they like to give him a little surprise.'

A few nervous laughs and uneasy silences, then a buzz of conversation broke out. Parnes cut it short by calling upon the two plainclothes WPCs at the end of the table.

WPC Nicola Palmer said they had been to visit witnesses still held in BRI Casualty and Intensive Care. One of these witnesses, Maelee Thomas, eighteen, Washbrook Street, St Pauls, had had a bullet removed from close to her spine. Firearms and ballistics lab reports indicated the bullet had been fired from a Smith & Wesson .38 revolver issued to Detective Chief Inspector Barnard.

Parnes said he wondered if that was relevant at this juncture, although, obviously, it was an issue that would have to be addressed in due course. He asked WPC Nicola Palmer whether the witness Maelee Thomas was aware of the provenance of her injuries; WPC Palmer conferred with her colleague WPC Sandra Metcalfe. WPC Metcalfe said she thought not, the witness was more concerned with who was looking after her baby. Shortly after this, Ms Nova Perrott, seventeen, Moxley Road, Eastville, entered the ward with Maelee's baby Liam, and in view of Ms Perrott's abusive language and behaviour they deemed it advisable in the patient's interests to leave. Inspector Parnes thanked them, and called the meeting to a close. It was 1434.

By 1438 Vic and Cromer were back on their Siemens terminal trawling through Winston Simmons' records and notes trying to figure out why, where and when he had turned into a killer called Baz.

21

The Channel One every-hour-on-the-hour news update came on at three. Rupert, who reckoned he'd had about one and a half hours' sleep in the last twenty-four, leaned back against a damp, white-distempered wall and watched Baz thrust the two-inch Casio through the bars of the cage where DCI Barnard sat handcuffed and bollock naked. 'Hey man,' said Baz, 'you on TV.'

There was no reaction from DCI Barnard but Rupert found himself scrutinising the tiny black and white screen, expecting to see himself at any moment.

All he caught was a brief glimpse of the DCI who was reported missing, then another guy, called Chief Constable something-or-other, who was reported dead. Then the update went into a story about a cat and a parrot who slept in the same cage together.

They were in Hillside, in the sub-basement. It was cold, damp, white-distempered, half-underground and smelled of cat piss. The sub-basement was built in a series of triple brick arches a hundred yards long with two sets of brick pillars over three feet thick. You could walk or drive a dumper truck along the middle row; the outside row had its windows knocked out and covered in blue polythene; and the inner row was divided into cells or cubicles with whitewashed cinderblocks. The cop was in one cubicle, the woman in another; a Security guy and his muzzle-taped whining Rhodesian Ridgeback in a third.

Whichever way you looked, all you could see was white brick-vaulted arches dwindling off in both directions, all identical, on and on and on for fucking ever . . .

Rupert started to count them, gave up, his mind wandering, drivelling off on its own, knackered by lack of sleep, thinking, What attracts cats to piss on cement bags?

Trying to focus, sort it out, pick through the wreckage, add up what was left. The way Rupert saw it the job had gone seriously pear-shaped and wobbly the moment they pulled the cop off the woman. Now, stuck in fucking Hillside with the fucking dog whining when they should have been back in the Smoke, it had turned into a right colostomy bag.

Arguments starting inside his head, with himself, with Baz. Arguing and looking for the point where it all went wrong, trying to remember the sequence of events that had led to this fucking hellhole. Seeing the pair of them sitting in the Land-Rover at the end of the allotments by the woman's house in Churchwood. Watching the cop go in. Waiting, as Baz said, for the man to get comfortable—

'Baz.'

'Yah?'

'We're not here to deliver, we're here to collect, right?'

'We already delivered,' said Baz. 'Now we collect. Seen?'

'Seen, yeah, sure, I'm not arguing with that.'

'You arguin' with you own fuckin' nerves, boy.'

'All I'm saying, Baz, what do we need these two for? Man's a fucking copper—'

Baz turning that dark heavy-lidded look on him. 'Man a fuckin' Beast.'

Rupert treading carefully, wanting to sound reasonable. 'OK, right, man's a fucking Beast. Fine. But that's not the point I'm trying to make, Baz. My point is why the woman? What's she done? Why the pair?'

Baz going silent, then: 'You want a know?'

'Yeah. Please.' Please seemed to get through: he always went for that public school shit.

Baz said shortly, 'They decoys.'

Fucking decoys? What the fuck was this? Wanting to say, Baz if you had two more braincells you'd have a pair. Instead, he grinned at Baz, said, 'Oh, right.'

Baz was grinning back now, thank Christ. 'Rupert, you so fuckin' dumb, all you brains grow is fuckin' hair.' He took hold of a handful, twisted and tugged it through his fingers. 'Heh-heh-heh.'

Rupert shoved his hair back in place and shook it, knowing Baz loved all that stuff. Then, forcing another grin, shrugging, aiming to sound apologetic: 'Yeah, well, my first run, man. Next time, I'll know, I'll be ready.'

That dry, resigned, matter-of-fact killer's voice. 'Yah. Nex' time.'

Rupert swallowed, tried to think of something to shift Baz's mood. 'So what we do is what? Use these two as a diversion, right? Set up something like The Moonglow?'

'Fuckin' Moonglow.' Baz looking even heavier.

Rupert backtracking. 'No, man, I mean like The Moonglow *should've* worked, hadn't been for that cunt Chingola.'

Barnard lightening up a touch. 'Heh-heh-heh. Man dead, you still badmouthin' the fucker.'

'Fucking right,' said Rupert. 'I mean, if The Moonglow had worked, it would've taken the heat right off the school, screwed up the raid and we'd have fucking walked it.'

'Sure,' said Baz. 'If shit was chicken, man never go hungry.'

'We'd be back in the Smoke by now.'

Both of them silent, thinking about it.

Baz said, 'What 'appen, 'appen.'

Rupert wondered about his five grand.

Baz shifted position, scratched his stubble, went tssssssss. 'Any job, always come a screw-up point, always come a point when the fish get spooked. Flash, they gone. Then you got a wait. You got a sit, you got a wait.'

Rupert, sensing an opening, tried to suss Baz out. 'You talking about this phone call? This guy Riad?'

'Heh-heh-heh. Stay on the case, Sherlock.' Then saying, 'One phone call, we out a this place.'

Rupert needed to push it. 'And these two? The cop and the woman?'

'While they lookin' for them, they ain't lookin' for us.'

Pushing it further. 'So we're going to dump 'em somewhere, then make the switch?'

'Heh-heh-heh. You could say that. We goin' a dump 'em somewhere.' That dry, matter-of-fact voice again.

Oh shit.

Unable to stop himself Rupert said, 'And this stuff we're collecting? What is it, Baz? I mean, you know, what's it worth?'

'Rupert.'

'What?'

'You runnin' off at the mouth again. Shut the fuck up.'

Baz looked out through the windscreen into the night. After a while he came back to himself, reached out, took hold of Rupert's wrist and twisted it to see his Bangkok Rolex. 'Man should be comfortable by now. We in there, you take the woman.'

Then Baz smacking the grey-haired cop twice across the mouth with the barrel of the Browning and asking him, *Who a fucking piss-stain' reptile now?* Meanwhile Rupert was pulling the woman away, looking at her but not registering anything other than she was naked; after the cop got hit, she didn't even resist but went like warm jelly and leaned on him. Baz telling her to get dressed, watching her pull on jeans and sweater, and then telling her to get a coat, and her taking a long ankle-length camel number and looking at him, looking at Rupert for permission; saying nothing but then opening a drawer and quickly stuffing a handful of white knickers in her coat pocket.

All Baz let the cop wear was his suit. He stuffed everything else he could find – shirt, socks, shoes, belt – in a carrier bag, cuffed him with his own plastics, and wrapped three-inch silver gaffer tape round the cop's mouth and eyes. Then he threw the tape to Rupert and the woman asked if she could have some tissue underneath, for her skin, and Baz said, Yah, why not?

In the Land-Rover Baz held the Browning on them

while Rupert taped up their knees and ankles. Less than twenty minutes and they were moving, no lights, through a three-hundred-yard covert up the scraggy poplar-lined back road to Hillside. There was a huddle of brick buildings at the foot of the hill; a gatehouse with iron gates and the main tarmac'd road behind it, workshops and a stable-block converted to garages.

Above them, floating over the ruff of bare trees round the forty-five-degree slope, the whole first floor of the massive grey block was lit up like an ocean liner, and outside the flat halogen floods blanched the top of the hill stone-white.

'Fucking Security, man.'

Rupert heaved the Land-Rover off the back road through a gap in the poplars. He flattened a swathe through stringy wet-looking black nettles for twenty yards and then switched off.

'Fucking Security.' Looking at Baz. 'All over the fucking place.'

'Yah,' Baz said. 'Fuck it.' He went to sleep.

So, as far as Rupert could tell, did Rae and the cop. The cop made snoring noises for ten minutes, making Rupert want to strangle him, then stopped.

4.45. Rupert's spirits sank into middle-of-the-night hopelessness. A dull shitty hate at being awake and alive but too catatonically tired to do anything about it. Everything was shit and telling himself it was only lack of blood sugar was no help at all. He lit one Camel, then another. They both tasted dry, dry and harsh, as if they'd been stuck behind a radiator for years. Shit and double-shit.

His smoke-laden breath coalesced into shapes like clouds on the inside of the windscreen. Ten minutes or an hour later, he didn't know – and what's more he didn't fucking care – he saw they *were* fucking clouds: clouds of frost. Jesus. He was dropping into sleep and banging up awake again, thinking Christ, twigs breaking, someone outside – but all it was, the Land-Rover's metal ticking down from hot to cold, cold to colder.

Six-thirty he woke Baz up.

In the back the other two shifted uncomfortably on the freezing metal floor, then seemed to fall back to sleep again.

Ten to eight Baz woke him up, offered him a baggie. One snort and his mind was off like a longdog.

Baz was saying something about Security changing over, a beige Cavalier come in and a white van gone out, so drive up to the fuckin' pole, man.

'What?' Rupert's hands and feet felt very big, but not connected to the rest of him. Dizziness, like snow falling—

'Fuckin' barrier, man. He the only guy there.'

Rupert trying to make his mouth work, ask Baz how he knew.

'Cause I keep my fuckin' eye open, Rupert. I seen three come out, one go in. Three out, one in, OK?'

'Yeah, but you don't fucking know for sure—'

Baz hit him. Another short punch. Rupert came awake.

'Shit, Baz, all I said was—'

Baz slapped the magazine into the Browning with the heel of his hand. 'All you said was what?'

'All I meant, how'd you know he's the only one?'

Baz slid a round into the breech. 'He fuckin' better be.'

Rupert backed the Land-Rover out, looked, and drove through the huddle of buildings, past a peeling sign saying HOSPITAL STAFF PARKING ONLY and on towards a black-and-yellow barrier pole next to a sectional wooden hut.

When they were about twenty yards away, a guy in a grey uniform with a yellow 'Security' shoulder-flash came out and put his cap on to wait for them. He was about six foot three, short-haired, pasty-looking, and had flattened his cap-peak to give it that Nazi-Guardsman look. In one hand had a clipboard. In the other was a short plaited rope lead. On the end of it was a Ridgeback, big as an Alsatian but reddish and more solid in the body.

'Fucking dog, man.' Rupert pulled up the handbrake. They were about ten yards away.

Baz glanced at the two in the back, grunted and hunched forward to shove the Browning in his back pocket. 'What you do, is when the dog jump you, you catch him by the two front leg and pull 'em hard, wide apart. That way, you split 'im an' his shoulderblades go straight through his fuckin' heart. He dead, man, dead in mid-air.' Glancing at Rupert holding the Land-Rover on the handbrake. 'Heh-heh-heh.'

When Baz got out, Rupert put the metal lock-tongues down on both doors.

The Security guy said, 'What's this, overtime?'

Baz said, 'No, man, we on a sub-contract.'

'No site work on Saturdays.'

'Yah, I know, but we ain't on site, we on timber clearance up the hill there.'

'Got a note?'

'Note?' said Baz.

Rupert saw the guy starting to get bolshy. Tipping his head back to look down his cap-peak at this gimpy black bastard. 'Yes, sir.' The voice wearily patient. 'A note from a main contractor, an authorisation, a pass.'

'Yah, I got a pass.' Baz patted the pouch of his sweatshirt, grinned at the guy, patted his back pockets and pulled the Browning. He held it two-handed in the guy's face from about four feet away and deliberately let the guy hear the safety snick off. 'You let go that dog-rope you both dead.'

Rupert watched them go up two coir-matted steps into the hut. He felt his bladder go shivery and wished he dared fuck off now, fuck off right out of it.

Baz came out backing carefully down the steps. He was holding the gun one-handed. He stepped to one side and motioned the Security guy out with the barrel. He emerged with the dog in his arms. Its legs and jaws were strapped up with the silver gaffer tape. So was the Security guy's mouth. He had no cap now and his face was going red from the weight of the dog. The dog was already struggling and whining in the guy's arms and the guy was trying to say things to it but couldn't because of the tape round his mouth.

Baz shoved the Security guy and the dog in between Rupert and the cop and said, 'You sure you got all that key shit right?'

The guy nodded.

'You ain't, you made you last mistake.' Baz made the guy tape his own wrists and feet, then taped his fingers together.

Rupert unlocked the passenger door and Baz knelt on the seat to hold the Browning on the dog and the three in the back. With his other hand he dug in his sweatshirt pouch and tossed Rupert a set of car keys. 'Beige Cavalier.' F Reg. Parked up on the back road, edge of the covert.

Rupert drove up the fresh scar of track that wound round the hill. It was rutted over a foot deep with construction plant tracks and sooner than stop and dig about for four-wheel drive, Rupert drove half on the road, half on the verge. Down below, a quarter of a mile off, the M32 was blazing with traffic.

At the top the track divided. One part led to a paved terrace piled with scaffolding and sheeted stacks of insulation blocks. The other part forked down beside the terrace to the lower of the two heavily buttressed basements. A double layer of battened blue polythene shielded the entrance.

'Back in there,' said Baz.

'Back in?'

'Yah, back in.' Baz got out while Rupert reversed and kept the Browning trained on the back of the Land-Rover. As it approached he pulled the polythene aside, letting it fall again once Rupert was in.

'That it. Stay there.'

Rupert switched off.

A dripping silence.

Cold blue light filtered through the windows into the triple row of arches. A torn-down plywood sheet which had been used as a cement-mixing board read:

    MALES   CUBICLES 1–10
    FEMALES CUBICLES 11–20

269

Baz got Barney out first and made Rupert rip the gaffer tape off his knees and ankles. When Rupert indicated the tape round his eyes and mouth, Baz shook his head.

'He ain't home yet.' He tossed Rupert a new-looking green spade with a shiny steel blade. A handwritten tag on the handle read LANDSCAPE USE ONLY. 'You keep you eye on them. And when I say you keep an eye, you *keep* an eye. You hear me nah?'

'Yeah, I hear you.' Still getting at him over that business in the band-room.

Baz prodded Barney over to one of the cells. Barney in his bare feet, trying to walk and keep his unzipped beltless trousers up at the same time.

Rupert saw Baz shove Barney through into Cubicle 10. Some banging, clattering, a few grunts, then Baz came back grinning.

'Beast is fuckin' caged, man. Not the same fucker they put me in, man, but near enough. You want a take a look?'

First thing Rupert saw as he walked past the row of cubicles to number 10 was they weren't cages at all. They were pre-war cream-painted drop-sided metal hospital cots. Kid-sized things about five feet by two on chipped white ceramic wheels. What somebody had done was fit lids on top of the cots. The lids were made of two-inch steel reinforcing mesh and fastened with jubilee clips. The steel had gone rusty but the clips were still bright. At the head and foot of the cot were thick leather restraining straps, gone blue and green with mould. Baz hadn't bothered with the ones at the head of the cot because the cop was already cuffed but he'd fastened the ones round his ankles. As Rupert walked in he saw the cop still had the silver gaffer tape round his mouth and head but Baz had taken it off his eyes. The cop tried to look up. His look said plain as day, 'You're fucked, son.'

The other difference was the cop was stark bollock-naked, crammed in and head down over his groin as if he was looking for his prick. The skin was already turning pink and blue under his patchy black body hair.

Baz was grinning as Rupert came back out. 'You see 'im? You see the man now?'

'Fucking hell, Baz.'

'Yah. Well now he fuckin' know. *Now he fuckin' know.*'

After that, apart from showing the cop his picture on the Casio, Baz ignored him.

Then for hour after hour all Baz did was shuffle up and down the tunnel of whitewashed brick arches, dragging his bad leg through the cement on the floor, saying *Shit, ring you fucker* at his mobile. The noise of Baz's trainers slithering and rasping was sandpapering Rupert's nerves, making him want to scream out *For Christ sake stand fucking still a minute!*

At twelve they ate the Security guy's thin Marmite sandwiches, and then Baz took the guy round to key in the time-clocks.

While he was gone Rupert took a look in the cubicles. The woman was closest in 2, the Security guy and his dog in 5, the cop in 10. All the doors had been taken off and stacked against the central brick pillars. The doors were painted gloss cream and long scratches and dents where they had been crowbarred off their hinges showed the bright metal facings underneath. They all had double locks, and grilles top and bottom, one for food, one for inspection.

Some fucking asylum.

At least the woman was holding herself together. She seemed able to do that. Remove herself, ignore it all. So far she hadn't cracked once. They said women could stand things better than men. She sat hunched in the corner of her cubicle, mouth still taped but able to see now, arms round her knees, collar-up, head down, avoiding eye contact. Baz's Casio in her taped hands like one of those handwarmer things his so-called parents and their friends bought out of National Trust catalogues to take to point-to-points. Rupert had given her the Casio to keep her quiet after Baz had shown the copper his picture on the screen but she was quiet anyway.

Pale and wiped out, but quiet. Nerveless even.

The one time he had dared have a go at Baz about what they were supposed to be doing he had caught her tilting her head to one side and seeming to smirk to herself. That faint mirthless smirk some women had that said what arseholes men were.

But she was holding up a lot better than that poxy dog. Thing hadn't stopped howling and whining since they'd got here. Huge crest of fur standing up all along its back. Surely to Christ Ridgebacks had been banned years ago? All they were ever bred and trained to do was rip the faces off blacks. Howling and whining. Guy seemed to have no control over it. Shit, why didn't Baz shoot the thing? Only a fucking dog.

At four o'clock, the sky growing dark, Baz took the Security guy round the site to set the lights and key in the time-clocks again.

Rupert, having already decided the job was fucked, rooted around in the Land-Rover and found the yellow AA first aid box. He took out the round-ended two-inch scissors, tilted back the passenger-side mirror, switched on the interior light and started to cut his hair off.

The scissors were blunt, stiff, and rust-stained. This fucking job, what else would they be?

After the first sawing-hacking attempts to get through a half-inch thickness of hair over his left temple, futility, self-disgust and frustration left Rupert close to tears.

Fourteen fucking years growing it and now this. It was all that black fucker's fault. He thought about asking the woman, Rae, to do it for him; then, remembering her smirk, thought she was just as likely to stick the fucking scissors in his neck.

Chopping and sawing. Jesus. His eyes actually beginning to mist over: it was pain as much as tears. He shut his mind off and soldiered on.

Baz came back, glanced at Rupert, put the Security guy back in his cubicle, the fucking dog whining worse than ever, taped up the guy's hands and legs, shuffled back over to Rupert, shoved his hands deep inside his sweatshirt pouch and stared at him.

Rupert had cut the hair off most of his head with his right hand. Holding the too-small scissors in his left, he couldn't make them work and had nicked the top of his ear. That side and the back had ended up a right fucking mess. So far he'd chopped most of it down to a series of uneven punk-style spikes and tufts between half an inch and two inches long. That and the streak of blood running down inside his ear made his head look like the skull of a chick that had fallen out of a nest and killed itself.

'Fuck you doin'?'

'Fuck's it look like? Don't want to be fucking recognised straightaway, do I?'

Baz shook his head, bent to pick up one of the brassy coils. He felt it, stretched it, dropped it back on the damp cement floor, the life already gone from it. He shook his head again. 'You lost you fuckin' brains, boy.'

Rupert held out the scissors. 'You fucking do it then.'

Baz shook his head, very slowly this time, watching Rupert saw away at the top of his forehead. He turned away, his face hardening into a fury of disappointment.

Then, like lightning, swinging back on him—

'You jus' fuck you self, you know that?'

'Just taking elementary precautions, Baz.'

'You hear me? You hear what I sayin'?' Baz's voice going high and strangulated, his eyebrows knitting down together, a thick blue-black vein showing between them. He shoved his face jaw-first at Rupert and spittle sprayed out all over Rupert's face. 'You jus' fuck you fuckin' self, you white piece a shit!'

Baz's mobile beeped.

22

Baz dragged himself over to the blue polythened entrance and stuck the short black aerial out. Rupert shut the interior light off and listened.

'Yah? . . . This is Baz. You? . . . Who? Shabba who? . . . Shabbahatin, right . . . OK. Where you fuckin' been, man? . . . What Riad said. No fuckin' storm here. You talk to Riad when? . . . What he say . . . Right. You know this Avonmout' place? . . . OK. You got how many? . . . Shit . . . No, two . . . Jus' me an' a kid . . .'

Baz glanced at Rupert. 'Tall, skinny, twenty-some-odd, look like a day-old chick. Like that . . . Yah. He the driver . . . Name a Rupert . . . No, man.' Another sour glance. 'He white. Got scraggy yeller hair . . . If you say so . . . Yah, I will. You too. Take care.'

Baz closed the aerial down. He shoved past Rupert, reached into the toolbox under the passenger seat, took out a box of shells, reloaded the Smith & Wesson, then checked the Browning. 'Turks. Eight a the fuckers.' He turned to Rupert, grinning. 'Boy, am I glad I ain't you.'

After two hours of phoning, faxing and ransacking computer terminal files, Vic and Cromer knew everything they needed to know about Baz and Rupert except where they were.

They knew Baz had made it to London from Jamaica as Winston Simmons. They knew he had a house and family in Brixton as Winston Simmons. They knew that he had a flat in North London as Brandon Baxter. That he was in Leyhill Open ten years ago as Brandon Baxter. That he was a witness to the heart attack and death of fellow-prisoner Clifford Uley. The file mentioned two other witnesses: Leslie Whybrow and Rupert Johnson-Lang. That there was an incident in Leyhill involving Johnson-Lang and a housebreaker called Redfern.

They knew that eight years later he was remanded to Horfield as Winston Simmons. 'When Barney planted him, John.' They knew that as a result of a fight with two whites he was sent to Hillside for psychiatric treatment and evaluation. That he was sent back from Hillside with a report describing him as STABILISED. The report also mentioned unspecified periods of restraint and enforced medication.

'Fuck me,' said Vic, 'where's that car-hire sheet?'

Cromer pulled it out from under a mass of curled-up faxes.

'"Name of Hirer: Robert Long".' Vic looked at Cromer. 'That's what they do, John, that's what the silly fuckers do.'

'What?'

'Pick a name that sounds the same. Something close so they think they'll remember who they are.'

'How?'

'Robert Long, Rupert Lang – forget the Johnson bit – mother probably got divorced and remarried.'

Cromer punched in the details. Compared to Baxter, Lang was a doddle. Adopted. Vicar's son. One conviction, three months growing cannabis, Leyhill Open. NOTHING FURTHER KNOWN.

Vic went back through their files. Rupert's was marked NO VISITORS AT OWN REQUEST. Baz's listed two for Leyhill – Evelyn Patterson, half-sister, and Joseph Patterson, her cousin – and two for Horfield: Joseph Patterson and Maurice Perreira.

While Cromer got on to the Met about Evelyn and Joseph Patterson, Vic spoke to Steven the doghandler at the Westminster Road Community Centre.

'How's it going, Steve?'

'Rough. Lads outside have just had another dust-up with the kids wanting their amps and gear back.'

'Why not give it to 'em?'

'I don't fucking know. Forensic have finished, so have we, but the Well says no, let 'em stew, teach 'em a lesson.'

'Sounds more like fucking punishment to me, Steve.'

'You said it. About fifty of 'em out there now. Like fucking Rorke's Drift in here. We're all barricaded in. Missis is going fucking spare.'

The red PRIORITY call button started flashing on Vic's phone.

'Why's that, Steve?'

'Got free tickets for the panto preview, haven't we?'

'How d'you get on with that warrant?'

'We didn't. Community Council brought pressure to bear.'

'Community Council? Fuck's it to do with them?'

'What happened this morning. Police brutality, victimisation, you name it. Everybody's turning shirty and they all want to bite lumps out of us. Blacks *and* whites. You should hear that guy Perreira. What a mouth he's ever got—'

'Bust him, Steve.'

'Leave it out, mate. Everybody thinks he's a fucking hero—'

'Listen, Steve. Tell your super to ring me if he wants, but I'm telling you as of now Maurice Perreira is a major drugs suspect and I want that fucking basement turned over. His place and the school. Got it?'

'Fucking hell, Vic—'

'Tell your Super to lay it on me if he wants, but get down there or this'll be another fuck-up and tell him I said so.'

'Fuck we supposed to be looking for?'

'Five kilos of fucking cocaine, mate.'

'Forensic got all that, they had it on the news—'

'The news is all bollocks, Steve. Regards to Buster.'

Vic put the phone down, the PRIORITY button still flashing.

Cromer said, 'Nothing on Evelyn. Recently died of cancer. String of Receivings down to Joseph Patterson. All minor but they think he gophers for the North London brothers.'

Vic picked up the phone. It was Parnes. 'Hallam – get the fuck over here fast as you can!'

Vic waited a moment. 'The fuck over where, exactly?'

'Jesus Christ, Hallam, the CC's office!'

Parnes and Sam Richardson and the Surveillance super had twelve-inch-to-the-mile maps of Bristol and surrounding areas spread out all over the CC's conference table. Parnes looked up to make sure that Vic had closed the door through to the secretaries. Then he said, 'Why are you being such a fucking pain in the arse, Hallam?'

Vic said, 'Because of the way every aspect of this fucking job's been fucking well mishandled.'

Sam Richardson said, 'If we can just knock it on the head there, gentlemen.' Glowering at the pair of them. 'George?'

The Surveillance Super switched himself on and said, 'We've heard from the network that a call emanating from Base Station 4877 Portishead has been made to our target number and that call has been answered. Tracing a call destination as opposed to a call source depends first of all, as you obviously appreciate, on decoding the appropriate computerised billing information. As far as scanning is concerned, there are various technical difficulties to do with signal strength, call duration, possibility of frequency switching as when, for example, a vehicle is travelling through the overlap between one cell and another. All the same, the network assures us that all their scan-record resources, hand-held and mobile, have been in operation and they are at present contacting their field engineers for results. If any. And that's it, basically.' The Surveillance Super stared at the CC's combined fax-phone. 'Ring, telephone, ring.'

A fax started jerking out:

RECORDED CALL FRAGMENT ENDS

V1 WHAT HE CALLED
V2 NAME OF RUPERT
V1 THIS MAN A COLOURED MAN
V2 NO MAN HE WHITE GOT SCRAGGY YELLOW HAIR
V1 YELLOW HAIR THATS GOOD THATS BETTER <LAUGHS>
V2 IF YOU SAY SO
V1 OK SEE YOU BE THERE
V2 I WILL YOU TOO TAKE CARE

CALL TIME 1638

CALL DURATION 73 SECS

PORTISHEAD 4877 >>> FILTON 4167

SCANNER PRELIM EASTVILLE/M32 J2

MORE FOLLOWS >>>

'M32, Junction 2.' The Surveillance Super laid a transparent plastic ruler on the map. 'Dog track, Eastgate Centre, supermarket, say between three and five hundred houses and Eastville Park.'

Sam Richardson said, 'Close off Junction 2.'

Parnes said, 'In the rush hour?'

The Surveillance Super said, 'They can get off at Stapleton and carry on up Bell Hill.'

Vic went on studying the map while they talked about diversions. Then he said, 'It's Hillside. They're in Hillside.'

Parnes said, 'What makes you think that, Hallam?'

Vic said, 'I don't think, Parnesy, I fucking know.'

Sam Richardson said, 'For Christ sake, Vic—'

Vic said, 'This guy's been there before. Before it closed down. He was there for three months. He knows what it's like, knows the layout, he's familiar. Where else does he know?'

The phone rang. The Surveillance Super listened,

'Quarter mile west of Junction 2?' He listened again. 'Similar north of Muller Road? Many thanks.' He moved the ruler slowly round the map and stopped. They all saw where it pointed.

Vic waited. Nobody said anything.

Baz said, 'Two minutes we out a here.' Rupert watched him drag his bad leg into Cubicle 10. As soon as Baz was inside Rupert moved quickly into Cubicle 2 and snipped the tape on the woman's ankles and legs. Then he pulled her to her feet and cut her fingers free. Her hand moved to the tape across her mouth. He grabbed her wrist. 'You yell, we're next.'

Baz waited until the cop looked up, waited until he was sure the cop still had that 'piss-stain' reptile' look in his eyes, said, You badmouth fucker, and shot him in the face. Barney's head was knocked back by the impact. He looked as if he was staring through the steel grille for someone who wasn't there.

Rae staggered. The sound of the shot banged up and down the length of the brick-vaulted arches. Rupert pushed her towards the Land-Rover. She had no feeling in her legs. He yanked the door open, piled her in, clicked the door shut.

Baz hauled himself round to the head of the cage, shoved Barney's lolling body forward and put a second .38 into the knob of bone at the top of his neck. The iron-grey head jerked forward and wedged against the top of the metal grille. That was it. The letter was posted, the message sent. Baz felt himself cleansed. Cleansed and replete.

A hoarse, whining noise: the Land-Rover's starter-motor—

'Fucking arseholes!' Rupert held the key down so hard he could feel the metal twisting. The starter dog-clutch spinning, sticking, starting to churn, throwing itself out again. Fucking hell. Fucking Land-Rovers. Fucking diesels. Fucking glowplugs. 'Get down! Get right down on the fucking floor!'

The engine caught. Holy shit—

Baz came out at a stumpy run. A thick blue cloud of diesel smoke billowed towards him. He shot orange stabs of flame into it. First the .38, then the Browning. Noise concussed up and down the passage. Then the battened blue polythene sheet was lifting and the Land-Rover was roaring away under it.

The battened sheet fell and clacked back into place.

'You white piece a shit!'

The dog was making muffled howling noises.

Rupert punched the starred and bloodied glass out and gunned the Land-Rover up to the top of the terrace. Blood, for Christ sake. Where was all that coming from? He felt the rush of cold air growing hot on the top of his scalp.

Rae, crouched down in the footwell, looked up. The left side of her face was streaked with radiating bright-red splatters. 'You've been hit,' she said.

Fuck off, thought Rupert – I've been hit and you're covered in blood? A warm wetness ran down his forehead into his eyes. Oh fuck. Wrestling with the steering. Oh fuck.

'Where?'

'I don't know. Somewhere on top of your head.'

They came out level with the terrace. Glaring floodlights everywhere. His head began to ache. Flashes of white pain. Then continuous like a hot iron being seared across his scalp: 'Ow, shit!'

'What's the matter?'

All his life women had been saying What's the matter. 'Can't fucking see, can I?'

She writhed herself up on to the seat. 'You better stop.'

'Fuck it.' He felt good about that.

He heaved the Land-Rover out through the glare of the lights and tried to pick out the rutted track winding round the forty-five degree slope. Christ in shit, he was practically fucking blind—

He slowed down. She dug in her coat pocket and thrust a wodge of white knickers at him. 'They're all clean.'

'I should fucking hope so.'

He wiped the blood off. There was a terrible smell of diesel: he wondered what else Baz might have hit.

She said, 'If you put a pair on your head, it might stop the blood running into your eyes.'

'Are you taking the piss?'

The Land-Rover rolled round the corner of the hill. Down below, blue lights were flashing all over the M32. Closer, a siren began yipping and a motorway patrol car, headlamps blazing, was heading up the main road to the gates.

'Fucking hell.' He switched off the lights and began reversing round the hill towards the back road and the culvert.

'If I were you I'd get out now.'

Shots from under the terrace, sounding flat in the open air.

'No thanks.'

The further he backed the worse the smell of diesel. Below, the loom of headlamps was swinging through the gates and up the tarmac to the gatehouse and stables. Fucking red-stripes.

He shoved the stubby transfer lever into four-wheel drive and heard it clonk. Thank fuck for that.

'Put your belt on, we're going over.'

The Land-Rover teetered on the edge, tilted down. Holy shit. It looked steep enough from the bottom. It was ten times worse from the top. A hundred and fifty yards, then a flat bit, then another hundred yards downhill to the back road through the covert. The whole length of it rutted and iced-up.

The steering bucked and spun through his hands. The wheels slid. God sake don't touch the brakes. Play it on the accelerator. Second and third best for grip.

Jesus Christ the thing was going sideways already. He felt the upside wheels lifting. Try not to wrench the wheel. Don't dab on the accelerator. Smooth changes. Stay off the brakes. Keep your left foot jammed against the bulkhead.

The Land-Rover lurched down on to all four wheels and immediately began to slew the other way. Fucking hell. He saw Rae start to rise above him, then slam down again. Oh Christ my fucking head.

Trouble was, these ruts, lynchets, whatever the fuck they were, were throwing the front wheels all over the place. He got it straight, reached for the second – *graunch* – got fourth instead.

They started rocketing downhill. The flat bit came rearing up at them. He eased off the accelerator and straightaway the back wheels started coming round again.

Fuck it. Shit or bust. He put his foot down hard.

Geronimo—

They hit the flat bit at what felt like sixty miles an hour but was probably no more than thirty-five. Their heads smacked forwards in unison towards the remains of the windscreen and then snapped back. He felt his arms wrench out of their sockets, the belt crushing his breath out. Then they were off the edge of the flat bit.

Flying. Engine screaming. Time slowing down. Waiting for the crash—

They hit fifty or sixty feet down the second slope. All the wheels, axles, shocks and springs slammed up into the bodywork. Metal and rubber screeched against each other. A smell of burning, and parking tickets, dried earth, old nuts and washers flying up through the cab. Rupert saw a stub of yellow carpenter's pencil shoot past his ears. The Land-Rover plunged and staggered, brought to its knees like a stunned beast, and then it shuddered, shook itself, came back up on its springs and roared on. He drove into the covert and switched off.

Jesus Christ what a magnificent piece of machinery. They sat there. Thick grey smoke began to surge out of the bonnet. The smell of diesel was overpowering.

'Right, that's it,' he said. 'Out.'

The grey smoke turned black and shot up in tongues of greasy orange flame.

The beige Cavalier smelled of dog and roll-ups. He put a hand up to his scalp. His fingers came away red and sticky. As he revved the engine he saw she was standing ten feet away watching the flames. Her eyes were shining.

Now all he had to do was get himself to Avonmouth. Blood, red-stripes and roadblocks permitting . . .

23

The negotiations had stalled.

Baz had seen the ball of orange flame bloom up over the trees from the Land-Rover and hoped the white piece a shit was still inside but when he saw the red-stripe turning off and the woman hobbling towards it, he figured he wasn't.

Catch up with him later would be nice.

Then the cops was all over the place, cars and a helicopter, and shouting and bawling at him through their loudspeakers and telling him what to do but he wasn't having any of that 'Mister Baxter this is the Police' shit. Say nothing, let the fuckers waste their breath. He still had the guy and the dog and they knew fuck about the cop the way they kept asking for him so it was still a chance.

All you got to do is watch which way the fish swim.

He had got himself fixed nice. In between the end cubicle and the brick-pillared entrance. That way he was covered from both ends and he could see the windows that had been knocked out. He had his bad leg stretched out on one cement bag, his ass on another, a pile of three more to rest his gun arm on. Laid out on creases in the top bag, three big fat ones, each with a nice little sprinkle, and another one half-smoked.

So, he was feeling good, feeling ready. Taking a peek out the polythene now and then, telling himself you been in shit all you life, you get in, you get out. All you got to do is watch which way the fish swim and when you chance come you take him by the hand and you greet him like a brother and you *go*—

Knowing he was scared. Heh-heh-heh.

The halogen floods had been pulled forward and set on edge. The stark white light blasted a fifty-yard gap across the frozen turf and blazed off the blue rectangle at the end. It reminded Vic of raw nights at Eastville dogs.

The police negotiator, DI Ted Hutchins, a tubby friendly looking guy with grey curly hair and a pink healthy face, was talking to Sam Richardson behind the armed response vehicles. The white long-wheelbase Land-Rovers and blank-windowed Transits had been drawn up in a semi-circle at the back of the floods.

Behind the vehicles, four black-clad police marksmen. Four more in position on the terrace above the entrance, two more below it on the lip of the white slope, flat out, legs splayed. Further back, police and civilian ambulances, then a queue of patrol vehicles and unmarkeds lining the track back up to where it forked. Twenty vehicles, fifty men and women, standing around in the freezing cold.

Fifty to one.

Small groups of men and women in anoraks, puffa jackets, dark blue police car coats. All wearing bulletproof vests, either over or under. All talking quietly about anything but being in at the death. All watching the blue rectangle.

'What you doing Christmas Day, John?'

'Going over to her lot.'

'Pauline's?'

'Yeah.'

'What's that like?'

'Old man's a churchwarden.'

'Glass of sherry and a bottle of Wincarnis?'

'Blue Nun, usually.' Looking puzzled. 'What's Wincarnis?'

Sometimes Cromer made him feel old.

'How about you, Vic?'

Thinking about Ellie. Her warm, generous, absent body. Her gorgeous arse. The empty flat. No fucking

curtains. For the first time in hours, thinking about Caroline—
Come and see me, will you?
Cromer rubbing his hands together. 'Got anything lined up?'
'Not a lot.' Wondering should he give Caroline a ring.
'Don't fancy Cricklewood then?'
'Fuck off, John.'
Sam Richardson came up. Hatless, wearing a dark blue crombie and black fur-lined gloves. Parnes behind him in a waxed jacket, DI Hutchins bringing up the rear in a police car coat.
Parnes said, 'How long you been here, Hallam?'
'Long enough.'
Sam said, 'Not a blind bloody word.'
'I noticed.'
All three gathering round, looking at him, waiting.
DI Hutchins said, 'Needs somebody who knows him.'
Sam said, 'You know him, you talk to him.'
'I'm not the negotiator, Hutch is.'
DI Hutchins shrugged. 'Man won't talk, I can't make him.'
Sam hunched his shoulders inside the crombie. 'I'm not asking, Vic.'
Walking up to the Land-Rover with the four-way PA, feeling wobbly, unsteady, as if he'd just toked down a four-inch joint on top of half a bottle of Grouse.
Sam said, 'All you've got to do is talk him out.'
Seeing the bulked-up marksmen in their long-peaked caps and groin-length flak jackets, their black strap harnesses, their Parker-Hale sniper rifles. Red-dot laser sights being ranged in, wavering over the stone facings surrounding the blue polythene rectangle.
The nearest pair were wearing alloy-rimmed anti-glare Polaroids. Night, the middle of winter. Round green-tinted lenses, making them look blind.
They treated him like male nurses. One told him where to stand. The other showed him the coiled-lead mic and told him to talk across it, not into it. They said it would make his voice clearer and he wouldn't have to

present his head.

Present his head?

Any case, they said, the griff was the target only had a two-inch .38. Fifty yards, shooting into the glare, a two-inch .38 was nothing. No risk at all. Unless of course he got lucky.

The target?

DI Hutchins came up and said that according to Mrs Webber – who was now in the BRI for shock, but had sounded coherent enough at the time – several shots had been fired. One creased the Lang kid apparently. Any case, the priority was DCI Barnard – and of course the Security chap and his dog. Get them out the job was done. Any help, he'd be glad to. Ducking back to stand beside Sam Richardson and Parnes behind one of the blank-windowed Transits.

Realising these guys were here to kill.

Thinking, Fuck that for a game of soldiers, then thinking, It's too late now—

A quick flash of driving pencil-slim steel through Frank Webber's neck and the flesh slicing open—

He made his mind a deliberate blank. Cleared his throat. Watched his breath fly up in the heat coming out of the back of the floods in front of him.

'Baz!' Jesus Christ it was loud. His voice came bellowing back off the terrace and walls.

Thinking the guy's up shit creek, don't beat him over the head, offer him a paddle: 'Baz! Are you OK? Is there anything you want?'

Baz leaning forward, peeking through the gap between the polythene and the wall. What the fuck was this? Angling the .38 into position.

'Baz! This is Vic Hallam! I said you OK? Anything you want?'

Baz got both hands on the .38, screwed up his eyes against the glare.

'Vic Hallam, Baz! You and I have met before!'

Hallan. He the fucker with the punch?

'This was outside the Palm Grove – two, two and a half years ago, remember?'

Hallan. That the fucker. Rabbit-punch in the neck.

'You slipped and fell – remember that?'

Sure. Fuckin' leg give way, you rabbit-punch me.

'Baz? The other officer who was there that night, Mister Barnard – he's with you, isn't he?'

You bet he with me.

'He OK?'

He fuckin' dead, man. Fucking piss-stain' reptile dead.

'How is he, Baz?'

You heard, Hallan. Only fucker he plant now is him fuckin' self. Heh-heh-heh. Was a good one. You hear that, Hallan?

'Look, Baz, we're all in a bad situation here. You want to talk about it, one to one, I'd be glad to. What d'you say?'

Baz seeing the glimmer of a chance: Keep goin', Hallan.

'I tell you what, Baz. You've got somebody else in there, haven't you?'

You bet.

'Mister Norris, site security, right?'

Right. And his fuckin' dog.

'The man's got nothing to do with any of this, Baz.'

He have now, Hallan.

'All he's on is two-fifty an hour.'

More fool 'im.

'Two pound fifty an hour for all this. Is he all right? Baz, is Mister Norris all right?'

He fine, Hallan. Fuckin' dog ain't so hot, but he fine—

'You don't need him, Baz. He's just one more to look out for. Could be a long night, man.'

You right there, Hallan.

'You show good faith, we'll show good faith.'

Heh-heh-heh.

'You let Mister Norris walk, free and unharmed, and we'll talk. You and me, Baz, see what kind of deal we can come up with.'

Deal? Now we gettin' there, Hallan. Now we gettin' to it.

'He walks, we talk. What d'you say, Baz, what d'you think?'

Baz thought the fish were beginning to swim his way.

'You've still got one of our officers, Baz. We're not going to do anything stupid, are we?'

Baz figuring. The guy was five cubicles away from the cop. So he heard the shots, but that's all. So did the woman. And they got the woman. So they know about the shots. But that's all they know.

'You've got nothing to lose, Baz, everything to gain.'

You better believe it, Hallan.

'Look, Baz, we know you've got a mobile. You can talk to me or anyone else you like, you don't have to show yourself. We can get this thing sorted and that's it. What d'you say, Baz?'

Baz thinking. Sure, I'll take the fuckin' helicopter, Hallan. Heh-heh-heh. When did the black guy ever get the helicopter? Not even in the fuckin' movies, man.

But a cyar, now. A cyar was a possibility. Yah . . . But where to? Not all a way to fuckin' London, man. No, back to St Pauls. Where the black people live. Yah . . . Seeing the chance coming, the fish turning—

Have to be a red-stripe. One that draw the crowd. Seeing the St Pauls kids coming round, rocking and wrecking the fuckin' thing, creating all kind a shit. An' you slip away, get down, see Mo Perreira. Yah. Was nice. The chance come, you say, Hey man how you doin' and you fuckin' go—

Was not only nice. Was fuck all else, man. Heh-heh-heh.

'Baz, I'm going to give you the number now. Ready? 0836 70 17 30. You get that? 0836 70 17 30.'

Baz wrote it down with his finger in the cement dust.

Vic said, 'You got any throat sweets, John?'

'It's the air.'

'I know it's the fucking air. You got any throat sweets?'

'I got half a Mars bar.'

'That'll do.'

Cromer, looking reluctant, pulling it out.

'Christ, John, who fucking paid for it?'

'Hallam!' It was Sam Richardson from the Transit. 'Give him whatever the fuck he wants!'

Vic, chewing, nodded.

'Just get him out here!'

Vic saw both marksmen had their rifles inside their coats. One said, 'Got to keep the baby warm.'

Vic's mobile rang.

'Hallan?'

'Yes Baz?'

'How you doin'?'

'Fine. You?'

'OK. You hear me what I say nah.'

'I'm listening.'

'All these people, all these cyars and shit, all go.'

'Right.'

'One cyar lef', right?'

'Right.'

'One a them big red-stripe.'

'Motorway patrol car?'

'Yah big, like that. All a doors open an' a boot. Seen?'

'Got it.'

'You come out, I come out.'

Shit.

'You hear me nah? You come out, I come out.'

'Yeah, I hear you Baz. And Mister Norris?'

'You want 'im, you got 'im. An' his fuckin' dog.'

'You'll let him go? You'll let him walk free, unharmed?'

'Be a fuckin' pleasure, man.'

'And the other officer?'

'You pick him up when you like. I ain't handlin' two a these guys.'

'Fair enough. What about me, Baz?'

'You drive the fuckin' cyar, Hallan.'

Vic thought about mentioning his arm.

'You got a problem with that, Hallan?'

'No.'

'You do you dead. Anybody follow, do anythin' like that, you also dead, seen? Now you tell me what you got, Hallan.'

'One, everybody leaves. Two, car. Three, Mister Norris. Four, out. That it? Everything?'

'So far.'

'Give me twenty minutes.'

'You got it.'

Baz leaned back and lit the half-smoked joint. Was three back ways out a the place. Take one a them. Any trouble, he'd be sitting in back, the .38 in Hallan's neck. Yah. Was good.

It took twenty-five minutes to move the vehicles out. Nobody said a word to Vic until the white Land-Rover with the four-way PA was ready to roll. Cromer came over, said Good luck and climbed in the back. Sam Richardson leaned out of the passenger door. 'Whatever you do, Vic, don't stand too fucking close to the cunt.'

'Thanks.'

Vic climbed into the red-stripe Rover 827i. The driver told him it had a bit of a sudden-death clutch. Then he said, Well, Vic knew what he meant. Vic said, Yeah, no problem. *No, not fucking much.*

He drove the car on to the frozen turf and parked it facing away from the blue rectangle. Then he opened all the doors and the boot lid and moved a couple of yards away.

'All ready, Baz!' He could feel his heart thudding against the bullet-proof vest and wished he'd got one that reached right down to his groin.

'Baz!'

'I hear you, Hallan!'

The battened edge of the blue polythene swung out and a big guy in a grey uniform took half a step out. His face was sweaty-white and he was carrying a bulky, strapped up reddish-coloured dog. Baz's arm reached round the guy's neck and touched a short-barrelled .38 to the bone behind his ear.

The guy took another half-step – he looked scarcely able to walk – and Baz appeared. He had his other arm round the guy's waist and they were so close together it looked like two drunks doing the tango.

The guy shuffled another couple of steps and then stopped. They were no more than four feet outside the stone entrance facade and the overhanging balustrade of the terrace was still protecting them.

'Hallan!'

'Yes, Baz?'

'Back the cyar closer up!'

'What about the doors?'

'Leave 'em!'

'Right, Baz. I'm getting in the car now.'

'Hallan!'

'What?'

'You get out, you get out facin' me. Nice an' close. Seen?'

'Right.'

Vic backed the Rover up to within a couple of yards of the façade. As he got out, the dog began to wriggle and whine in the guy's arms. Vic heard Baz say Shit and the guy say Sorry and knew this was the moment.

He put his right shoulder down and charged into the dog and the guy's midriff. The dog yelped, the guy doubled up, and, as Baz was swinging his gun-arm round on to Vic, red dots began to dance all over Baz's head and body.

Sharp cracking shocks of high-velocity rifles splintered the air. Baz pitched forward, pulling the Browning automatic, firing blindly at Vic. Chips of stone, gravel flying, a thrumming, whirring noise and Vic felt his right leg sledgehammered from under him. There was no pain though—

He saw Baz staggering round as if hit by invisible punches, his face skeined with blood and more patches on his sweatshirt. He was trying to lift both guns on to Vic, the automatic blasting off on its own, but his arms had gone too heavy.

Still grinning and laughing away.

A final, flat crack and Baz took another one to the head, spun and fell. The fish scattered, turned into shards of light then nothing.

24

They all told him he was lucky, and Vic, who was floating halfway down a warm cocktail of morphine and relief, was inclined to believe them until the bastard pain hit.

The surgeon told him he was lucky: it was only a simple fracture of the tibia because the high-velocity bullet that caused it had spent most of its kinetic energy on the wall and if the ricochet had struck anything else but bone, and that only glancing, the tail-wag would have ploughed deep cavitation tracks through blood vessels and flesh and they would be into compound fracture and muscle wastage, and Vic would have been left with one leg shorter than the other.

In his light woozy state Vic thought about Baz and whether he was turning into him or whether he already had and was dead and this was what happened.

But no Sergeant Hallam you've been very fortunate and this .38 in the upper right thigh here – he started probing and scraping and three searing flashes of pain later Vic knew he was still alive – looks to *me* as if it's missed everything *vital*, male and femoral so to speak, although it's close enough to the nerve to give you a chance of sciatica in years to come.

Something heavy clanked into a steel kidney dish.

'Sutures please', and some vigorous tugging and stitching went on. Vic could see his red and blue thigh being shoved about like a piece of topside. So Sergeant you've lost precious little apart from blood which is a stroke of luck, eh?

Vic felt too happy and sick to say anything.

A blue and white cap and a green mask and a bare, surprisingly hairy arm holding something in a pair of forceps. 'This is the little beggar. We're going to have to turn you on your tummy for the other one—'

Other one? Christ, how many more?

Vic heard a retreating voice saying, 'Ah, yes, laceration and bruising, this may hurt a bit', and his consciousness went sliding all over the place like a handful of frogspawn.

'Lucky to get a room on your own.' Looking up, seeing Cromer and finding himself laid out on top of a hospital bed in a white shift that tied up the back and barely covered his bollocks. Two drips in the back of his left hand, one in his right, his mouth dry and chemical-tasting, as if he'd had one of those dentists' air-suction things stuck in it for hours. His right thigh and left shoulder were throbbing out of time with each other, his left buttock ached like a horse had kicked it and from the knee down his right leg was in plaster to the ankle.

'What's time, John?' His voice thick and his lips sluggish.

'Twenty past ten.'

'What, at night?'

'Yeah. You've been out three hours.'

'Fuckin' hell.'

'Why?'

'Couldn' ring Ellie for me, could you? Number's in the wallet somewhere.'

Hearing Cromer rattling around in the small wardrobe, watching him opening the wallet as if half a dozen used johnnies were about to fall out.

'This 0121 number?'

'Yeah.'

'What shall I tell her?'

'Say I'm all right, tell her whatever fucking ward I'm in.'

'Right.'

'Send her my love, all that shit.'

Cromer serious, copying the number down. 'I'm locking your wallet in the locker. Key'll be under the pillow.'

'Yes John. John—'

'What?'

'Just tell her. Don't make a fucking performance out of it.'

'Right.' Cromer moved awkwardly close to Vic and tucked the locker key under the pillow. He pushed Vic's lank, stiff hair back.

What the fuck—

'Still got blood in your hair.'

'Oh, right.'

Cromer standing there looking at him, determined to get something or other off his chest.

'What is it now, John?'

Cromer said, 'Looked like touch and go in the ambulance. You were soaked in blood from the waist down.' Shaking his head, his eyes going moist. 'You were dead lucky, mate.'

'Yeah. Thanks for the grapes.'

'What grapes?'

'Right. What fucking grapes?'

A nurse came in from the brightly lit corridor outside and made Cromer leave. The nurse's plastic name-tag read JODIE TYLER STAFF NURSE. He thought about asking her if she knew Ellie then decided his mouth wasn't up to the chit-chat. She took his temperature and his pulse and gave him a drink of water out of a beaker with a kid's mouthpiece on it. A nice-looking dark-haired girl with big eyes, quite plump, and she smiled at him as he sucked and dribbled at the beaker as if he was a baby on the breast. Putting the beaker down, she said, 'You were lucky to get in just before Christmas, we're usually packed out with dossers on the cadge.'

When he asked about another jab or something, she said twelve, they did a drug-trolley round at twelve. Then she put a buzzer thing under his right hand and said if he got any really bad pain just ring the bell.

Half-eleven, Sam Richardson and Parnes appeared. They had a sweet smell of scotch about them and were looking pretty fucking pleased with themselves. They asked him how he was and what the doctors said, then

Sam nodded and clopped his fur-lined gloves together. 'Well, you're in luck, Vic.'

'That's right,' said Parnes, smiling down at him.

Pair of smugfuckers standing there half-pissed.

'Yeah,' said Vic, 'looks like it, doesn't it?'

Sam told him Perreira had coughed when the doghandler Vic had talked to found the cocaine. Now he was offering to name names for a light sentence but they didn't think he knew anyone they or the Met didn't know, so they were deadbatting that one until he came up with something better than he had already.

Apparently, said Parnes, there was a double trapdoor and staircase under the stage left over from the war – the kids and teachers had used the basement area as a shelter from the bombing. Why the windows were seven foot off the ground. There were still hanks of raffia and old cardboard milk-bottle tops down there, the doghandler said, so the kids could pass the time lacing the raffia through the straw-holes in the cardboard tops and then join them up into shopping bags for their mothers. Sam said he'd heard the same thing up north – they'd done it to keep the kids quiet. Parnes said there was a passage through to the coal cellar then on to the boiler room under Perreira's flat. The doghandler told them the cocaine was under a load of slag and rust inside the old boiler but the dog had sniffed it out.

Vic said, 'Good old Buster.'

Parnes said, 'Who's Buster?'

'Friend of mine.'

Anyway, Sam said, Vic would get a mention on that one. As for the Baxter thing, they both agreed that took fucking guts, mate, and that would be another mention, obviously, but until things were more sorted out at the top they couldn't say anything for definite. Not at the moment. When Vic asked what was happening over Maggi Reed and the Webber business Sam clouded over and said one thing at a time, Vic. Parnes said his understanding was, from a meeting he and the CC had had immediately prior, all that was being knocked quietly on the head in view of what had happened.

Vic said, 'Anything on the Lang kid?'

Sam said, 'Avonmouth have picked up the car. They found some ladies' knickers covered in blood on the passenger seat but nothing much else, was there, Parnesy?'

'Not so far, no.'

'Well, good luck, Vic.'

'Thanks.'

Rupert had left the Cavalier with a lot of other nightshift bangers in a big meat-packing and processing plant carpark 400 yards from The King of Prussia. He got out, pulled his sweatshirt hood over his head and started to walk. At first the cold air did him good. Then he began to feel a bit thin on the ground and had to stop and sit down in a corner shop doorway. The shop was dark and boarded up but a woman in her thirties with a baby in her arms came straight out and told him she'd had enough of fucking junkies so he could fuck off out of it.

He walked on, keeping to the dock fence, steadying himself from time to time on the V-shaped galvanised iron railings. They were trellised in barbed wire, triple-spiked and freezing to the touch. The air smelled of tar, sulphur dioxide, frozen meat and poultry carcasses. The state he was in, Rupert knew he'd reached the end of the world.

It was nearly as cold inside The King of Prussia. He asked for a pint of Guinness because it was supposed to be good for the blood. The landlady, a woman in her forties with a face like a boiled ham and cold blue eyes, was sizing him up as if she had just decided to throw him out. He saw why when he looked at his crusted hand holding out a blood-stained fiver.

'It's all right,' he told her, 'I've been in a fight. Well, actually, I got mugged.'

It was the 'actually' that did it. She took the money and told him there was a sink in the Gents where he could wash himself. She gave him his change and a couple of white paper napkins printed with red bells and green holly. The water in the sink was freezing cold and the napkins disintegrated.

When he came back there were four jowly-looking guys at the bar in overcoats with short dark hair and tashes. There were three more younger kids in leather jackets and jeans standing over by the door.

Dark liver-coloured eyes looking at him.

The oldest guy said, 'You from Baz?'

'Yeah, I'm from Baz. You Riad?'

'From Riad.'

Searching his memory. 'Oh, right. You're Shabbahatin, right?'

'Sabbahatin, yes.'

'Sorry.'

Sabbahatin shrugged, leaned forward, looked up under Rupert's sweatshirt hood. 'What's this?' He reached out, put his hand on the back of Rupert's neck. The landlady had gone into the other bar. He could hear her washing up glasses. Sabbahatin's hand was warm, rough-skinned. He pulled Rupert's head forward, looked carefully at the clotted lumps of hair. 'How you get this?'

'I got creased, man.'

Rupert thought it sounded all right until Sabbahatin said, 'Why?'

Why? Jesus Christ—

'Fucking police, wasn't it?'

'How?' The 'H' sounding very sharp and hard.

'Waiting for you, man. You didn't fucking ring.'

Sabbahatin nodded at the young guys. 'Their vessel was delayed. Was a storm. Riad said he told you.' Leaning forward, looking exasperated. 'He tell me he say to Baz one, two, three times how the vessel containing the goods was delayed and was riding out the storm off Swansea—'

'Yeah, but—'

Sabbahatin laying it on hard now. 'Riad said Baz was screaming at him like a woman. Riad said Baz had lost his ring.' Waiting, challenging Rupert.

'Oh no. Not Baz.' Shaking his head. 'Not Baz, man. Never.'

'So why shout and scream?'

'I don't know – Baz didn't know what the Bristol Channel was – probably thought it was the River Avon—'

Sabbahatin looked at the streak of blood again. 'Tell me about this.'

Rupert lit a Camel, giving himself time to go over his story. The filter end was smudged with blood. He drew the smoke in. It tasted faintly of iron. 'We're hiding out, right? This big old joint Baz knows. Waiting for you to fucking ring, man. One minute we're sitting there, the next bang – they're all over the fucking place—'

Sabbahatin said something to the kids by the door. They pulled the rags of curtains aside to look out.

'Where?'

'Fucking miles away. Up the M32.'

'The what?'

'Near the M4.'

Sabbahatin said something else to the kids by the door. One of them went out. Sabbahatin turned back to Rupert. 'And Baz?'

'I don't know, man. They came in—'

'Came in where?'

'I told you. This big joint. Place you phoned Baz. I split, I took off.'

Sabbahatin nodded, suddenly looking bored. 'You drive, like that?'

'Got down here, didn't I?' Taking down half the Guinness. It tasted acid. Probably nobody else had had a pint all week. 'Fucking hell, man, I turned up, didn't I?'

The kid who went out came back with a magazine-size AA road atlas, 2.4 miles to 1 inch scale. Sabbahatin flicked slowly through it, held it open on pages 34–35. 'Show me.'

'M32, Junction 2.'

Sabbahatin traced the blue motorway line with his middle finger, and stopped. 'Is no Junction 2.' He had the exact same half-closed-eyes look as Baz.

You fucked up, boy.

Rupert going sweaty, twitchy. 'Fucking is, man.'

'Where?'

Rupert spread the atlas wide open. Junction 2 was buried right down in the centre crease. 'There. That's it.'

Sabbahatin took the atlas back without a word. He and another guy with a tash and a Lux-U-Hire key-ring spent a minute tracing out a route which avoided the M32 and the M4/M5 interchange and went north along the A38. The other guy took the atlas and left.

Sabbahatin stood up and said, 'OK. We go now.'

'Where?'

Holding out an arm towards the door. 'Now.'

Outside there was a heavy-set young guy standing by a dark-green Granada and a silver-grey Scorpio estate, also from Lux-U-Hire. Behind them was a white U-Haul Leyland DAF 400. The heavy-set young guy moved, opened the door of the van for Rupert. The back was full of open cardboard boxes with rolls of gold and silver wrapping paper sticking out. As Rupert went to get in, Sabbahatin spoke to the young guy. The young guy put a thick arm round Rupert's neck, held something hard in the small of his back, patted him down, then up between the legs and right round the balls. When Rupert turned round the young guy was putting a pistol-grip pump-gun back inside his jacket.

As though nothing had happened, Sabbahatin said, 'You drive on your own. You got a car in front, car in back, all you got to do is follow. OK?'

Rupert sat in the cab and looked at the Christmas paper behind him. 'This is the delivery, right?'

Sabbahatin stood at the door and said, 'You just drive, OK?'

'On my own?'

'Yes.'

'Taking a risk, aren't you?'

Sabbahatin said, 'No. You the one taking the risk.' Then he said, 'Think about it.'

Rupert turned the key to check the fuel. There was

almost a full tank. 'You mean if we get stopped?'

Sabbahatin shook his head. 'No. If *you* get stopped.'

'You just drive on?'

Sabbahatin gave him the bored look again. 'No.'

'What then?'

'We come back for the goods. You get in the way, too bad.'

Rupert glanced round at the boxes, turned back to Sabbahatin and tried to sound casual. 'So what we carrying?'

'Heroin.' Dry and matter of fact. 'Seventy-three kilos.' *We ain't here to deliver, we here to collect.*

Rupert heard himself say, 'Stick-a-pin, man.'

'What?' Irritable and harsh, as if he was hawking up.

'How much?'

'How much? I just told you how much.'

'No – how much am I getting?'

'How much Baz tell you?'

'Baz and I agreed on five. Five grand.'

'So why you asking me?'

'Baz isn't here, is he? Who gets his share?'

Turning away. 'Fucking shitheads—'

'Hang on. What if I have to, you know, stop?'

Sabbahatin gave him the look. 'You don't. You piss on the floor and you shit in your pants.' He slammed the door and walked over to the Granada.

You piss on the floor and you shit in your pants.

No chance of getting paid. Every chance of getting shot. No idea of where he was going. Heroin worth anything between fifty and ninety grand a kilo. He twisted the key in the ignition. There had to be a way. Had to be.

Rae discharged herself from the BRI just before midnight. She rang Maggi from a plexiglass booth in Casualty Reception. The phone burbled a dozen times before Maggi answered.

'Yes?' Cautious, ready to cut off the nuisance call.

'Maggi, it's Rae.'

'Hang on.' Sounds of movement, the telephone being

put down, picked up, then Maggi, more alert, 'Rae?'

'Yes?'

'Sorry, I took a Nytol. Look Rae, where are you, how are you?'

'The BRI—'

'My God.'

'I'm all right. I'm fine. It's just that stress thing they do, make you hang about, keep an eye on you—'

'I rang and rang. The police were having a bad fucking hair day. They wouldn't say anything. Were you there?'

'Yes.'

'At Hillside?'

'Yes.' Rae waited. Maggi didn't answer. 'I'd have phoned earlier but they only just told me I could go. Maggi . . .'

'Yes?'

'Maggi, I know it's late but can I come and see you? I need to talk, get this, you know, over, out.' Waiting for a response. 'I promise I won't throw up.'

Silence, then: 'How'll you get here?'

'Taxi. I'll get a taxi.'

'OK. Good. I'll watch out for you.'

'Thanks, Maggi—' The disengaged tone.

Maggi's house was a Victorian mid-terrace in Southleigh Road, Clifton, dark grey stucco, lined to look like Georgian stone, with narrow twelve-pane windows on two floors and a six-pane dormer in the roof. Southleigh Road had a restaurant at one end and a pub at the other and was just the sort of place Rae would have chosen had she been able to afford it.

Fucking Barney. Fucking Frank . . .

Maggi was wearing a black linen kimono. They kissed cheeks in the hall and Rae smelled night-cream. Maggi led the way to the dining room. White walls. Modern Rennie Mackintosh furniture, high-backed and black-lacquered. The table sat on a big afghan runner over bare boards and a white-enamelled French stove glowed in the cast-iron Victorian surround. Apart from two square yellow-and-white abstracts on the walls which she didn't like, Rae loved it. And wanted it.

'Come on through.'

Ceiling-height folding double doors with large cracked-glaze white china knobs and fingerplates led into the sitting room. More white walls. Two white linen sofas covered in red and blue Navajo throws faced each other across another black-lacquered table. There was another white-enamelled French stove. Maggi pulled a bottle of Montrachet from a plastic cooler and poured all of it into two large thick-stemmed Dartington glasses.

'This is wonderful, Maggi.'

'Sit down.'

Maggi patted the sofa beside her and pulled her legs up under her.

They had a long sensible adult talk about what had happened, including possible interviews and money, and Maggi said she was going to talk Channel One or somebody into something bigger. Another bottle of Montrachet and Rae found she had freed up completely and was on a really good high. It was as if the hard bright point of light Barney had done his best to put out had relit itself. She didn't know whether it was the wine or reliving the experience or just being in the warmth of Maggi's house instead of dank old Ashton, but she knew she was enjoying it – had enjoyed it, right from the get-out—

You yell, we're next.

Oh boy.

Splashed with blood, feeling like an accomplice, going over the edge—

Maybe crime, excitement, death, was a revitaliser?

Maybe that was what Frank got out of it, with the nurse. Cutting everything loose . . .

Was it Frank?

Nothing from Frank.

Even better.

She had been upstairs, twice, to the small separate loo, and both times had pushed her nose into the bedroom and adjoining bathroom. The first time it had all seemed a little too severe, too Philippe Starck, all white with artfully placed jars, bottles and flasks of Bristol blue; but the second time, slightly drunker, she loved it, give or take a jar or placing, and she wanted to be in it, walk through it, alter it. And have it, have it all.

Maggi watched her return, arms folded, appraising her. 'You know what I think, Rae?'

'What about?'

Maggi closed her eyes, smiled slowly to herself and opened them again. 'I think it's going to take you a long time to come down.'

'How d'you mean?'

'From all this.' She stretched her feet out towards Rae, put her arms up, yawned and arched her back, watching Rae to see if she was looking at her. 'I've never seen anyone so – energised.'

'I know.' Rae swilled the last half-inch of wine round her glass. It was getting warm. 'You think that's wrong? I mean, those guys, they were real sleazebags, scumbags, toerags, they didn't even get on with each other. Oh shit – I don't know, Maggi—'

Maggi pulled her kimono tight. 'You fancy them?'

'God no.'

'Not even the blond one?'

'God no. It wasn't like that, it wasn't like that at all. I mean, they'd seen me stark naked.' Looking straight at Maggi but getting nothing back. 'As far as they were concerned I just didn't bloody well exist. Most of the time it was just bloody boring and bloody cold. Then, when they both went for it – they had no brakes, Maggi. They didn't care, either of them. Basically, they didn't give a fuck.'

Maggi smiled.

'I think that was what got me.' She drained the glass. 'No brakes, more fun.'

Maggi stood up and dumped the bottle upside down in the cooler. 'You want to stay here tonight?'

'With you?'

'If you want.'

In bed, under the rough cotton duvet, Maggi leaned

up on one elbow and pushed Rae's hair back behind her ears. 'You know, you're my first widow.'

Half-ten in the morning, and Caroline had arrived. It was the ward's busy time when the consultants did their rounds, but after the surgeon had seen Vic and because Caroline was in uniform, the ward sister let her stay.

She had drawn the sliding blind to shut out the light from the corridor and was sitting by the bed holding both Vic's hands when Ellie walked in.

Vic said, 'Ellie, this is Caroline. She's a colleague of mine.'

Ellie looked at their intertwined fingers. 'I can see that.' She held out her mittened hand so that Caroline had to let go and stand up. 'Hello Caroline.'

They talked about Vic and the weather and Ellie's freezing cold trip down the M5 in the 2CV and what that was like, then there was a gap.

'Well,' Caroline said, talking to Vic but pretending to include Ellie, 'it doesn't look as if you're going to be doing much over Christmas, so why don't you give me a ring?'

Ellie said, 'He's going to Birmingham.'

Vic said, 'Oh no I'm not.'

'Well, whatever,' Caroline said. She bent down and kissed Vic on the lips. Her mouth was as soft as ever. 'Just give me a ring.' She smiled at Ellie. 'Bye. Happy Christmas, Vic.'

'And you,' said Vic.

'And you,' said Ellie as Caroline opened the door. Caroline gave Ellie another smile, raised an eyebrow slightly at Vic and pulled the door firmly shut.

They heard her heels on the vinyl corridor.

'Stab stab stab,' said Ellie.

'Not going to fucking Birmingham. Not fucking well enough.'

Ellie pulled the screens round the bed. 'Let's have a look at you then.' She pulled the sheet off the frame over his legs, stood the frame on the floor and professionally inspected his wound-dressings. 'Mm.'

'See? I told you. Not fucking well enough.'

Ellie shoved her hand up his shift and caught hold of him. 'Oh yes you are.'

His prick was standing up like a lighthouse.

She climbed carefully on to the bed, straddled him and pulled her knickers to one side. Vic had a momentary flash of Webber and Ellie with her legs in stirrups; then thought, Well, why not, if that's what it takes, so be it.